OUTSTANDING PRAISE FOR KATE COSCARELLI AND *LEADING LADY*

"Immensely enjoyable . . . Coscarelli is a master of plotting and a whiz at folding delicate layers of satire."
—*Los Angeles Times*

"Crackling entertainment."
—*Publishers Weekly*

"Kate Coscarelli is a born storyteller . . . She has a gift for creating characters and situations that make you care what happens next."
—*Palm Springs Desert Post*

"Fast and furious. Coscarelli cuts into the belly of the Hollywood beast and reveals the desperation within."
—Warren Adler, author of
War of the Roses

"Kate Coscarelli has a way with words. She is, in fact, one of today's premier storytellers. She just turns her imagination loose and lets fly with a story that moves like a rocket. No other current novelist, except for Sidney Sheldon, keeps the plot moving as swiftly as she does."
—*The Desert Sun*

W9-AQJ-363

LEADING LADY

KATE COSCARELLI

ST. MARTIN'S PAPERBACKS

LEADING LADY

Copyright © 1991 by Kate Coscarelli.

Cover design by Ann Twomey.

Library of Congress Catalog Card Number: 90-27080

ISBN: 0-312-92844-0

Printed in the United States of America

St Martin's Press hardcover edition/August 1991
St. Martin's Paperbacks edition/August 1992

10 9 8 7 6 5 4 3 2 1

*As always, this book is dedicated
with love to my husband Don,
the leading man of my life.*

Acknowledgments

Bouquets of roses to my agent, Joan Stewart, and my editor, Maureen Baron, for their comments, their criticism, and their faith.

1

Childhood should not end suddenly. It should fade away slowly, etched by an accumulation of small truths that eliminate innocence and gradually bring the harsh portrait of life into sharp focus. But it does not always happen that way. For many born on this earth there is no childhood at all. From the moment of birth these tiny ones are engaged in a day-to-day struggle with reality as they grimly try to survive poverty, abuse, and neglect. For others, there is a sudden stinging occurrence that drains them of all innocence and leaves them forever suspended somewhere between being a child and becoming an adult.

One cold February night in the 1930s Bunny Thomas experienced such an event.

Bunny was not an ordinary child. More than just pretty, she was beautiful in all the ways the western world acknowledges beauty. Her eyes were large and china-blue and rimmed by a thick fringe of dark lashes. At will she could summon tears, big golden drops of water, that would hover briefly in her eyes and then flow down her velvety white skin, leaving a silvery streak of moisture on her round, pink, adorable cheeks. She was petite, fine-boned, and fragile, small for her age. Her hair was thick and dark red, and although it was not curly, there were little tendrils of fine silken threads, wisps of glorious hue, framing her face.

Bunny was as sweet as she was physically lovely. Life

had given her no reason to be otherwise. Never a word of anger had been directed to her from the moment she was born, for she was the center of her mother's life. No child had ever been more adored or cherished, in spite of the fact that she had never known her father, who had fled from the responsibilities of marriage and parenthood immediately upon learning that his seed was about to bear fruit.

Laverne Thomas was not surprised when her husband left her. Her father had deserted his family too, leaving her and her mother alone and dependent on the kindness of friends and relatives. Because she had learned early on never to place too much hope and trust in a man, Laverne had heeded her mother's advice and started a secret savings account right after her marriage. Although Harvey Thomas didn't make much money and they were never able to afford to live anywhere except a rooming house, Laverne secretly went through his wallet and pockets every night and extracted a little something for her account. She never took enough so that he would notice, but in five years it began to add up to a nice little nest egg, enough to provide her and her baby with food to eat and a place to live when he abandoned her. Laverne supplemented her income by doing piecework on her sewing machine at home, sewing lace on fine corsets and brassieres.

When Bunny was three years old, Laverne entered her in a photographer's contest and learned that the camera loved her daughter almost as much as she did. Bunny received first prize—a ten-dollar gift certificate at the department store—and suddenly Laverne's sights were lifted skyward. Why waste years waiting for Bunny to grow up and marry a wealthy man, when she could take her to Hollywood now and make her a star? Surely the studios would welcome her daughter with open arms when they saw her. Enthusiastically, Laverne predicted Bunny Thomas would someday be the greatest star the movies had ever known.

Having struggled all her life merely for survival, Laverne at long last had a dream, one so compelling that it carried her through the next five years of drudgery, laboring to make enough money to bring the dream to pass. Working days as a clerk at Woolworth's and nights slaving over her sewing machine, Laverne pinched her pennies until they squealed. At the same time, she managed to provide her daughter with all the things she believed necessary. She sewed costumes in exchange for Bunny's elocution and dancing classes. Staying up nights to work on them, Laverne received a pittance for the finely-crafted outfits, which the dance studio sold to the other students at a considerable profit. Laverne drove herself relentlessly in pursuit of her dream.

When at last they finally said good-bye to Kansas forever and boarded a bus for California, both mother and daughter had high hopes and great expectations. Fortunately, they didn't know how impossible their dreams were, nor how many similarly hopefuls had set off for the golden land and found nothing but disappointment and dust.

After three weeks in Hollywood, when Laverne had just begun to glimpse the futility of her quest, the dream unexpectedly came alive again. Bunny was cast in a movie. Although her part was small, she was outstanding in it. Without effort, her twinkling eyes and merry smile stole every scene in which she appeared, and, miracle of miracles, she was now actually on the cusp of stardom.

Laverne checked Bunny to make sure she looked perfect.

The beautiful child was wearing a delicate white lace dress that fell loosely from her shoulders to a flounce just above her knees and was gathered at the waist by a wide pink satin sash. She had on white stockings and black patent-leather Mary Janes. Her long, thick hair was pulled back from her face by a pink ribbon, and around her neck was a gold, heart-shaped locket. But when Bunny looked up at her mother, her eyes showed how truly troubled she felt.

"Mama, I don't want to go unless you come too."

"I'm sorry, baby, I can't. Not this time. But everything is going to be fine, I promise you. Now, tell me again what you're going to do," she said, barely able to keep the apprehension and the agony out of her own voice.

"Not again, Mama, please. I know what you said—" She was interrupted by a knock at the door.

"Honey, get your coat. The car is here for us. Hurry now. We must go. We'll talk about it on the way over."

Dutifully, Bunny put on her little blue velvet coat and matching hat. Laverne pulled her own worn black wool coat over her gaunt frame, and they left the run-down garden apartment on Hollywood's Gower Avenue. Outside, a black Packard limousine awaited them, its uniformed driver holding the door open.

As the car carried them westward, Laverne cuddled her little daughter close. She wanted to soothe and encourage her, and convince her that she must do everything just right or all would be lost.

"Now, darling, tell me again, one more time."

"Oh, Mama . . ." Bunny protested.

"Again, Bunny. It's very important."

With a deep sigh, the child repeated the words that had been drilled into her. "I'm to be sweet and nice and smile. I'm to pretend he's the director and do everything he wants me to do without complaining or crying or getting sick. Even if it hurts. Will it really hurt bad, Mama?"

"It might, honey. It might. You must be prepared for it to hurt, and then if it doesn't, you'll be happier. But above all, do everything he tells you to do. If he says smile, you do it. If he says cry, you do that too. Understand?"

"But why can't you be there with me just like on the set?" the child asked plaintively. She had never had to do anything without her mother before.

Laverne looked at her darling child's upturned and troubled face, and her courage almost failed her. Almost. "It's not possible, sweetheart. Mr. Baker has invited you to spend the night at his house alone. He doesn't want your mother there."

"But why, Mama, why?"

"He has his reasons," she replied, trying to sound encouraging. "Now, you must remember that how you behave tonight is very important to both of us. Remember that Mr. Baker likes you a lot. He's the most powerful man in Hollywood, and he has promised your mama that he is going to make you a big star. You know what that means, don't you?"

Bunny nodded her precious little head and repeated again the words her mother had drummed into it for the past five years. "A star has lots of money and lives in a big house with a swimming pool and servants and lots of pretty dresses."

"And?" her mother prompted.

"And everybody in the world knows who she is and loves her."

Laverne nodded. "Good. Now, you want everybody in the world to know you and love you, don't you, darling?"

"I guess so," Bunny responded without conviction.

But Laverne knew exactly how to control her daughter: "And don't forget that a movie star can have her own puppy to live in her room and sleep in bed with her."

"I'm going to call it Muffin," Bunny said, her face brightening at the prospect of having her very own soft little puppy to hold.

The car pulled up and stopped in the circular driveway at the entrance to the large Tudor mansion. A butler came down the steps to greet them. Twilight had given way to early winter darkness, and the lights of the house streamed warmly from the windows and the open door.

"Give Mama a nice kiss now, and be a good girl, sweetheart. Pretend this is just another movie. Now, what are you going to do?"

"I'm going to sparkle, Mommy, just like you told me," the child replied, her eyes filling with tears and her voice quivering.

"That's right, my darling baby. And remember that Mama loves you more than anything in the whole world. Now I'll be right here to pick you up first thing in the morning, don't you worry about that."

The beautiful child kissed her mother on the cheek and reluctantly stepped out of the car. The butler smiled and took her hand gently to lead her into the house. Just before she passed through the huge portal, Bunny turned for one last look at her mother, the agony of separation visible in the tears in her eyes.

"Just keep thinking about Muffin, darling, and it'll be morning before you know it," her mother reassured her.

As Laverne settled back into the thick cushions of the luxurious sedan to be driven home, she closed her eyes and tried to push away the doubts and the loathing that filled her. It would be a miserable night for her too, but in the long run it would all be worth it, she reminded herself over and over. Her daughter would be the biggest star in Hollywood. She would be a legend in her own time. All Bunny would lose would be her illusions about men and romantic love. And it was never too early for a young girl to know the truth about that.

2

1949

Laverne Thomas slammed down the receiver of the white telephone in her bedroom. She strode to the butler's call button beside her bed and punched it as hard as she could, taking out some of her frustration and anger on the tiny brass button.

Within moments there was a knock at the door, and she snapped, "Come in." She was pacing the floor, trying to decide what her next move would be. She must not make a mistake or everything would be lost.

"Is there something you wish, ma'am?" the slightly

round, bald butler asked, a hint of a British accent coloring his words.

"Hugh, have Randolph bring the Rolls—no, not the Rolls, the Oldsmobile—around to the front door, and tell him to make sure the tank is full. I have an errand to do, and I don't want to run out of gas."

"You don't want him to drive?" Hugh asked curiously. His employer rarely drove anywhere herself.

"Obviously!" she retorted, and it was apparent that she was extremely upset.

"Ma'am, is there something I can do? You seem . . ."

She started to tell him to mind his own business, but Hugh had been a good employee for more than six years, and had proved on many occasions to be shrewd as well as discreet.

"Hugh, I just got a call from the studio. Bunny was just seen checking into a motel out in the San Fernando Valley with that nasty little punk, Timmy Horton."

"How did they find out about it?"

"The desk clerk recognized her and called Louella, who didn't waste a minute before calling Gordon Baker. Fortunately, Baker's in London, but his secretary called me immediately. I've got to get Bunny out of there before somebody else sees her."

"Take my advice, ma'am, let Randolph drive you. If that Horton person gives you any trouble, you might need some support. Randolph's not a man to be trifled with, and he's very fond of Miss Bunny. He wouldn't want to see her hurt in any way."

"Perhaps you're right," Laverne conceded. Who was she trying to fool anyway? The servants knew the problems she'd been having with Bunny for the past two years. Ever since her sixteenth birthday she'd been on a rebellious streak, sneaking out of the house at every opportunity.

"Take the Rolls too, ma'am. Let that silly little rascal know with whom he's dealing."

"Thanks, Hugh. I appreciate your advice."

Laverne went to her closet and pulled out one of her

Chanel suits. Although she and her daughter had lived well for the past nine years, she was still as thin as ever, and Coco Chanel's trim little suits blazoned with buttons, braid, and jewelry suited her perfectly. It was not easy managing a child who had become America's darling, and as her daughter approached womanhood, control had become increasingly difficult to maintain. Gone was the gentle, malleable child; in her place there was a moody, secretive teenager who resented the constraints of stardom and often seemed hell-bent on destroying her reputation and her career.

Seated in the backseat of the Rolls on its way up the canyon, Bunny's mother tried to put away all thoughts of Gordon Baker's wrath. More than once in the past couple of years, he had called her in to berate her about Bunny. He had told her in no uncertain terms that he expected her to make sure Bunny appeared to be a virgin. When the proper time came for his little star to marry, he wanted the public to believe that her white wedding gown was absolutely unsoiled. He warned Laverne that if there were any scandal—any at all—Bunny's career would be finished.

Laverne had assured him that there was no need to worry, but the pious mouthings of the lecherous man galled her. Gordon Baker was the self-appointed guardian of the nation's morals. Thank God, the moviegoing public had fallen in love with Bunny in her first starring role, otherwise she would have been just another of the deflowered little girls Baker had promised to make into stars and hadn't.

Fortunately for Bunny, his taste was limited to prepubescent girls; by the time she was twelve, Laverne had found it almost impossible to force her daughter to visit Baker's home. Bunny knew she didn't dare refuse, but she tended to get sick and feverish as the time approached. After Bunny's last visit, Laverne was coldly informed that she had spent most of the night in the bathroom throwing up. The situation had been solved, however, by Bunny's rapidly sprouting breasts, which offended Baker, and so the command performances, mercifully, had ceased at last.

Laverne opened her handbag and checked again to make sure that she had plenty of cash. She would pay off the clerk who had called Louella, and anyone else who might have recognized her daughter.

At last the car drove into the driveway of the Coral Reef Motel. Before the chauffeur could get out and open the door for her, Laverne was out of the car, shaking her head at him and telling him to wait.

Behind the desk sat a large, overweight woman with long red fingernails and frizzy blond hair. She was reading *Photoplay* magazine. Laverne approached her cautiously.

"Hello, are you by any chance the person who called the newspaper?" she asked softly.

"Yeah . . . who are you?" The woman was wary. She'd heard that the vice cops had women now, and she needed to be careful.

Laverne smiled. "I'm the mother of the young woman you called Louella about, and I want you to know how much I appreciate your kindness." As she spoke, she opened her purse and pulled out the first bill.

"No kiddin'? You're Bunny's mom?" she asked, her eyes glued to the fifty-dollar bill. It was more money than she made in a week. "How'd you find out?"

"Louella's a dear friend of mine, and she knows how closely I watch over my daughter," Laverne lied, her hand going back into the purse and extracting another bill of equal size.

"Oh yeah? Does your kid do this kind of thing often?" the woman asked, dreams of riches dancing in her eyes as she stared at Laverne's purse.

"Never. This is the first time, and I can only attribute it to her not being well. The doctor gave her some of that medicine they call 'antibiotic,' and it's really confused her. That awful young man has taken advantage of her poor health, I'm afraid," Laverne replied, and laid the bills out on the desk. "Now, could you give me a key to the room she's in so that I can rescue her?"

The woman snatched the bills and put them in the

pocket of her skirt. "Probably too late for that. They've been in there for more'n two hours."

"We mustn't assume the worst. May I have the key, please?" she insisted, keeping the friendly smile pasted to her lips.

The woman shrugged, pulled a key from the row of boxes and handed it to Laverne. "Why not? The jerk only paid me for an hour anyway."

Laverne smiled gratefully. "Thank you. After I take care of this little matter, you and I will have a nice talk."

Turning on her heel, Laverne marched out the door. She signaled to Randolph to follow her as she walked toward the row of one-story rooms. When she reached the door marked 24, she said softly, "Wait here. I'll call you if I need you."

Quickly, she inserted the key, turned it, pushed open the door and stepped inside, startling the two young people in the bed.

"Bunny, get up and get your clothes on this minute!" she snapped.

Bunny immediately rolled off Timmy Horton's nude body and stared in astonishment. "Mama!" she squealed.

"Jesus!" the skinny young man exclaimed, pulling at the sheets to cover his erect penis.

"Both of you get your clothes on!" Laverne ordered. "Now! And if you don't do as I say, I have someone outside who will come in here and help me do it for you."

Bunny had never been able to defy her mother openly. Her rebellions were always covert and secret, and she quickly grabbed at her clothes and hastened to cover herself.

Timmy Horton, however, was not too intimidated to ask as he scurried to get dressed, "How the fuck did you find us?"

"Don't you use that kind of language with me, you nasty little hoodlum! And it's none of your business," she retorted. "Just let me warn you that if one word of this ever gets around, it will be the end of your career in Hollywood, understand? You're nothing but a dime-a-dozen actor. You could disappear from the face of the earth and nobody would care. Do you get my drift, young man?"

"Jesus, ma'am . . . it was Bunny's idea to come here, not mine!" Timmy replied defensively.

"Shut your filthy mouth!" Laverne spat angrily. "One word from me, and you're dead in this town. Now get out of here before I have our bodyguard fix that funny face of yours so you'll have to spend the rest of your life peddling newspapers."

There was such menace in her voice that Timmy Horton believed every word she said. Half dressed, he ran from the room, almost colliding with the muscular chauffeur waiting outside.

Bunny handled the situation as she did almost every difficult moment in her life—by weeping. As soon as they were alone, Laverne's manner changed. Gently, she helped her daughter button her skirt, and her words became silky and soft.

"There, there, honey. He took advantage of you. I know that. Come now. Let's go home. Mama will help you take a nice warm bath and fix you a big cup of your special tea."

Sobbing hysterically, the young woman allowed her mother to dress her and lead her out of the room into the car.

"Wait there for Mama, darling. She has to take care of something. Randolph, watch her for a minute, will you? I need to talk to that creature inside again."

Organizing her face into a serene smile, Laverne strode into the office.

"Everything okay?" the woman asked sardonically.

"Everything is just fine, thanks to you. Nothing had happened, bless the dear Lord. They were still drinking some awful wine he had brought to lower her defenses, but I got there just in time. Now, I think you should be properly rewarded. I know you did this out of the goodness of your heart to protect an innocent young girl and didn't expect anything at all, and I also know that you'll never tell anyone about this . . . will you?" Laverne asked, drawing three more fifty-dollar bills from her purse.

Astonished that she was getting even more money, the woman shook her head and held out her hand. "No ma'am. Mum's the word. Believe you me."

Laverne's smile was steely as she handed over the money. "Good, because if it does get out, I'll know who talked, and I'll have the vice squad descend on this place and close it up forever!"

Stunned by the venomous threat, the woman watched mutely as Laverne sailed imperiously out the door. "Jesus, what a bitch," she murmured softly when she was alone once more.

Later, while Bunny was in the huge marble tub soaking in scented bubble bath, Laverne fixed a pot of her daughter's special tea. She stirred in two envelopes of sleeping powders and then sugared it heavily, the way Bunny liked it. Tonight was no time to worry about calories.

3

Laverne sat in front of the huge mahogany desk, humbly listening to Gordon Baker pontificate. He had been told the story of Bunny's escapade, and he was in a cold fury. He, of course, blamed her mother.

"This is a pretty mess. You should get down on your hands and knees to thank Louella for calling me immediately. If she had chosen to tell that story—or even hint at it—everything would be finished. You know that, don't you? Have you called her yet? Or sent her a gift?"

"Of course I called her, but—"

"Send her something! And no penny-pinching. I want her to get a gift from you that will make her feel like the Queen of England," he thundered.

Laverne wanted to snap back that the whining lump

of a woman was already almost as powerful as the Queen because of the studio heads' impossible toadying to her, but she kept her silence.

Angered at her lack of response, he goaded her. "Buy it at Tiffany's—and make sure there are diamonds in it, understand? She saved your brat's career."

"I'll do it this afternoon," she assured him.

"Good. Now, it's time we dealt with that little tart of yours. We'd better get her married before she gets herself in real trouble. Have you had Dr. Shepherd check her over to make sure she's not in a family way?"

Laverne nodded. "He did a D and C on her yesterday just to make sure," she replied, trying to put out of her mind the grim scene in the doctor's office. Dr. Shepherd did whatever G.B. wanted, but to protect himself, he did prophylactic surgery rather than scrape a uterus he knew was carrying a fetus, and risk breaking the law.

"This could have all been avoided if you had watched her more closely. Where is she now?"

"She's home in bed. The doctor told me to keep her sedated until tomorrow, because she's going to have bad cramps for a day or so."

"She's supposed to report for work Monday morning. Will she be up to it by then?"

Laverne took a deep breath and clenched her fists to keep her hands from revealing her nervousness. "Please, Mr. Baker, don't make her play that part. She's too mature for the role of Emily. She's a beautiful young woman now, and she hates having to bind her breasts and pretend to still be a little girl. She doesn't want to do it."

Gordon Baker looked down from his Olympian position at the ugly and scrawny woman cringing before him and was offended. How dare this repulsive bag of bones question him!

"Beautiful young women are a dime a dozen, madam, especially in this town. The day Bunny Thomas ceases to be a darling child, her career is over," he snarled, and then switching to brisk abruptness, he terminated the discussion. "Thank you for stopping by."

Puffed up by his own ego and the certitude of supreme power, Gordon Baker had no idea how seriously he had underestimated his opponent. Laverne Thomas's instincts for preservation were finely tuned. She knew that she had to win this battle, or Bunny's career would, indeed, be over. Her last three movies had not been huge at the box office, and Laverne did not intend to let Baker milk her career dry and then cast her out.

"Then I'm afraid that Bunny won't be reporting on Monday. I've already called both Louella and Hedda and confided in them that my daughter has been ill and needs a rest. The item will be in their columns tomorrow—that I am taking my daughter on a much-deserved vacation to Hawaii for several months."

Nobody told G.B. what to do. "If she's not there at seven on Monday morning, she'll be in violation of her contract, and she'll be finished in this town, my dear lady." His words dripped with menace.

Laverne was geared up for the battle. "I don't think so, G.B.," she replied poisonously, using the nickname that was reserved only for his equals, of which there were very few.

Instantly Gordon Baker sensed that he had before him a more formidable woman than he had assumed, and he suspected she would risk everything to protect her daughter's career. He was fairly certain that she would cause an immense scandal if he crossed her. "What exactly is it that you want?" he demanded.

"I want you to let her grow up on the screen so that she can continue to be a star. She is, after all, almost eighteen," Laverne replied, satisfied that he had perceived her threat.

Gordon Baker sat silently staring at the woman before him, sizing up her determination. With all his peccadilloes, he was a canny and instinctive genius. His next words startled Laverne. "On one provision. She has to get married."

"What?" Laverne asked, surprised not just by his sudden acquiescence, but by the strange demand.

"A wedding. A big extravaganza. It will show everyone that she is now an adult, and put her back in the spotlight. A husband will also cool down those hot little pants of hers."

Laverne was amazed at his ingenuity. Of course. A husband. But who would it be? "We'll need a groom," she replied.

"Submit a list of possibilities. Now, good day, Mrs. Thomas."

On the drive home, Laverne pondered the problem of picking a suitable consort for the young queen of Hollywood. Naturally he would have to be young and attractive. It would be a storybook wedding. The marriage of America's princess to her handsome prince. Just like Cinderella. Right . . . that was the idea. Perhaps she should even give a ball?

Later that evening, when Bunny was awake enough to understand the importance of the news, Laverne told her that she would not have to pretend to be a child anymore.

Bunny smiled groggily. "Did Mr. Baker say it was all right that I didn't want to play Emily?"

"He understood completely. He was very sweet about it all. So . . . I have a plan."

Bunny sat up and pulled Muffin, her tiny and fluffy white poodle, from the foot of the bed to cuddle in her arms. She smiled contentedly as the dog nuzzled her and licked her face.

"Bunny! How often have I told you not to let that dog lick you on the mouth!" Laverne scolded.

"He's cleaner than most people I know," Bunny protested, as she always did.

"Well, I've decided to give you a party on your birthday. A big, beautiful party. After all, you will be eighteen years old—a grown woman. We'll let the world know. Think of it as your coming-out party. You'll be the world's most famous debutante."

"But Mama, my birthday's less than a month from now. How will you get it organized that fast?"

"G.B.'s going to help me. I called him this afternoon,

and he said it was an excellent idea, although the studio will only foot half the bill. We're going to take over the Coconut Grove for the night. What do you think of that?"

"I love it. Who will we invite? I don't have many friends."

"You have millions of friends, darling. Just let Mama take care of the details."

The guest list was like an open casting call for eligible young males. Laverne did not confine herself to actors. She invited young men who were college football stars, and sons of the wealthy and powerful. The studio's publicity department pulled out all the stops, and within a few short days the world was poised and waiting for the big event. *Life* magazine agreed to send reporters and photographers to the party, and *Look* promised the cover. After all, Bunny Thomas was growing up, and the world cared.

The publicity became so heated that Laverne asked G.B. to pick up the whole tab, and he agreed on the provision that he have veto power on the choice of the groom. Laverne gave it to him.

Bunny's formal was created especially for her by Orry-Kelly, one of the top costume designers in Hollywood. Laverne eschewed the color white because there was still a big wedding to be faced, and she didn't want to bore the public. She chose instead a pale peach silk tulle, demure yet low-cut enough so that her daughter's voluptuous cleavage would be revealed for the first time. She also decided that Bunny needed to lose some weight. The night of the party, she would be presented to the world as a shapely young woman, and all baby fat had to go. Her waist must be tiny, and that might be difficult, because eating was one of Bunny's greatest pleasures.

Dr. Shepherd was helpful, as usual. He gave Laverne some pills; but when they kept Bunny from sleeping, he obliged by providing more pills to help her to rest. Bunny lost weight rapidly. Any concerns that her mother might have about all the medication evaporated with Bunny's high good humor and energy.

The night of the party arrived. The palm trees in the Grove were festooned with gigantic silver flowers. Tables, draped in pale green linen, bore large silver baskets of peach roses. Place cards held by tiny silver bunnies had been made especially for the occasion by Tiffany's. At Bunny's request, Benny Goodman and his orchestra were hired for the evening.

With her hair pulled off her face and arranged in a cascade of auburn curls down her back, Bunny was radiantly beautiful, no longer the pouty, adorable star-child of more than two dozen successful pictures, but a slim, voluptuous, and desirable young woman. It was the happiest night of her life.

Through it all, Laverne kept her eyes open, watching, observing, occasionally making notes on a tiny pad she carried in her evening bag. She studied her daughter's reaction to each of the young men who claimed her attention, intent on choosing a groom Bunny would like.

Gordon Baker and his wife Rowena made an appearance, but they did not stay for dinner. Baker hated big parties, and although his wife would have enjoyed staying and experiencing the obsequious attention everyone lavished on her, he would not permit it.

The success of the party was so great, with pictures of Bunny emblazoned on the covers of magazines and prominently featured in newspapers, that Gordon Baker was moved to announce that Bunny Thomas had been given the coveted role of Lily in the upcoming movie based on *Homespun,* the best-seller by the popular novelist, Mary Van Pouk.

For a week after the party, Bunny was walking on air. She had given her telephone number to many of the handsome young men who had danced attention on her, and they all called, intending to invite her to dinner, to football games, and to dances. Only a very few of the calls actually got to Bunny, however. Her mother screened them all first and rejected those she considered unsuitable. In spite of the fact that the party seemed to have strengthened Bunny's career, Laverne was mindful of the reasoning behind Baker's stipulation that her daughter marry. The princess needed a proper consort to service her needs, or there would be a terrible risk of her running wild and destroying herself.

Of the four young men Laverne allowed to take Bunny out on a date—in her own car, with Randolph driving—only Frank Hunter was judged by Laverne to be a fit suitor. He was tall with blond hair and brown eyes, a senior at Stanford University and the heir to a fortune. Although it was expected that one day he would join his father's prestigious law firm, he was fascinated by Hollywood and the movies. From the moment he first held the supple and exquisite Bunny in his arms, Frank was madly in love, and when she agreed to go to Palo Alto to be his date for the senior prom, he was in paradise.

Laverne chaperoned her on the train trip, but she allowed Bunny to attend the prom with Frank alone, upon the strict terms that Bunny permit him no liberties sexually. Everything proceeded as planned. Bunny had a marvelous time, since she was once again the belle of the ball. But the next day Laverne insisted that they return home. Frank followed soon after, and because Laverne had made certain that the hormones raging in the young couple's bloodstreams were not given an opportunity to get them into trouble, it was not long before he asked Bunny to marry him.

When Laverne called Gordon Baker to announce the engagement, he was pleased. Not only would the wedding draw the cream among film celebrities, but the wealth and social standing of the young man's family would attract the socially prominent as well. Baker had only one condition: Bunny had to complete her role as Lily before the wedding could be announced, and the wedding date had to coincide with the release of the film.

The plan orchestrated by Laverne and G.B. was executed without incident. *Homespun* was a hit, and Bunny's performance was lauded by critics everywhere. She was no longer just a cute little star-child, she was now recognized as an actress too.

The marriage was hailed as Hollywood's event of the decade, but three months after the ceremony, something happened that, amazingly, no one foresaw. Bunny Thomas got pregnant.

4

Frank turned over and looked at the clock. Good God, it was almost nine! Normally an early riser, he threw back the covers and slid out of bed, berating himself for wasting the best part of the morning. He was becoming as much of a slugabed as his wife.

Striding to the window, he grabbed the cord to the drapes and pulled them noisily open. "Good morning, sleepyhead," he said brightly. Frank was nothing if not cheerful and exuberant from the moment he first awakened. "Time to rise and shine. Come on, now. Have breakfast with me for a change."

Bunny groaned and turned over. "I don't feel like getting up. I'm too tired, and if I eat, I'll just start throwing up again."

Frank stretched his long, nude, muscular body down onto her side of the bed and put his arm across her.

"Come on, darling. Stop thinking about your nausea so much. Try telling yourself you'll feel fine, and maybe you will. How about it?"

As he spoke he nuzzled into the masses of hair concealing her face and tried to find a patch of flesh to kiss, but she turned away from him.

"Just give me a chance to wake up, okay?" she muttered crossly into the pillow.

"Honeybabe, if I leave you, you'll go back to sleep

again, you know you will. Come on, now. We haven't
eaten breakfast together in weeks, and I want to look at
your beautiful face and have somebody to talk to instead
of Hugh. He's okay as far as butlers go, but the sun
bounces off that shiny dome of his and almost blinds me,
so come on," he teased, stroking her back lightly with
the tips of his fingers.

Bunny was awake now, and the pressure of his body
against hers and the feathery touch of his fingers began
to arouse her. She turned her face to his and rested her
lips against his mouth, not kissing but just touching as
she whispered, "I want something else for breakfast."

Frank responded to her arousal with his own.

"So do I, baby, but the doctor said—"

"Screw the doctor," she whispered, raising her leg and
wrapping it around him. "I want you inside now."

It was an invitation no virile young man could resist
for long, and soon their bodies were entwined in a passionate embrace, which was not destined to reach a sat-
isfying climax.

"What the hell is going on in here?" Laverne asked in
a stentorian voice.

Startled, the young pair looked up without uncoupling.

"Jesus Christ!" Frank howled. "Get the hell out of
here!"

"Not until you get the hell out of my daughter!" Laverne barked back, her hands trembling with indignation,
causing the china on the silver tray she was carrying to
rattle. "Dr. Shepherd told you not to have intercourse,"
she continued, her voice filled with rage, "at least not
until she's in her second trimester, and that's not for
another week. Now stop it this very minute!"

"What business have you got barging into our room
without knocking?" Frank asked, moving off his wife, his
passion wilted by the fracas. He reached down and pulled
the sheet over them both.

"I did knock, but when there was no answer, I came
in. What are you doing home at this hour anyway? You're

usually at the tennis court long before now," Laverne replied defensively, not backing down an inch.

So intent were the two adversaries in their exchange of hostilities they didn't notice that Bunny's initial shock had changed to distress, until she began sobbing loudly.

Frank tried to gather Bunny into his arms, to comfort her. But she turned away from him, nearly hysterical. Nothing he said seemed to have any effect on her, and finally he gave up. Reaching out, he grabbed his robe off the chair, wrapped it around himself and got out of bed.

Laverne, meanwhile, set the breakfast tray on the table in the bay window and approached the bed, saying, "There, there, darling, everything's going to be fine."

Frank turned on her. "By the time I get out of the shower, I want you out of the bedroom, Laverne, understand?"

"You will not tell me what to do, understand?" she mimicked him.

Furiously, he stomped into the bathroom and slammed the door, but when he emerged twenty minutes later, shaved and showered, he was surprised to see that the room was empty. Both Laverne and Bunny were gone.

He dressed quickly in a pair of white tennis pants and T-shirt, slung a white cable-knit sweater around his shoulders and headed downstairs. There was no one in the dining room, but Hugh appeared almost immediately.

"Would you like your usual scrambled eggs, sir?"

"Where's Mrs. Hunter?" he asked.

"Miss Bunny is in her mother's room, I believe," he replied stoically, and Frank got the distinct feeling that Hugh knew everything that had happened that morning.

"Forget breakfast. I'll have an early lunch over at the club. Tell my wife I'll be back this afternoon by three."

Frank climbed into his car, feeling frustrated and helpless. Moving into the house with his mother-in-law had been a mistake, even if Laverne had insisted that the house was Bunny's and not hers, but he'd really had no other choice. With still a year of college to finish, and then law school, with no money other than his allowance from his father, he had been forced to acquiesce to Bunny's entreaties to live with her mother. Well, he'd tried, and it hadn't worked. Now the only thing for him to do was to ask his parents for a loan so he could get them a place of their own. He knew their marriage was never going to make it unless they got away from that virago of a mother-in-law.

Later that afternoon, when Frank returned home, Hugh met him at the front door and said, "Miss Laverne is waiting for you in the library, sir."

"Well, let her wait," Frank snapped confidently. His mother and father had been sympathetic to his plight and had promised whatever financial help he needed to set up his own household.

"Where's my wife?" he asked, moving past the butler. Hugh hesitated.

"Well, where is she?" Frank demanded in irritation.

"I believe she's in her room, sir, but—"

Frank brushed past him, murmuring, "But nothing," and raced up the stairs. He was just about to open it when he noticed there was new hardware on the door, as well as a shiny new brass keyhole. What the hell was going on? He turned the knob but it didn't budge. The door was locked!

"Bunny," he called, knocking. "Open up. I've got some exciting news." There was a short pause, and then the lock turned and Bunny opened the door. She was still wearing her nightgown.

"Good Lord, have you been in bed all day?" he asked.

"Mama had Dr. Shepherd in to examine me. Everything's fine, but she insisted that I stay in bed the rest of the day, just in case." She drooped toward the chaise and sank down on it, pulling the mohair coverlet over herself.

"In case of what?" Frank asked in exasperation.

Bunny's lower lip began to jut out as it always did just before she went into a crying spell. "You know . . . she was upset that maybe you had hurt me this morning."

Concerned, Frank sat down beside her and took her hands in his. "I didn't hurt you, did I, honey?"

Bunny shook her head, but the tears were fast approaching, and Frank wanted to head them off.

"Good, well, I've got some great news. I talked to Mother and Dad, and they've agreed to set us up in a place of our own. Isn't that terrific? I stopped at a realtor's office, and he told me there was a great apartment on Roxbury that would be perfect for us. I said I'd bring you over to see it tomorrow, and if you like it, we can sign the lease. What do you think?"

Bunny looked up at him in astonishment, her tears forgotten. "What are you talking about?" she asked in alarm.

"Sweetheart, I'm talking about us, our marriage. We need to get away from your mother for a while, can't you see that?"

"But this is my house. Why would I want to leave this beautiful place for a junky little apartment?"

It was apparent to Frank that Bunny had no understanding of his frustrations. "This isn't really your house, darling," he explained patiently. "Your name might be on the deed, but it's your mother's house. She runs things here, and I just can't live under her domination any longer. Surely after that miserable scene this morning, you can understand that, can't you?"

As fervent as Frank's plea was, he realized he might as well have been talking to the wind. Bunny was not about to change her living arrangement.

But not wanting to antagonize her husband, she turned on her considerable charm. "Frank, honey, what happened this morning was an accident. Mama apologized to me and promised it would never happen again. Never. In fact, she even had a new lock put on the door to make sure that we'd never be disturbed. Didn't you notice it?"

"Yeah, I saw it, but that doesn't change the fact that we need to have a life of our own."

"Darling," Bunny said softly, leaning close to him.

"School starts for you next week, and Monday I have to do wardrobe and makeup tests. They've reorganized the schedule to get my scenes completed before I get too fat, so we're both going to be too busy to bother with an apartment." She reached over, kissed him tenderly and said, "Besides, Mama and I are a team. I'm not sure I could work if she wasn't around to take care of things for me. Please be a little patient with her . . . please? For my sake?"

Helplessly, Frank looked at his lovely wife and realized that Laverne had won again. Not only could he not resist his wife when she asked him sweetly, but the notion of her running a household suddenly seemed ludicrous. He had married a star, and he would never be able to turn her into a housewife, even if he wanted to. It was not long before they were in each other's arms, and with the new lock safeguarding their privacy, Bunny was soon begging him to continue what they had started earlier in the day.

Later, with Bunny's warm softness cuddled up against him, Frank consoled himself with the knowledge that Laverne might be able to manage his wife's career and her life, but she damned well couldn't give her daughter the kind of loving he could.

5

1951

Frank's eyes locked with Laverne's in another of the countless standoffs they'd had in the three years since he had married the celestial Bunny Thomas, and suddenly he'd had enough.

"How dare you send Mrs. Wells packing without so much as a word with me? She was the best nursemaid we'd ever had for Chelsea, and Chelsea loved her!"

"I had my reasons!" Laverne snapped.

"Your reasons! Your reasons, bullshit! You didn't like her because she didn't approve of the way you coddle that daughter of yours. Can't you get it into your head that Bunny is a mother now with responsibilities to her child?"

"Bunny's responsibilities begin and end with herself, understand?" Laverne replied indignantly. "She's not some cow who breeds children and cleans up their messes. She's a star! You knew that when you married her. And if you don't like the way I run this house, then you're free to leave at any time. Be my guest."

"Well, maybe it's time for me to do just that. You want your daughter back? Well, you've got her. I'm tired of listening to her moan and groan anyway, but I'm taking Chelsea with me, you hear? I will not leave my daughter in your twisted care." The determination of his voice was framed in anger and disgust.

"Your daughter? Your . . . daughter!" Laverne spaced out her words menacingly. "The nerve! Did you carry her in your belly for nine months? Did you give up your figure for her? Did you vomit every morning and suffer labor pains and endure the agony of giving birth, or were you, as I recall, working on your backhand at the tennis club while Bunny was hemorrhaging on the delivery table? As a matter of fact, just what did you do to create that child except screw her mother?" Laverne retorted.

"I'm not going to let you turn Chelsea into a quivering, crying mound of blubber like you did Bunny!" Frank insisted.

"You better not cross me, Frank," Laverne said in a heavy, threatening tone.

"How're you going to stop me, 'Mama'?" he sneered. "Especially when I tell everybody that my wife lives on pills—pills to go to sleep, pills to wake up, pills to take off weight, pills to calm her nerves, pills to get her going so she can work . . . pills she doesn't even know she's taking. My God, she's only twenty-one years old, and she's a walking bag of chemicals, thanks to you."

If his taunts hit their target, she did not let it show.

Instead she smiled and replied, "You'll reveal nothing about my daughter or her private life, or I'll tell the world that she threw you out of the house because she found out you were queer."

Although he tried to retain his composure, he failed. "Who would believe that?" Frank asked less confidently.

"Everybody. Especially when I provide the details about that one-night stand you had in . . . let's see, I believe it was in your freshman year, and the young man's name was Gorski." She paused to gather momentum. "Yes, the exalted and revered Adam Gorski's son, as I recall. Just think how awful it would be if that little tidbit of scandal about the only child of one of our most respected Supreme Court justices made its way into the newspapers. Dear me, why, I do believe it would cause your father's dearest friend no end of heartbreak, wouldn't it? Not to mention the embarrassment of having a homosexual for a son."

"You bitch, you wouldn't dare—" he began angrily, but she cut him off.

"I wouldn't dare? You seriously underestimate me, Frank. It would be a juicy story, especially since Justice Gorski is such a pious man and so utterly conservative. What would he do, do you suppose? Would he disown his son or defend him?" she responded, her words laced with acid.

"We were just a couple of stupid kids, and I was drunk!" he protested, but it was obvious that Laverne's words had touched him at a vulnerable point.

"Yes, well, just remember that Bunny tells me everything . . . everything, you understand? Every little intimate thing you've ever whispered in her ear, I know." Her eyes glittered as she narrowed them with evil satisfaction. "I also have that pitiful little letter he wrote to you when you got married, and it's safely tucked away in the bank vault. Poor little fairy poured out his heart, didn't he? Told you everything about his feelings and apologized for seducing you, didn't he, huh? Is it really possible to be seduced by someone of the same sex if you don't have any inclination at all? I wonder."

"How did you get that letter? Did Bunny give it to you?" he demanded.

"How I got it is none of your business. I was only doing what was necessary to protect my daughter."

"You're disgusting! No wonder Bunny is such a mess."

"How dare you talk about her like that! I want you out of this house today and forever!" Laverne declared. "And you damned well better behave yourself and keep your mouth shut about us or I'll cover you and your family and your fancy friend with so much dirt you'll never be able to wash yourself clean again. You know the tabloids would just love this story."

With that final threat tossed into the air, she turned away and left him standing alone, beaten into submission. He looked around at what was left of the half-eaten breakfast on the long, baroque dining room table. The smell of the poached eggs congealing on the plate in front of him made him nauseous. With one sweep of his arm, he cleared the table, sending china, glass, food, and linen crashing to the floor, splattering the walls and furniture with orange juice, coffee, strawberry jam, and egg yolk. God help him, he would never eat another egg again as long as he lived.

In one nasty spiteful moment, his marriage had been terminated. He would lose contact with the pretty little daughter he loved so much, and he would never again hold the gentle and soft child-woman he had married. Laverne had succeeded in squashing him as easily as if he had been a cockroach under her heel. If only it had been his own reputation, he would have fought the bitch tooth and nail, but there were others at risk now, and he couldn't smear them just to set his own life in order. Damn her!

Frank threw the napkin down on the splintered Haviland china, the sterling silver, and the shards of Baccarat crystal, thinking how pleasurable it would be to smash every piece of the expensive and pretentious luxuries in-festing this house. He hated every bit of it. He abhorred Laverne's pitiful attempts to buy gentility and breeding. Although born to wealth and privilege himself, Frank had been taught to avoid ostentation; money was to be spent discreetly or not at all. Laverne's compulsion to have nothing but the most expensive status-labeled goods at all times was an obscenity.

Resisting the impulse to do any more damage, he left the room, crossed the marble entry hall, and dashed up the grand staircase. He hesitated briefly outside his wife's door, tempted for only a moment to go inside and beg her to bring Chelsea and come with him. But realizing the futility of such a request, he walked past to his own room. What an utter ass he had been to think he could have any kind of a decent relationship while that harpy was pulling his wife's strings every moment of the damned day.

He had just begun to take his clothes out of the drawers when he heard a gentle knock at the door. Hoping that perhaps it was Bunny coming to renounce her mother's iron grip and declare that she wanted them to be a real family, he turned quickly and pulled the door open. Standing there, however, was not his wife, but Hugh, the butler.

"Madam asked me to come up to help you pack," he said gently.

Frank remained motionless for a brief moment of de-spair, then said, "Good idea. Look, Hugh, you know what's mine. Pack everything up and I'll let you know where to send it. If by any chance my wife asks where I am, tell her she can reach me at the Racquet Club in Palm Springs. I'll be there for the weekend, and then I'll probably take a room somewhere near law school."

"Yes sir. Would you like me to pack a small bag to take with you?" the butler replied kindly. The young chap had stuck it out longer than anyone on the staff had expected, and everyone liked him. He had never failed to be kind and courteous to the servants, unlike the matriarch of the house. Mrs. Thomas treated everyone like slaves, except Hugh himself, of course, because she was too intimidated by his British accent and haughty demeanor to try it.

"Thanks a lot, Hugh. I'm going to take a shower and dress. I feel like somebody just pissed all over me."

An hour later Frank left the house. As he was leaving, he knocked at Bunny's door, but she never emerged from her room or spoke to him again. She left all of the divorce arrangements to her mother. Frank's attorney eventually secured visiting privileges with Chelsea, but by that time Frank had dropped out of law school at UCLA and joined the Navy, where he received a commission and an assignment to pilot training in Pensacola. Shortly after his divorce from Bunny was final, he returned home on leave to marry Anne Mathews, a San Francisco debutante who immediately got pregnant with her first heir to the Hunter fortune.

When President Eisenhower finally brought the conflict in Korea to an end, Frank returned home and was accepted at Stanford Law School. By that time, he and Anne had two children, and Frank was too busy to pursue his relationship with Chelsea with any serious kind of determination. At first he had written to her regularly and never missed sending gifts on her birthday and Christmas. He had tried too, on several occasions, to make an appointment to visit her, but Laverne always managed to find some excuse to postpone or cancel it. Even his attempts to talk to Chelsea on the telephone were thwarted. Doggedly, however, he sent gifts and letters to her; but there was never a reply or acknowledgment, and after a while it began to seem too futile. Chelsea probably didn't even know who he was anyway, he rationalized after missing her birthday one year, and although he tried to rekindle his determination to keep in touch with her, in reality she had become only a reminder of the miserable years under the same roof with Laverne, a time he preferred to forget entirely.

What Frank did not know was that the picture Bunny

and Laverne painted for Chelsea was that of a man who
was spoiled, self-centered, and irresponsible. As she grew
up, she knew nothing about his having served his country
with distinction in Korea or that he was devoted to his
children and his new wife, or that he had tried on countless occasions to see her. And although she often dreamed
about having a loving father, someone who would hold
her and love her and protect her, the man of Chelsea's
dreams bore no resemblance to Frank Hunter. He looked
more like Jimmy Stewart.

6

1961

Chelsea came home from school to find the Bekins moving van parked in front of the house. Thinking that perhaps it was just there to deliver another antique—
Grandma was always buying more antiques—she paid it
little attention. She had other things on her mind, and
was eager to talk to her mother. She just hoped Bunny
hadn't taken to her bed again with one of her "spells."
Chelsea hated it when Bunny wasn't feeling well, which
was most of the time lately.

She dashed into the entry hall of the huge Georgian
mansion and was startled to find it in complete disarray.
Bewildered, she wondered what was happening. Furniture was being moved out of the house, not in!

Chelsea hurried into the kitchen to ask Hugh what was
going on, but only Linda, the cleaning woman, was there.

"Linda, where's Hugh?"

"He's gone, honey. Didn't he tell you he was leaving?"

Chelsea was astounded. "Leaving? What do you mean
leaving? Where did he go?"

"Your grandma hasn't paid him for over two months,
and he just couldn't hang on anymore. He has a mother

to support over in England. He felt awful bad about going. I guess that's why he didn't tell you."

"But why didn't Grandma pay him?"

"She hasn't paid anybody. I got nowhere to go or I'd be outta here too. Didn't she tell you nothin'?"

Chelsea's experience in life had taught her to dislike surprises, because they were invariably bad, but she didn't want to hear the worst from Linda.

"Is my mother here?"

Linda looked down at the box of Royal Doulton dishes she was packing and replied, "She's got one of them migraines again. Your grandma's in the library. Better talk to her."

Chelsea whirled around and headed back across the wide marble entry hall to the walnut-paneled library. When she swung the heavy, carved wooden door open wide, her worst suspicions were confirmed. Instead of the perfectly coiffed and Chaneled grandmother who usually sat at the large antique desk, she saw a woman in a cotton wrapper with a scarf tied on her hair. Laverne wore no makeup on her face, and her gaunt features and sharp nose etched a portrait of an aging woman drowning in a deluge of bills. Startled, Laverne looked up, and Chelsea was surprised to see that her grandmother was crying. She rarely cried, because Bunny shed enough tears for the whole family.

Chelsea picked her way gingerly through the litter of boxes to the couch, pushed a stack of papers aside and sat down primly, with her knees together, just as she had been taught. "What's happening, Grandma?"

"Your mother's contract was dropped by the studio. They haven't paid us a cent since Gordon Baker died. I was able to sell the most valuable pieces in the house to Marcy Greer, who's decorating Martin Nelson's new house in Bel Air, and she's giving me a good price. It'll keep us going until Bunny gets another job."

"Are we going to have to sell the house?"

After a long pause Laverne replied in an almost inaudible voice, "It's just too big to run without a staff. I owe everybody, and the attorney says the studio won't pay us unless we sue them. But I don't dare do that. Bunny's reputation would be destroyed. God knows what terrible lies they might tell about her." Laverne did not seem to be talking to her granddaughter as much as ruminating aloud.

"Why is the studio doing this to her? She's a big star," Chelsea protested vehemently, echoing the phrase she had heard her grandmother use frequently over the years.

"Over the past twenty years she's earned millions for those creatures at Taurus, and now they say the public isn't interested in her anymore. They say she's a has-been. Would a has-been still get so many fan letters every week?" Laverne asked angrily. "Bunny Thomas is still the most beautiful woman in the world!"

Chelsea went to her grandmother and put her hand on her shoulder to comfort her. "I know, Grandma, I know. Don't worry. Mom just needs a rest. Maybe it would be a good idea to move to a smaller house, then you'd have more time to take care of her and have less to worry about."

Laverne found herself somewhat consoled by the quiet determination of her granddaughter. Chelsea was not the petite, gorgeous child Bunny had been, but she was bright and steady and resourceful. Laverne stroked her grandchild's bright golden hair, looked into the somber brown eyes and smiled.

"You're such a good girl, Chelsea. What would I do without you?"

"I'll go change my clothes and help you. We'll get all this stuff packed up in no time at all," Chelsea said, moving away. She always felt uncomfortable when her grandmother tried to be affectionate, although she loved it when her mother held her in her arms and cuddled her. Grandma was so thin and bony that she had shied away from her touch even as a little girl. Gran was all angles and points, whereas her mother was all soft cushions and curves. Chelsea responded eagerly when her mother hugged her.

"Good," Laverne said briskly, her determination and resolve restored by her grandchild's easy acceptance of the situation. "I'm going to call Mr. Wilder right now and tell him to find us a rich buyer for this house. There's a perfectly charming little cottage over on Camden that's for lease. It should do us nicely until things get straightened out. It even has a maid's room and bath over the garage. With the money from the sale of the furniture, I should be able to start paying Linda a salary again."

"We could do the housework ourselves and save the money," Chelsea suggested. "It might be a long time before Mom works again."

"Nonsense, Chelsea. How would it look? We must never let the world know that we have money troubles. It would spoil Bunny's image."

"But everybody'll know something's wrong when we sell our furniture and move to a littler house, won't they?" Chelsea asked.

"I'll just say that we're taking a small place here, because we plan to build a bigger home in Palm Springs."

"But that would be a lie. Nobody will believe it," Chelsea protested.

"In this town, everybody lies and everybody knows it, but everybody believes anyway."

Chelsea shook her head, perplexed. Grown-ups were so strange. She climbed the big staircase, running her hand along the slick alabaster banister, thinking that she would have to tell her teacher that she could not go skiing with her class next month. It would have been fun, but now it was quite obviously out of the question.

Chelsea was a most unusual child. She never put her own wishes above the needs of others in the family. What she wanted never seemed to be important enough. Bunny was the star of the house. What was good for her was good for everyone. It was a fact of life, and she accepted it.

She stopped at her mother's door, put her hand on the knob and looked over her shoulder to make sure that no one would see her going inside. Surreptitiously she tip-

toed across the room, as she had done so often, and sat
down beside her mother's still form spread across the
bed. Gently, she lifted the tendrils of auburn hair away
from Bunny's beautiful face, so serene and tranquil. Tenderly she touched the softness of the cheek, and from the
moisture she felt, Chelsea knew that her mother had probably cried herself to sleep again. Poor Mom. She was
either hysterically happy or just plain hysterical. She
didn't seem to have any moods in between, and she hadn't
had any good periods for a long time.

As much as she hated the thought of having another
man in the house, Chelsea almost wished that Bunny
would find someone new to love her and make her laugh
and be happy again. The last one, David Gorhan, hadn't
been as bad as the others. At least he never hit Bunny
like Stan did. God, Chelsea had hated Stan. She had only
been eight years old when Mom had married him, and
the two years he had lived in the house had been the
worst. When he and Mom came home drunk and started
fighting, Chelsea hid under her bed. Thank Heaven for
Grandma, she thought. Right after the night he blackened
Bunny's million-dollar eyes and cut her soft pink lip,
Grandma went to the store and bought a shotgun. She
told nobody about it except Chelsea, warning her not to
touch it, because it was loaded and ready to go.

Just thinking about it again made Chelsea smile. There
was skinny little Grandma, pointing that shotgun at big
old Stan, telling him to get out or she'd shoot him where
it would do the most good—wherever that was. He
didn't believe her, but when she pulled the trigger and
put a hole in the wall over his head, he turned around and
ran down the steps and out of the house as fast as
he could go.

Bunny moved slightly, and Chelsea got to her feet
gingerly. She mustn't wake her, or Grandma would be
angry. Quietly, Chelsea walked across the room and sat
down at her mother's beautiful vanity table. The pink
marble top was cluttered with bottles of makeup and
perfume. Silently, she pulled open the bottom drawer

and took out the long black velvet box in which her mother kept her jewels.

As Chelsea lifted the lid, she caught her breath with joy. Every time she opened that box to look on the jumble of sparkling jewels, she felt just as Long John Silver must have felt when he opened his chest of treasures. How beautiful everything was!

With her slim fingers she carefully pulled the chains of gold and diamonds away from the strands of pearls. As she always did, she draped one strand after another around her neck. First the long black baroque pearls with the sapphire and diamond clasp, then the triple strand of satin-smooth pink pearls that were the size of the marbles in her Chinese checkers game. She especially loved the clasp on those. It was a flower with white diamonds in the petals and a pink diamond in the center.

She had just picked up the square-cut emerald and diamond ring when she heard someone in the hallway. Quickly, she swooped the necklaces off her neck, dumped them back in the box and dropped the ring on top of them. Playing with her mother's jewelry was her own little secret, and the clandestine excitement would be spoiled if anyone ever found out. She hurriedly stashed the box into her schoolbag and sneaked out of the room.

Her heart slowed its racing when she saw that the noise had merely been one of the men carrying a small bombe chest from her grandmother's bedroom. As soon as he was out of sight, Chelsea ran into her bedroom and slammed the door shut behind her. She had just had a disturbing thought. Suppose they would have to sell Mom's jewels? She pulled the black velvet box out of her schoolbag and caressed it tenderly.

Hearing her grandmother's voice in the hall outside her door, she slipped the box of jewels inside the case of her bed pillow. Later tonight, after everyone had gone to sleep, she'd be able to put the box back in her mother's room without anyone knowing she'd been playing with it.

7

Bunny's eyes felt as if they had been covered with rubber cement. She tried to open them, and although they moved slightly, the lids just wouldn't lift enough to let the light in. Turning over on her stomach, she tried to close off her thoughts so that she could drift back into sleep. Her mind, however, was awake, no matter that her body was still heavy with slumber and her eyelids too heavy to move. Damn!

Bunny wondered hazily what time it was. Was it morning or night? Afternoon or evening? She hadn't the slightest idea. God, she hoped it wasn't the middle of the night. Suddenly, remembering the depressing news about the termination of her contract, her eyelids flew open, but she could see nothing. Shit. It was the middle of the night!

She turned her head and looked at the tiny jeweled clock beside her bed. She could just make out the time on the radium-numbered dial. The long hand was on the four and the short hand on the three. God, it was only twenty minutes after three in the morning. She must have been out since noon, when Mama had given her the sedative to calm her nerves after that nasty letter came from the studio. Bunny lifted her head and reached over to turn on the light. As she moved, a smell of ammonia wafted from beneath the covers. Oh God no, she lamented, I've wet the bed again. It always seemed to happen when she took more than one pill and slept too long.

Disgusted with herself, she sat up and stripped off the wet silk nightgown, shivering as the cool night air touched her warm damp body. As she got to her feet, a feeling of momentary vertigo caused her to clutch at the bedpost to steady herself. Once she regained her balance, she made her way into the bathroom.

Creeping along the pink onyx floor, she snapped on the light and sat down on the toilet. Nothing happened immediately, so she reached across to the sink where she always kept a pack of Camels. She withdrew a cigarette, lighted it with a match from the glass dish filled with matchbooks from famous places, and took a long, deep drag of the soothing hot smoke. God, that felt good. Feeling a little better now that there was some nicotine in her blood, she stood up and went to the great pink onyx tub in the center of the room and turned on the water. She would take a long, hot bath, and get rid of all the ugly body odors. She hated to smell bad. A bath also would take up some of the time until the rest of the house would be awake.

As the steaming water gushed from the mouth of the huge gold-plated fish at the end of the tub, she dumped bubble bath from a cut-glass decanter into the water and watched the foam rise. One of the joys of her life was this bathroom. When she looked around at its beautiful beveled mirrors and handsome appointments, the shower stall with her name etched into its glass door, the exquisite rows of glass bottles of the most expensive perfumes, she was reassured that she was indeed a star, no matter what that dreary letter had indicated.

Only when her eyes drifted from the surface of things and looked deeper into the reflection of herself in the mirror did her mood darken again. Who was that ugly creature looking back at her? She couldn't be a star. She was a hag. A fat hag with thighs and belly all dimpled and bulging, breasts too big and pendulous to be sensuous, eyes too red and vacant to intrigue, mouth too slack to tempt. Nobody wanted her anymore. The studio didn't want her. The public didn't want her. She was over thirty and finished. What was she going to do with the rest of her life?

She sat down heavily on the wide ledge of the tub. The cigarette in her hand fell unnoticed onto the thick white fur rug and began to smolder. With her face in her hands, hiding from the reflection peering at her from every wall in the room, Bunny handled her problems in the only way she knew. She began to weep.

Nobody knew how to weep like Bunny did. Deep inside her she had an endless wellspring of tears and an infinite abundance of sobs, deep and wrenching and heartfelt. Weeping to her was far more than a Pavlovian response to an emotional situation. It was her refuge, her escape from reality or blame or responsibility. When she wept, everyone around her felt guilty and compelled to promise her anything, anything that would stop the heartrending sounds of her sorrow.

On that night, however, Bunny's distress had left her totally vulnerable, for no one was around to be moved by her tears. She was all alone. Her ever-watchful mother was sound asleep, exhausted from a long day of anxiety and unaccustomed physical effort. Hugh, who was a light sleeper and often prowled the corridors of the house checking windows and doors, was gone. Linda, whose room was over the garage, away from the main house, had left to spend the night with her boyfriend. Only Chelsea might have heard the sobs, but she had been moved to a room away from her mother's when she was having night terrors at the age of eight. Laverne had insisted that the screaming child be placed in the room farthest down the hall so that Bunny's beauty sleep would not be disturbed, and there the child had stayed.

Unconsoled, Bunny could weep for hours until her eyes were swollen shut, her nose clogged with mucus, and her throat raw from the depth of her sobbing. In the midst of her emotional uproar, and without her seeing or understanding what was going on around her, the insidious spark from her fallen cigarette began to snake across the rug, escaping the flame-proof marble room and nipping at the more vulnerable wool carpeting of her bedroom. Suddenly there was a flash of combustion as the flame reached the heavy damask draperies on the window, then the room became an inferno.

Through her tears Bunny finally heard the roar of the flames and felt the heat. Her chest still heaving with her sobs of despair, she looked up and saw that she was a prisoner of the flames engulfing her bedroom. Instinctively she jumped to her feet and attempted to flee, but she was in danger of fiery, painful immolation if she stepped out of her marble room. She picked up the burning rug and heaved it into the flames and out of the bathroom. She slammed the door, safe for the moment, only the moment. The room was filling with smoke, and it was becoming increasingly difficult to breathe.

For the first time in her life Bunny was truly alone. If she was going to be saved, she would have to do it herself. She could just see the headlines: Hollywood's Most Beautiful Star Dies in Her Bathroom! No! It wasn't going to happen that way. Not yet. Just a moment ago she was miserable enough to kill herself, but not now. Now she wanted to live. She went to the leaded glass window over the tub and tried to open it, but sealed by steam and rust, it would not budge.

She picked up a heavy crystal decanter filled with bath salts and threw it at the window, but the colored glass only cracked and the decanter fell back and smashed on the floor. Desperately she looked around for something bigger. Smoke filled the air, and it was hard to see anything. The scale! The hated scale that revealed her excesses and made her life miserable, she'd use that. Paying no attention to the pain she felt as the shards of broken glass tore into the soft flesh of her pampered feet, she grabbed the scale and slammed it into the large decorative window, hitting it again and again and again, until it flew open and the smoke was sucked out into the night air.

But Bunny was not out of trouble yet. Black smoke came billowing under the door, reaching out to the clear night air. She snatched one of her large Turkish towels, doused it in the water in the tub and then shoved it against the bottom of the door to hold the deadly black cloud back. When she saw that it worked, she did the same to all of the towels in the room, building a wall of moisture between herself and the inferno beyond.

The water was still running in the tub, spilling over its edge and swirling about the room, mixing with the broken glass and the blood streaming from the deep cuts on her feet. Unmindful of the pain, Bunny went to the open window, thrust her head out and began to scream for help.

She screamed and she screamed, in a voice big and loud, a voice she had never heard before, coming from a woman she had never known. A woman determined to save her own life.

The great mansions in Beverly Hills are not far from each other. Land had been precious there even in the thirties when the houses were built. If they had lived in the wilds of Malibu or the open spaces of Encino, it is possible that Bunny Thomas might have failed not only to save her own life but her mother's and daughter's as well, but they lived in Beverly Hills, next door to the Jack Benny house. Mary Benny heard the noise, awakened her husband, and called the fire department.

Bunny's screams aroused Laverne, who raced from her bedroom and down the smoke-darkened hallway, only to be turned back by the flames. Right behind her was Chelsea, her eyes wide with fear. Clutching each other, sickened by terror and sorrow at the realization that they could do nothing to save the woman who was the center of their lives, they stumbled down the staircase, the flames following them closely. They dashed out the door and into the arms of the arriving firemen.

Laverne immediately began to beg the men to save her daughter. "Please, please, get her! She's upstairs in that room by herself."

By that time the entire house was a blazing inferno, but miraculously, the fireman replied, "It's okay, ma'am. We're gettin' her. Look up there . . . here she comes!"

Laverne and Chelsea looked up, to the rungs of the ladder pressed against the side of the house, and there was Bunny, in the nude, with her ample bottom waving in the air as she made her way quickly out of the broken bathroom window, climbing rung by rung down to safety, while the firemen skillfully aimed their hoses to keep the scorching flames from burning her.

As soon as she touched the ground, a blanket was wrapped around her by another fireman, and she turned to smile at him. Laverne was dimly aware that there were flashbulbs popping everywhere as she and Chelsea both rushed to Bunny, grateful, joyful, and happy. Bunny stretched out her arms in a dramatic gesture of love, gathering her family to her. The blanket fell, and newspapers everywhere carried the picture of Bunny embracing her loved ones. Her modesty was protected only because her daughter managed to step in front of her just in time.

No one noticed that the child was tightly clutching a bed pillow in her arms.

8

Amid much fanfare and attention by the press, the star was hustled into an ambulance and transported to the emergency room at Cedars. There, the slivers of glass were removed from her feet by the city's finest plastic surgeon, who had been routed out of bed by the hospital's administrator. Bunny was admitted for observation and possible effects of smoke inhalation and wheeled into a luxurious room reserved for the city's most influential people. Chelsea followed her grandmother into Bunny's room and, curling up on a chair, fell asleep.

Although Laverne requested that Bunny be given a shot to calm her nerves, the excited young woman refused to take anything.

"Mama, no, please! I don't feel like going to sleep. I'm much too excited. Turn on the television and see if we're on the morning news!" she exclaimed.

"Bunny, darling, do what the doctor says. You've got

your nerves all worked up, and you need to rest," Laverne insisted, in the gentle but firm manner that usually worked with her daughter.

"No, Mama. I've already had more than fifteen hours of sleep today. I want to stay awake," Bunny insisted stubbornly.

Laverne knew it was useless to try to force her daughter to do anything she didn't want to do. She had learned that to control Bunny effectively she had to use guile and persuasion. She turned on the television, and sure enough, they were the lead story. Mercifully, it was a slow news day, and every channel showed pictures of the star and her family in front of the blazing mansion. Padding the story, the reports reached back into the past and showed clips of Bunny's most successful films and heralded her as one of Hollywood's brightest stars. They referred to her as a heroine whose cries for help had not only saved her own life, but those of her family.

Laverne watched the news with satisfaction. When it was over and Bunny finally fell asleep, Laverne woke Chelsea and took her to the Beverly Hills Hotel, where they checked into a bungalow. Clutching her pillow, Chelsea crawled into bed, but Laverne had no time to rest. It was already morning, time for her to swing into action. Bunny must be kept in the news as long as possible. She called newspaper editors, the wire services, and the television news departments and invited them to a press conference, promising that Bunny herself would appear and tell the story of her rescue from the fire. Then she called the city fire department and scheduled a visit two days later. She asked that the firefighters who had been at their home be present so that Bunny could personally thank each one of them.

With those events scheduled, she called her favorite saleswoman at I. Magnin's and asked her to send over several of their finest nightgowns and robes in Bunny's size, as well as some clothes for herself. Maxwell Holly, the celebrity hair stylist, however, proved difficult.

"Please, Maxwell, you must come to the hospital tomorrow to do Bunny's hair. You're the only one I trust to bring out her radiant beauty . . . please," she cajoled.

"Mrs. Thomas, you haven't paid me for the last two months. I can't afford to work for nothing anymore," he protested. "It's not like it was when she was top box office, you know. She hasn't made a successful film in ages."

"I promise you faithfully, I absolutely swear on my daughter's life, that you will receive payment in full as soon as the insurance company pays me for the loss of everything we own."

"You lost everything?" he asked, curious.

"Absolutely everything. We were barely out when the gas lines exploded. The house went up like a haystack, there was nothing the firemen could do to save it. We were lucky to get out alive, but we lost everything—even my daughter's jewels . . . all gone . . . there's nothing left," she said, dropping her voice dramatically.

"Was everything insured?" he asked, suddenly interested. Bunny Thomas's fascination with gems was well-documented, for a succession of wealthy lovers over the past few years had wooed her with expensive baubles and bangles. Bedding the great star was costly, but most men felt they'd gotten their money's worth, in ego satisfaction if not much else.

"Absolutely. Our finances will shortly be quite liquid, Maxwell."

"Okay, what time do you want me at the hospital?"

"No later than nine. I want her to look exquisite when she leaves the hospital to come home later in the day."

"Home? I thought it burned down," he questioned her.

"Slip of the tongue," Laverne hastened to explain. "Home is now a bungalow at the Beverly Hills Hotel, until I can find another suitable residence. I would also appreciate it if you would bring Nadia to do Bunny's makeup."

That accomplished, Laverne began to write out a list of things that she needed to do, people she still needed to call. Reaching into the pocket of the robe she'd worn the night before, Laverne patted a stiff piece of paper. Thank God she'd had the presence of mind to snatch up the check she'd received for the sale of the furniture. It would take care of their expenses until matters were settled with the insurance company. She closed her eyes and said a little prayer. She was rid of that big white elephant of a house at last, and without any loss of face. No one would now ever have to learn how close they had been to financial disaster.

The clothing she had ordered was delivered to the hotel by noon. Laverne looked quickly through the garments and chose a simple black suit and white silk blouse. She had already showered and put on makeup, which the hotel had sent in earlier from its sundries shop. The Evins pumps were a little big, but she had no time to wait for others to be brought. She had to get to the bank and deposit the check immediately so that she would have some cash.

Before leaving the hotel, she checked to see if Chelsea was awake, and found her still sleeping soundly, hugging the pillow that she'd brought with her. For just a moment Laverne felt a brief flicker of gratitude that her granddaughter required so little attention. Quietly she closed the door, left a brief note instructing Chelsea to call room service if she was hungry, and promised that she would be back in a few hours.

As soon as she finished at the bank, Laverne took a taxi to look at the ruins of the once-glorious mansion, hoping that perhaps one of their cars had been spared. In the bright sunlight, the devastation was shocking. Only minutes after Bunny had been rescued, the flames had reached the gas lines and exploded, burning the house to the ground. Nothing was left but two giant brick chimneys rising from the black and smoky ashes, stretching to the sky like two giant arms raised in supplication to heaven. She looked with dismay at the wreckage of the garage, where only the burned and twisted metal skeletons of their cars remained. Would she ever again feel rich enough to buy another Rolls-Royce?

She shrugged off the doubts and the regrets. Even though everything they had was gone, it was for the best. It was time to start afresh. She whirled about and returned to the waiting cab.

"Where to now?" the driver asked.

"The Oscar Garland Agency . . . do you know where it is?"

"Sure do, lady," he retorted.

Laverne settled back into the seat. Hilda Marx was one of Bunny's biggest fans, and she was also one of the savviest agents in town. Bunny would need better representation than she'd been getting from Rupert Doan. It was time to make a change—a very fast change. In Hollywood, the first thing one did when times were lean was to find a new agent.

9

Hilda Marx was not accustomed to having people arrive at her office without appointments. One of the strongest, most powerful agents in the business, she had proven beyond a doubt that a woman could negotiate as toughly as any man. She had a roster of big clients, and she never represented anyone in whose talent she did not believe wholeheartedly.

The daughter of a famous actress and a top movie business attorney, she had cut her teeth on the business and had grown up learning the intricacies of studio contracts. Her father had taught her the importance of cutting the right deal, and her clients benefited from her expertise and were grateful to have her working for them.

Moreover, she had a sincere interest in her clients' careers and welfare.

A tall, broad-shouldered woman, Hilda was considered more striking than pretty. She usually wore tailored suits and was always simply but perfectly dressed. To her secretary's surprise, she agreed to see Laverne Thomas.

Although she was kept waiting for ten minutes, when Laverne was finally ushered into Hilda's luxurious office, she was greeted warmly.

"Laverne, I was so sorry to hear about your house burning down last night. It must be terrible to lose everything you own," Hilda said sympathetically, pulling her tall, lean body from the leather chair and reaching across the desk to shake hands. The light coming from the huge window behind her cast a halo around her head as it bounced off the shiny, naturally bright red hair that was so curly she had to have it straightened regularly in order to maintain the sleek chignon at the nape of her neck.

Laverne looked directly into the agent's hazel eyes and put a suitably distressed look on her face and replied, "Yes, but I'm very thankful that everyone survived."

"I heard on the news this morning that there were no servants in the house. Was that a misprint?" she asked slyly. She needed to know just how candid this woman intended to be.

Laverne looked down at her hands and replied, "I could tell you it was the staff's day off, but it would be a lie." She sighed and then admitted, "I let them go because Bunny's contract was dropped by Taurus, and without her income, we can't continue to live in the style to which we've become accustomed."

"Mmm, too bad," Hilda murmured, pleased that Laverne was playing it straight. "So what can I do for you?"

"Bunny's career has hit a low point, Hilda," Laverne admitted candidly. "Taurus kept putting her in one mediocre film after another, and Rupert Doan didn't have the balls to stand up to them for her."

"There's not much an agent can do for a contract player,

Laverne," Hilda replied, her bright eyes watching Laverne closely.

"I know that, but he's lost faith in Bunny. I can tell
by the way he's always apologizing for the studio and
making excuses for them. An agent is supposed to be on
his client's side, damn it," she said angrily.

"You want the Garland office to sign her?" Hilda asked,
pressing the tips of her slim and very white hands together
and touching her chin thoughtfully.

"I don't want just the Garland office, Hilda, I want
you. I want someone who recognizes her ability and potential and who will go to bat for her."

"Why is it so urgent that you make a change right
now?" the agent asked.

"Because that damn fire last night has put Bunny in
the news, and you know what short attention spans these
producers have. I want someone who will orchestrate her
comeback, get her a big film as quickly as possible, before
the fuss dies down. With the right part, she'll deliver box
office, I promise you." Laverne spoke with passion and
conviction, for she believed every word she said.

"What about the contract with Rupert?"

"It's a handshake. I can terminate it today with a letter.
Will you take Bunny on?" Laverne asked anxiously.

"I could tell from her picture in the paper that she
needs to take off at least thirty pounds."

"All she needs is incentive," Laverne responded
quickly. "She overeats only when she's upset and depressed."

Hilda punched a button on her desk, summoning her
secretary. The woman arrived with steno pad in hand,
and Hilda dictated a quick letter to Bunny's agent, firing
him. When she finished, she said, "Type it on plain paper
and prepare it for Bunny Thomas's signature. Then give
it to Mrs. Thomas to take with her."

After the secretary left the room, Hilda swiveled her
chair around so that her back was to her visitor. She
stared thoughtfully out the window for a few minutes.
As suddenly as she had turned away, she turned back and

said in a serious tone, "Laverne, even though you're her mother, I believe you're right about Bunny. Her potential has never come even close to being tapped. You get her thin, and I'll see that she's cast in Rick Wehner's next film."

Laverne was astonished by the suggestion. "Good God, he makes those heavy 'cinema verité' movies that play mostly in art houses. What would Bunny do in one of those?"

"Act, my dear. And she'll do it without a lot of makeup or an expensive wardrobe or perfectly coiffed hair. People get tired of watching actresses who do nothing but look pretty and decorate the scene. We're going to push her over the edge, and she'll either fly or she'll fall flat on her face. It's the only chance to resurrect her career."

"Oh God, that's scary," Laverne said, shaken by the thought. Could Bunny really make it on her ability alone?

"Rick wants to break into the mainstream with his own kind of films. The only way he can do that is to cast a major star and have her perform brilliantly. He's a great director, and if it works . . . well, take a guess what will happen. An Academy Award nomination? Her choice of juicy scripts? All of the above, but best of all, she'll be respected. And how many pretty faces in this town ever experience that?"

Laverne listened closely, memorizing every word as she stared into the agent's eyes, which had seemed to harden into marble. God, this woman was formidable, she thought. She would be either a great ally or a deadly enemy.

"So . . . what do you think?" Hilda said quietly.

"I think we'll try it your way," Bunny's mother replied.

"You won't be sorry. I've seen all of your daughter's films, and I think the studio's squandered her talent. I've seen the depth of her pain shining through those bright eyes of hers."

Laverne was unnerved by the remark. "Pain? What pain do you see in Bunny?" she asked nervously, and then in an attempt to cover her own unease, said, "Why, she's a dear, sweet person, very easy to get along with, and extremely happy when she's working."

Hilda Marx drew a long filter-tip cigarette from the gold Tiffany case lying on her desk, put it between her lips and lit it. As the smoke curled up toward her eyes, she smiled sardonically.

"I see her as a woman with secrets . . . deep, dark secrets . . . that perhaps no one will ever know. Mark my words, she'll be a different actress altogether if we find a director who will tap into them and put her emotions on the screen."

Laverne left the office with the letter for Rupert Doan in her hand and a worried look on her face. Was it possible that dear, sweet, lovable Bunny was still suffering from those terrible nights with Gordon Baker? No, it wasn't possible. It just couldn't be. Bunny had not mentioned a word about the subject for years.

10

Chelsea heard the knob turn on the door to her bedroom at the hotel, and she quickly closed her eyes and pretended to sleep, knowing it was Grandma checking to see if she had awakened. She didn't feel like talking, didn't feel like anything except being alone.

She couldn't stop thinking about the fire. It had happened so fast. At first it had been exciting, watching the flames envelop the house, seeing her mother being rescued, but now that the cold reality of loss had set in, she felt miserable. Everything they had was gone—all the clothes, books, toys, and dolls that she cherished, everything. Yesterday when she had talked to her grandmother about moving to another house, it had seemed like an adventure, but now that the only home she had ever known had vanished, she was frightened. She found it hard to believe that she would never wake up in her lovely pink bedroom again, never open the window and smell the citrus blossoms, never run down that giant curving staircase with her hand skimming the highly polished banister.

The door closed silently and she knew her grandmother had gone. She opened her eyes to study the unfamiliar surroundings. The room was pretty, done in blue and green, but nothing like the house that had been her home. She closed her eyes tightly once more, trying to shut out the memory of what was and would never be again.

She squeezed the pillow she had carried with her, the small soft down pillow that she had slept with all of her life, and felt the box she had slipped inside the case. At least she had saved her mother's precious jewels. How happy Mom and Grandma would be when they found out they had something beautiful left.

Cautiously she sat up and swung her legs over the side of the bed. Padding barefoot across the carpet, she opened the door and looked out into the sitting room. Everything was silent. She decided that her grandmother had left again, but she explored the bungalow to make sure. She found the note, and picked up the telephone to call room service. She hadn't been in a hotel for years. When she was little, she and her grandmother often went on personal appearance tours with Bunny, but that had stopped when Chelsea was eight years old and began to ask questions about the strange men who were always in her mother's bed in the morning.

She started to order fresh raspberries and cream but stopped when she remembered what her grandmother had told her about needing money. Instead she asked merely that they bring her an orange, a glass of milk, and a doughnut. Grandma would have a fit if she caught her eating a "greasy doughnut," because she never allowed anything like that in the house. She said it was too much of a temptation for Bunny. Poor Mom. She was always hungry, it seemed, and everything she ate made her fat.

It was strange, because Grandma was skinny and so was she.

While waiting for her breakfast to arrive, Chelsea went back to the bedroom and got the case of jewels. One by one she extracted the beautiful pieces from the case and laid them on top of the coverlet. It made her happy just to look at them. Grandma was always saying that Chelsea was a Gypsy just like Bunny, because she loved jewelry so much. She smiled in satisfaction, imagining the delighted look on her mother's face when she saw that her precious trinkets had survived.

It turned out to be a long, lonely day. If she'd had some clothes or some shoes, Chelsea would have gone out for a walk, but all she had was the cotton nightie she had been wearing when they escaped from the house. She looked through the boxes that Magnin's had delivered, but there was nothing in them for her. Perhaps Grandma would remember to pick up something.

After breakfast she read through the guest-informant magazine, played several games of tic-tac-toe with herself on the hotel stationery, and finally turned on the television. After watching reruns of *I Married Joan* and *Our Miss Brooks,* she turned off the set. Television bored her almost as much as the whole process of making movies bored her. Of course, she loved to go see her mother's films, but there were very few movies that interested her. Chelsea was not cut out to be a spectator. She liked to be doing things all the time.

Later, after she had a hot bath, she called room service again and ordered herself a cheeseburger, a Coke, and a plate of french fries. She had just hung up the telephone when she had another good idea and had them include a rich hot fudge sundae with lots of nuts and whipped cream and two cherries. Eating all that would use up some of the time, and it would serve Gran right for leaving her stranded here alone all day. Grandma never let her eat the stuff all her friends ate.

When the maid came in to clean up, Chelsea tried to

start a conversation with her, but the woman, whose English was poor anyway, was eager to finish and go home.

Alone again, Chelsea decided to take the jewelry out of the case and try it on once more. While she was preening in front of the mirror with the ropes of pearls draped around her neck, the emerald and diamond ring perched on her finger, and the sapphire earrings drooping from her tiny earlobes, she suddenly had an inspiration. Quickly, she pulled back the coverlet, and when she had finished arranging the jewelry artfully across the wool blanket, she made the bed again. It looked a little lumpy, but no one would notice that.

She was excited at the prospect of leading Bunny into the room and sweeping back the coverlet to reveal the treasure. How thrilled her mother would be when she learned how brave and smart her little girl was to have saved her jewelry! When oh when were they ever going to get there?

It was twilight before she heard a sound at the door. Finally, her family had arrived. Chelsea ran to her mother, who sat in a wheelchair, both feet bandaged and elevated. She was startled to see Bunny looking so happy and radiant. Her hair looked wonderful, all fluffed out and wavy. Her makeup was perfect, and she was wearing a new velvet robe in blue with a wide lace collar that framed her face.

Chelsea started to give her mother a hug, but Laverne intervened.

"Don't mess your mother up. There's a reporter from the *Times* waiting outside to interview her and take her picture for a feature in Sunday's paper," Laverne said sternly. "I probably shouldn't have let him come before the press conference tomorrow, but his offer was too good to pass up."

"Hi, darling," Bunny said, reaching her hand out to touch her daughter's arm. "Have you been alone here all day?"

"Oh dear Lord," Laverne exclaimed. "I forgot to ha'

some clothes sent over for you, Chelsea. Well, you'll just have to wait in the other room."

"Mama, why can't she stay in here with me?" Bunny asked, seeing the stricken look on Chelsea's face.

"Don't be a fool, Bunny. You and I are all dressed up, and there is the poor little neglected waif in the same nightgown she was wearing when the fire broke out. Use your head!" she snapped. "You know how reporters grab on to a thing like that and make you look bad."

Bunny squeezed her daughter's hand and said regretfully, "Sorry, sweetie, your grandma's right. Do you mind waiting in the bedroom? I promise this won't take long."

Chelsea backed away, trying not to let her feelings be hurt. Uncomfortable at the center of attention, she tended never to make scenes.

"I'll be okay, Mom. Smile pretty for the camera."

"That's a good girl. As soon as we're finished, I'll have room service bring dinner in, and the three of us can talk," Laverne said, her voice softer and more conciliatory now that everyone was doing as she asked without making a fuss.

There was a knock at the door, so Chelsea turned and fled from the room. Feeling sad and unwanted, she pulled back the coverlet, swept up the jewelry and shoved it quickly into the black case. Then she tucked the velvet box under her pillow and climbed into bed. Mom's big surprise would have to wait until another time.

Listening to the muffled voices of the adults on the other side of the door, Chelsea heard her mother's high tinkly laugh many times and wondered what in the world she was so happy about. It took her an hour to fall asleep.

Bunny didn't finish the interview until almost nine o'clock in the evening. The reporter, an attractive young man who was a fan of hers, was reluctant to bring the conversation to a close. When he finally left, Laverne went into the bedroom to find out what Chelsea wanted for dinner, but she found her granddaughter asleep.

"Well, our little girl's in dreamland," she reported to Bunny.

"Poor baby, this whole ordeal has probably exhausted her. Maybe we ought to just let her sleep," Bunny commented. Then, taking a small bottle of medicine from her bathrobe pocket, she asked, "Mom, will you get me a glass of water?"

"Where did you get those pills?" Laverne asked suspiciously.

"Relax, Mama. They're just pain pills, that's all. The sutures in my feet are killing me."

Laverne got a glass of water from the bar in the sitting room and handed it to her. "Are you sure you should be taking those on top of all that wine you just drank?"

"For God's sake, no nagging, please. I just can't handle it tonight. Besides, I only had two glasses of wine. Somebody had to drink with the guy, since you insisted on having only tea."

Laverne pursed her lips with disapproval. "He drank half a glass, and look, the bottle's empty. You're the one who did most of the drinking."

"What the hell. I needed something to make me feel better about everything. You know it isn't easy being sparkling and brave after all I've been through the past couple of days." The expression on her face became very sad, and her lips formed themselves into the adorable pout that had charmed the world.

"I know, baby, I know," Laverne said sympathetically, feeling contrite for having criticized her. "But now you really ought to have a little something to eat. Suppose I order us a nice cup of chicken broth and a salad?"

"Ugh, I'd really rather have a steak sandwich with some french fries," Bunny replied.

Laverne knew she was in for a battle. "Look, darling, I promised Hilda Marx you'd lose weight—not just a pound or two, but a lot. You've got to curb your appetite, particularly now that you're not getting any exercise at all."

"I know, but I just don't want to start right now. I'm

hungry, damn it. I want something I can sink my teeth into, and a salad and soup just won't do it." Nothing made Bunny more belligerent than being denied food.

Laverne decided not to press the issue, knowing it would just bring on an emotional scene, and she'd eventually lose the battle anyway. "All right, I'll have them broil you a small filet, but no french fries. You'll have to make do with a baked potato."

"You know I can't stand to eat baked potatoes without sour cream," Bunny said stubbornly.

Gritting her teeth angrily, Laverne went to the telephone and ordered what Bunny wanted. Tomorrow she would call Dr. Jack and have him bring her some diet pills. There was no way she was going to get that weight off her daughter without a little help.

While they were eating dinner, they discussed their financial situation, and Laverne explained to Bunny that they would be basically solvent as soon as the insurance company settled all of their claims.

"But wasn't there a big mortgage on the house?" Bunny asked.

"The sale of the land should just about take care of that. The swimming pool and tennis court are still in good shape, and the value of the property has gone up considerably since we bought it fifteen years ago."

"But where are we going to live?" Bunny asked, spreading her slice of sourdough bread with a thick coating of butter.

"We'll rent a little place right here in Beverly Hills, where we'll still be in the middle of things," Laverne replied, surreptitiously moving the butter dish out of her daughter's reach. Where in the world had this child of hers gotten that ravenous appetite?

"Nice places are expensive. Will we have enough money?"

"The loss of your jewelry should bring a tidy sum. Thank goodness I kept everything insured at its market value. It cost me a pretty penny, I can tell you, but I was always nervous about being robbed. With you parading around all the time and being photographed wearing all those jewels, I figured it was only a matter of time before somebody nailed us."

Bunny sighed and leaned back in her chair. "I know we need the money, but I do hate the thought that all my beautiful jewels were destroyed. I'll probably never own anything like them again."

Laverne got up quickly and wheeled the table away from Bunny before she could eat more.

"I know how much you loved your trinkets, baby, but they were a problem for us anyway. I was going to sell some of the bigger pieces, but I hated taking them away from you. Believe me, having them burned up was the best thing that could have happened. That fire was a godsend."

"You really believe that?" Bunny asked curiously.

"In a strange way, yes, I most certainly do."

Bunny was pensive for a long moment, and then she said very softly, "It was my fault, Mom. I started the fire."

Laverne made a quick reflexive movement as she looked around to make sure there was no one else in hearing range.

"What are you talking about?" she asked, lowering her voice too. "The fire chief told me it was probably caused by the insulation wearing off some old wiring."

"I woke up in the middle of the night and went into the bathroom. I was groggy from the sleeping pills. You know what an awful day I'd had with the news from Taurus. Well, anyway, I apparently dropped a lighted cigarette on that fluffy rug, and it burst into flames."

Laverne moved close enough to her daughter so she could whisper.

"Don't you ever, ever say that again! You hear me? I know how these damned insurance companies work. They make you pay through the nose for years, and then when something happens, they try to find a reason not to pay you. You didn't mention this to anybody at the hospital, did you?"

Bunny was insulted. "Of course not! You might think I'm stupid, Mama, but I'm not."

"Then you just stick to that story you told—you

couldn't sleep, so you decided to take a bath. You had the door closed so as not to awaken anybody, and when you were finished bathing, you found yourself trapped in the bathroom, because your bedroom was an inferno."

"Mama, please don't talk to me like I'm still ten years old and can't think for myself. I'm the one who made up that story, remember?"

Laverne looked at her daughter in despair. God help her, she wouldn't be able to let her out of her sight until she got the insurance money in hand. Bunny was a bright, sensible girl, but when she'd had too much to drink or too many pills, she was liable to say anything. It was even worse when she was in love. Then she felt she had to blab everything to the guy in her bed. Lord, would life ever be simple?

A change of subject was in order, Laverne decided. "Well, at least if we live in Beverly Hills, Chelsea will benefit from their great school system, although the new trend seems to be to put kids into boarding school."

"I'd hate that," Bunny said. "I like having her around."

"Don't worry. Private school is not one of our priorities," Laverne said flatly. There was no way she was going to let Chelsea out of the house, because she needed her to keep tabs on Bunny. Her granddaughter was, in fact, far more reliable and trustworthy than anyone she knew. Bunny was eighteen years older than Chelsea in chronological age, but somewhere in her short life span, Chelsea had already passed her mother on the path to adulthood. Laverne sighed as she looked at her beautiful daughter and wondered if she would ever grow up.

"I think I better go to bed. I'm starting to feel a little woozy," Bunny muttered.

"I told you not to take those pills on top of that wine. Come on, I'll help you wash up and get into a fresh nightgown."

"I don't feel like washing up. The makeup can just stay on until tomorrow morning," Bunny said, yawning widely.

"You know it's bad for your complexion to sleep with

your pores all clogged up with that goo. Come on, I'll
do it for you. All you have to do is sit still and relax,"
Laverne insisted, pushing the wheelchair toward the
bathroom. It wouldn't be the first night that she'd had
to put her star-child to bed.

Chelsea, who had awakened and was listening to their
conversation from behind her bedroom door, was in a
state of shock. They didn't want the jewelry! She'd done
a bad thing by saving it. Now what would she do? Her
grandmother would be furious if she found out.

Chelsea crept back into bed in the darkened room and
waited silently until both women had gone to bed. When
the place had been quiet for enough time to assure her
they were asleep, she sneaked into the room where they
had been eating. Ravenously hungry, she ate what was
left on their plates.

11

Chelsea was afraid to leave the hotel bungalow, since
she couldn't very well carry her pillow with her, and there
was no place to hide the jewelry box without risking it
being found by the maids. As soon as the stores opened,
Grandma had dashed out to pick up things they would
need, and she remembered to buy a skirt, blouse, and
shoes for Chelsea. She forgot, however, to buy underwear, and so Chelsea had to take a pair of the lace panties
the store had sent for her mother and pin them on. They
were much too big for her and the lace scratched her
skin, but she pinned them to her blouse so they wouldn't
fall down.

Although the other clothes fit her, she didn't particularly like them because they were so plain and unstylish.
Her grandmother always bought her such drab, service-
able outfits, making her feel like a dolt at school. But

Laverne would silence her pleas with a sharp remark: "Little girls don't need to be fashion plates," or "We have to save our money now so that when you're grown, we'll be able to afford stylish things for you." It never occurred to Chelsea to compare her meager wardrobe with her mother's closets full of gorgeous clothes, because Bunny, after all, was the star in the family. But Grandma wore only the best too, so it didn't seem fair to Chelsea that she never, ever, got to pick out anything for herself, even though she was now twelve years old.

All afternoon the bungalow was filled with visitors. The hairdresser and makeup people arrived to get Bunny ready for her press conference. Hilda Marx appeared shortly after two with Bick Martin, a new publicity agent she had hired. Chelsea drifted around on the periphery, indulging in her favorite pastime of trying to piece the adult conversations together and figure out what was going on.

Grandma spent most of the afternoon on the telephone with the insurance companies, and from the tone of her voice, Chelsea could tell she was upset. She heard her threatening them with attorneys and lawsuits. Life had suddenly become very interesting.

When it was time for Bunny to leave for her press conference, which was to take place in one of the hotel's public rooms, Chelsea asked her mother if it would be okay if she ordered an early dinner for herself. They'd had only a small salad for lunch, and she was hungry.

"Don't bother your mother now, child," Laverne scolded. "She has to have her head clear for the press conference. Besides, you're going with us. The press will be expecting to see the whole family together."

"Do I have to?" Chelsea asked, panicked at the thought of leaving the bungalow unguarded.

"Yes, now come on. Move yourself!" Laverne commanded.

Hilda Marx intervened. "It's a great idea, Laverne. Come here, honey," she said, directing her attention to

Chelsea. "I want you to push your mother's wheelchair into the room, okay?"

Chelsea realized she was trapped. There was no way she could avoid going with them. "I'll be with you in a second," she said, turning and running toward her bedroom before anyone could stop her.

"Chelsea!" her grandmother barked in exasperation.

As soon as she was in the room, she slammed the door shut and locked it. Grandma would be hot on her heels in a moment, and she needed to do something about the jewelry. Scanning the room anxiously, trying not to be distracted by the angry knocking on the door and her grandmother's imperious orders to open it, she could see no place to hide her treasure. There was only one quick place to stash it, between the mattress and box spring. Tonight she would have to find a serious hiding place.

Her grandmother was livid when she opened the door, but Chelsea emerged with her head down and whispered, "Sorry. I had to go to the bathroom," as she brushed past her, hurrying to her mother's chair. The quickest way to escape her grandmother's ire was to assume a properly penitent attitude immediately. Chelsea had learned very early in her life that it was easier to absorb wrath than to try to defend her position.

The press conference was well-attended, especially by the Hollywood foreign press, because Bunny was still a huge star overseas. Flanked by her new agent and press representative and gowned in an exquisite mauve lace dressing gown, Bunny dominated the scene. Being a star was what she was, and when the lights were turned on by the television newsmen, her own inner spotlight went on, and she glowed with self-confidence and pleasure. She handled the questions adroitly, with just the right amount of self-deprecating humor. When one of the Hollywood columnists, who was known for her soppy, sob-sister approach, asked her how she felt when she thought she might burn to death or be disfigured, Bunny seized the moment and made the most of it.

Her eyes bright with rising tears, she looked at a point

just above the last row, so that her eyes would be wide open in photographs, and replied, "All I could think about was that I was cut off from my little girl, and I prayed to the good Lord that she would be saved." She turned her famous profile to the crowd and looked back at Chelsea, who was standing behind her. She reached toward her daughter, who responded on cue, lowering her head just enough so that her mother could take her face in her hands and kiss her gently on the forehead. Chelsea, who had been playing the role of the adored child all of her life, knew better than to get too close and risk mussing her mother's hair and makeup, and the resultant scene was picture-perfect.

The flashbulbs popped furiously, and even hard-edged Hilda Marx felt a lump in her throat. My God, she thought, Bunny Thomas really was an actress, a totally natural one. She looked across at Laverne and saw that she too was moved to tears. What a trio they were!

After about twenty minutes Bick Martin took the microphone and said, "Three more questions. That's all. Miss Thomas has been through a terrible ordeal."

The reporter from the *Herald* who had been sitting quietly in the front row taking notes asked: "Miss Thomas, do you have any idea how the fire started?"

Bunny took a deep sigh and replied regretfully, "No . . . but I surely hope they find out soon. I'm not sure I'll ever have a sound night's sleep until I know exactly what caused it."

The reporter started to ask a follow-up question, but Bick ignored him and pointed to a woman from United Press.

"Have any of your fabulous jewels been recovered?"

"I understand they're combing through the ashes as we speak," Bunny answered quickly. "It was a terrible fire, you know, the house was completely destroyed. I'm sorry to lose those beautiful jewels . . . as well as everything else I owned, but I'm not going to weep over a handful of rocks and minerals when my dearest treasures, my family, were spared."

Jesus Christ, Hilda Marx thought, we ought to run this broad for president!

The next reporter threw Bunny a curve. "Miss Thomas, just a few hours before the fire started, there was an announcement from Taurus that they were dropping your contract. Seems like you're on a run of bad luck, doesn't it?"

Bunny had been handling the press since she was just a little girl, and they did not intimidate her in the least. Instead of being ruffled, she smiled sweetly and paused for only a second before replying, "The fire was more than just bad luck. It was tragic. I lost everything. My daughter's baby pictures, the Oscar I won for *Homespun* and the Golden Globe for *Dancing Days* . . . all the little pieces of memorabilia that meant so much to me." She paused dramatically, and then, with her chin raised in dignity, she said the words exactly as Hilda had instructed her, "But the separation from Taurus was at my request. Movies are changing, and I want to change with them. The men at Taurus have a very narrow view of Bunny Thomas. Under contract with them, I would never be permitted to appear in a Rick Wehner film."

The controlled atmosphere erupted in a torrent of shouted questions from the surprised reporters, who began yelling to make themselves heard above the din. "Rick Wehner?" "Isn't that a stretch for you?" "Why would you do that, his films never make any money?"

The questions were coming so thick and so fast that Bunny could not respond properly to any of them. Bick leaned over Chelsea and ordered, "Move her out of here fast, kid."

Chelsea immediately pulled her mother's wheelchair away from the table and headed out of the room.

"What are you doing, honey?" Bunny protested, not quite ready for her moment to end.

"What Mr. Martin told me to do, Mom. Hold on, here we go!"

As they left the room, Bick Martin could be heard shouting that there was absolutely no arrangement with

Wehner, and that Bunny's remark only represented a feeling she had about the direction her career should take and that she was still in a state of shock and had appeared against the advice of her personal physician.

Hilda Marx and Laverne walked slowly back to the bungalow, following Bunny's wheelchair.

"So . . . what did I tell you?" Laverne asked smugly.

"I've got to hand it to her," Hilda replied. "She was brilliant. She did exactly what we told her to do . . . and then some. She must be a director's dream."

"So where do we go from here?" Laverne asked.

"I've already talked to Rick. He's got a screenplay that's perfect for her, but now that he knows for sure she'll do it, he wants to tailor it to her."

"How long will that take?"

"Rick doesn't work fast. He's a stickler for detail. I'd guess it will take him a month . . . six weeks . . . whatever. He doesn't work on a schedule. He's an artist."

Laverne was upset. "But . . . where does that leave us? Bunny will be yesterday's news in six weeks."

"No, she won't," Hilda replied. "I'll make damn sure of that. By the time Rick's ready, the financing and distribution of the film will be all set. Trust me. We'll make the announcement at a party the agency will give for her to celebrate her becoming one of our clients."

"You're going to give a party for her?" Laverne asked suspiciously. "Who's going to pay for that?"

"Our agency isn't planning to settle for just a percent of a single artist's salary anymore. There are lots of ways to cut the pie and get a bigger slice. We'll represent everyone, writer, director, stars—the whole package—and on top of that we'll get a percentage of the picture. You'll see."

Laverne looked doubtful. "I can't imagine the studios letting you get away with that."

"The studio system is a dinosaur . . . with just about as much future as those reptiles had. Believe my words," she said with assurance. "And Bunny Thomas is going to be in the forefront of a new wave of filmmaking that will sweep the industry clean."

Laverne listened and was convinced. She thought Hilda Marx was one of the sharpest, most intense people she had ever met.

After Bick and Hilda had gone, Bunny and Laverne talked about the future far into the evening. Bunny was stimulated by the attention she had received and excited about the new turn her career was taking.

Chelsea waited until they had retired to their room, and when she was sure they were asleep, she sneaked out into the garden. Using a hand trowel, which she had filched from the gardener's truck earlier, Chelsea proceeded to dig a hole under the shrubbery outside her window. Although the ground was soft and moist, it was slow work digging a hole deep enough not to be disturbed by gardeners planting flowers. Her arms were tired and her hands blistered by the time she was satisfied. Then she set the jewel case, which she had wrapped in a large piece of plastic cut from the shower curtain, in the deep hole and buried it.

When she had finished tamping down the dirt, she looked around to find something to mark the spot. There had to be some way, she thought, that would be permanent. It might be a very long time before she dared come back to retrieve the case, if ever. There was a wooden window ledge just above the site, and with the edge of the trowel, she gouged a small wedge into it. It wasn't much, but it was the best she could do, because she was exhausted and one of the blisters on her hand had begun to bleed.

She tiptoed back into the bungalow, washed the dirt off her hands and knees, crawled into bed and fell soundly asleep.

12

Anne Hunter read the headline and then silently passed the morning paper to her husband, who was just finishing his breakfast and the *Wall Street Journal*. Frank scanned the article, then looked up at his wife and said quietly, "Thank God they all got out all right."

"What do you suppose caused the fire?" she asked, sipping her coffee and nervously pushing at her dark hair.

Frank shook his head. "I'd bet my life it wasn't an act of God. Bunny was probably in a stupor of some kind and dropped a cigarette."

Anne looked out the window of the breakfast room through the cypress trees to the amethyst sky reflected on the calm waters of Monterey Bay. It was going to be an unseasonably warm clear day on the peninsula, and she had been looking forward to her morning walk through the forest until she had seen the story in the paper. After almost eight years of marriage and two beautiful children of her own, she still found herself troubled by the unresolved relationship between her husband and his first child.

Biting her lip, Anne finally gave voice to the subject that Frank had declared closed years ago. "Honey, don't you think you ought to make some attempt to see Chelsea? After all, she is your daughter, and you haven't seen her since she was just a baby, really."

Frank, whose boyish good looks had matured into distinctive handsomeness, shook his head and turned the page of the paper.

"It's no use. If you'll recall, I tried five years ago when I was in L.A. for the bar association convention, but I couldn't get past that witch Laverne. As soon as she heard my voice, she started threatening me with that old homosexual crap, and I got disgusted and hung up on her."

"It's such a shame. I'll just bet that Chelsea doesn't even know you've been sending money to support her."

"She's my child, Anne. I have an obligation to support her whether she knows about it or not."

Anne sighed in exasperation. "It's not just the money, Frank. I think it's important for her to know she has a father who loves her and cares about her." She stopped for a breath and then continued, "I'd hate to think that if something happened between you and me that you'd pull away from Jeremy and Lisa."

Startled by the implication in her words, Frank took her hand in his and squeezed it gently. "Honey, you know better than that. Those children mean everything to me . . . and nothing in the world will ever happen to the two of us, ever." He reached over and kissed her on the cheek.

Anne was as different from Bunny as any woman could be. Born to wealth, she had graduated from Vassar with a degree in American History and had planned to teach school, but had been discouraged by her parents who felt it unseemly for her to take a job from someone who needed the salary. Bright and energetic, she had turned to volunteer community work and was organizing a school library program when Frank Hunter returned after the break-up of his celebrated marriage.

Two months after his divorce was final, Frank married the not beautiful but not unpretty young woman who had been brought up with the same advantages and values as he had. Although others advised her not to rush, telling her he was on the rebound and might regret his hasty plunge back into matrimony, Anne had loved him enough to take the risk. Just to be sure, however, she had gotten pregnant on their honeymoon in France, and produced a son nine months later.

After he had finished law school and passed the bar, Frank joined his father's firm in San Francisco. Because he wanted his children to live outside the city, he and Anne chose to make their permanent home in the Carmel area, and so they had built a home on two of his father's ocean-front acres on the Seventeen Mile Drive. Specializing in tax law, Frank opened a small office ‘- Monterey and commuted into the big city only two days each week. Both heirs to substantial fortunes, the young couple worked hard, lived in a comfortable but not ostentatious style, and kept their names out of the newspapers. Having had one brief but intense experience in the public eye, Frank wanted no more of it.

One morning, two days after the fire, Frank arrived at his office in San Francisco and was startled to learn that Laverne had called and wanted to talk to him. Reluctant to expose himself to more vituperation, he called Brian Delaney, the attorney who had handled his divorce settlement, and told him to find out what she wanted.

"I read about the fire in the paper. Suppose this has something to do with the call?" Brian asked.

"I would guess so." Frank sighed and remarked, "She probably wants another advance on the trust."

"Frank, when are you going to learn to say no to that bitch?"

"Look, Brian, I know I don't have to give her anything more than the settlement stipulates, but I don't want my child to suffer because her grandmother is a pain in the ass," Frank replied, and remembering the conversation with his wife, added, "Tell her she'll get the money, but I want Chelsea to come visit me for a weekend. After all, she's got a half brother and sister she's never even met."

"Now you're talking. How much do you want to give her?"

"Find out how much she needs."

Later that afternoon Brian called Frank back after he had talked to Laverne.

"First of all, she wants ten thousand immediately to tide her over until she collects the insurance on the house and the jewels. Frank, I don't remember, but didn't you give Bunny some of that jewelry?"

"I sure did. I gave her a ring with a three-carat square-cut diamond and a matching emerald, and on our wedding day, my grandmother presented her with a triple strand of very fine old pearls. Natural pearls, not cultured. As I recall, Bunny had them restrung with a clasp that had a fairly good-sized pink diamond in it. It cost a bundle, but I had to admit it was beautiful. My grandmother was upset that she'd changed them. You tried to get it back, remember? I wanted to give it to Chelsea when she was grown, but Laverne insisted she'd lost them."

"Well, maybe we ought to check to see if she makes a claim for them," Brian said. "We could haze her a little if she did."

"Hey, forget it, friend. That stuff is all in the past. What did she say about Chelsea visiting me?"

"Said it was fine with her, but she had to ask Chelsea if she was interested. She'll let me know tomorrow."

At dinner that evening, after the nanny had taken the children upstairs to get them ready for bed, Frank told Anne the news.

"Do you think she'll come?" Anne asked, now a little nervous about having initiated an encounter that might prove to be emotionally unsettling for everyone concerned.

Frank shrugged his shoulders. "How would I know? I have no idea what kind of person my daughter is. Do you think we should mention it to the children?"

Anne was cautious. "Not until we know for sure she's coming. It will be too difficult to explain if she doesn't show up."

The Hunter family needn't have worried. Laverne called Brian the next day and said that Chelsea had no desire to see her father and would certainly never go to visit him at his house.

Frank was disappointed but not surprised. He was fairly certain that Laverne had successfully poisoned his daughter's mind against him.

"What about the money, Frank?" Brian asked. "That old harridan claims it's your fault not hers that the kid has no use for you."

"Give it to her, but deduct it from the trust principal," Frank snapped, "and remind her that she's stealing from her granddaughter's future."

Brian Delaney was not a lawyer who believed in giving up a good cause. "Look, I don't think you should just lie down and play dead with those women, Frank. You've got a right to see your own kid, and the divorce settlement so stipulated," he said with annoyance.

"You're forgetting laches, my friend, laches. If you fail to exercise a right, you lose it legally. And I haven't really pressed to see Chelsea for years. Any judge would have serious doubts about the sincerity of my interest in her after all this time."

"Look, let's call a spade a spade, Frank. You haven't seen Chelsea because Laverne threatened to embarrass you publicly with that one little indiscretion in college. That's the only reason you haven't had a closer relationship with your daughter. Besides, who'd believe that baloney anyway?"

"Brian, I know you mean well, but I've got a wife and two children to protect now, not to mention my friendship with Evan Gorski."

"This won't be the last time she extracts money from you, buddy. You know that, don't you?" Brian said, frustrated by the situation.

"Don't let it bother you. I've had enough hassles with Laverne to last me a lifetime."

Frank put down the telephone and stared out the window thoughtfully. "Evan's never admitted to his homosexuality," he said to his wife, "and he never will, because of his family. But that's his business. His family is very important to him. Only his sister knows, and she's fiercely protective of him. I'll never forgive myself for telling Bunny his name, and keeping those letters, so Laverne could find them."

Anne nodded with understanding. "Evan is such a nice person, but he's not strong either physically or psychologically."

"I know, and that's why I've avoided any kind of public attention. If there wasn't a wellspring of money for her to draw from, I feel almost certain that Laverne would shoot off that mouth of hers just to be spiteful." He

paused and added softly, "That's why I refused to run
for Congress last year when the party approached me.
Laverne's always hated me, you know, and I don't want
to do anything that might draw her fire." He took her
hand and squeezed it. "So, just let it be, darling, but
thanks for caring."

When the conversation ended, Frank went into his
study and opened the drawer of his desk to take out the
newspaper clipping showing Chelsea standing behind her
mother's wheelchair at the press conference. He studied
it closely for the sixth or seventh time. Of his three children, Chelsea was the only one who looked like him, and
the resemblance was remarkable. Poor kid, he thought,
Laverne must hate it.

13

After less than a week in the hotel bungalow, Laverne
received the money from Frank and rented a furnished
house in the Beverly Hills flats, just north of Santa Monica
Boulevard on Crescent Drive. It was not big or fashionable or luxurious, but it was in the right neighborhood,
and the scaled-down lifestyle was in keeping with Bunny's
new image, that of serious actress. The insurance company was suspicious of the origin of the fire as well as
the complete loss of Bunny's jewelry. Not a single jewel
had been found in the ashes, and it was readily apparent
the claim would not be soon settled.

Chelsea was enrolled in a public school for the first
time in her life, but she adjusted easily, as she always had.
Unlike some children, who grow up thinking they are at
the center of the world, Chelsea always knew that her
role was a supporting one. Bunny was the star, and as
she had heard her grandmother say over and over, there
was room for only one star in the family. Chelsea had

never demanded much attention, and she was unspoiled, appreciative, and fairly content with her life; but above all, she was extremely self-reliant and dependable. Other families might have considered her a treasure, but Laverne and Bunny simply took her good qualities for granted.

Rick Wehner's screenplay eventually arrived, and it was brilliant. The part of Camilla was as juicy as they came, and Hilda Marx delivered on her promises for financing and distribution. She convinced Columbia that Wehner would deliver a film that would not only be Academy Award dynamite, but popular in the overseas market, which would cover their downside risk. A smooth talker with a reputation for picking winners, Hilda was very persuasive. Besides, the more impossible the dream, the more irresistible it was to Hollywood's executive ego. Everybody dreamed of taking the big leap and landing in a mountain of money.

Rick insisted that the picture be shot on location in London, where he made all of his films and where he could surround himself with a crew with whom he was comfortable. Bunny and Laverne had been warned that it might be a very long time before they returned to California, because Rick Wehner refused to be held to a tight schedule and he edited as he filmed, often going back to reshoot scenes that didn't work. It was expensive and not efficient, but Wehner contended that art could not be created on a deadline.

Chelsea was at a stage in her life when friends were of utmost importance. Told that she would soon be relocated on the other side of the world, where she would know no one, she rebelled for the first time. Laverne had no sympathy for the teenager, and was, in fact, outraged by her granddaughter's unusual burst of defiance.

"No, you may not stay here!" Laverne declared flatly. "Your mother wants you with us, and the last thing she needs is to be worrying about you when she has more important things going on in her life. Have you got any idea how much the success of this picture means to all of us?"

Chelsea did not back down as she usually did.

"Please, Gran, this is a lovely house. Couldn't I just stay here with the housekeeper? Really, I'd be just fine," she pleaded.

Laverne was outraged by her grandchild's unusual impudence. "The nerve!" she exploded. "Just who do you think you are, anyway? I can't afford to pay for a house and a housekeeper just for you. Now, get your things packed, Chelsea. I'm sick of listening to your complaints!"

Chelsea had never been effective at arguing, because she was forever cursed with the ability to see the other person's point of view, and she had to admit that it would be an unwarranted extravagance to maintain a house and a servant just for her. Her friends had advised her to throw a monumental temper tantrum, but since she had never done it, she wasn't at all sure she knew how. So she dragged herself to her bedroom and slumped into a chair to contemplate the grim months ahead. She'd be in a strange country, Mom and Gran would be busy, and she wouldn't have any friends at all. It was a bleak prospect. Picking up her telephone—a luxury her grandmother allowed her because she didn't like having the line tied up with teen talk—Chelsea called her best friend, Tara Lynn, whose father was a television actor.

"What's wrong, Chelsea? You sick?"

"I lost the war, Tara. Gran said Mom'd be worried if I stayed here alone with the housekeeper, and she's afraid she'll lose her concentration." Chelsea knew better than to admit to anyone that they were short on money.

"Nuts!" Tara replied. "What about school? Don't they give a damn about what you want?"

Suddenly Chelsea felt that she had to defend her family. "It's just that Mom's career is the most important thing. After all, she's the one who makes the money."

"Yeah, well, my dad does too, but he never makes us go with him. Mom and my brother and me always stay here at home, near my friends. He says it's important that we live like normal people," Tara Lynn responded.

"It's different for you. You've got a mother and a father."

"Where's your dad? Maybe you could stay with him."

Chelsea snickered. "I haven't even seen him since I was two years old. He's probably forgotten I even exist."

"What a louse. Hey, I've got an idea. Suppose I ask my mom if you could stay with us? I've got twin beds in my room, and we could pretend we were sisters!"

Chelsea replied wistfully, "Gosh, that would be fun, wouldn't it?"

"I'll ask her and my dad tonight at dinner."

Chelsea tried not to get her hopes up, afraid that it was unlikely Tara's parents would agree to take a strange young girl into their house for an unspecified period of time. If they did, however, Gran certainly couldn't use the money angle against her.

Tara called back later in the evening. "Hi. My folks said they'd be happy to have the daughter of Bunny Thomas stay with us. Dad says your mom's a screen legend."

"Oh, Tara, that's terrific. Let me talk to my mother and I'll call you back," Chelsea replied.

Hanging up, she rushed to her mother's room, where Laverne was giving her daughter a back rub. Unschooled in the art of persuasion or manipulation, Chelsea did not bide her time, nor did she take her case to each of the women individually. Instead, she simply blurted out the proposal breathlessly.

Laverne did not even look up to see the brightness of her granddaughter's eyes or the pathetic hope gleaming from them. "Chelsea, the answer is no. Now stop pestering me. Your mother simply cannot be worrying about you being on the other side of the world."

In desperation, Chelsea turned her attention to her mother. Although it was unlikely that she would intervene, Bunny was now her last best hope. "Mama . . . please. I don't want to go to England. I won't know anybody there. They'll think I talk funny . . . please . . ."

Without even bothering to lift her head or look at the

distress on her child's face, Bunny sided with Laverne. "Your grandmother knows best, honey. Besides, it'll be good for you to see what it's like living in a foreign country and making friends there." All of Bunny's schooling had been on the lot at Taurus with other child actors, and she hadn't the slightest understanding of Chelsea's desire to live an ordinary life.

Without another word of supplication, Chelsea retreated to her room and called Tara to thank her politely for the offer which she had to decline. The next day she refused to go to school, pleading a headache and sore throat. Worried that she might become ill and delay their departure, Laverne allowed her to remain in bed for the last few days of their stay in Beverly Hills, which suited Chelsea just fine. She couldn't bear the thought of saying good-bye to the school and the friends who had come to mean so much to her in the past few weeks.

14

Working with Rick Wehner turned out to be the most demanding, exhausting experience Bunny ever had. Never in her entire career had a director expected so much from her both intellectually and artistically. Each night she would return home to the rented West End flat with barely enough energy to put a few morsels of food in her mouth before falling into bed. She was so drained emotionally and physically that the pounds melted off her tiny frame, and her fine bone structure emerged. The once plump, rounded, and girlish actress gradually turned into a woman of haunting beauty and grace.

Laverne observed the transition with a mixture of pride and alarm. Rick allowed his crew to view the dailies with him, and although he forbade any actors to see the footage, he did relent and allow Laverne to join them at the late evening screenings. She was mesmerized by the performance her daughter was giving, because although she had always known Bunny was a star, she had never really understood the depth of her ability as an actress, and it threatened her. Laverne had created Bunny the star; how could she have overlooked the profoundness of her daughter's talent when Hilda Marx and Rick Wehner, both strangers, had seen it?

To add to her feelings of concern, Laverne was not welcome on the set. Rick Wehner allowed no one outside his small, efficient band of crew members to observe. For the first time in her daughter's life, Laverne found herself almost totally shut out of the process of making the film. Because their relationship was so intimate, Bunny noticed her mother's hurt feelings and tried to make it up to her. During the first few weeks, she would return home in the evening and relate the entire sequence of the day's events. But as she got deeper into the character she was playing, the work became more emotionally demanding, sapping all of her energy, and she begged off.

"I'm sorry, Mama, but I just can't go over every detail of the day. I'm too tired," she pleaded. "Rick makes me explain every little movement, every single word or smile or frown. He says I must know why I'm doing things, and I'm just too wrung out to do it again for you."

"You're working too hard, sweetie. Do you want me to talk to him about it?" Laverne suggested sympathetically, hoping that her daughter would invite her into the relationship with Wehner. Bunny, however, was alarmed at the suggestion.

"Absolutely not, Mama! Rick would be furious with you, and with me too. He feels this role in *Wintersong* is the watershed of my career, and I believe him. Please, I'll be very upset if you say anything to him," she said with all the force and emphasis she could muster. Then, seeing the determined expression on her mother's face, she switched to a wheedling tone. "Besides, if you annoy him, he might stop letting you see the dailies, and I don't want that to happen."

The threat worked, but Bunny leavened the blow with a smattering of flattery. "You do think I'm doing all right, don't you? You're the one whose judgment I trust most, you know." Bunny touched her mother's arm and smiled fetchingly, and Laverne was reassured. The manipulator incarnate was not immune from manipulation herself. This film couldn't last forever, she rationalized, and when it was over, Bunny would be hers again.

One night several weeks later, the evening fog was unusually thick even for London, so thick that although Laverne had promised to take Chelsea to the theatre, she decided not to venture outside. Cabs could be very scarce after the show on nights of such low visibility, and when she had asked her granddaughter if she would mind staying home, Chelsea had, as usual, been agreeable. Because she was so preoccupied with Bunny, Laverne had failed to notice how withdrawn Chelsea had become. The young girl spent most of her time at home in her room reading or at her desk sketching. Laverne had no idea what she was doing, nor did she have much curiosity, and sensing her lack of interest, Chelsea never offered to show her sketches to her grandmother.

Usually Bunny was home by eight in the evening, but an assistant called Laverne and told her not to wait dinner since they were going into overtime and food would be brought to the set. It had happened before, so Laverne was merely annoyed. All day she had looked forward to the moment when her daughter came home exhausted and submitted to a rigorous back massage and a cozy cup of hot water with lemon before being tucked in for the night.

Laverne settled into one of the big easy chairs by the front window so she could see the lights of the Rolls-Royce when the driver finally brought Bunny home. She opened Katherine Anne Porter's long awaited new novel, *Ship of Fools,* and began to read.

An hour passed, then two, then three, and Laverne found herself reading each page two or three times without being able to absorb what she'd read. Finally she slammed the book down on the small antique table beside her chair and got to her feet. How dare that man work her daughter so long! She marched to the telephone and dialed the set, but there was no answer. Good. They must have finished, and Bunny was on her way home.

Laverne put the kettle on the stove to boil some water and went into Bunny's room to make sure the maid had turned down the bed and laid out a fresh nightgown and slippers before she left. The room felt a little chilly, so she turned up the gas in the grate in the fireplace. Everything looked warm and comfy and inviting; not that Bunny would notice, she thought. She'd be so exhausted, she would probably need help undressing and removing her makeup. Laverne checked the vanity to make sure that Bunny's special cold cream and astringent and moisturizers were set out and that there were plenty of tissues in the box.

Going back into the kitchen, she turned the fire under the teakettle down to simmer. Then, only because she was on her feet and nervous, she walked down to the end of the hall and checked to see if Chelsea was asleep. The room was dark and quiet, the young girl snuggled under a massive goose-down quilt.

Back in the living room, Laverne sat down once more in the chair and picked up the book, though she had no intention of actually reading it. It was important that Bunny not suspect how much her tardiness distressed her, because lately she had sensed her daughter's resentment at her ministrations.

Laverne maintained the pose for more than half an hour before she became sufficiently agitated to get to her feet and begin pacing. Where the devil were they? Looking out the window once more, she saw that the fog had lifted enough for her to see as far as the street. If they were just leaving when she had made the call, then surely Bunny should have been home by now . . . unless, God forbid, there had been an accident on the road!

No sooner had the thought formed than it took on the shape and texture of reality. That had to be it! Bunny was lying somewhere out there injured, bleeding, needing help. Good Lord, what should she do? Her knees began to shake, and she was dizzy with the certainty that she must do something, but what? In God's name, what? Without thinking, she rushed down the hallway to her granddaughter's room. She had to talk to someone; she could not bear this terrible burden alone!

As soon as she entered the room and snapped on the light, Chelsea was wide awake. "What's wrong, Gran?" she asked, sitting up.

"Bunny's not home, and it's almost midnight," she babbled, the stress in her voice pitching it an octave higher. "I called the set almost an hour ago, and no one was there!" Laverne sank down on the bed.

Chelsea reached out and put her arms around Laverne's thin, bony frame to comfort her. "Don't think the worst, Gran. Come on, there are lots of good reasons why she's not at home. Don't dwell on the worst."

Laverne was not consoled. "What are you talking about? Where could she possibly be?"

Chelsea, whose wisdom far exceeded her years, was much more observant than either of the other women in her family suspected, and she hesitated to say what she really thought, because she disliked revealing the extent of her own knowledge. The last thing she wanted was for her grandmother to realize how much insight she actually had.

"I'll just bet she went out for a drink or a bite to eat with Rick so that they could talk over a scene or something," she suggested shrewdly, trying to frame her words with the ingenuousness of a child and hoping her grandmother would put the proper adult twist to them.

"That would be nonsense, Chelsea. She needs to be in bed asleep so she'll have the strength to work tomorrow. The camera can see fatigue better than we can," Laverne said, missing the implication entirely.

Chelsea said nothing in reply. How could adults be so thick? Couldn't Gran see that Mom had fallen under the spell of Rick Wehner completely? Chelsea had often seen her mother madly in love, and it was quite obvious to her that this was another one of those times.

"I'm going to call Rick at his home and see if he knows anything," Laverne said, getting to her feet.

"Don't . . ." Chelsea called, as she watched her grandmother sweep out of the room. Oh Lord, she thought, as she fell back on the bed. What a scene this was going to be!

15

Rick held the telephone out to Bunny, but she shrank from touching it and shook her head vigorously. She couldn't bear the thought of talking to her mother. Not now. Not tonight. Not at this moment of sublime intimacy. No, she would not let this beautiful night of lovemaking be spoiled by her mother's plaintive demand for her to come home. Above all, she would not allow herself to be made to feel guilty and irresponsible. Not this time.

Her firm resolve was short-lived, for Rick refused to let her hide. He believed that difficult situations were made worse if ignored, and he had nothing but contempt for Bunny's propensity to run away from emotional problems.

"Come on, love, you've got to tell her sooner or later. Might as well be now. You can't spend your whole life avoiding sticky situations. Just tell her you're going to be staying with me. That's all. You're a big girl, darling. Stop acting like a child."

Realizing that it was impossible to ignore the demands of both Rick and her mother, Bunny wrinkled her nose at him, sat up and reached for the telephone, letting the sheet that was covering her nakedness slip down and expose her large, full breasts. Rick stared at the bright pink areolas that contrasted so sharply with the whiteness of her skin. As she took a deep breath and sighed, he could not resist reaching out with his fingertips and gently tracing a circle around the roseate flesh. He was amused at how quickly the nipples hardened, rising even more swiftly than his own instant tumescence.

"Hello, Mama," she said, looking up into Rick's eyes and lying back on the pillow languidly.

"Bunny, you could have at least had the decency to call me! You knew I'd be worried half to death about you!"

"I'm sorry, Mama, but we worked so late . . ." she answered, her voice trailing away as Rick stripped the sheet from the lower part of her body and let his fingers travel softly down to the bright auburn little bush which he tugged at gently until she spread her legs open for him.

"Honey, I think you're making a mistake getting involved with Rick," Laverne began. "You know what a reputation he has with women. The last few months have been a terrible strain on you, but you mustn't let him use—"

A small involuntary gasp escaped from Bunny as Rick's finger glided gently inside her. Laverne could not avoid hearing her. With the sixth-sense awareness that comes from knowing someone as intimately as she knew her daughter, Laverne did not have to witness the scene that was being played out on the other end of the line to see it in her mind's eye. With a pragmatism that comes of years of living with a star, she knew the competition was too stiff. There was no way a mere mother could compete with an attractive virile male for her daughter's attention. She must retreat gracefully and choose a more favorable battlefield on which to fight for control. Laverne dropped her voice an octave lower and turned the volume control to sweet.

"Baby, now remember, you must have a good night's rest. The camera sees every little tired line and wrinkle and records it forever, honey," she said softly. "Tell Rick to let you come home early tomorrow so I can give you a good rubdown after your bath. Give me a call if you have a chance in the afternoon. Good night, now."

Although Rick's caresses had become more sensuous and demanding, and her body was responding to him eagerly, Bunny was not yet ready to end the conversation. She had one more crushing bit of news for her mother, and she needed to say it at this moment in time when nothing really mattered except Rick's touch.

"I won't be home tomorrow night either, Mama. Rick wants me to move in with him." Her words were thick with a naked passion and desire she cruelly made no attempt to conceal from her mother.

Ever alert to the dramatic potential of a moment, Rick picked up immediately on her feelings and exploited them by moving over on top of Bunny and sliding himself quickly inside.

Laverne knew exactly what was going on, and she was outraged. Her daughter was such a little slut. It would serve her right if she spat out her fury and disgust, slammed down the telephone, packed her bags and left her to destroy herself. But Laverne was too smart for such a reckless impulse, having learned long ago that one could not control others without keeping a tight rein on one's own responses.

"This is no time for rash decisions, honey," she said, her voice dulcet and fluid. "We'll talk this over when we're alone, when you're . . . in a position to think more clearly," she continued, hoping her double entendre was not lost on her lustful child. "I'll come to the studio tomorrow, and we'll have lunch and talk it over rationally."

"No, Mama," Bunny gasped thickly as her body rose and fell with each of Rick's thrusts. "Rick doesn't want you there . . . you know that. He says you . . . distract me when I'm working." Bunny had trouble holding onto her thoughts and her words, which were being smothered by her erotic yearnings for release.

Her mother tried to respond. "But, sweetheart . . ."

Unhearing, Bunny continued, stimulated by the involuntary voyeur on the other end of the line. "No,

Mama . . . you won't talk me out of it this time," she gasped breathlessly. "I'll have somebody pick up my clothes and things tomorrow," she finished, her voice beginning to drift as she sank deeper into the well of passion, her body responding to the urgency of Rick's demands, moving rapturously with them. God, it felt so good to have a strong, loving man inside her. Nothing in life could match the feeling. She dropped the telephone on the bed, and it slid off the sheet to clatter to the floor unnoticed, her mother's presence suddenly forgotten. All that mattered to her in the world was this moment and this wonderfully strong exciting man inside her. He was the only man who had ever understood her needs and desires, who had tapped into the fountainhead of her emotions and taught her to use them to please herself and to portray them in her work. At long last she had found the man who could satisfy her physically, intellectually, and artistically. He was wonderful!

As Laverne listened to the heavy breathing and moans of the two rutting bodies, she was disgusted beyond measure. The little fool! Once the picture was over, Rick Wehner would have as much interest in Bunny as he would have for a firecracker on the fifth of July. He had never had an affair with an actress that lasted more than a week or two beyond the final wrap. His only true passion was for his film, and nothing else was sacred to him. Even Hilda Marx had cautioned Bunny to be careful and not let herself be consumed by him, but her warning had gone unheeded. Bunny had no instinct for self-protection where men were concerned. None at all.

Laverne slammed down the telephone, grimly consoled by the knowledge that when the affair was over, she would be the only one who could pick up the pieces of Bunny Thomas and put them together again.

16

Chelsea knew something was wrong when she went into the kitchen the next morning and her grandmother was not there presiding over the preparation of her mother's breakfast tray.

"Where's Gran?" she asked Letitia, their live-in housekeeper and cook.

"In her bed still. I fixed you a bit of Wheatena, since the weather is on the chilly side. Better hurry. Bertie should be here shortly," said the tall, angular woman with gray streaks in her brown, bobbed hair.

Letitia Hamilton had lost her young husband and both parents in World War II, and although she was an intelligent and well-educated woman, she preferred to work as a domestic servant because she liked being part of a family. She particularly liked her new situation because she loved the sweet but neglected young Chelsea, adored the childlike Bunny, and respected the hard-edged and tough-minded Laverne.

"I better check on her to see if she's all right. Has my mother gone to the set?"

Letitia shook her head and continued to ladle the cereal into the bowl. "I took a peek into her room, and unless she tidied it up herself, which is most unlikely, I'd say she did not sleep in her bed last night."

Without saying a word, Chelsea turned and sprinted for her mother's room. Sure enough, the bed was untouched. She hurried across the hall and gently knocked at her grandmother's door. When there was no answer, she turned the knob and peered in. With the shutters closed, the room was quite dark, but she could see that her grandmother was still huddled under the thick down quilt. Quickly, the young girl went over to the bed and touched her grandmother's cheek.

"Gran, are you okay?" she asked in alarm. "Should I have Letitia get the doctor to come over and see you?"

Laverne opened her eyes and looked up, and after a lengthy moment she replied, "Go on to school, honey. I'm sick at heart, that's all."

Relieved, Chelsea sat down on the bed. "It's Mom, isn't it? She's gone to stay with Rick."

"How the devil did you know that?"

A small shadow of a smile passed over Chelsea's lips, but she suppressed it immediately. Adults were so impossibly strange. Did they really think that kids were deaf, dumb, and blind?

"I could tell by the way she gets out of bed at the crack of dawn every morning without complaining, that she was in love again," Chelsea replied.

"Rubbish. She's excited about the role she's playing, Chelsea, that's all," Laverne replied irritably, turning over to get up.

Though Chelsea had learned to keep things she knew to herself, she was growing up and beginning to resent being treated like a child.

"Gran! When has Mama ever been happy about going to work? The only time she's ever alert and energetic is when there's a handsome man around for her to impress."

Laverne looked more closely at her granddaughter. Was it possible that this small child had turned into a real person without her noticing? Nonsense. Chelsea was simply parroting something she'd overheard.

"Who's filling your mind with that kind of garbage? Have you been talking to the help again?" the older woman asked sharply, getting out of bed and pulling on her heavy cashmere robe.

"Gran, her name is Letitia, and she's the only help we have, and you know as well as I do that she never gossips. She doesn't have to. I've got eyes in my head, you know. Besides, I'm glad Mom's found somebody. She's so dreary when she doesn't have a man mooning around and telling her how ravishingly beautiful she is every minute of the day."

"All right, if you think you know so much, Miss Smartass, then you also know what a mess she'll be when the big romance is over, as it will be very soon."

With the unjaded romanticism of the very young, Chelsea responded, "But maybe this time it will last, Gran. Wouldn't that be nice?"

Laverne shuddered at the thought but was immediately relieved when she thought about Wehner. Instead of moaning about the situation, she should be rejoicing that Bunny had chosen somebody so assuredly temporary. Rick Wehner was most definitely one man who would not be around very long. She smiled at her grandchild and announced, "That is simply not a possibility, Chelsea. Take my word for it. Now you better hustle or you won't be ready when the car arrives."

At eight sharp Bertie Masterson pulled up in front of the house in his antique Bentley and waited for Chelsea to come outside. A World War II vet who had broken both his legs at Dunkirk, Bertie was plagued with frequent bouts of painful neuralgia and had difficulty working. He was dependent on odd jobs to supplement his pension. Driving Chelsea to school every morning and picking her up in the afternoon was the best of the lot, and he was happy that the grandmother had refused to put up the money to board the girl at Mrs. Chenoweth's school. Of course, the Americans didn't pay him much, but it was enough to buy petrol for his beloved car, which he had inherited from an old war buddy. Next to his wife Zellie, the Bentley was the most important thing in Bertie's life, because it gave him freedom to move about and see things, and more importantly, it permitted him to drive his wife to the countryside on weekends.

Bertie checked his pocket watch and saw that it was getting late. He didn't want to sit and wait if Chelsea wasn't coming, but neither did he want to drag himself out of the car, a painful maneuver at best, unless it was absolutely necessary. He'd give the child a bit more time. Poor youngster. Living with her famous mother and that cheap old biddy of a grandmother must be no bed of roses.

To his relief, Chelsea suddenly burst through the door and raced down the walk to the car. As usual, she climbed into the front seat beside him.

"Sorry I'm late, Bertie. Family problems."

Putting the car into gear and pulling away, Bertie asked, "Nothing too serious, I hope?"

Realizing she might have said too much, Chelsea changed the subject immediately. From the time she had been able to talk, she had been programmed never to discuss things that happened at home with anyone, ever. Laverne had drilled into her head the belief that anyone, no matter how nice, was capable of taking even little bits of information and turning them into stories that the tabloids would buy.

"My grandmother was just annoyed with me for dithering around and being late. So, where are you and your wife going this weekend?" she asked, deftly changing the subject.

"Windsor Castle again, I suppose. It's Princess Margaret Rose's birthday, and Zellie says there's sure to be interesting people about. She's filled an album with photographs she's snapped with her box camera."

Ordinarily Chelsea loved her little chats with Bertie, but today she only pretended to listen because she was preoccupied with the prospect of moving again. Although she liked the school and was doing well in her classes, Margaret Ashford was the only friend she had made since she arrived. As one of the few day students, Chelsea was considered an outsider and treated distantly though civilly by the other girls.

That afternoon as she was walking down the road to the spot where Bertie usually waited to take her home, Margaret came running down the walk in her gym bloomers.

"Chelsea, wait up!" she called breathlessly. "I have to ask you something."

Chelsea stopped and watched her long-legged friend churn up the dust of the gravel path with her sneakers.

"What's up, Maggie?" Chelsea asked curiously.

Coming to a halt, Margaret screwed up her face and grimaced. "Don't call me Maggie. It's a perfectly dreadful nickname."

"I'm sorry, Margaret," Chelsea apologized, "but I see Bertie's car coming up the road, so tell me quickly what's going on."

"Wills is bringing a chum home for the weekend, and Mum thought it might be nice if I brought one too. Can you come? Do say yes. We'll have ever so much fun. Everybody says that my twin is a lot nicer than I am, and I so want you to meet him. I just know you'll get on well."

Chelsea was surprised and pleased by the invitation. "Gosh, Margaret, I'd love to . . . but I'll have to talk it over with my grandmother."

"Ripping. Must dash or I'll be late and Miss Givens will give me the devil," she said, trotting off and then calling back over her shoulder, "Just bring your things to school in the morning, and we'll take a bus to the train station. Mum likes us to dress up a bit for dinner, so bring your best dress, and don't forget a pair of sturdy boots because Wills loves to take long hikes in the woods and so do I."

Suddenly she turned around and yelled, "You don't by any chance ride, do you?"

"No, but I wish I could," Chelsea called back.

"Wills will teach you. The horses love him too. See you in the morning."

All the way home Chelsea ignored Bertie's chatter and concentrated on the best method of approaching her grandmother. Getting permission to visit the country estate of the Ashford family would ordinarily present no problem, especially if she pointed out that Margaret's father was an earl. But with her mother away, Chelsea feared that her grandmother would not want to spend the weekend all by herself. Laverne was always so busy fussing over Bunny that she never had time to make friends of her own.

The atmosphere in the house that evening was even more morose than Chelsea had expected it to be. Ignoring her daughter's instructions to stay away from the set, Laverne had not waited for someone to pick up Bunny's things but had packed them and taken them to the studio herself. When the guard at the gate telephoned the set, he was instructed to take the packages and refuse Laverne entry. Humiliated, she had returned home stone-faced and furious.

Now, hours later, her anger was replaced by self-pity. How could that ingrate of a daughter treat her so cruelly?

As her bedtime approached and there was still no letup in Laverne's mood, Chelsea decided she could wait no longer.

"Gran, Margaret's mother invited me to spend the weekend at the Ashford country estate. I hate to leave you all by yourself, but I really would love to go. Margaret's my best friend, and I'm all caught up on my schoolwork. Please, I really want to go. Letitia said she'd be happy to stay on and keep you company." Chelsea exhaled as she got it all out quickly.

Laverne was sitting in front of the bay window staring at the street outside, so consumed by her overwhelming rage and hatred that she did not hear a word Chelsea was saying.

Patiently Chelsea tried again. It had never been easy to get her grandmother's attention. "Gran, I know you're unhappy about Mom, but she'll be okay. Please, listen to me, will you? I need to pack my things so I can take them to school with me tomorrow." Still receiving no response, Chelsea decided it was time to crank up the sales pitch and try appealing to her grandmother's snobbery. "You know, Margaret's father is an earl, and I've heard that they have one of England's most beautiful country houses. They raise jumpers, and Margaret says their stables are the best in the country . . . they must have lots of money too."

Wearily, Laverne raised her hand to silence Chelsea. "Not now, child. Can't you see I have more important things on my mind? Please, just let me alone. I'm in no mood to listen to your nattering away about school things."

Frustrated, Chelsea returned to her room and threw herself on the bed. If only her mother were here. She'd let her go. Upset as she was, Chelsea's eyes remained dry. As a small child she had learned that her puny little tears weren't worth shedding in the same household with the master weeper of them all, and now she realized she would have to be more secretive and devious about getting things done. Suddenly she had an idea.

Being careful not to make any untoward noise, she crept into her grandmother's room and shuffled through the papers on her desk to find the telephone number she needed. When at last she saw it, she quickly committed it to memory, and then tiptoed into the kitchen. Closing the door so that she would not be overheard, she picked up the telephone and dialed the number. Rick Wehner answered, and she said, "Hi, this is Chelsea. Would you tell my mother that it's very important that I talk to her?"

"Look, young lady, if your grandmother has put you up to this, forget it. I'm not going to let her upset Bunny as she usually does—"

"Please, Mr. Wehner," Chelsea interjected, keeping her voice low but raising the intensity level of her plea, "my grandmother doesn't know I'm calling. I just need to ask my mother a question, that's all. If you don't believe me, you can ask her for me, okay?"

Relenting, Rick gave the telephone to Bunny.

"Hi, honey, are things pretty terrible there?" she asked.

"Not so bad, Mom. Are you okay?"

"Everything's just great, darling. Rick has been wonderful for me. I can't tell you how good I feel."

Chelsea loved to talk to her mother when things were going well. Bunny could be the dearest, sweetest person when she was happy, which was all too seldom.

"I'm so glad. Of course, Gran's not too thrilled, but she'll be okay. Mom, my new friend, Margaret Ashford, the daughter of a real earl, has invited me to spend the weekend at their country estate. Would it be okay with you if I went?" she asked.

"What does Gran say?" Bunny hedged. She wasn't accustomed to making decisions about her daughter without her mother's guidance.

"I can't even get her to talk to me. You know how gloomy she gets when she's in one of her moods. Letitia says she'll stay all weekend and keep her company."

"I don't know . . ." Bunny hesitated, afraid to make a decision all on her own, even to a question as simple as the one her daughter had posed.

"Please, I need your help, Mom. You know I never ask for much. Let me do this one thing," she pleaded.

Unsure, Bunny turned to Rick and sketched out the situation for him. "For God's sake, let the kid go," he responded immediately.

That was all the reinforcement Bunny needed. "Of course you can go, darling. Have a good time . . . and tell your grandmother that Rick said he would be showing dailies to the crew on Tuesday evening, and if she likes, he'll leave word at the gate to let her in. If she decides to come, she can have dinner with us beforehand, but Chelsea . . . tell her to be nice, will you? It will make it all so much easier for everybody."

"I will, Mom, I will. I love you," Chelsea said gleefully.

"I love you too, honey. Have a good time."

Chelsea sat in the kitchen for a long time planning her strategy. There was no point in giving Gran any good news at this time. Now that she had permission to go, the last thing she needed was for her grandmother to snap out of her doldrums and start meddling in her weekend plans. No, no. The best way to control the situation was simply to leave things as they were. Leave her grandmother brooding and let her get angry when Letitia informed her why Chelsea did not return from school tomorrow evening. Then, when she came home on Sunday, she'd have Rick's invitation to cool matters down. Perfect. Humming a little tune, Chelsea went into her bedroom and began to pack for her exciting weekend, pleased that she had managed to arrange things so neatly.

17

Chelsea had seen many beautiful mansions in her young life in Hollywood and Beverly Hills, but she had never seen anything quite as magnificent as the Ashford country house. It was as beautiful as Manderlay in her favorite old movie, *Rebecca,* but without the forbidding overtones. Set on the highest of a series of undulating hills covered with a carpet of thick grass, the mansion rose up before them in all its red-stone beauty as they broke through the clearing in the woods. A forest of magnificent Scots pine trees, larch, spruce, and beech, interspersed with quantities of wild cherry, ash, holly, and quickwood, surrounded the road.

"It's gorgeous, Margaret. Has your family always owned this place?" she asked, filling her eyes with the beauty surrounding them.

"Not always, just since 1780, actually, and it's much smaller than it was then."

"How big is it now?"

"With the tenant farms and all, just under fifteen thousand acres, I believe, but when the first Earl of Ashford acquired it, it was four times that size. All these beautiful trees were planted then. The house itself was built by our family and designed by John Carr and Samuel Wyatt, two of the greatest architects of their time. A brilliant plasterer named Joseph Rose did a lot of the work inside. Wait till you see Papa's library."

"Fifteen thousand acres!" exclaimed Chelsea, a child of Beverly Hills, where a half acre was a huge estate.

"Papa says that ten thousand is the minimum size to support a place like this. We have eight different departments to manage things, like the wood yard that does the forestry, the home farm, which tends a thousand acres around the house, and the dairy, which provides milk cream and butter for the house and a restaurant in the village. Besides that we have a stud farm where we board mares and foals for a number of owners. It's a big business, really."

"You must have a lot of people working here," Chelsea exclaimed.

"My, yes. Papa says they exchange high wages for a steady income and a lovely place to live. Everyone is happy here because they are part of a community where everyone cares about everyone else, and no one is ever poor or lonely."

"Why would anyone ever want to leave?" Chelsea asked.

"Not many do. We're always somewhat overstaffed, but Papa tries to strike a balance. Most of his decisions must be made on cold economic terms, but he also has to consider the goodwill and welfare of the people."

Chelsea hung on every word her friend uttered, feeling that within just a few hours' time she had stepped from a very ordinary workaday modern world into a land of enchantment. She was even more impressed when she was ushered into the great entrance hall. Marveling at the marble staircase that divided halfway up into two grand staircases going in opposite directions, she exclaimed, "My gosh, Margaret, this is absolutely the most fantastic house I've ever been in."

"A lot of the credit goes to Mum. Daddy married her for her money, you know," she said airily.

Chelsea was aghast. "How can you say such a thing?"

"Well, it's true," Margaret said with a wicked giggle, "but that isn't the whole story. Her father was one of those wealthy financial wizards of Wall Street. He was a widower, and Mum was his only child. After her debut, he sent her on a grand tour of Europe, which I understand was the thing to do back in the thirties. Unfortunately for my grandfather, she decided to stay in London with some friends, and while she was here, she met a dashing young officer in the RAF." She chuckled and rolled her eyes. "That romantic young man was my father. Well, the war started but she refused to go home, which distressed Grandfather terribly. Against his wishes, she joined the Red Cross and did all sorts of things, like driving an ambulance. When it was over, Father was a true hero, with a bit of a limp and his chest covered with medals, and it was swoontime for them both. Without telling a soul in either of their families, they had a quiet civil service and became man and wife and set about having babies."

"How romantic!" Chelsea exclaimed. "But wasn't there a problem, her being an American and all?"

"Oh no! Titled European families love rich American girls. Besides, Mum was beautiful and young and virginal, and everybody adored her." Margaret shrugged. "Even if anybody had objected, it would have made no difference to Father. He loves her quite madly still. Sometimes they bill and coo so much that it can be bloody uncomfortable to be around them."

"You ought to be thankful you have a mom and dad who're together," Chelsea remarked, and then covered her unwitting revelation by asking, "What about your mother's dad?"

"Oh, eventually Grandfather came around and they were reconciled. He died the year my sister was born, and left Mum millions and millions, and Papa was able to put the house back into proper shape. Come on, that's Mum's study down there at the end of the hall. I'm so anxious for you to meet her."

Chelsea allowed herself to be pulled along the gallery, past impressive portraits of nobility, which she promised herself she would inspect more closely later. Margaret knocked at the heavy wooden door and, upon being summoned, they entered.

As they stepped into the charming, wood-paneled room lined with bookshelves on one side and leaded glass windows on another, Chelsea could not remember ever entering a room that felt quite as comfortable and warm and inviting.

A woman with blond hair softly fading to white was

seated in a brown leather wing chair with a book in her lap. She looked up as they approached. Then she opened her arms, and Margaret rushed to her for a welcoming hug. Chelsea watched at a distance, until Margaret pulled away and said, "Mum, this is Chelsea. She's from the Colonies too."

"Shame on you, Margaret. It's rude to call the United States the Colonies. Chelsea, I'm so glad you could come for a visit." Her voice was both cool and warm at the same time, just like her smile, Chelsea thought.

"Thank you. I'm really happy to be here. This is the loveliest house I've ever seen," she replied, her eyes fixed on Evelyn Ashford's exquisite face. She had never seen anyone quite like her. Raised in a community where a woman was expected to battle age and wrinkles to the death with scalpels and makeup, Chelsea suddenly found herself witnessing the beauty of aging with grace. Margaret's mother looked to be well into her forties, but she was wearing no makeup, and although there were fine lines around her eyes and mouth, she possessed a loveliness that was almost ethereal. Her bright blue eyes were ringed with thick, curly lashes almost as pale as her hair, and Chelsea was astounded to realize that eyes could be beautiful without mascara. Her skin looked clear and soft, and there was a hint of color in her cheeks that was also natural. When she spoke, Chelsea could see that her teeth were white and perfect and not capped, and her voice was mellifluous and soft.

"Why, thank you, Chelsea. I must confess that I feel the same way. You must have Margaret take you on a complete tour. It has a lot of interesting little secret places where she used to hide when she wanted to get away from the world."

Her words were tinged with the barest hint of a British accent. In spite of all her years in England, she still sounded like an American. Chelsea liked her immediately.

"Has Wills arrived?" Margaret asked.

"He certainly has. He and Tim have been here since two this afternoon. It seems they were released early to allow the faculty to attend the funeral of someone on the staff. They should be back from their ride by now."

"Is it all right if Chelsea sleeps in Nancy's old room?"

"I suspected you'd want her as close to your room as possible, so I've already had it made up, dear," Evelyn Ashford replied with a gentle smile. "Dinner will be at eight, but I would like for you to be in the library by seven-thirty so your father will have a chance to meet our guests before we sit down."

Margaret gave Chelsea a few minutes to look around the beautiful bedroom that was to be hers, with its bed canopied in layers of bleached linen edged with handmade lace, its needlepoint rug, and the vanity table in front of tall windows that looked down on the rose garden below. "Indeed, it's a lovely room, because Nancy always has the best of everything, but come on," Margaret urged. "It'll be getting dark soon, and I so want to see Wills."

As they hurried downstairs and out the door, Chelsea asked, "Who is Nancy and why would she not want to spend every night of her life in that gorgeous room?"

"She's my older sister, and she's in school in Paris studying music. She's a prissy one, so bloody full of airs. Speaks French all the time and thinks Wills and I are barbarians," Margaret replied, and then giggled breathlessly. "Which we are when she's around. Wills says she brings out the beast in us."

"What's the big rush?" Chelsea asked.

"I can hardly wait to see Wills. It's been almost a month since we were last together!" she exclaimed, breaking into a trot. Although Chelsea was almost as tall as Margaret, her friend was moving at such a brisk pace she had to break into a full run to keep up with her. They dashed past the training ring, and Margaret yelled, "Wills! Wills!"

Suddenly, from around the corner of the stables, a young man in weathered riding boots and breeches stepped out and waved his arm. "Hello!" he called.

Once more Chelsea stood by and watched her friend embrace another one of her beloved family, only this time Margaret did it with unreserved enthusiasm and excite-

ment. Chelsea wondered where people ever got the idea
that the British were stiff and undemonstrative.

"Wills, I want you to meet Chelsea. She's from Hollywood."

Wills grinned and responded, "Well, hello there, Hollywood Chelsea. I'd offer to shake hands with you, but
I've been brushing Galahad down. Good to meet you."

Another young man appeared. Although he too was
attractive, he was a bit on the plump side, his hair a bright
orange-red. Chelsea was introduced to Tim Dodson.

Margaret began chattering immediately. Apparently,
she and her brother were very close, and she had a lot of
things to tell him. As they talked, Wills returned to his
job of brushing the beautiful black stallion. Chelsea
watched silently, and observed that although there was
a similarity in height and coloring, the twins did not look
at all alike. Wills's hair was thick and wavy and as light
in color as his mother's, his cheeks rosy and his nose
lightly sprinkled with freckles. Both were tall, but Margaret seemed skinny and a bit awkward, whereas Wills
was lean and lithe. He had heavy eyebrows and thick
lashes, and his eyes were blue. His teeth were white and
perfect, and he had a bright smile that was punctuated
by deep dimples on both cheeks. Chelsea had never met
a young man of her own age who was as grown-up and
graceful as Wills Ashford appeared to be, and she had
certainly never seen anyone quite as handsome, even by
Hollywood standards. She was terribly impressed.

When he finished grooming the horse, Wills insisted
on walking Chelsea through the stables and introducing
her to each of the horses by name. He gave her sugar
cubes to feed each one and insisted that she pet them and
make friends.

By the time they sauntered back up the hill to the house,
it was twilight, and Chelsea found herself trailing behind
the other two with Wills.

"So, you don't ride? Well, we'll have to fix that starting
first thing in the morning. Margaret will find something
for you to wear, and we'll begin in the ring with Marbella.

She's a lovely patient old mare. Have you ever been on a horse at all?"

"Well, my mother has a picture of me sitting on Trigger when I was about two, but I honestly don't remember ever doing it at all."

"Trigger? Who is Trigger?"

"Roy Rogers's palomino. You know, the cowboy in the movies?"

"Of course. I do love your American movies, you know. And your mother is really a beauty. Funny, you don't look a bit like her."

Chelsea made a face and replied, "Well, thanks a lot."

"I'm frightfully sorry that came out so badly, but what I really meant to say was that I thought you were a lot prettier than she is."

Chelsea was startled by his remark. She had always been compared unfavorably to her mother in looks. Somewhat flustered, she replied, "My mother says I look just like my dad. He was quite tall and blond, like I am. Both my grandmother and my mother are short, petite women. I looked like a giant to them when I was ten, and now I tower over them both. Gran is always threatening to set a brick on my head."

"Don't let her do it. I think you're perfect just as you are," he said quietly, and Chelsea responded by blushing. Nobody had ever complimented her so nicely.

George Ashford was a big handsome man, loving and warm, with cheeks ruddied by the outdoors and huge bushy eyebrows that hovered above his bright blue eyes. He poured lemonade into highball glasses on the portable bar that had been wheeled into the massive library. He served the younger people with as much deference as if they were honored adult guests, and chatted amiably with them. Once more Chelsea found herself smitten. Was there anything or anybody in this magnificent house that was not perfect? she wondered, gazing around at the high vaulted ceilings of the huge library, magnificently done in ornate plaster and painted in gilt and blue. The room was ringed on three sides by tall windows that looked out onto the formal gardens, and the highly polished wooden floors were inlaid with darker woods in a pattern of swirling leaves.

They dined at a long antique table set with crystal goblets, lace tablecloth, Wedgwood china, and sterling flatware. Though it was all beautifully formal, the food was simple, nutritious, and plain. Chelsea found herself devouring the rack of lamb, fresh garden vegetables, and homemade dark bread.

She was seated next to Wills but did not converse with him because the earl directed the conversation and drew everyone into a discussion involving topics of the day. Chelsea felt terribly ignorant, and she vowed to begin reading the newspaper to find out what was going on in the world. The only papers that were avidly read in her household were *Variety* and the *Hollywood Reporter*.

After dinner the family and guests retired to the library, where the earl and his wife settled down in front of the fire to read, and Margaret challenged Tim to a game of checkers. Wills pulled a chess set from the cabinet.

"How about a match, Chelsea?"

Feeling stupid, Chelsea replied, "I don't know how to play."

"Then you must let Wills teach you, my dear," the earl declared. "It's the only true game of skill. There's no luck involved, you see. With my son's guidance, you'll learn quickly. He was beating me regularly by the time he was eight years old."

Wills was a patient teacher and Chelsea a good student. She soon learned that she had a pronounced affinity for the game, but the evening passed too quickly, for in no time at all it was time to retire.

Promising Wills she would meet him downstairs before breakfast for her first riding lesson, Chelsea climbed the stairs with Margaret, who remarked with a giggle, "Well, I must say I expected my brother to like you, but I never thought he'd fall head over heels."

Her cheeks reddening, Chelsea looked down. "He just

feels sorry for me because I'm such a clod and don't know how to do anything, that's all."

Inside Margaret's room, which was pretty but not nearly so fussy or beautiful as Nancy's, Margaret threw herself on the bed and hooted loudly. "I know my brother better than anyone, and he cannot abide people he considers ignorant or stupid. You're the first girl I've ever brought home that got more than a nod from him. Thank heavens old Tim is here, or I'd be spending the weekend alone, I'm afraid."

"I'm sorry," Chelsea apologized, knowing full well she wasn't sorry at all. She loved hearing that Wills liked her, because she liked him too.

"Well, I'm not. I knew that eventually I'd bring home somebody he'd like. Since he's my own brother and I can't have him myself, I want to be the one to choose the girl for him. And it looks as if I finally did it," she said smugly.

"So that was your scheme, was it?" Chelsea asked with feigned outrage. "You wanted me here for him and not for yourself. I thought you liked me as a friend."

Margaret sat up instantly, concerned that she might have hurt Chelsea's feelings. "Oh, but I do. And that's the beautiful part of it. Wills means all the world to me, and I can't bear the thought that someday he might fall in love with some strange woman who might loathe me."

"Nobody could loathe you, Margaret. You're a lovely person," Chelsea said, sitting down on the bed and putting her hand on the other girl's shoulder to reassure her.

"Oh yes they could. Nancy has always felt that the Lord played a terrible trick on her when he put a nasty little sister in the house to plague her," she said dolefully, and then brightened as she added, "And I do so love to make her life miserable."

"Margaret, that's awful. I can't imagine you making anyone miserable," Chelsea protested.

"You haven't met my sister. She's the world's worst tattler. It's always, 'Mother, stop her from doing that,' or 'Father, will you please speak to your dreadful daughter and make her behave.' "

"Sounds like you enjoy making a nuisance of yourself," Chelsea said with a grin.

"As a matter of fact, I do consider it my mission in life. Come on. Let's go through Nancy's things and find you some proper riding attire."

Later that night, as Chelsea snuggled under the warm down comforter, she reflected on how lucky Margaret was to be surrounded and sheltered by a loving and caring family.

18

Years later, when she was a grown woman, Chelsea would look back upon that first weekend at Ashford Hall as being the most luminous time of her life. In those few short hours, she developed a love for horses and riding, a desire to become a skilled chess player, and a respect for the institution of the family that she had never really known before. And without fully understanding her own emotions, she fell in love. Wills Ashford became the focus of her young life, and when it came time to say goodbye to him, the imminent separation was excruciatingly painful.

The four young people found themselves standing at the train station, awkwardly searching for words that would express what they were feeling. Casual good-byes were sufficient for Margaret and Tim. They had, after all, been cast together only because they had been deserted by the other two. Wills made idle chatter, his eyes fixed constantly on the pretty girl whose presence had instantly enriched his life. At the sound of the approaching train which would carry the boys away, Chelsea at last found her voice.

"Thank you so much, Wills . . . I had a terrific time," she said, looking up at him and wishing she could think of something memorable and witty to say. She wanted to leave a lasting impression on him.

"I did too. I'll be back home in three weeks, after exams. Do you think you could come back with Margaret then?" Wills asked.

Chelsea looked at the smug smile on his sister's face and replied shyly, "Well . . . if I'm invited."

"You are invited . . . anytime," he said quickly.

"Here, here now, brother, let me do the inviting of my own friends, will you?" Margaret replied cheekily, and then seeing the expression of concern on both their faces, she added quickly, "Mum loved her too, and so did Father. Chelsea is welcome at any time."

Overwhelmed with delight at the prospect of another weekend, Chelsea could only nod quickly.

"It's settled then," Wills called as he stepped up onto the train and disappeared from their sight.

Filled with joy and anticipation, Chelsea was nevertheless well-prepared for the onslaught of anger that greeted her when she arrived home.

"Well, well, little Miss Smartass has finally decided to honor us with her presence," her grandmother said as she whipped open the door.

"Gran! Didn't Letitia tell you where I was?" she asked, feigning surprise and chagrin.

"She most certainly did, and don't you ever, ever go behind my back to your mother again! Do you hear me?" she said angrily, gripping Chelsea's upper arm and squeezing it painfully as the young girl passed through the doorway.

Chelsea wanted to scream back that she had a right to ask her own mother's permission, but she had learned as a very small child not to get drawn into a fight with her grandmother, who vented her fury on everyone around her except Bunny. Chelsea knew that the only way to survive the storm was to weather it in contrite silence, a technique that spared her the frequent spankings that had been a hallmark of her early life. So with eyes downcast she mumbled her apologies and promised never to ever do anything like that again, but she shed no tears.

For Laverne, it was like punching a cream puff. Chelsea's very refusal to fight back baffled her, and she found it tiresome to rant at someone who simply absorbed everything and gave nothing back, no resentment, no excuses, no real remorse . . . and no tears. Her granddaughter was a stone.

As Chelsea maintained her still, silent pose, her mind was racing. She must find a way to make her grandmother want her to go back to Ashford Hall again. If her grandmother had any idea how important it was to her, she would exact punishment by refusing to allow her another visit. She must not utter a word until she knew exactly the proper words to say.

Finally, in frustration, Laverne ended her tirade. "Damn it, get yourself washed up. Letitia has dinner ready for us. Go!" she snapped, giving her granddaughter an angry shove.

As they sat at the dinner table in silence, Chelsea decided it was time to play her trump card.

"I sure wish I could go with you to see the dailies on Tuesday," she said casually, picking at the lamb stew and trying to avoid the carrots.

"What are you talking about?" Laverne asked sharply.

"Gran, don't tell me you've forgotten?" Chelsea asked, feigning a shock so genuine, an observer would have remarked that all the acting talent in the family was not centered in Bunny.

"I don't know what you're talking about."

"Didn't you read my note— Oh, no!" Dropping her napkin, Chelsea jumped up from the table, raced into her bedroom and retrieved from her bureau drawer the note she had carefully prepared the night before she left. Hurrying back to the table, she dropped the envelope in front of her grandmother's plate.

"I'm so sorry, Gran. I meant to put this on the kitchen table, but I was in such a rush to get to school Friday morning, I forgot and left it in my room."

"You'd forget your head if it wasn't attached to your body," Laverne said as she opened the envelope and began to read.

As she pretended to concentrate on buttering a slice of bread, Chelsea felt the atmosphere in the room change. She sneaked a look at Laverne's face, saw the slight smile break at the corners of her mouth and knew that happy days were here again.

Reading the note twice to savor the words, Laverne picked up the small silver bell beside her plate and tinkled it lightly. Letitia appeared promptly.

"Yes, ma'am?"

"I just wanted to tell you that the lamb stew was excellent. I think we'll have a few oatmeal cookies with our tea. Would you like that, honey?" she asked, turning her eyes on her now beloved granddaughter.

"Sounds great."

"Now, tell me about your weekend," she said, grandly conferring upon her daughter's child the blessing of her undivided attention.

Picking her words carefully, Chelsea described the handsome earl and his beautiful wife, as well as the magnificent house and grounds. She painted a picture of nobility, of privilege and wealth, of servants, of magnificent horses. These were the things that would interest her grandmother. She made no mention of the warmth and love and family feeling, nor their affectionate and generous acceptance of her, nor did she say a word about Wills.

Now in an expansive mood, Laverne listened and was suitably impressed.

"Well, I'm delighted to know that you're making some decent friends for a change. Do you think they might ask you back again?"

"Not likely. After all, I'm really nobody to them, you know. Although Margaret is my closest friend, there are loads of other girls at the school who are dying for an invitation."

"What do you mean, you're nobody, Chelsea? After all, your mother is one of the greatest stars in the world. She's one of America's 'royals,' " she declared grandly. "You mustn't put yourself down."

"I guess you're right, Gran. Mama used to be called the Box-Office Queen, didn't she?" and immediately upon uttering the words, Chelsea cursed her own stupidity.

"What do you mean 'used to be,' you silly child? Just you wait. She'll be back on top again, I promise you."

"She's the best, isn't she?" Chelsea said, anxious to put her grandmother back into a comfortable mood.

"Yes, she certainly is, and she's the most beautiful woman in the world." She smiled benignly at Chelsea. "I just wish you looked more like her, dear."

19

Laverne appeared at the scheduled dailies and was greeted warmly by Bunny, who looked slim, confident, and radiant. Even Laverne had to admit grudgingly to herself that her daughter looked better than she had in years. At her best, there was no one who could touch her for true glamor and star quality, nor even come close.

Watching as Bunny clung to Rick's arm during dinner and nestled her body as close to his as the armrest on her chair would permit, Laverne said a little prayer that the long-legged, craggy, notorious womanizer would run true to form. What would she do with herself if she were to be shut out of Bunny's life permanently?

Later, in the screening room as the house lights dimmed, she closed her eyes and tried to pull herself together. She must concentrate on the dailies, must be able to discuss them intelligently and fairly, and she must, above all, not let her prejudices against Rick Wehner poison her opinion of the scenes she was about to see.

Dailies are monotonous to watch, at best. Although Rick's editor had synchronized all the scenes with sound, it was a seemingly endless repetition of takes, the same scenes over and over. Since the director was known for his quest for excellence, he tended to print many takes, and even when his actors came close to perfection, he always asked them to try once more to attain it.

It was a very long evening. Usually Rick scanned the previous day's work every morning on a moviola, but on Tuesday evenings he indulged himself in the luxury of watching the week's work with selected crew members who were invited to give him their opinions afterward. He never allowed his editors to begin cutting scenes together until after the Tuesday session. Laverne looked around and saw that many of the men and women had pens and paper and were taking notes in the dark. The final decision would be the director's alone, but his fellow workers knew their opinions were respected.

Not much time had elapsed before Laverne realized that Bunny's performance in this film could very possibly bring her an Academy Award nomination. Even her mother saw a new dimension to her work, a deeper, more sensitive performance than Bunny had ever given before, a performance that was not dependent on tear-sodden eyes to convey emotion. Laverne congratulated herself for having secured the clever Hilda Marx as her daughter's agent. It had been the right move at the right time, and although she had to put up with Rick temporarily, in the long run it would be worth it.

After the screening, when Bunny rejoined the group, they all moved to a conference room where trays of cookies and hot coffee had been set out. Once everyone had filled their plates, Rick opened the discussion.

Nibbling at her sandwich, Laverne kept quiet because

she had no fault to find with Rick's direction. Bunny was being displayed at her very best, and that was all that concerned her, but she listened carefully nevertheless, just in case someone asked for an opinion.

As the discussion began to wind down, Rick did ask for her comments, and she wisely opted to tell the truth. "I can only say that Bunny has never been better. You've managed to bring out the talent that I always knew was there." It was the most generous credit she had ever given anyone.

As the evening came to an end, Bunny stopped to hug her mother and whisper in her ear, "Thanks, Mama. Rick says you can come to the set tomorrow. I'll leave word at the gate."

Laverne's heart sang as she drove home. She could go to the set, be helpful and darling and cooperative. That's all she needed to be, for now anyway, because it was patently obvious that Rick Wehner could at least be trusted with her daughter's career. Perhaps she ought to call Hilda and bring her up to date.

Hilda was delighted to hear from Laverne, and especially gratified by her enthusiastic approval of Rick Wehner's work.

"I'm so glad you called, Laverne, because no news from a set is usually bad news. I'll begin to spread the word around. Good buzz on a film can never start too early."

"Have you got anything else lined up for her when this is finished?" Laverne asked anxiously. "She's going to need something quickly when this is over."

Hilda's ears were sharp and she picked up the nuance of anxiety in Laverne's tone.

"You're not telling me everything, are you, Laverne? What are you worried about?"

Laverne decided to confide in Hilda. After all, they were on the same side where Bunny was concerned. "She's in love with him. They're living together."

There was a long sigh on Hilda's side of the line. "Oh, Jesus, he's at it again. Well, that's Rick for you. At least he's running true to form. It has nothing to do with love, you know. He'll ditch her when the film's shot. Can she handle it?"

"Only if she has another job to occupy her, but I'll have a mess on my hands if she doesn't."

"That's all she needs—a job?" Hilda asked skeptically.

"Trust me, Hilda."

"Damn. I wanted to wait until the movie opened, but if you say it's necessary, then let me get to work on it and see what I can do. Thanks for calling."

"I'll keep in touch," Laverne signed off, pleased that Bunny now had an agent who cared about her personal welfare as well as her career.

20

With Laverne happily involved with Bunny's film once more, Chelsea was again left to herself, which was the way she liked it. At one time in her life she might have wished for more attention from the members of her family, but she had learned to live without it, and now she regarded any interference in her affairs as intrusive.

Best of all, however, Laverne encouraged her to cultivate her friendship with Margaret, and every weekend that Margaret spent in the country, Chelsea was invited to join her. Even on those visits when Wills wasn't able to come home because of some activity at school, the hours spent at Ashford Hall were joyous. She and Margaret became very close friends. Chelsea quickly graduated from riding the slow old mare to a livelier horse, and they spent hours riding and exploring the countryside.

As the days flew swiftly by, Chelsea tried to ignore the signs of imminent change. The thought of leaving her new home in England and the school where she had settled into a comfortable niche was bad enough, but it was almost unbearable to contemplate leaving Wills and

Margaret and the idyllic country life of the Ashford family estate.

Laverne, on the other hand, impatiently watched the progress of the film, daily ticking off the scenes completed and happily watching the amount of work to be done dwindle. On the lonely evenings at home, she began to gather up their possessions, and when they were within a week of wrap date, she had the trunks and suitcases brought into the house.

One evening at dinner, Chelsea finally asked the dreaded question: "Gran, when are you planning to leave London?"

"I'm not sure, because your darling mother won't face the fact that we're leaving at all. She has some foolish notion that she'll be staying here in London with that man."

"If she does, we'll stay too, won't we, Gran? Surely we wouldn't go back to California without her, would we?" she asked, hope flooding her very being.

"Don't be ridiculous, Chelsea. Your mother's not staying in London and neither are we. Filming will be finished in about another week, two at the most, and as soon as Rick releases the cast, we'll be on our way."

"But what about looping her lines . . . won't she have to stay here for that?"

"That could be months from now. Rick Wehner basically edits his own films, and I understand he's very slow and meticulous about it. No, it's written into the contract that she must return if she's needed, but since most of the film has been done on a sound stage, not much if any looping will be required. Hilda Marx didn't want her tied up too long, and so she negotiated a very high rate of pay for her to return here."

"But Gran, suppose Mom won't leave? She told me that she loves Rick and he loves her."

"Sure he does," she snapped sarcastically. "Rick has a big love affair with all of his leading ladies, but as soon as the movie is over, so is the romance. He may be a genius, but he's nothing but another Hollywood user. Are you going to be home this weekend?"

"If it's all right with you, I'll be going to the country again. Wills, uh . . . Margaret's brother is riding one of the horses in a dressage event, and they've invited me to go with them." It was the first time she had slipped and mentioned his name.

"Wills . . . what kind of a name is that?"

"It's short for William. He's Margaret's twin, but he's not around much, what with school and horse shows and stuff. I understand he's a perfectly marvelous rider." Chelsea had learned to bend the truth to fit the situation.

Laverne's curiosity was piqued, however. "Margaret has a twin brother? How come you've never mentioned that before? Is he nice?"

Chelsea shrugged her shoulders and replied offhandedly, "Mmm, I guess . . . for a boy." There was no need for her grandmother to know that she and Wills were inseparable on the weekends when they were together. Her friendship with him was so special that she couldn't bear the thought of it being sullied by any of her grandmother's remarks. It was perfectly all right for Margaret to scheme and plan for her to marry Wills and become a real sister, but she didn't want her grandmother to have anything to do with that part of her life.

That night when she said her prayers, Chelsea asked the good Lord to grant her mother's wishes for a long and steady relationship with Rick. How perfectly divine life would be if her mother would marry Rick and settle down here in London to live forever.

21

Laverne was sitting in a chair off to the side, trying to be as unobtrusive as possible. Ever since she had been allowed on the set, she had tried to be invisible, and so she chose her positions carefully, close enough to see and hear everything that was being said and done, but always out of Rick Wehner's line of sight.

Because the director preferred to shoot on sound stages rather than on location, he wrote his scripts so that most of the action took place in rooms that could easily be constructed with three walls and no ceilings. He had been criticized for not opening up his films and going outdoors more, but he felt his actors benefited from not having to battle the elements or work in uncomfortable locations.

Most of the scenes for *Wintersong* took place in large, beautiful rooms decorated with antiques. His art director had done a brilliant job of creating the sets on the sound stage, none of which would be struck until Rick was completely satisfied with the scenes on film. Consequently, every square inch of the huge sound stage on which they were working was being used, and it was sometimes tricky business just to move the lights and the camera equipment from one set to another. Laverne made it a point to stay alert and out of everyone's way.

Since she was taking great pains to be discreet, her daughter seemed comfortable having her nearby, and Laverne even managed to be affable and good-humored, which was not her usual style. She often reflected wryly to herself that while Bunny might get the Oscar, she was the one who was giving the greatest performance.

Frequently, while she was massaging the kinks out of her daughter's neck, Laverne made little suggestions, which Bunny was at first reluctant to try, but when she finally did and earned compliments from Rick, she became eagerly receptive to her mother's ideas. It was a satisfactory arrangement on the surface, but underneath, Laverne fairly seethed with resentment. She had always been a force with whom directors and producers had to reckon, and she hated being treated like a nonentity.

The cast and crew worked six full days a week, and Laverne was one of the first to arrive on Saturday morning. She had gotten home on Friday evening to find a letter from Hilda Marx that she was anxious to show to Bunny. As the crew members trickled in and attacked the table of coffee and rolls, Laverne began to pace impatiently, checking her watch every five minutes. The gaffers were at work setting the lights for the first setup of the day, the makeup artists were waiting for the star to arrive, and everyone began to mill about uncomfortably. Rick Wehner had never once been late arriving, but it was now more than an hour past call time, and no one had seen or heard from him.

Laverne began to grow anxious. Suppose there had been an accident . . . suppose her daughter was lying on a road somewhere, hurt, needing attention?

She tried to calm her fears, breathe deeply, and think of something else, when suddenly the man she had come to loathe stormed through the door.

"Get Paul into my office as fast as possible! Greg, kill those lights. We won't be doing the fainting scene today . . . in fact, we may never do it. Now move! We've got some serious reorganizing to do."

Without even acknowledging Laverne's presence, Rick pushed past her, and she knew instantly it was time for action.

"Wait a minute!" she snapped, grabbing Rick's arm. "Where's my daughter?"

"Let go of me!" he warned, murder in his eyes.

Laverne was not afraid of any man. "I'll let go of you when you tell me where Bunny is!"

Realizing that he would not get rid of her easily, he said angrily, "Come into my office and I'll tell you, Mother Witch." He shrugged her off roughly and marched toward his tiny private office, Laverne's slight but steely frame tight upon his heels.

When they were in the office alone with the door closed, he whirled on her.

"The minute I saw you I should have quashed the whole deal. That pretty little mess you foisted on the world is as stinking as you are!"

"Where is she?" she demanded.

"She took my car and tried to run me down when I attempted to stop her. The bitch almost killed me."

"**Bunny** did that? I don't believe you. She won't even kill flies. When did she leave?"

"This morning about six. She said she was finished with the film, that she'd never come back to the set again."

"But you haven't filmed the crucial final scene yet." Laverne's anger was dissolving into bewilderment at her daughter's unusual behavior.

"Don't you think I know that!" he snapped.

"Bunny is a professional. What could you have possibly done that would have driven her to say such a thing?"

Rick sank into his chair and put his face in his hands. "We had a terrible fight last night . . . all night. She wouldn't let me sleep. God, the bitch is crazy!"

"But everything seemed to be going so well yesterday."

"I know. We had a special dinner last night. I let her have some wine for the first time. I figured, what the hell. She's been a perfect angel ever since we started the movie." He leaned back and looked up at Laverne, who was still standing in front of him.

"That was your first mistake. She doesn't handle alcohol very well," she snapped. "Then what?"

"She insisted we go to Italy and get married as soon as we wrapped. I told her it was impossible, that I had to go right to work in the editing room because I'd promised the distributor the final cut would be ready by April so postproduction could start."

Laverne sat down and finished the story in a tightly controlled, sarcastic tone. "So she said, fine, that you could get married here in London, and she'd cook and take care of you while you were working, and when the film was finished, you'd have your honeymoon."

"How the hell did you know that?" he asked in astonishment.

"You're such a smug, self-satisfied jerk, you're pathetic. You actually think you can take a woman's emotional temperature with your cock."

"Don't give me any of your man-hating shit, you old hag!"

Laverne spoke with deadly calm. "Don't call me names.

I'm the only person who can save your damned movie! Then what happened?"

"I tried to reason with her, but she wouldn't take no for an answer. She said she was pregnant, and that to avoid a scandal, I'd have to marry her."

Narrowing her eyes, Laverne said thoughtfully, "That's strange. I've never known her to threaten anyone, ever. When she can't have her way, she usually turns on herself and starts crying. So what did you say to that?"

"I didn't have any choice. I told her the truth. I've got a wife and two kids."

On occasion even the cynical Laverne still had the ability to be surprised at the duplicity of men. "I thought that was all over and you'd gotten a divorce."

Rick took a deep sigh and looked through the glass partition at the crew members milling about outside, sneaking glances into the office.

"We're divorced, yeah, but we're still together. We've never been separated for longer than it takes me to make a picture. This is between us, understand? Strictly between us," he said, lowering his voice significantly.

"Listen, you bastard, let's get one thing straight. The last thing in the world I want is for her to marry you. So where the hell is this phantom family of yours?"

"I have a farm in the south of Ireland," he said softly. "My wife breeds horses there. She has no use for city life."

"Then how come you screw around with your leading ladies like you do?" she asked in bafflement.

"It's the way I work," he said sullenly. "My wife understands it now, but she just didn't want to keep on being married. Said it made her look like a bloody fool."

"Now I've heard everything."

"Look, your daughter can't have that baby, understand? I know a doctor in Knightsbridge—"

"I'll just bet you do," Laverne snarled, and got up to leave.

"Where are you going?" he asked.

"To find what's left of my daughter and try to patch

her together so she can be on the set bright and early Monday morning ready to work. How many days will you need her to finish your movie?"

"Five . . . no, six, to be safe. But look, I can't have her mooning around making me out the villain because I got her pregnant and won't marry her."

"Lucky for you that's not quite the way it is with my daughter. Oh, you may've broken her heart and disillusioned her and made her miserably unhappy, but in spite of your manly virility, that's all you did, Rick." Laverne looked down at him witheringly as she stood at the door with her hand on the knob.

"What do you mean?" he asked suspiciously.

"Bunny's not pregnant."

"How the hell do you know?"

"When Chelsea was born, I decided that my little Bunny, the most beautiful woman in the world, the greatest star, would not be a brood mare for a bunch of assholes whose cocks are bigger than their brains, so I arranged with the doctor to tie her tubes. Your seed did not make her pregnant. Nobody's will."

"So she was deliberately lying to me?" he asked. Though there was relief in his voice, Laverne also detected a trace of chagrin. Men were so disgustingly vain.

"Not really. The poor baby was just hoping it was true, I would guess. I saw no reason to tell her what we did. She might foolishly try to have it undone. I know what's best for her."

"God, you really are a monster."

"I'm just a woman living in a man's world. Now, on Monday, you're to follow my lead to the letter. Is that understood?"

"And if I don't?"

Laverne paused and looked down benignly upon him. "You will. I not only understand my daughter, you see, I understand directors like you who think of themselves as artists. You'd sacrifice anything or anybody for your damned movie. I just hope for your children's sake you never feel it necessary to kill your firstborn."

She whipped open the door and marched out with her head high. At last she was in control again.

22

Twilight was settling on the grounds surrounding Ashford Hall, casting a lavender glow on the forest and burnishing the stream with an amethyst brilliance that emitted little sparks of light as the water brushed across the rocks, making it seem as if fireflies were dancing on the water. All of the crepuscular beauty went unnoticed by Wills and Chelsea, who were walking their horses to cool them down in the ring just beyond the broad stand of trees. The young couple had been riding all afternoon through the woods and across the fields of the Ashford estate in a thoughtful and sad silence. Both of them knew that this would be their last day together for a long, long time.

As the stablehand took the reins from them to lead the horses away, Chelsea finally said the words they had both dreaded to hear.

"I guess Margaret's told you that we'll probably be going back to Los Angeles very soon."

"She did mention it. She'll miss you awfully. You're the best friend she's ever had," he said as they walked toward the house.

"I think of her as a sister. Leaving London is going to be the hardest thing I've ever done."

Wills shook his head and laughed. "I jolly well hope that you don't think of me as a brother."

Chelsea shook her head and smiled, not sure how she should respond.

For the first time since they had known each other, Wills took her hand in his. Without looking at her, he asked, "Will you promise to come back as soon as you can? I don't think I can bear your leaving if you don't."

Chelsea wanted to say yes, but she simply didn't have the power to make such a promise. "I'll try, but I don't have much influence in my family."

"Mum's promised to write your mother and ask her if you can spend summer vacation here with us."

Chelsea's heart lifted. Maybe her life here at Ashford Hall wasn't over. "That would be nice. I can't think of anything I'd rather do more. This place seems more like home to me than any place I've ever been."

"Look, I'm not much good at writing letters. If I don't write, don't think for a minute that I'm not thinking of you."

"I'll keep that in mind," she said with a smile.

"It's been great, Chelsea. Don't forget us."

"I could never forget you, Wills," she replied honestly.

There was so much in their hearts that they wanted to say, but they did not yet have the maturity to put their feelings into words, and they parted.

Chelsea was not permitted to return to Mrs. Chenoweth's school the following Monday, because she had to stay home and help Letitia pack.

Just as she had promised Rick, Laverne delivered Bunny, sober and ready to work. Everyone on the crew noticed that the pecking order had been radically altered. Laverne sat in a chair beside the director at all times, and Rick found it necessary to relay every word of direction through her to his star. Bunny would neither look at him nor listen to him, and behind her back the crew snickeringly referred to Laverne as Rick's new leading lady.

Laverne, to her credit, made Bunny do everything just as he wanted without interference or criticism. While she detested him as a human being, she respected his talent. Bunny was back on the road to being the greatest star in the world, and this time nothing, absolutely nothing, was going to stop her.

In the face of such determination and control, Rick was more than a bit subdued. The young woman who had been doing Bunny's makeup came to him at the end of the first day and said she had something important to tell him in private. When they went into his office, she said quietly, "Rick, Bunny seems awfully listless."

"She's just getting into the part, that's all. That's how she works. Remember, her character is supposed to be depressed."

"But the pupils of her eyes are dilated. I just know she's on something."

"Look, forget it, okay? Lots of actors take things to keep them going. Her scenes were perfect this morning."

"Maybe so, but I walked into her dressing room and caught her mother giving her an injection."

"What goes on between Bunny Thomas and that mother of hers is nobody's business, understand? Have you mentioned this to anyone else?" he asked warily.

"No! I wouldn't do that," she protested, upset that he seemed to be turning on her.

"Good. Now just keep your mouth shut so I can get this damned picture finished!" he declared, and strode out of the office.

True to his word, Rick called it a wrap the following Saturday evening. To celebrate, he had food and champagne brought in for the cast and crew, but Bunny and Laverne did not stay around for the party, which was a relief for everyone. An eerie atmosphere of uncertainty and doubt had settled on the set, and everyone was affected by it, particularly the other actors in the film, who had struggled to retain their concentration in the last days of shooting.

While Bunny was waiting in the limousine for her mother to collect her belongings, Laverne went to have a last word with Rick.

"I did exactly as I said I'd do. Now, I want your faithful

promise that when you get into that editing room you will do your best for my daughter."

"Whatever I do will be for the benefit of my film."

"You can rest assured that no one wishes you well more than I do," Laverne said quietly and with great sincerity. She wanted her last conversation with him to be a pleasant one. Bunny's performance was now in his hands. "Good-bye, Rick. If you need Bunny to loop any lines, I'll try to make her available."

"My sound man is the best in the business, and he says it's unlikely. But thanks anyway." He looked down at the tiny woman thoughtfully and then asked in a low tone of voice, "It was heroin, wasn't it? You were shooting the stuff into her to keep her going."

Looking him straight in the eye, Laverne said flatly, "What a ridiculous idea! I would never give my daughter drugs. I've been giving her injections of vitamins, that's all. Since she went on a diet to slim down for this film, she tends to be anemic. Good-bye, Mr. Wehner. My best to the wife and kiddies."

The next morning, Bertie drove the Thomas family to Heathrow. Wrapped in cocoons of their own concerns, neither Bunny nor Laverne had the slightest idea that Chelsea was miserable. As the plane took off, the young girl pressed her face to the window to watch the land recede, and she vowed that someday, somehow, she would return to England and to the Ashfords, who had given her a chance to experience family life as it ought to be.

23

Chelsea dropped her schoolbooks on the hall table and listened for the sounds of life to tell her who was in the house and what was going on. They lived in a big house on Maple, which they had rented fully furnished. Catalina was singing in the kitchen while she prepared dinner, which was a clear sign that Laverne wasn't home, because Laverne liked quiet in the house. Since there was a vacuum cleaner going, her mother probably hadn't yet returned from the studio either. Bunny was about to begin work on her second film since she'd finished *Wintersong*. That film had recently opened to respectable business and outstanding reviews for Bunny's performance.

Chelsea took a deep breath of blissful solitude. Life was so pleasant when her mother and grandmother were not there stewing about all sorts of things in which Chelsea had no interest. She picked up the mail and went through it listlessly, since she rarely got anything. There were lots of bills. Gran and Mom were spending money again, but it wasn't a worry because her mother's agent had negotiated some very good contracts.

Chelsea was just about to drop the stack of envelopes when she noticed a strange stamp. Quickly she separated that envelope from the others, and happiness flooded through her. The postmark was London, and she knew it was from Margaret. She had often wished over the past year that Wills might write to her, but she was content to hear from Margaret, which happened all too rarely.

Clutching the envelope tightly, she hurried up the stairs, dashed into her own bedroom, closed the door and locked it tightly. Her relationship with the Ashford family was the only thing in her entire life that was hers alone, and it was important to her that neither her mother nor her grandmother insinuate themselves into it in any way.

She put the letter down on the lavender-skirted vanity table and stared at it, cherishing the moment. She wanted to rip it open and devour every single word on the page, but the letter was an event too precious and rare to be consumed in one greedy bite. She picked it up once more and turned it over, luxuriating in the feel of the fine quality linen stationery and smiling at Margaret's flourishes and swirls. Her friend had the fanciest handwriting she had ever seen.

Tucking the letter inside her sweater, she walked slowly down the stairs, letting the heat of the unread missive warm her being just as an unspent penny burns a hole in the pocket. With measured steps she went into the kitchen to get a Coke from the refrigerator.

Catalina looked up from the thin strips of white veal she was preparing for dinner and smiled. "You home early, Chelsea. You okay?"

"I'm fine, Catalina. No, I'm more than fine, I'm perfect. Isn't it a glorious day?" she responded with a beatific smile.

Catalina was instantly curious. The young one didn't usually have much to be happy about in this house of nerves. "You gotta boyfriend, no?"

Chelsea was suddenly on the alert. What had she done to reveal so much to a woman for whom English was a second language?

"Of course not, why would you ask such a dumb question?" She stuck her head in the refrigerator to get the bottle of soda as well as to cool off her reddening cheeks. She hated for anyone to see her blush.

"You got one a them boy shines in your eye, chiquita. Catalina can tell. Say, I baked you some cookies."

"Thanks. Gran forgot to leave me lunch money, so I'm kinda hungry," she replied, snapping off the bottlecap and then scooping a handful of oatmeal cookies off the dish.

Catalina's lip curled. "Why you not tell Señora to give you money? You go hungry alla time."

Chelsea shrugged her shoulders. "It's okay. She's got more important things to worry about than my lunch money. What are we having for dinner tonight?"

"Veal picatta, potatoes Chantilly—"

"Who's coming for dinner?" Chelsea asked, alarmed at the prospect of sitting through another interminable meal, listening to people babble about movies for hours.

"Señora Marx and a couple of men."

Chelsea was relieved. "Oh good. It's probably strictly business then, and they won't expect me to join them. Tell Elena to be sure not to set a place for me. I've got lots of homework."

"Come down when you feel hungry, chiquita. Catalina take good care of you."

The housekeeper-cook shook her head as she watched the reedy young teenager leave the kitchen, thinking sadly how alone and neglected the girl was and how little trouble she caused anyone in the house.

The precious letter still warming her flesh, Chelsea carried her soda and cookies up the winding, ornate staircase, across the oriental rug in the upstairs gallery and into her room. When the door was once more locked tightly, she laid her forage on the desk and then took the letter out to feast on it again. She took a sip of Coke, nibbled at a cookie, then carefully slit the envelope open with the sharp silver opener on her desk.

She read it through one time to garner its information quickly. Then she read it through again to make sure that she had understood it correctly. Only on the third reading did she begin to assess the possibilities.

At last she laid the three thin pages of script on her desk and looked out the window thoughtfully, sipping and nibbling at the only food she'd had since breakfast. She had so much to think about now.

Today had started out like almost all the days of her life, with her grandmother rushing from the telephone to her mother's bedroom, talking, talking, talking, making deals, making plans. Then school, where she endured boredom until time for her art class, the happy hour of her day. Now this letter, which brought joy mixed with great apprehension. Chelsea had learned to expect little from life. She knew that as only a satellite revolving around the star in the family, her wishes and dreams were of no importance.

Ever since her departure from London the year before, she had kept in touch with Margaret. At first they had written each other weekly, but although Chelsea continued to answer her friend's letters on the day she received them, the time it took Margaret to respond began to stretch out gradually, until it was almost two months between letters. And Wills had written her only once. There were even times nowadays when she began to wonder if the lovely memory had really happened or if it had sprung full bloom from her overactive imagination.

The telephone rang three times before she could bring herself to pick it up and return once more to the reality of her life as she lived it now.

"Chelsea," her grandmother snapped. "What took you so long to answer the phone?"

"I was in the bathroom," she lied. Through the years she had developed quick reflexes when it came to answering her grandmother's questions. Always try to find a response to which there could be no rebuttal.

"I'm going to be late getting home, and Hilda's bringing a couple of producers from Europe, who . . . well, you wouldn't understand, but it's an important night, Chelsea. Bunny's on her way home, and I want her to be at her best, understand? So don't go bothering her with anything. Now, I've got to stay here and thrash out this wardrobe situation, so I'm counting on you to help your mother relax. Get her into a warm tub and massage her legs and feet. She's been standing all day for fittings."

"I'll try, Gran, but she won't like it. She says my fingers aren't strong enough."

"That's because you're lazy. You've got bigger hands than I have. Put some energy into it for a change. Check that green silk pajama outfit I bought her yesterday and see if it needs pressing, and be careful when you cut off the tags."

"I hear Mama coming up the stairs, Gran. Look, I hope it's okay if I eat in the kitchen tonight, I've got a ton of homework—"

"I haven't got time to talk. Now get going and do as I told you."

Three hours later Chelsea watched with relief as her

mother glided languorously down the stairs to greet her newly-arrived guests. Bunny looked sparkling and rested, but her young daughter was exhausted. As she walked slowly back to the seclusion and peace of her own room, Chelsea flexed her tired fingers and longed for the time when they would again be rich enough for her mother to have her own masseuse on call.

Just as Catalina had promised, there was a tray of food waiting in her bedroom, and Chelsea attacked it ravenously. As soon as she had polished off every morsel of the delicious dinner, she sat down to finish her homework. She tried not to think about the tantalizing invitation she'd received to spend her summer vacation in England with Margaret and her family, but it was almost impossible to put it out of her mind.

24

Three days after Margaret's invitation arrived, Chelsea was ready to approach her grandmother. She had called the airlines to check on the cheapest student airfare available, and was happy to find that she had enough in her savings account to pay for almost half of her ticket. Looking over all her summer clothes, she realized that she had outgrown most of them. She had started getting her periods, and she had not only grown taller, but her breasts were much larger and her waistline thinner. Her mother's closets were filled with designer clothes, but they were all much too small.

The night before filming was to begin on Bunny's new picture, Chelsea went into her mother's room, where her grandmother was helping her get ready for bed. The massage and facial completed, the actress was about ready to climb between the sheets.

"Hi, darling," Bunny greeted her daughter. "Come give Mommy a good-night kiss."

Chelsea went over, planted a tiny peck on her mother's cold-creamed forehead and smiled. "Are you excited about the new picture, Mama?"

"It's going to be a great film, I guarantee you," Laverne said confidently.

"I sure hope so," Bunny said doubtfully. "The last one I did, *Marketplace,* looks like it might be a disaster. I still don't know why Hilda rushed me into it the minute I finished Rick's film. I'm glad it's not going to be released before the Academy Award nominations are in. God, there sure aren't many directors around as good as Rick."

"He's not that good. Besides, you're the one who made that performance, not Rick Wehner, so get those thoughts right out of your head," Laverne said sharply. "In spite of the reviews, *Wintersong* isn't exactly gang-busters at the box office."

"It's got legs, Mama," Bunny said. "It's still playing in a lot of theatres."

Chelsea listened impatiently, afraid that her grandmother would suddenly decide the conversation was over and eject her from the room before she'd had a chance to make her proposal. It was important that she do it in front of Bunny. Although her mother wasn't a strong ally, she was better than nothing.

"Gran, Margaret Ashford has invited me to come to England for the summer. Would it be okay if I went?" she asked quickly, and she could feel her heart racing. Please, please let her say yes, Chelsea prayed silently.

"Out of the question, I need you here," Laverne said without entertaining the idea for a single moment.

Chelsea looked at her mother and pleaded for support. "Mama, please. I really want to go. I can get a student airfare, and I'll use the money in my savings account."

Laverne was indignant. "Young lady, you have one helluva lot of nerve getting your mother upset on an important night like tonight. She needs her sleep, so just forget it."

Ordinarily Chelsea never pressed for anything, but she couldn't bear the thought of denying herself the chance to go to England. It was time to risk all.

"It's not very much to ask, and I want to go. I really want to go so much," she begged desperately. "I'll do anything you want me to do, but please think about it. Don't just say no, Gran."

Unfortunately, virtue is often its sole reward. Because she was a quiet, obedient, helpful child, Chelsea had no chips with which to bargain.

Laverne's voice was cold with fury. "Get out of this room now! Your mother's starting work tomorrow, work that will keep this beautiful roof over your head, keep the cook in the kitchen to fix your meals, the maid to clean your room and wash your clothes. How dare you upset her?"

"Why do you need me here, then? You've got Catalina and Elena to help you. Why do I have to be here?" Chelsea persisted doggedly.

Suddenly the mother whom she had hoped would lend her support and encouragement in this one all-important matter deserted her. With a few, benign words, Bunny delivered the coup de grace to Chelsea's hopes. Reaching out to take her daughter's hand, Bunny smiled sweetly at her daughter as tears filled her eyes.

"Don't blame your grandmother, darling. She knows how much I'd miss you if you weren't here at night, and I just couldn't stand having you so far away. I'd die with worry. Please forgive me, precious, but I love you too much to let you go." Bunny was a master at killing with kindness.

Despondent, Chelsea returned to her room to write Margaret and tell her she couldn't come. Her disappointment was almost unbearable. She couldn't remember when she had felt so bereft of hope. Was this all that life had to offer her?

25

Hilda sat at her desk and stared at the telephone as if it were a rattler ready to strike. Any minute it was going to ring, and she'd probably have to suffer another of Laverne's attacks, which were becoming more frequent as the days passed and she still had not been able to find a good picture for Bunny.

She was just not mentally prepared today for the abuse she knew was forthcoming, because she felt miserable and guilty. For nine years now she had been closely associated with Bunny Thomas and her family, not only as an agent, but as a family friend and confidante. In spite of the fact that Bunny had received an Academy Award nomination for best actress, in *Wintersong*, Hilda was not proud of her own performance as an agent. Of course, she could blame the disaster of *Marketplace* on the fact that she had been forced to rush Bunny into it to get her over the Rick Wehner romance, but since then there had been nothing, zilch, zip, zero except leaden turkeys that could not get off the ground.

Why the hell didn't Laverne fire her? Why, indeed? Because her record with every other client was excellent. She had a roster of stars that was the envy of every agent in the industry. Why was she failing so miserably with Bunny?

The telephone rang and she shuddered. A moment later the secretary buzzed and announced that it was her lawyer, Sandy Shapiro, on the telephone. Relieved, Hilda snatched up the receiver.

"Hilda, honey, I haven't heard from you for a couple of weeks now, and I was just checking on you," he said. "Everything okay? You know I promised your mother on her deathbed that I would watch out for you, but I haven't been doing such a good job lately."

"Everything's fine, Sandy," Hilda replied without conviction to the elderly attorney who had been a family friend for so many years.

"How's Sergio, honey? Has he found a job yet?" he asked, trying to keep the edge out of his voice.

"He'll be okay, Sandy. Honestly, he will. I really have to try to pull the strings a little harder. You'd think that with all the connections I have, I could get him a decent gig once in a while."

"It's not your job to take care of him. He's supposed to take care of you. Since when is it your responsibility if your husband can't get a job?" he asked irritably.

"Sandy, you're beginning to sound like a Jewish mother. Look, we've been over this a hundred times. Sergio's a dancer, a good one, too good to take just any kind of job. Besides, I make enough money so he shouldn't have to do shit work," Hilda responded defensively, although she too was beginning to suspect that her handsome young husband had married her only for her money.

"Well, what else is new?" Sandy asked, changing the subject. "How's Bunny Thomas and that harridan of a mother nowadays?"

"Sorry you asked. Bunny hasn't worked in almost two years now, and her mother is driving me nuts."

"I heard Bunny's gained a ton of weight."

"You heard right. She just slouches around the house eating. On top of all that, they're desperate for money, so desperate, in fact, that Laverne agreed to take Bunny to talk to Hector Dilworth today."

Sandy whistled and commented, "That snake-oil salesman? I'd sure hate to see her in one of his pictures. They're the pits."

"True, but if he likes the way Bunny looks, he'll pay her a million dollars to star in his next schlock epic."

"It won't do her career any good, honey."

"Tell me, but she needs to do something, for God's sake. Everybody considers her box-office poison, and any work is better than none at all. I'm waiting to hear from either Dilworth or Laverne now, and I have a terrible feeling it's going to be bad news, whichever way it turns out."

"Well, good luck, sweetie. Let's do lunch next week. Whattya say?"

"Love to."

Hilda sat and looked at the telephone for perhaps ten more minutes, then, deciding that she couldn't wait any longer, she dialed Laverne's number. Chelsea answered.

"Hi, Chelsea, is your grandmother back yet?" she asked when she heard the young woman's voice.

"No, Hilda, she and Mom left hours ago. She didn't say where they were going."

"Well, she'll probably call me when she gets back. So how's college?" Hilda was extremely fond of Chelsea, who had grown up to be a graceful and beautiful young woman, hardworking and selfless. In a world where children from loving and caring families were dropping out, doing drugs, and protesting everything, nice little Chelsea had turned out perfectly, and she had done it without any help from her whining mother or her bitchy grandmother.

"School's great. I'm a senior now, you know. Look, Hilda, sorry I have to run, but I'm late for work," Chelsea said hurriedly.

"I didn't know you had a job. Where are you working?" Hilda asked curiously.

"At a small jewelry lab in Westwood. I set stones in rings, do sizing, junk like that. Most of it's boring, but since I intend to be a jewelry designer after graduation, it's good experience. Want me to leave a note to have Gran call you?" she asked, obviously anxious to end the conversation so she could be on her way.

"Yeah, go ahead and do that. Nice talking to you."

Hilda put down the telephone and resumed her vigil, now thinking about the young woman who lived in the house with Laverne and Bunny. She shuddered. God, it must be hell around there nowadays.

The telephone rang again, and when the secretary announced that it was Laverne on the line, Hilda took a deep breath. She had a premonition that this was not going to be pleasant.

26

Chelsea put down the telephone, ran a brush through her long blond hair, and stepped into a pair of patched and embroidered bell-bottomed jeans. It was the age of Aquarius, and she enjoyed the comfort and ease of the current style. Wearing jeans and soft gauze shirts also fit into her budget, since she didn't earn much money, and her grandmother certainly didn't have any money to give her.

She dashed out of the house to the garage. Laverne had sold everything but the Lincoln, and there was now room for Chelsea to park her little Volkswagen bug inside, where it stayed relatively clean.

Chelsea drove her car to the lab where she worked and hurried inside. Jake, the owner of the small, independent wholesale jewelry lab, simply called "Jacob's Jewels," was there working, and he looked up to smile and greet her. Short but powerfully built, Jake was in his early forties and balding, and he had a smile that illuminated his face when he was happy. And he was always happy to see Chelsea. Not only was she dependable and efficient, he found her brighter and even more beautiful than the gold and the diamonds that were part of his life. Married and relatively happy, Jake nevertheless had made Chelsea part of his fantasy life.

"Hi there, pretty girl. You're late again."

"I know, Jake, but I had to finish a paper for tomorrow, and it took me longer than I thought. So what do you want me to do today?"

"What about the GIA exam, did you pass it?" he asked,

inquiring about her course at the Gemological Institute of America, which was situated just a few miles from her home in Santa Monica.

Chelsea put her hands on her slim hips, cocked her head saucily and smirked. "Yeah, I did, as a matter of fact. Now will you believe me about that cornflower-blue sapphire from Sri Lanka? Wasn't it as good as I said it was?"

Jake looked up at her and grimaced. "God, I hate smart broads. Get to work, or I'll fire you."

"Fat chance. Nobody else will work as cheap as I do. Did you put some Cokes in the cooler for a change?"

"I did, as a matter of fact, and in celebration of your now being a certified gemologist, I'll even pop for the pizza tonight."

Chelsea groaned. "Oh no, we're not going to work late again, are we? I've got serious studying to do."

"Well, if you can get sixteen grandmother rings set with the right combination of birthstones, eight watch-bands shortened, and eleven rings sized before sundown, we won't. How fast can you work?"

"Not fast enough. Let's get going so I can get out of here. When are you going to start telling Mr. Holzman not to promise overnight service?"

"When the cow jumps over the moon."

It was after ten o'clock when they finally closed the lab and Chelsea headed for home. She had just turned the car off Sunset Boulevard into the lower Bel Air gate and was approaching the street on which her family now lived, when she noticed a lot of activity. There were dozens of parked cars, people milling about, and flashing lights on the normally quiet, dark road. What was going on? As she inched closer, she realized that all the activity was happening at her own house, and it was obvious by the police cars and the ambulance parked in front that there was serious trouble. Good God, had something happened to someone in her family?

Unable to drive any farther, she parked her car at the

side of the road and began to push her way through the people crowding around the gate, but she was stopped by a police officer.

"Sorry, young lady. Nobody's allowed inside the gate, now move on!"

"But I live there in that house," she protested.

"Yeah, sure, you're the tenth person who's told me that in the last five minutes. Jesus, people will say anything to satisfy their ghoulish curiosity!" the young man said disgustedly, continuing to block her way.

Grabbing her wallet out of her purse, she waved her driver's license in front of his face. "Look, look at this! See the address!" she yelled angrily at him, pulling at his arm in frustration, but it was too dark and he was too busy trying to keep the gathering crowd from pushing forward.

"Keep your hands off me!" he ordered her roughly. "You damned hippies are really a pain. Now please get back, everybody! We've got a dying woman coming out of that house, and we have to get this road cleared so they can get her to the hospital."

"Who's dying? For God's sake, what are you talking about?" Chelsea yelled desperately, clinging to the policeman's arm tenaciously and trying to force her way past him.

In other less volatile times, the young officer might have been willing to listen, but this was the dawn of the seventies, and young men and women with long hair and wearing blue jeans were considered the enemies of law and order. Besides, the ambulance was coming down the road, and he didn't want anyone stepping into its path. Using his nightstick to extend the length of his arm and form a barricade with his body, he pushed a little too hard. Chelsea's head happened to be in the way and his nightstick hit her sharply just above the eye. Dazed, she staggered backward and fell to the ground as the ambulance drove by her. Without even realizing he had hit anyone, the policeman jumped on his motorcycle and sped off, determined to overtake the ambulance and provide it safe escort. He was on an important mission. That was Bunny Thomas in there, and she was almost dead.

27

Laverne rode to the hospital in the ambulance with her daughter, holding her hand and crooning words of comfort.

"Everything's going to be all right, darling. Trust Mama. Please, honey, hold on just a little longer. Try, darling, try for me. You know how much I love you. Don't leave me," she whispered fervently, trying with her own force of will to keep her daughter alive. "Everything's going to be good for you again. You're the best and the most beautiful. Nobody else even comes close. You've got to have faith in yourself and the future." Her words tried to make contact with her daughter's spirit, while in her heart Laverne sought help from a deity that until now had little presence in her thoughts or her life.

Eyes ringed with deep circles of distress, the pale woman lying on the gurney was too weak, too far along the path to another life to make any kind of response. Bunny Thomas's first attempt at suicide had come within minutes of being successful and was foiled only by that particular instinct that gives mothers second sight when their children are in imminent danger.

It had been a long, terrible day. Hilda had called early in the morning to tell her that she had managed to convince Hector Dilworth to let Bunny read for the female lead in his multimilliondollar epic, *Sandbar*.

Laverne took instant umbrage at the suggestion. "Absolutely not! It's an insult. Bunny has never been asked to read or test for a part in her entire career!" she fumed.

"Why in the hell should she do it for some low-life producer who does nothing but big-budget schlock?"

Hilda kept her voice deadly even as she replied, "Either she reads or she's out. It's that simple, Laverne. Do you want her to work or don't you?"

At the very moment that Hilda's call had come in, Laverne was elbow deep in a pile of unpaid bills, trying to decide which must be paid without fail and which could wait for a while, and she was getting desperate. Laverne had no choice but to back down, even though it galled her to do it. "I'll ask her and get back to you tomorrow."

"Tomorrow's too late. Dilworth wants a big name, and Elizabeth Taylor will consider doing it for two million and points. He's a cheap bastard, so I suggested that Bunny might do it for one and points, because I know how badly you need the money. Actually, I'm surprised he's hedging. It's quite possible that I cut the price too much and he's suspicious and wants to see what shape Bunny is in."

Dollar signs began dancing before Laverne's eyes. God, a million-dollar fee would make them solvent again, but she was wary of jumping too quickly.

"Suppose I say that Bunny will do it for that price, but we want half up front. No fiddling around four months to get the contract negotiated, understand? We want the money as soon as possible, and no reading. If word got around that she'd read for a piece of crap like that, it would be humiliating. He wouldn't dare ask Elizabeth to read. Can't he just look at Bunny's films?"

"Hector doesn't go to the movies. He says that just because he makes them doesn't mean he has to waste his time looking at them too."

"Hooray for the new Hollywood," Laverne muttered scathingly. "What kind of a role is it?"

"A glamorous movie queen on the skids and looking for a rich husband. She manages to get an invitation to cruise on the yacht of an Onassis-type billionaire, along with a bunch of other strange characters, and they get lost at sea."

"Sounds like a *Gilligan's Island* retread. Are there any scenes in the water? Bunny can't swim, you know. They'll have to use doubles."

"We'll cross that bridge when we come to it."

"Very funny," Laverne replied.

Hilda took a deep breath and returned to serious counseling. "Laverne, take my advice. If you want this deal, Bunny will have to go see the guy. If I go back with a counteroffer, he'll pass, I just know it."

Laverne trusted Hilda's instincts about deals. "Okay, suppose I take her to his office just for an informal chat. Will he go for that?"

"I think so. I'm pretty sure he just wants to see her, and that massive ego of his demands that she come to him. He'll be available between three and four this afternoon at his office in Burbank. Is she in good enough shape to go?"

"Give me a few hours and she will be."

Since the part called for a glamorous movie queen, Laverne decided that Bunny should look as gorgeous as possible. Rousting her daughter out of bed, she left her at Elizabeth Arden's, where she was treated to the works, including a massage, leg waxing, a facial, a manicure, and a pedicure. It was a routine that Bunny loved, and something she didn't often have now that money was tight. Laverne spent the time prowling through the designer clothes at Saks, where she found a white suit with a jacket that would hide the thickness girdling her daughter's waist.

It was almost a quarter to four when they arrived at Hector Dilworth's office, but Bunny looked amazingly good, and when she looked good, her vitality returned along with the sparkle in her eyes. Unfortunately, they were kept waiting for more than twenty minutes, and with each tick of the clock, Bunny's sparkle dimmed as she sank once more into her dank well of self-doubt. Why in God's name, Laverne fretted, did her daughter, the beautiful star, the Academy Award–winning actress, have so little confidence in herself?

"You look gorgeous, darling," her mother whispered encouragingly.

"Why are we doing this, Mama? I don't have to beg for a role, do I?"

"This isn't just any role, sweetheart. He's already agreed to a million dollars for just two months' work. For that kind of money, don't you think he at least deserves a chance to see you and talk to you?"

"I guess so," Bunny replied listlessly.

"Just think, if everything works out and you do the film, we'll be able to afford a nice, long vacation afterward. I understand there's a beautiful hotel in Hawaii, the Mauna Kea, where the three of us could go for a visit. It's supposed to be the world's most luxurious hotel."

"I hate the beach, Mama, you know that. I have to spend all my time hiding under an umbrella to keep from getting sunburned, and I detest the water, especially the ocean with all those nasty little squiggly things in the sand. I'd much rather go to Paris. The shopping is terrific, and the food is the best in the world. Besides, it's so romantic there. Remember Claude?"

The mere sound of his name sent bells of alarm ringing in Laverne's memory, but she smiled sweetly and patted her daughter's hand reassuringly. "Forget Hawaii, then. Paris, it is. We'll get a suite at the Ritz and have café au lait and croissants in bed every morning," Laverne assured her. The mention of the scion of one of the great wine families who had almost enticed her daughter into marrying him and settling down in the vineyards made Laverne shudder. Paris was definitely not the place they would vacation, no matter what kind of promises she made now.

Hector Dilworth lived down to all her expectations of him. Young, no more than thirty-five, dressed in black leather and sporting a huge diamond ring, he did not bother to get up from his chair when the women entered his office, nor was there any smile or sign of welcome. He simply waggled his hand insolently to indicate that they should sit down in the chairs in front of his desk as he continued talking on the telephone. Laverne knew instantly that she had made a terrible mistake in bringing her daughter here. If their financial position had been even just a hair more secure, she would have gotten up and walked out on the smug bastard.

They waited a humiliating four or five minutes while he complained about his Ferrari's engine troubles with a mechanic. Without pausing in his conversation, he shoved a script across the desk to Bunny and mouthed the words, "Page twenty-six," to her. She looked at her mother askance, and Laverne nodded, giving her permission to open the script and look at the indicated scene. When Dilworth finally put down the telephone, he wasted no time on niceties.

"Miss Thomas, if you don't mind, I'd like you to read that page for me."

"Aloud?" she asked in surprise.

"Really . . . this is a very cold reading. She doesn't even know what the story line is, Mr. Dilworth," Laverne interjected, trying not to let her outrage slip through the words on her tongue.

"Yeah, yeah, you've got a point there," he said, nodding and lifting his eyebrows. "Besides, what's the use? It would be a waste of everybody's time anyway. Now that I've seen her, I can tell she's not right for the part. Sorry to drag you in here like this, ladies." His smile was forced and his eyes dead with lack of interest.

Now that there was no longer any reason for Laverne to rein in her fury, she didn't even try. "Then why in the devil *did* you drag us in here?" she asked angrily.

"Well, you know, the price was right. Too bad she isn't." Then he laughed nastily and commented, "I'm a sucker for a bargain, I guess, but after I talked to your agent, I checked into the figures on her last coupla films and found out she's poison at the box office nowadays."

"They were bad films, Mr. Dilworth, but she was great

in them. Bunny got outstanding reviews, you know, or is it possible that you can't read?" she snapped waspishly. "She's a big star, as big as Elizabeth Taylor. You're lucky she even considered being in your stupid movie!"

Standing up to indicate that it was time for them to leave, Dilworth replied offhandedly, "Yeah, sure. Thanks for coming in. Good-bye, Miss Thomas, and good luck. By the way, there's a great little fat farm down in Tecate where you can get that lard burned off you in no time at all, and it doesn't cost a fortune. Tell 'em I sent you."

When the ambulance arrived at the hospital, a crowd of photographers and reporters were already waiting at the entrance to the emergency room, pushing and shoving to get a picture of the star at death's door. Once inside the hospital, however, even Laverne was not allowed to accompany her any farther.

"I'm sorry, but you'll have to stay out here in the hallway. She's in shock from loss of blood, and her heart is fibrillating. We'll do the best we can," the charge nurse exclaimed as Bunny was wheeled away from her mother. Disconsolately, Laverne obeyed and sat down on the bench in the cold hallway, shivering and wishing she could erase every minute of this, perhaps the last day of her child's life.

They had gone directly home from Dilworth's office, with Bunny weeping so violently that the costly makeup became a blurry smear. Her face looked like a palette on which an artist had swept his brush back and forth across the colors until there was no longer any definition between them.

Disturbed by her daughter's distress, but not unduly alarmed, because Bunny was given to great bouts of crying over the most trivial of slights, Laverne had done her best to console her by bathing her face and putting her to bed. To make sure she relaxed and got a good night's rest, she had given her two Valium tablets rather than the usual one, and left her when she was sure she had gone to sleep.

Now, sitting on the hard bench in the hospital, Laverne was drenched in remorse. Why in God's name hadn't she checked on her more often? Why hadn't she realized how upset Bunny was, and why had she spent all that time on the telephone, berating Hilda Marx and then vainly trying to set up appointments with other powerful agents who would not even take her call?

She should have realized that Bunny could not possibly tolerate such a brutal rejection, and she was angry with herself for not being alert to the signs of danger. Bunny had talked about suicide several times in the past, but it had never seemed to be a serious threat, and her daughter had never, ever done anything this self-destructive. Bunny was in fact an exceedingly fearful person, afraid of pain and illness and terrified of death. The memory of finding her daughter struck her once more, and she covered her eyes with her hands, trying to shut the ghastly vision from her mind, but it was useless. Her eyes seemed to look through the flesh and bone of her hand to the grisly scene that was burned in her mind forevermore. Even now the horror was as fresh as the moment she walked into Bunny's bedroom and saw her daughter's bed covered with blood, and the scissors she'd used to slash repeatedly at her wrists lying there . . . how could she have tolerated the excruciating pain she had inflicted on herself? She must have gone mad!

The minutes ticked away slowly, and with each passing moment, Laverne's hope for her daughter's life diminished. What was left for her if she lost her baby? Bunny was her life. She was the reason she got out of bed each morning, the only reason she took a breath. If her daughter died, she would die too.

A hospital attendant brought papers for her to sign, and she tried to focus on them but could not think, and her hand was so weak, she could not grasp the pen tightly enough to write her name. "Later, please," she whispered. "I'll do it later."

Laverne had been waiting less than an hour when she felt a gentle touch on her shoulder. She looked up at Chelsea's face, surprised to see the girl's eye was swollen almost shut.

"My God, Chelsea, what happened to you?"

"I was coming home just as the ambulance was taking Mom away. The cop was having trouble keeping people out of the road, and he accidentally hit me. How is she?"

"I don't know, but I'm so glad you're here."

Chelsea sat next to her grandmother and put her arm around her thin shoulders to comfort her and wait with her through the night.

A razor-thin strand of dawning sunlight was just slicing through the horizon when one of the doctors emerged from the room where Bunny lay. He looked tired and spent. It had been a grueling night for him too.

Both women got to their feet anxiously, but he asked them to sit down and drew up a chair to talk quietly with them.

"I think we're over the hump, Mrs. Thomas, but I have to tell you it was touch and go there for a while. I'd hoped we wouldn't have to give her blood, because there's always the chance of hepatitis, but I had no choice. In fact, we gave her five units. We had to use the paddles to get her heart beating regularly, but she's stabilized now. I'm sending her to intensive care for the night, and although we stitched her up as best we could, I've asked one of the plastic surgeons to take a look at her later this morning. What in God's name did she use to chew up her wrists like she did?"

"A pair of barber shears . . . scissors . . . dull ones," Laverne said quietly.

"I've gotta tell you, I've seen suicide attempts that failed before, but this one was for real. It was definitely no stunt to get attention. It's hard to believe a person could do that to herself. Had she taken anything?"

"Valium . . . twenty milligrams. She had a very bad day, and I wanted her to relax."

"Well, I'll let you see her for a minute, and then I think

you should both go home and get some rest. What happened to you, young lady?"

"It's nothing. I had a run-in with a policeman's nightstick, but I'm fine. Really, I am. It wasn't that hard a blow, it just caught me at a bad spot."

"Did you lose consciousness?"

"Not really . . . well, maybe for just a moment or two."

He looked closely at her eyes. "I'm sending you to X ray. That's a real goose egg you've got there. Nurse, get a wheelchair over here!"

"No, I don't think—" Chelsea began to protest, but Laverne shushed her.

"Do as the doctor tells you, Chelsea. I can't afford to have two injured people on my hands. Now, I'm going in to see Bunny, and you go on home when you're finished."

28

Chelsea's injury turned out to be a mild concussion, and she was advised to go home and rest for a day or two and put ice packs on her eye to reduce the swelling. While the doctor was examining her, she managed to wheedle from him permission to visit Bunny for a few minutes.

"Okay, young lady, I'll let you see her, but just for a brief look, okay? Your grandmother gave the nurses a hard time when she was asked to leave after five minutes, so I don't want any trouble from you. Your mother's conscious now, but she's been to hell and back, so be careful what you say."

"When do you think she'll be able to go home?" Chelsea asked.

"Too soon to tell. We've got her on a seventy-two-hour hold, although she's too weak to be much of a danger to herself now. Later we'll determine whether or not to extend it for a week. By that time we should have her firmly established under the care of a good psychiatrist."

"I really need to see her and convince myself she's okay."

"Hey, she's not okay, but she's alive. Remember that. Now tell me honestly, is there any reason that I should consider restricting your grandmother's visiting times? Does she upset Bunny?"

"Oh Lord, no. They're as close as any two people can be. Mom couldn't get along without Gran," she replied.

Looking down at the pale vestige of the only parent she had ever known, Chelsea was overwhelmed by sadness and pity. Poor Mom. She was so fragile and easily hurt, yet she was a dear, sweet woman without a speck of hatefulness in her. Tenderly, Chelsea traced her fingertip lightly across her mother's cheek. Even as a little girl, Chelsea had always felt more grown-up than her mother, and like Laverne, she was fiercely protective of her. Now she felt utterly helpless. Wasn't there anything she could do to ease her mother's pain?

At Chelsea's touch, Bunny's eyelids fluttered and she opened them. For a moment there was no sign of recognition, and then she whispered, "I'm sorry," and two big tears hovered on the lids of her pain-filled eyes then spilled down her cheeks.

"Oh God, Mom, please don't cry, please," she begged fervently. "Everything's going to be fine from now on. I promise you. After tonight, we're not going to have any more troubles. Wait and see. Just get well, Mom. Gran and I couldn't make it without you."

A small wisp of a smile brushed across her mother's face, and her eyes closed again. The nurse signaled for Chelsea to leave, and she backed out of the room.

Her grandmother was sitting at the kitchen table drinking a cup of tea when she got home, and there was a desperation in her eyes that Chelsea had never seen before.

"I saw Mom, and she's sleeping nicely, Gran, and you

ought to get some rest too. Mom's not the only one who's been through hell and back . . . so have you," she said, going to the refrigerator to get some ice for her swollen eye.

"With the troubles we've got, I don't know if I'll ever get to sleep again."

Exhausted and with her head still throbbing, Chelsea sat down and tried to comfort her grandmother.

"Is it money you're worried about or Mom?" she asked.

Laverne rubbed her forehead nervously and said bitterly, "Both. I owe everybody in town, and I used what little cash I had to buy your mother a new outfit and get her groomed at Elizabeth Arden's for an interview this afternoon that turned out to be a big fat bust . . . no, it was worse than that, it was the cause of your mother's suicide try this evening. Oh God, if I could just relive this day and do things differently."

"Everything's going to work out fine, Gran. It always does," Chelsea said encouragingly.

"The annual lease payment on this house is due in two weeks, and if I can't make it, we'll be out in the streets."

"We'll move to an apartment. What do we need with this big house anyway?"

"I don't even have the cash to rent a place, my dear child. It's gone. I'm broke . . . flat broke . . . and I owe everybody or almost everybody in town. They even stopped my subscription to *Variety* and the *Reporter*." Laverne sighed. "Well, I'm going upstairs to bed. Turn out the lights. Maybe if I get a few hours sleep I'll be able to tackle our problems tomorrow. Good night."

Laverne pulled her tired, thin body to a standing position and shuffled out of the room. As Chelsea watched her go, an idea began to germinate in her mind. If they were as desperate as Gran said, then maybe now was the time to reclaim the cache of jewels from the hotel grounds where she had buried them more than nine years ago. They might just provide the solution to their problems, financially at least.

The next morning Laverne was dressed and ready to

leave for the hospital when Chelsea emerged from her room. Looking at the clock, her grandmother said crossly, "How in the world could you possibly sleep with your poor mother lying in the hospital near death? I couldn't even get my eyes shut."

It never occurred to Chelsea to resent her grandmother's unsympathetic attitude, and she responded with a singular lack of ego. "I'm sure it was the pills the doctor gave me. They knocked me out."

Putting down her coffee cup, Laverne's expression was a mixture of alarm and annoyance. "What kind of pills?"

Going to the refrigerator to get a glass of juice, Chelsea replied, "I don't know. He just said I needed a good night's sleep. Nothing serious, Gran."

"Thank God. The last thing I need is to have two invalids on my hands," Laverne said with a sigh of relief.

"I'll be okay, but I probably ought to do as he says and stay in bed most of the day. I'll stop in to see Mom this evening."

"I just don't understand why you had to get in an argument with a policeman. Couldn't you have just explained nicely who you were and shown him some identification? What's wrong with you young people anyway? None of you seem to have any respect for the law anymore."

"It was an accident, Gran," Chelsea protested, shaking her head, but the movement made her suddenly dizzy and she had to hold onto the refrigerator door to brace herself. Laverne seemed not to notice.

"Well, I've got to be going. If Hilda Marx calls, tell her what happened and ask her to call me at the hospital."

"I'm going to try to sleep. I'll have the answering service pick up, okay?"

"That'll be fine."

Half an hour after Laverne had gone, Chelsea was dressed and ready to go to school. She had decided she couldn't afford to waste a day lying around in bed, concussion or not.

29

Bunny Thomas was in the headlines again. The tragedy of her suicide attempt was detailed in newspapers and television broadcasts all over the globe, and the millions of fans who had loved her since she was a little girl swept the tabloids off the stands, sent cards, telegrams, flowers, and letters expressing their sorrow. After two days of this attention the hospital had to put extra security guards on duty to ensure her privacy. Bouquets of flowers arrived in such quantity that they were diverted from her room, which was already filled to capacity, to the children's ward. Schoolchildren wrote her letters telling her they were praying for her recovery. Hilda Marx herself was astonished at the outpouring of love for the actress.

"Damn them!" she swore to Laverne as another huge sack of mail was delivered. "If they'd gone to see her recent movies, this would never have happened."

"Well, I think it's pretty obvious that the world still wants to see her. They just haven't liked the movies she's been in, that's all," Laverne commented.

The two women were standing in the hall outside Bunny's room while a photographer took pictures of the star who had been dressed in a frilly bedjacket, made-up, and coiffed for the camera. Now that she was again the center of attention, Bunny was cheerful and happy once more.

Hilda, however, was suffering terrible guilt for having exposed her client to the harsh rebuff of Hector Dilworth. But today, on the third morning after Bunny's violent attempt to take her own life, Hilda had come with something more than apologies to offer.

"When's she going home?" Hilda asked Laverne, keeping her voice down so that Bunny couldn't hear her.

"The psychiatrist said I could take her home tomorrow, if I promised to bring her into his office for sessions at least twice a week."

"You said you would, I hope. She's going to need a

lot of psychological help, you know," Hilda commented, suspicious of Laverne's real intent.

"I think it's a lot of hooey, but I agreed, of course, although I'm not sure any psychiatrist will be interested in a patient who can't afford to pay. However, she'll be a lot better off at home with Chelsea and me than she will be in here."

"How soon do you think she'll be back on her feet?"

"What are you driving at, Hilda?" Laverne asked sharply.

Hilda smiled, and for the first time in a long time felt good about something she was going to tell Laverne. "Well, I talked to a few people over at the Academy this morning, and it seems that there is an unexpected opening for a presenter at the awards ceremony next week. Think she's up to it?"

"Who the hell's on their deathbed and can't make it?"

"Evelin Bascombe. I hear she's gone into a deep depression over that mess her son is in."

"No wonder. He's her only child. She must be devastated," Laverne said, sympathizing with another woman's problems with her only child.

"It's so sad. Sandy says the D.A. is going for murder one."

"That's tough. So what award was she supposed to present?"

Hilda paused and then announced softly, "Best actor."

Laverne's heart took a sudden lurch. Good God, what a chance this was. "Bunny will be there," she responded immediately. "Go, right now, and call them back and accept before they change their minds. This might be just the incentive she needs to get her on her feet again."

"I've already accepted, Laverne. You think I'm crazy?" Hilda said with a smile. "But you've only got six days to get her in shape. Can you do it?"

"You know I can . . . it's just that," she began, and paused. She hated to let people know her troubles, but Hilda was different. She was on their side. "It's just that I'm flat broke and up to my eyeballs in debt."

If Hilda hadn't felt so guilty about having let Bunny be humiliated by the miserable Hector Dilworth, she would have ignored the comment, because Laverne already owed her a great deal of money.

"How much will you need, Laverne?"

Desperate as she was, Laverne shook her head. "I don't want to take any more money from you, unless I can't work anything else out. I already owe you too much."

Hilda was surprised. Laverne had never turned down a loan before. "Don't you think it's time you hired somebody to manage Bunny's business affairs? She's made a lot of money over her lifetime. What happened to it all?"

"It wasn't all that much money, Hilda, and we've got a lot of expenses. Besides, I can't afford to give anybody five percent of what Bunny earns just so they can tell me where and how I can spend money. They're all a bunch of parasites anyway," Laverne replied with disgust.

Hilda sighed and shrugged her shoulders. "Well, if you change your mind, I can give you the names of a couple of reliable managers. Are you sure you don't need some cash? Does Bunny have a dress that fits her?"

"There's got to be something in all those closets that will look good on her."

Before leaving, Hilda had one thing she had to say. "Laverne, I'd have never sent her to see Dilworth if you hadn't been so desperate for money."

"Yeah, I know. If anybody's to blame, it's me," she said sadly. "But you can bet your sweet ass she'll never have a reason to try that kind of thing again. Not while I'm alive."

Through the years, Hilda had built up a deep and abiding animosity toward the sharp-tongued and pushy Laverne, but the depths of the pain in her eyes was touching.

"You've taken good care of her. She's lucky to have you."

"Yeah sure. Well, thanks for the Academy Award show. It won't pay the bills, but it sure as hell won't hurt for a zillion people to see her again. Maybe something good will come of it."

"Don't worry, I'll get something going. Make sure she looks beautiful," Hilda said as she turned to leave the building.

"She is beautiful, Hilda, the most beautiful woman in the world, and don't you forget it."

30

Just as Chelsea pulled her grandmother's Lincoln into the driveway of their house in Bel Air, Laverne came storming out the front door.

"Where the hell have you been, young lady?" she demanded angrily.

The long-legged slim young blonde slid easily out of the car and responded gently, "Gran, I told you I had to go to the cleaners to pick up Mom's dress for the ceremony tonight, and they weren't finished pressing it."

"Where is it? I hope you didn't wrinkle it putting it into the trunk," she said crossly.

At twenty-two Chelsea was a fine-boned, graceful beauty who bore almost no resemblance to her mother. Her striking good looks were obviously Frank Hunter's legacy to his daughter. Now, she pushed her hair back from her face, opened the trunk hood and carefully lifted the green satin Dior gown for her grandmother's inspection. "See, Gran, it looks perfect. You can't even tell where they let it out at the waistline. Now quit worrying. Mom will look gorgeous tonight. Is she feeling okay?"

"She's fine, but I just wish we'd had time to get something new for her to wear," Laverne said, twisting her hands nervously as they went into the house. "Maybe I'm not doing the right thing letting her do this so soon after the . . . accident."

Chelsea sighed. They had been going over the same ground for two days now, and she was getting tired of listening to her grandmother's anxieties. "Look, Gran, cool it, will you? Mom hasn't been offered a decent script now for more than two years, and if she doesn't get a job soon, we're going to have to give up the lease on this big house and move to an apartment. You said so yourself. This is a great opportunity to showcase her and let everyone see that she's in good shape and ready and able to work."

"She's still too heavy," Laverne moaned.

"It's better to have her a little too plump than prowling the house night and day, smoking all the time, unable to sleep because of the diet pills."

"I should have called one of the designers and asked for the loan of a gown . . . everyone will know she's wearing an old dress," Laverne fretted.

"Oh please, Gran, we've been over all this a million times. I called everywhere, and nobody had a dress that would fit her, and they didn't have time to alter one. They've got their hands full with paying customers getting ready for the Academy Awards. They haven't got time for freebies."

"Damn them all. They were more than eager when she won for *Wintersong*."

"Yeah, well, times change. Nothing stays the same. Mom was on top for a while after she got the Oscar, but then she made two big bombs and two mediocre pictures. Here, I'll hang this up on the door where the hem won't trail on the floor. I've got some groceries in the car to bring in."

"Where did you get the money?"

"I've got a job, remember? It doesn't pay much, but it does pay a little."

Half an hour later Chelsea called from the kitchen, "Gran, get Mom downstairs for something to eat. I've made some scrambled eggs and toast for dinner."

Ten minutes later, as the eggs congealed on the plate, Chelsea ran up the stairs to find out what was going on.

The scene she encountered in her mother's bathroom was predictable. Bunny was sitting in front of her vanity weeping, as usual, and Laverne was nervously trying to pin a large hairpiece of sausage curls onto her daughter's head.

"What's wrong, Mom?" Chelsea asked, although she knew exactly what the problem was. The hairdresser who had been scheduled to come to the house to do Bunny's hair had announced at the last minute that Laverne had to pay the long-overdue bill in cash or he wouldn't come, and she didn't have the money. So Laverne was valiantly trying to make do with a hairpiece.

"I can't appear in front of the whole world looking like a scarecrow," Bunny wailed.

"You'll look gorgeous no matter what your hair looks like, Mom," Chelsea said, trying to be encouraging, but the hairpiece was crooked, and it looked like a bird's nest set awry on the top of her head. "But if you don't stop crying, your eyes will be a mess. Come on, now, we've got lots of time. I think you both ought to come down-stairs and have a bite to eat, and we'll talk about it." Taking her mother's arm to get her out of the chair, she pleaded, "Let's go. We can solve the problem while we eat." Food was always an irresistible temptation for her mother.

The two women followed her down the stairs, and as they ate the light meal, Chelsea gazed at her mother thoughtfully. Perhaps now was the time to broach a sub-ject that would have undoubtedly been rejected in calmer times.

"Mom, I've got a great idea. All the young people wear their hair like mine, parted in the middle and hanging straight. It's the fashion. Why don't we just brush out your long hair and let it hang the way it did when you were a little girl. As the fan mags used to say, it's your crowning glory."

"I'm too old—" Bunny objected.

"No, you're not! You're only thirty-nine, Mom."

Laverne listened to the exchange thoughtfully. She was

beginning to respect her granddaughter's opinions, for she had grown up to be clear-headed and forceful, so different from the emotionally unstable Bunny.

At last Laverne spoke up. "It's worth trying. Chelsea, run upstairs and get me the brush and comb," she said, getting up to take the hairpins out of Bunny's hair.

Ten minutes later the thick auburn hair was brushed into a shining mass that fell below Bunny's shoulders. Parted in the middle and billowing outward, it overwhelmed the star's tiny features. They decided something was needed to pull the hair away from her face, and they all went upstairs to rummage about in Bunny's chest of drawers. It was Chelsea who found the solution in a box of memorabilia Taurus studios had sent to them after the fire: the rhinestone tiara her mother had worn when she played a child queen. Exultant, Chelsea slipped it on her mother's head and pulled the hair back from her face. Suddenly, the years fell magically away and Bunny looked like the star-child she had once been.

"Let's see how it looks with the dress," Chelsea suggested.

As Bunny stepped into the green gown that turned her eyes into emeralds, Chelsea looked at her mother critically. Something was wrong. The heavily beaded collar was too top heavy with all that hair hanging over it. Without a word she took her mother's manicure scissors and began to snip at the threads.

"Stop that, Chelsea! You'll ruin the dress, and she won't have anything to wear!" her grandmother squealed in alarm, grabbing her arm.

Chelsea brushed her away. "Let me alone, Gran. I know what I'm doing. This collar is just basted on. I'm sure the cleaner removed it before cleaning the dress."

Because she was being very careful, it took her about fifteen minutes to take out the stitches and remove the small pieces of thread, but when she was finished, the effect was even better than she had hoped. The unadorned deep neckline showed her mother's cleavage at its best, and the simple design of the gown looked new and fashionable.

Studying herself in the full-length mirror, Bunny was delighted with what she saw. "It looks just great, honey. You're a genius! Oh dear, how I wish I still had my beautiful emeralds to wear."

"No way, Mom. You shouldn't wear anything but the tiara, believe me," Chelsea insisted. "That's why I took the collar off the dress, it was too much. Believe me, you'll make all the other actresses look like overdecorated Christmas trees tonight."

"She's absolutely right, darling," Laverne concurred. "Now, let's get started on your makeup. Here, I'll help you out of the dress. I think maybe we should use a little green on the eyes, what do you think, Chelsea?" Laverne asked, deferring to her granddaughter's judgment for the first time in her life.

An hour and a half later Chelsea helped the women into their mink wraps and into the limousine. Fortunately, they had managed to keep the limo service paid in full, because they used it only when absolutely necessary. First they would pick up the two actors who were to be their escorts for the evening. Laverne had tried to arrange for a hot name about town for her daughter, but she'd had to settle for a former leading man who managed to keep himself busy with television game shows and bit parts.

As the long white Lincoln pulled away, Chelsea smiled ruefully and muttered, "So long, Cinderella. Get home before your coach turns into a pumpkin."

She looked at her watch and hurried into the house. She couldn't waste a precious moment of this valuable night, the night she had chosen to do something that had been postponed far too long. She just hoped to God the buried treasure was still where she had put it all those years ago.

· 31

As soon as she was sure that Bunny and Laverne were on their way, Chelsea changed her clothes quickly, alerted the answering service to pick up, and then got into the Lincoln. As she pulled out of the driveway, she checked the clock and saw that it was just a few minutes past five. She was right on schedule.

At the Beverly Hills Hotel she gave her keys to the parking attendant, trying to keep her head down. Although through the years she had avoided photographers as much as possible, a few pictures of her had made their way into the fan magazines, though not enough to make her face familiar to the general public. She had to be careful, however, because in Beverly Hills the parking attendants knew everybody and were frequently paid to tip off the paparazzi when stars appeared.

That would not be a problem tonight, since all of the photographers were at the Academy Awards. The Polo Lounge, too, would be almost empty, because the tourists would be in their rooms watching the show on television.

Chelsea stopped at the front desk and asked for her key. She had been in the hotel only once since they'd lived there just after the fire, and that had been a few hours earlier, when, with her hair tucked into a short black wig of her mother's, she had checked in as Harriet Parker from Dubuque, Iowa, and gotten a room for one night. It had been expensive, but she was afraid to go prowling about the grounds unless she was a registered guest.

In her room she took the suitcase from the closet where she had left it earlier in the day and opened it once more, to make sure she had everything she needed. She just hoped she had planned properly.

Turning on the television set, Chelsea saw Army Archerd interviewing arrivals at the award show. As she watched him, she slipped out of the green skirt she had worn that morning while checking in, and changed into a pair of black pants and a black turtleneck sweater. She had deliberately chosen a black wig in order to be less visible to the roving security men in the darkness of the evening, and had also dyed a pair of her old sneakers black.

When she was ready, Chelsea picked up the large black purse she had bought at Ohrbach's and put in the small gardening tools, gloves, and two flashlights, just in case one didn't work. It was time to go. She turned up the volume on the television set and placed the "Do Not Disturb" sign on the door. With a little luck, she'd be back with the plunder in less than an hour. She just hoped the ceremony would run long, so she'd be able to see her mother present the best actor Oscar.

No one was in the hallway as she made her way quickly to the stairs and hurried down. The lobby was empty too. Still, she was glad she had reconnoitered the area early in the day. Moving slowly so as not to be noticed, she found a door that would take her outside. Things looked different in the darkness, but she was finally able to locate the bungalow where she had stayed after the fire. Although the lights were on inside, it was quiet. Whoever was staying there was probably out for the evening.

It would have been better to locate the spot where she had buried the jewels during the daylight hours, but she hadn't dared to prowl about in the shrubbery. She just hoped her memory was reliable.

Chelsea stepped off the path into the area between the bungalows and walked around to the back. Without using her flashlight, she ran her fingers gently across the edge of the windowsill, trying to find the wedge that she had cut nine years before. She felt nothing, nothing at all. Damn! They had probably painted and filled it up. Snapping on the flashlight, she examined it more carefully, but she could see nothing that looked like the indentation she had made. Was it the wrong place?

Frustrated and angry with herself, she went to the adjacent window and examined that sill, but it yielded nothing either. She returned to the original spot and looked it over once more. Perhaps she should try scraping off the paint. No, that would leave telltale evidence and would make a noise. She switched off the light and hunkered down so she could think without looking over her shoulder. There was only one thing to do. She must choose the spot she thought was right, hope that her memory was accurate, and begin to dig. With her time so limited, she had to make good use of it. She tried to conjure up again the image of herself digging the hole, and as she did so, she crawled to the spot she saw in her mind's eye and began to dig.

The soft, well-watered earth yielded easily to the sharp spade, and within minutes she had dug down more than ten inches. Remembering, however, that she had buried the jewels much deeper, she vigorously continued to attack the soil. She must hurry. If this wasn't the place, she would have to dig somewhere else. Suddenly, before she had gone more than another six inches, her spade struck something that did not give. Dropping the tool, she began to pull the dirt away with her hands. Although it took her a few minutes, she was able to determine that she had, indeed, remembered accurately. Less than an hour from the time she had entered the garden, she had filled in the hole and was on her way back to her room, the unopened and muddy prize tucked into her cheap handbag.

Just before entering the hotel proper, she tried to brush the dirt from the knees of her pants, but it was useless, for in her vigorous labors, she had ground the soil into the fabric. Thank God she'd brought gloves or her hands would have been a telltale mess.

She stepped through the door, saw a bellman coming her way, and decided to brazen it out.

"Sir," she called to him, "where can I buy a copy of the newspaper?"

"Down that hall and to your left, ma'am," he replied, without even looking directly at her, anxious not to be diverted from whatever his appointed duty of the moment was.

"Thank you," she replied to his back as he passed her. Swiftly, she crossed the hallway and ducked into the stairwell.

Once safely in her room, she bolted the door, checked the television to judge how fast the award ceremonies were proceeding, and decided that she would have plenty of time to inspect her package. She spread out newspapers on the table, and placing the mud-covered and moldy booty on the papers, she gently began to unwrap the package.

The plastic was amazingly intact. After nine years of burial in its muddy grave, the man-made material was pockmarked with mildew but showed no signs of serious deterioration. The velvet box inside was also intact, but it was damp and discolored, its clasp and hinges stiff with rust, its once soft pile flat and rank with the musty mildew odor.

Chelsea said a silent prayer of hope as she tried to force the box open, telling herself that the jewels inside were all products of the earth itself, that a few short years in their natural habitat would not destroy them. At last the clasp broke, and as she lifted the lid, the box gave up the treasure it had hidden and protected for so long. Excitedly, Chelsea carried it to the bed and gently spilled the contents onto the middle of the spread.

Suddenly there was a knock at the door. Anxiously, Chelsea swept the spread down to cover the jewels and raced across the room. "Who is it?" she called, bracing her body against the door to keep anyone from entering.

"The maid. Would you like the bed turned down?" the voice called.

"No!" Chelsea responded. "Not tonight."

"Would you like fresh towels?" the maid asked.

"Nothing, thank you."

When she was positive the woman was gone, Chelsea sprang into action. There would be plenty of time to gloat later. She had to get moving.

Hurriedly, she checked the closet and got a laundry bag. Gathering up the dirty plastic and jewel case, she stashed them inside the bag, along with the garden tools and the flashlights, which she then deposited in the suitcase she had brought with her earlier in the day. Carefully, she gathered up the jewelry and slipped it piece by piece into her large handbag.

Tossing the crumpled up newspapers into the wastebasket, she tidied the bedspread and went into the bathroom to wash up. After changing back into the dark green skirt and brown shoes, she studied her reflection in the mirror to make sure that it would be the same young woman checking out who had registered earlier in the day. With everything in its proper place, she called the desk.

"Please send up a bellman for my suitcase. I'll be checking out," she said crisply.

Holding the purse tightly under her arm, Chelsea followed the bellman downstairs to the cashier, who questioned her short stay.

"I see you just checked in today. Was everything all right with your room?"

"Yes, but I have to leave."

"Are you aware that you'll be charged for a full day?" she asked.

Rummaging in her purse for her wallet as she replied, Chelsea did not look up at the woman.

"Of course. I had no idea I'd get my business here finished in one day or I wouldn't have bothered getting a room. But that's my problem, not yours."

"Have you incurred any charges in the restaurant or the bar this evening?" the young woman asked.

"No, nothing at all. I've been too busy," Chelsea replied, paying the bill in cash, and thinking how true that statement was. Airily, she then handed the stub to the bellman and asked him to have her car brought up. When the Lincoln arrived, Chelsea gave the bellman and the driver each a dollar and drove off. She had seriously considered stiffing them for their tips, because the evening's caper had already cost her a month of lunches, but she didn't have enough nerve to do it.

When she was out of the hotel's driveway and humming along Sunset Boulevard, she gave out a long yell of victory. "Yahooo!" she shouted at the top of her lungs.

Step three on the path to her family's financial salvation had been successfully accomplished. The first step had been the night she saved the jewels from the fire, the second, the night she buried them. What a smart little kid she had been!

Now she had to figure out a way of getting as much money as possible out of the jewels, without getting herself in trouble with the law.

32

In a time when glamor was passé and young women no longer sprayed their hair or wore makeup, when male anti-heroes were sex objects and denim the fabric of choice for parties and restaurants, Bunny Thomas was an anachronism. In her long career from adorable star-child to world-famous beauty to serious actress to has-been, Bunny was a product of the old Hollywood studio system, which did not endear her to the new wave of serious filmmakers. Along with her talent as an actress, however, she had one asset that neither time nor a radical change in taste could destroy. She possessed star quality, that ineffable essence that at its best made the world worship her presence, and at its worst, left her unable to cope with neglect.

Her star quality was in high gear the moment she glided gracefully across the stage at the Academy Awards presentations, the audience rising as one to give her a standing ovation. She had, after all, been a star since she was nine years old, long enough to have become an institution, beloved enough to have become a legend. At events such as the Academy Awards, where the competition was murderous, no one could touch her, nor even come close, because of the magnetism of that star quality. Also, it didn't hurt that people were responding sympathetically to her tragic attempt at self-destruction, which had been thoroughly detailed in the press. As she stood at center stage with her arms outstretched to gather in the love that was flowing toward her, all eyes were fixed on the long, green satin sleeves. Was it possible to glimpse a bit of bandage peeking out at her wrists?

Suitably overwhelmed by the tidal wave of affection washing over her, Bunny waited regally at the microphone while the industry paid homage to the star she was, once and forever, the world hers again for a few brief moments. At last she spoke, her eyes glistening, the expression on her face radiant, her voice mellifluous, her beauty unsurpassed. When finally she announced the winner, it was redundant, for although another person walked off the stage with the statue in his hands, it was apparent to everyone that it was she, Bunny, who had won the moment.

Backstage, the photographers clustered about, snapping their flashbulbs at her, the reporters shoving one another to get near her, frantically shouting questions at her though she had not appeared in a film for almost two years. Bunny was indeed a legend in her own time, and although legends had their pictures splashed across magazines and newspapers, no one offered them jobs commensurate with their exalted standing.

At the gigantic party afterward, everyone kissed the air beside her cheek, told her she looked "fantastic," and deplored the fact that they had been out of touch. And although everyone promised to call her soon, no one mentioned a specific date. The gushing attention made Bunny euphoric, but Laverne was realistic. The adulation, the worship, would all be forgotten when tomorrow's newspapers were put out with the trash. Standing on the sidelines, she made it a point to remember the names of every single producer and studio executive who fawned over her daughter, and in fact jotted them down so that no one would be overlooked.

The following morning, list in hand, Laverne called Hilda Marx.

Hilda, still feeling guilty for having sent Bunny to see Hector Dilworth and exposing her to his crude insults, picked up the phone right away. Most of the time, Hilda took Laverne's calls immediately, for the simple reason that it was easier. Bunny's mother had a way of tormenting secretaries until she got what she wanted.

"Good morning, Laverne."

"Did you see the awards last night?"

"Yes, I certainly did, and I must say Bunny looked great. The dress and the hair looked fantastic. Among all those sausage curls and glitter, she was a standout. I was also glad to see she'd lost a couple of pounds." Much as she hated herself for doing it, Hilda often found herself using Bunny's yo-yo weight as an excuse for her own miserable failure to obtain desirable roles for her.

"She's on her way down now, Hilda, and you know how easily she can take it off. Did you know that she talked to Sven Young after the show, and he mentioned something to her about *Queen of the Night*. Isn't it just about to go into production?"

"There's only one good female part in that film, and she's a fourteen-year-old drugged-out groupie. Sorry."

"That's weird. He must have had too much to drink. Well, how about Cleve Somper? Isn't he doing *Farewell and Good-bye* for Columbia?"

"Yes, but they've got serious script problems, and I know for a fact that Bancroft has already been offered the lead. The only other part is much too secondary for a star of Bunny's standing."

As Laverne continued reading off the names of the men who had approached Bunny cordially, Hilda listened and assured her that yes, she would call everybody possible and talk about how great Bunny was, and that if she got any leads at all, she would call Laverne immediately.

Chelsea had made a fresh pot of coffee and mixed a can of frozen orange juice before she left for school, and Laverne poured herself a cup and a glass and sat down to drink them. Life was so damned difficult. She didn't know what she would do if something didn't come through for them soon.

Bunny slept late, as she usually did, and when she finally dragged her sleep-laden body out of bed and downstairs, Laverne was in the study sorting through the mountain of bills, trying to portion out their meager funds to extend their credit as far as possible.

"There's orange juice and coffee in the kitchen. Chelsea fixed it before she left," Laverne said without looking up.

"I'm hungry, Mama. I haven't had a bite to eat since dinner last night," Bunny complained with that special whine in her voice that appeared whenever she was demanding something she didn't really need, especially food.

Exasperated, Laverne set down her pen, turned slowly toward her daughter and fixed her eyes upon the disheveled figure in the faded robe and worn mules. Only the white bandages on her wrists kept her mother from snapping at her impatiently. Sucking in her breath, Laverne said softly, "You may have a nice big glass of orange juice and a cup of coffee, honey, but that's all for now. Let your blood sugar get elevated so you won't be so ravenous, and then I'll fix you some dry toast. After that, I expect you to go upstairs and wash your face. You promised me faithfully you would take off your makeup before going to bed, and you didn't do it."

Even the slightest word of remonstrance was too much for her, and Bunny reacted instinctively in the same way that a weaker animal submissively rolls onto its back when cornered by a stronger opponent. She sank to the floor and began to weep.

Through great gulping sobs of despair, she managed to choke out her distress. "I can't help it if I was too tired to do it last night." Deep shuddering breath. "I'm still weak, Mama." Wail. "And I'm so tired all the time." Sob. Sob. "I need food to keep me going." Hiccup. "And why should I starve when I'm not working anyway?"

Laverne looked at her daughter in despair. She knew it was nothing more than one of Bunny's hungry scenes, designed to melt her mother's determination to make her thin. She wanted to grab her and shake her out of her self-pitying orgy, but she could not ever speak crossly to her again. Never.

"All right, darling, now stop crying. Go on in the kitchen and get your juice. I'll be in in just a few minutes to fix you some breakfast."

The words were no sooner out of her mouth than Bunny's tears were shut off as suddenly as if she had simply turned the handle on the faucet. Pulling herself to her feet, she made her way to the kitchen.

When she was alone again, Laverne put her head down on top of the pile of bills for a brief moment of rest. Tentatively she touched her left breast. It was still there, that tiny swelling, and it seemed to be a little bigger and a little harder. Snatching her hand away quickly, she told herself it was nothing. She couldn't possibly have something so perfectly gross as cancer.

33

Chelsea did not go directly to class the morning after her treasure hunt, but instead went to the bank in Westwood Village where the week before she had rented a safe deposit box. At exactly ten o'clock, when the doors of the bank opened, she went in to put the jewels where they would be safe not only from thieves, but from the eyes of her grandmother. The only piece she kept out was a small platinum ring set with an emerald and a diamond mounted side by side and matching in size, which, if her memory served her, had been her mother's engagement ring. Made for Bunny's tiny hands, Chelsea managed to squeeze it onto the small finger of her left hand. It would be the perfect piece with which to begin her quest for security.

When the day's classes ended, Chelsea went straight to the lab. Jake was at lunch, and so she would have at least an hour to herself, as she had planned.

Turning on the light and donning the magnifying spectacles, Chelsea pulled the ring from her finger and examined its stones. Her trained eye told her they were of the finest quality. The diamond had only one very tiny feather and was probably a G or better color. The emerald was a dark, rich hue, typical of Colombian stones, and quite clear, which was good. Quickly and expertly, taking care not to put any pressure on the stones, she released the prongs and removed them from the setting. Determined to waste nothing, she examined the ring. With a few alterations, she could mount two synthetic sapphires—one faceted, one star—and make an interesting piece that could be sold for a modest amount of money, which would look nothing at all like the original.

The old setting, however, was of little importance. She had to do something with the gems themselves, for that was where she could get a significant amount of cash quickly. They had a huge hospital bill to pay, as well as the lease payment on the house. She opened her notebook, looked at the sketches she had done during the night, and decided to begin work on the mounting for the emerald. Since Jake always had plenty of gold and platinum on hand, she knew she could borrow the materials from him and replace them after she made her first sale.

Working with warm wax, she molded a small sculpture of the setting. Inspired by the design elements of the emerald itself, she fashioned a chunky square ring and then cut facets at the edges and the four corners. Placing the emerald into the sculpture, she cut away the wax so that it would fit perfectly in a bezel flange. Using tiny tools, she gently scraped and whittled until the proportions pleased her, occasionally plunging the wax into cold water to harden it in order to keep the edges sharp and neat. She made the top of the bezel thin so that it would fold easily over the stone when it was at last set into the mounting. After the casting was done in eighteen-carat gold and the ring was polished, she planned to surround the emerald with an enameled vine of ivy leaves on which there would be tiny dew drops of one-point diamonds.

She was hard at work when Jake came in and peeked over her shoulder. Her employer was very dark, with a perpetual five o'clock shadow, and although he would not be so shallow as to admit it bothered him that she towered over him a good six inches, he still preferred to converse with her when they were both sitting down. He pulled up a stool next to her and asked what she was doing. Chelsea had her answer prepared.

"Look, Jake, if I'm ever going to make it as a jewelry designer, I need to see if my work will sell. I talked Mom into giving me the stones out of a couple of old rings she hasn't worn in years."

Jake reached over, picked up the emerald and examined it closely. "Looks like good quality. Where you gonna sell it?"

"I'm not sure," she said hesitantly, which was the truth. "Maybe at the Saturday-night sale at the bazaar in the village."

"Forget it, kiddo. That stone's worth serious money," he said, then laughed sardonically.

"What's so funny?" she asked curiously.

"I just thought of a story Holzman told me. He was traveling in Hong Kong or Bangkok or someplace like that and he saw this beautiful emerald ring surrounded by diamonds, and the cost was, well, too cheap to be believed. But he could tell it was the real thing, and good quality too, so he buys it for his wife. He pays his money, the guy wraps it up nice and pretty, it's a gift, see? But when he goes through customs in New York, they look at it and tell him it's a piece of glass. He takes another look, and sure enough, they're right. It is glass."

"I don't understand. He's a jeweler, how could he have made such a mistake?"

"Kiddo, the only mistake he made was letting them take it to wrap up. They pulled the old bait and switch routine, and he fell for it." Jake turned away, still laughing, and started back to work.

"You mean they switched rings on him?"

"That's it. Remember, never let a piece of jewelry get out of your hands once you decide to buy it, unless you're shopping at a reputable store. Look, tell you what, I'll talk to Holzman, and maybe when you finish the ring, he'll sell it for you," Jake offered.

"Thanks, Jake, but I don't think so. He'd have to jack the price up too much to get his commission, and the ring could sit there for months. Maybe I'll go down to the Jewelry Mart and see what I can get from somebody there."

"Good idea, now let's get to work. We've both got a lot to do. Sorry, kiddo, but I can't afford to pay you to work here on your own stuff. You've gotta size three rings this afternoon, fix six broken clasps, and shorten two watchbands."

Guiltily, Chelsea shoved her own work aside. "Sure, Jake. I'll get on it right away. We'll start my hours now."

"Good girl. And I don't mind you workin' in the lab on your own time. Just keep track of the materials you use, okay?"

"Of course I will, Jake. I don't expect anybody to subsidize me," she said indignantly.

Jake raised his hands in mock alarm to fend her off. "Down, girl, down. I just think that in business it's important for everybody to know exactly where things stand."

"Listen, Jake, if there's one thing I want in this world,

it's to stand on my own two feet. I don't want to be dependent on anybody, ever."

"Yeah, but everybody needs a friend sometime."

Chelsea stayed in the lab for hours after she had finished the work for Jake that night. She became so involved in finishing the design and making the mold that she completely lost track of time; but along with the ring, she was also formulating a plan that would bring her cash quickly. Inspired by Jake's story of the bait and switch routine, she decided to make two rings, identical in all respects except that only one would hold the real emerald.

Chelsea arrived home long after midnight and was relieved to find that both her mother and her grandmother were sound asleep and she wouldn't have to make conversation. She went into the kitchen to fix herself a snack, but as usual, there wasn't much except carrots and celery and lettuce. Laverne kept Bunny's appetite in check by simply keeping her cupboards bare.

Wishing she could have afforded to stop at Dolores' for a cheeseburger, Chelsea heated a can of chicken gumbo soup and ate some saltines before going to bed. As she passed the table in the hallway, she saw that a letter had been left on the credenza. Excitedly, she snatched it up and bounded up the stairs. It had been months since she had heard from Margaret.

Closing the door behind her, she stretched out on the bed to read the letter from the friend she had not seen for almost ten years. The letter was long and amusing. Margaret had a marvelous sense of humor and a delightful ability to put her thoughts into words. As Chelsea read of the doings of the Ashford family, the years seemed to fall away and she was engulfed in memories that had grown sweeter with the fullness of time.

Chelsea relished every bit of news. Margaret was busy studying journalism at a small college in London, and Wills continued at Oxford, where he was concentrating on the humanities and economics. Margaret reported that since he was interested in politics, he had decided to become a barrister, although at the present time he was more devoted to the Beatles than the law and he was driving everybody bonkers on the weekends playing "Hey Jude." Margaret added that he was still fascinated by the American cinema, and he was annoyed that the Academy Award went to *Patton* rather than *M*A*S*H*, which he felt was a comic masterpiece. She also reported proudly that he was a shoo-in for the Olympic riding team.

The earl was having trouble with his ulcer again, but his wife was healthy and still played tennis every day. Margaret had a beau, three years older than she was and from a proper family. No mention was made about Wills having a girlfriend, but Chelsea knew that if he did, Margaret would be too tactful to mention it. Ashford Hall was so long ago and far away, that Chelsea was grateful for the occasional reminder that such happy times had really existed.

Exhausted, she forced herself to stay awake long enough to finish studying for her classes the next day. She rarely allowed anything to interfere with her schoolwork, and had not once failed to make the dean's list at the university. From the first day she had entered kindergarten, she had found school a haven from the bizarre world of moviedom, for neither her mother nor her grandmother had the slightest interest in things academic. In fact, they found her addiction to books and studying a little unnatural, which suited Chelsea just fine because she tended to be secretive. Deprived of her family's attention or interest when she was a child, she now had little to share with them.

After much searching the next day, Chelsea finally found an importer in downtown Los Angeles with a huge inventory of colored stones, both real and synthetic. With his help, she was able to match the emerald in size, shape, and color with an inexpensive synthetic stone, and then she worked night and day until the two rings were as identical as it was possible to make them. When they were finished, she showed only the real one to Jake.

"It's magnificent, kiddo!" he exclaimed, examining the workmanship with a loupe.

"So, what do you think I should ask for it?"

"God, that's tough. Setting a price on colored stones is a lot less exact than on diamonds," he hedged, "but I'd guess the ring would retail at least around eight or nine thousand. If you want a more accurate appraisal, take it down to Jeth Goldstein at the mart and find out what he'll give you."

Chelsea was indignant. "He buys estate jewelry and out-of-pawn stuff, Jake. He won't give me anything!" she protested.

"Hey, hey, I didn't say sell it to him. I just said find out what he'll pay. In the long run, kiddo, that's all jewelry is worth, you know—the price somebody will pay you for it. Appraisals and price tags aren't worth the paper they're written on."

Jake was right, of course. Why hadn't she thought of doing that herself? "I'll go down there after classes tomorrow."

On the drive home that evening, she thought long and hard about what she would do with the rings. Selling the jewels outright was just as illegal as tricking someone into buying the fake ring thinking it was real. After all, the jewelry really belonged to the insurance company now, and the idea of selling the real stone from her mother's engagement ring depressed her. Why not try to make some money off the gems without actually selling them outright? Either way she was taking a risk. By the time she got home, her mind was made up.

34

Early the next morning, Chelsea drove up to the valley to place the advertisement in the classified section of the *Green Sheet*:

EMERALD RING, distress sale. Three-carat fine stone, deep green color, unusual setting. Must sell this week. Best offer. Will show only at bank or jewelry store. Send telephone number. PO Box 276.

It looked pretty good. People were always trying to buy something cheap, she reassured herself, and headed back to the freeway. On Wednesday she'd check the box and see if there were any answers. If this little gambit worked, she'd have enough money to do it again in another town. She tried not to think too hard about what she was doing because she didn't want a sudden attack of conscience or ethics to cripple her ability to make serious money quickly. It was a matter of life or death, she told herself. Financially, Gran seemed at the end of the line, and if something wasn't done soon, they'd all wind up on the street.

On her way to the UCLA Research Library, she stopped to see Jake, who told her she ought to go home and rest.

"That eye of yours looks worse, kiddo. You shouldn't have come back to work so soon."

"Don't worry about it, Jake. I'm a fast healer," she replied uncomfortably. She hated to be incapacitated in any way.

"How's your mom doin'?"

"Okay, I guess. I haven't been home much, but Gran's keeping tabs on her, as usual."

"How'd things work out with the psychiatrist?"

"Gran fired him as soon as she got Mom home. She hates shrinks, but Mom needs something," she replied, shaking her head. "Whenever she's neglected, she gets very unhappy. She has no inner resources."

"Maybe your grandmother made a mistake in getting rid of the shrink, huh?"

"Probably, but we really don't have the money to pay him anyway. A few months ago she let our medical insurance policy lapse, and Mom's hospital bill is going to be astronomical."

"Aren't you worried she might try it again?" Jake asked, watching her closely. Chelsea was such a sane, level-headed young woman, it was hard for him to associate her with a pampered, self-absorbed movie star like Bunny Thomas.

"I hope not—God, I hope not—but I wouldn't rule it out," Chelsea replied, grateful to have someone with whom she could discuss seriously personal things.

"Why do you say that?"

"Well, she's the kind of person who needs to be at the center of attention all the time." She sank down onto the stool next to him and looked away thoughtfully.

Jake reached across and touched her hand lightly. "One way or another, she's going to have to learn how to deal with loneliness, kiddo. The public is a fickle lover."

"It's not that way, Jake," she said, looking up into his eyes. "It's not the crowd she needs, it's somebody to love her. And she hasn't got that."

"Well, she's got you and your grandmother . . ."

"It's not enough, Jake. Not enough," she said with a deep sigh. "Mom needs a man around to love her and cherish her. I keep trying to tell my grandmother, but it's like talking to the wall. Gran's hated every man who's ever touched my mother, including my father. But I just know that if Mom ever found the right person, it would mean all the difference in the world to her. She's a very loving woman." Her voice was sad as she looked down at her hands in thought.

Jake looked at the bowed head of the young beauty so near and yet so far from him. Most blondes reminded him of spring with their white skin, pink cheeks, and blue eyes. They were like living, breathing bouquets of wild-flowers. But Chelsea was different; she was a blonde of autumn, with hair like the golden sunset on an October day back in Indiana, and eyes brown as the dark earth after harvest. Even her cheeks with their tinge of red on her tawny skin reminded him of the falling leaves of a maple tree. He often wondered if her lips would taste as sweet as syrup.

"That's the first time I ever heard you mention your dad," he said, shutting off his libidinous imagination before it got him into trouble. The last thing he wanted to do was frighten her away with the unwelcome advances of an older, married man.

"What's there to mention? I haven't seen or heard from him since I was a little girl."

"How come?"

Chelsea shrugged her shoulders. "I honestly don't know, Jake. He's always been a taboo subject around our house. Gran made me promise never to talk about him in front of Mom. He must have done something terrible to her."

"And what about you, pretty girl? How come you never have a date on Saturday night?" he asked.

"I'm too busy for guys, Jake. What with school and Mom and Gran and working for a slave driver like you, I haven't got time for that kind of stuff."

"That kind of stuff! Sweetheart, that kind of stuff is what makes the world go around. Why, when I was your age, all I could think about was girls . . . big ones, little ones, short ones, tall ones . . ." he said with a salacious grin on his face that made Chelsea giggle.

"Jake, I've always suspected you were oversexed," she retorted.

"Uh-oh, my wife's been talkin' again!" Jake said, laughing.

Chelsea stood up to go. "I was just teasing. Look, I've got to finish some research at the library today without fail. The paper's due on Monday, and the art books can't be checked out."

"I'll be here slaving away. Stop and get us a pizza, will you? I'm not gonna take time for dinner."

"As long as you're paying," she said as she walked toward the door.

"God, you're cheap! Yeah, of course I'm payin'. Get pepperoni on my half. No mushrooms. Bring a six-pack of Cokes. We'll both need some caffeine to keep us awake."

Later that evening, after they had been working together, talking comfortably for three hours, Jake decided to call it a night.

"I've had it, and so have you. Go on home now and get some rest," he insisted.

"You go, Jake. You've been at this all day, and I'm still fresh. I don't want to quit on this ring until I've found some way to get this square peridot into the round setting. I should be finished in less than an hour, and I'll be back as soon as my classes are over tomorrow, okay?"

Jake reluctantly agreed and left, but Chelsea stayed until well past midnight working on a pendant design for the diamond from her mother's ring. Inspired by an old comb she had seen in the window of an antique shop, she wove thin wires of white gold into a delicate filigree that seemed lighter than air. She had tried to buy platinum but had learned, to her chagrin, that fine platinum wiring was no longer pulled, which meant that the lovely platinum filigrees could no longer be made.

When she had the wire in a form that pleased her, she carefully laid the three-carat stone into the fragile nest to see if it would look as she had imagined it, and was delighted with the result. The texture of the metal contrasted beautifully with the hard brilliance and mass of the stone. Excited by her success, she wanted to continue until she finished, but a glance at the clock told her it was too late. Suddenly she became aware that her neck and her back were aching almost as much as her head, and her injured eye was burning with fatigue.

Carefully, she packed the diamond and the unfinished setting into a small velvet box, then slipped it into a secret zippered pocket she had sewn into the lining of her jacket. When all the jewelry and precious metals had been stowed safely into the huge old vault, she turned out the lights and set the burglar alarm.

As she drove home through the now quiet streets of Westwood, she thought about her coming escapade and again felt a sickening lurch of fear in her stomach. Would she be able to pull it off successfully, or would she botch everything and wind up in jail? Only now did she fully understand what an economics professor had meant when he said there were no great rewards without great risks.

35

Laverne sorted quickly through the mail, ignoring the bills, the junk advertisements, and even a letter from England for Chelsea. Damn them, where was the check Frank's lawyer, Delaney, had promised her? She sorted through it again, and this time she found it, tucked between an envelope of free food coupons and a Saks catalogue. She ripped it open, saw the amount, and relief surged through her. Thank God for Chelsea's trust. It wasn't the first time it had pulled her through a financial crisis. She got out the checkbook and began writing checks: first the hospital and the rent, the utilities, and the grocery store. There was just enough to cover all the important bills. That done, she hurriedly dressed and raced to the bank to deposit the check.

When she returned home, she felt like a new woman. She was just about to go upstairs to get her daughter out of bed when the telephone rang.

"You're not going to believe this, Laverne," were Hilda's first words.

. "Believe what?" Laverne asked warily, afraid that the agent was going to tell her something that would ruin the first good day she'd had in ages.

"Hector Dilworth called me this morning. Want to hear what he had to say?"

"Don't tell me he had the gall to say he wants Bunny for his shitty movie," Laverne said bitterly.

"You've got it. He saw her on the Academy Awards show and he was impressed."

"What did you tell him?"

"That the price had gone up. If he wanted her, it would now cost two million. I told him everybody was sending me scripts for her."

Laverne's heart skipped at the thought of suddenly coming into that much money. "And what did he say to that?"

"He told me I was a no-good dirty name beginning with a C, and offered a million and a half."

"No kidding? Should we take it?"

"Not on your life. And certainly not after the way he treated your daughter."

"I admire your principles, Hilda, but Bunny's got to go to work or she's going to go to pieces again," Laverne replied and added, "Besides, we're broke. I just paid most of the big debts hanging over my head, and I'm out of cash again."

"Well, I'd hate to see Bunny pushed into a part that will do her career no good at all just for the money. Especially since she's being considered for the part of Annabel in the movie version of *The Beyonder*."

"Are you kidding me? She's been offered that?" Laverne gasped, astonished.

"Mike Stern himself called me. I was as stunned as you are. It's a role any actress would kill for. I thought Glenda Jackson was a shoo-in after she got the Oscar for *Women in Love*, but apparently Mike's determined to cast the part off the wall. Even though the play was a huge hit, he feels that the movie will have to be quite different to succeed."

"But Annabel is a killer. Do you think Bunny will be accepted in that kind of a role?" Laverne asked doubtfully, still thinking about the two million dollars for the part in Dilworth's blockbuster.

"Come on, Mama," Hilda needled, "you should be the last one to doubt your daughter's talent and ability. Yes, I do think she's a strong enough actress to play against type."

"What kind of money will they pay?"

"I'll get the most I can for her, but isn't it really irrelevant? This is a great part, a challenge for her that will pay off in the long run."

"It's hard to think in the long run when the short run might kill us. How much? Take a guess."

"I'm sure I can get half a mil . . . maybe more, if I forgo the points . . . Look, my ten percent is going to be a lot less too, you know," Hilda said irritably.

"One more question, Hilda," Laverne said. "Stern isn't one of those directors who would just want to exploit the notoriety of her suicide attempt. Why is he suddenly interested in her?"

"I asked him, and he said he hadn't even thought about her until he heard her name mentioned on the newscast. That's the way it is here in Hollywood, you know. Out of sight, out of mind."

"Didn't he just see her at the Academy Awards? She was pretty damned visible there, you know."

"He's been holed up somewhere with the screenwriter, trying to finish the script. I guess he didn't watch it on television. He gets really wrapped up in his projects."

"Okay, let's go for it," Laverne decided, "but get as much money as you can, and keep negotiating with Dilworth too."

"Why, for God's sake?"

"So that when you get him up to two million or two and a half, even three, you can tell him to shove it up his ass."

Hilda laughed. "I'm tempted, Laverne, but I don't have time for that kind of game. Sorry. Besides, a good agent never alienates anybody. Congratulate Bunny for me. Tell her I still think she's the best."

36

Chelsea drove up to the valley to pick up the two responses to her advertisement, and upon returning home, found another letter waiting for her on the hall table.

Margaret Ashford's news was both exciting and disturbing at the same time. She and Wills were being treated to a tour of the United States as a birthday gift. The schedule called for them to be in Los Angeles for four days, less than a month from now. No mention was made of a hotel and so Chelsea knew they expected an invitation to stay at her home. It was the least she could do after all the kind hospitality they had extended to her when she was just a child.

As much as she wanted to see Wills and Margaret again, she was distressed at the prospect of their seeing the haphazard, unconventional way in which she and her family lived. Without a staff of servants to maintain it— even Catalina had been gone for four months—their house was in serious disarray. Bunny had never been expected to pick up after herself, much less do housework, and although Laverne had energy enough, she spent it all on her daughter and her career. Looking around at the coating of dust on the crystal chandelier, Chelsea sank down in despair on the carpeted stairs amid the bits and pieces of debris that had accumulated since the last time she had vacuumed weeks ago.

What with school and working, Chelsea just didn't have the energy to tackle the vast job of keeping the place tidy, and even if she did get it into passable condition, how could she entertain her friends properly in a house this big without servants? There was no shame in living simply, but to live pretentiously, as they did, would look unbearably foolish. For the past three years she had been trying in vain to convince her grandmother to move into a comfortable, efficient apartment that they could manage without help; but no, she insisted on trying to live on a grand scale, as she had when Mom was a child star and the studio was paying her regularly and handsomely.

Dejected, Chelsea got up and went to her room, so she would not be interrupted while reading the rest of her mail. Since her bathroom was the only place she ever had any privacy at home, she went in, locked the door behind her, and sat down on the edge of the tub. One response to the ring advertisement came from a woman in Santa Barbara who happened to see it while visiting her sister in Encino. She wrote that she had been looking for something unusual for her husband to give her for her birthday. The other came from a man in Tarzana whose wife loved emeralds. Both gave telephone numbers for her to call.

She looked at the time. Perhaps she should run over to the market, pick up some milk and stuff for Mom, and make the calls from a pay telephone.

The call to Santa Barbara seemed the most promising. After hearing a description of the ring, the woman expressed her eagerness to see it, and Chelsea sensed that she could afford to pay the six thousand dollar price she quoted. The man from Tarzana said it was too much money, but maybe if his wife saw it and liked it, they could make a deal. He was clearly looking for a bargain.

Chelsea agreed to bring the ring to a jewelry store in Santa Barbara on the following Friday at two in the afternoon, where the woman could have it appraised by a jeweler she trusted. Chelsea told the man in Tarzana that she had another buyer who was interested, and if it was still available, she would call him back at a later time. A sixth sense told her not to call the man again. There was something about him that made her uneasy.

Friday morning Chelsea was careful not to mention that she would be leaving the house for several hours. Past experience had taught her that the only safe way to get away from her grandmother's demands was simply to disappear and explain later. The bright, clear, sunny day would have made the drive up the coast a pleasure if she hadn't been so nervous about her coming escapade. At a gas station, she had the tank filled, then pulled the car around to the back and went into the ladies' room carrying a small valise. Ten minutes later she emerged wearing the clothes and dark wig she had worn to the Beverly Hills Hotel to retrieve the buried jewels. She checked to make sure none of the station attendants saw her in her disguise as she returned to the car and drove off. So far so good.

Once in Santa Barbara, she located the jewelry store and then parked the car four blocks away on a quiet, somewhat isolated street. Using a purse mirror, she applied heavy makeup to her normally scrubbed face and added a small fake hairy mole she had made from rubber cement and a few hairs plucked from her own eyebrows. She glued it at the corner of her mouth, where it would move when she talked or smiled, and it looked remarkably realistic. It was a trick she had learned from a makeup artist on one of her mother's movies. He had told her that people tended to focus their eyes on such things, diverting them from other facial characteristics, and it was a more effective disguise than anything else.

When she arrived at the jewelry store, she saw a woman who looked as if she might be Mrs. Thornton, but when Chelsea approached her, she realized she had made a mistake. Suddenly her courage deserted her and she began to imagine all sorts of terrible scenarios. Perhaps this was a setup the police had arranged to catch people selling stolen jewels, and she would be arrested and carted off to jail. Perspiration broke out on her scalp underneath the heavy wig, and she nervously ran her fingers around the edge to make sure that none of her blond hair had slipped out.

A salesman asked if he could help her, but she shook her head mutely. No sense in letting more people than necessary hear her voice. The minutes ticked away slowly, and her fear mounted to the point that she was about to bolt and abort her life of crime before it got properly started, when a tall, lean woman, looking to be in her forties pushed through the door and walked toward her.

"I'm Mrs. Thornton . . . are you Miss Mason?" she asked, smiling.

Chelsea merely nodded, for her tongue suddenly seemed to be stuck to the roof of her mouth.

"Good. I'm so sorry to be late, but my horse went lame this morning, and I had to walk him back. Then I had a miserable argument with my stable boy and had to fire him. I suppose you have the ring with you?"

Reaching into the right-hand pocket of her jacket, Chelsea felt for the box with the label on the underside, took it out and opened it.

Her eyes brightening at the sight of it, the woman lifted the beautiful ring from its velvet resting place.

"Why, my dear, this is exquisite! How can you bear to part with something so absolutely splendid?"

Chelsea smiled weakly and said her lines as effectively as even Bunny Thomas would have. "I wish I didn't have to. My dad gave the ring to my mother just before she died ten years ago. She never got a chance to wear it."

"Do you have your father's permission to sell this beautiful thing?" she asked sharply, suddenly concerned that the girl might have spirited it away from her father without his knowing it.

"He died last month . . . after a very long illness, and . . . I've a lot of bills to pay. I don't have much choice. I've got a little boy, and my husband left me. I need the money or I wouldn't . . ." She paused and looked down at the ground sadly, wondering if the story was good enough to keep the woman from trying to bargain her down too much.

"I'm sorry. Do you mind if I have Mr. Donovan check out the stone for me?"

"I'm sure it's a good one. My dad never bought anything but the best," Chelsea said quietly. "But I was told not to let it out of my sight. No offense, ma'am," she said apologetically.

"Of course not," Mrs. Thornton reassured her. "This is a very reliable company, but we'll keep the ring where you can see it at all times."

Chelsea kept her head down and her hands in her pockets while the jeweler checked out the ring with his loupe. When he finished, he said he would like to talk privately with Mrs. Thornton. The ring was handed back to Chelsea, who put it into the case, returned it to her pocket and waited while Mrs. Thornton conferred with him in his office. She was back in less than five minutes.

"Well, Miss Mason, I've decided to offer you three thousand for the ring. Cash, of course."

So much for compassion and hard-luck stories, Chelsea thought cynically. The woman was really playing hard-ball, offering only half of the asking price. Was this just the opening gambit on a negotiation, or had the jeweler downgraded the stone in an attempt to kill the deal so he could sell her something himself?

The only real alternative she had was to walk away. It was the best way to find out if the woman really wanted the ring or if she was just looking to steal something cheaply.

"I'm sorry but I can't possibly sell it for that low a price yet. You're the first person who's seen it, and I got lots of replies to the ad," she said, and started backing toward the door very slowly. If the deal fell through, she decided, it would fall through. Suddenly she felt relieved. Maybe she wasn't meant for a life of crime after all.

"Wait!" Mrs. Thornton said quickly, taking her arm to stop her. "Let's talk about it some more. Why don't you tell me exactly what you want for the ring?"

"I thought I made it real clear that I needed six thousand," Chelsea said firmly.

"Yes, I know that's your asking price, but surely . . ." She hesitated, then changed her approach. "Look, Mr. Donovan says the stone is fine, but that under the circumstances, four thousand is a fair price. Perhaps a jeweler could ask for more, but that's a different situation from yours. Now if four thousand is agreeable with you, we can go right over to my bank and you can take the cash home with you."

Chelsea repressed a smile. Although the real ring was worth a good deal more, she suddenly wanted to make the deal with this woman. All compunctions she had about cheating the wealthy Mrs. Thornton had vanished along with her nervousness, because now the lady was seriously trying to cheat her.

Giving her one more chance, Chelsea looked troubled and said, "Couldn't you possibly make it five thousand, Mrs. Thornton? I was told it was worth about eight."

"Mr. Donovan thinks I shouldn't pay more than three, because he says that's all he would give you for it, but since I know how badly you need the money, I'm willing to throw in an extra thousand. I do like the ring, and it won't be the first time I've overpaid for something I wanted."

Chelsea hung her head and fingered the two boxes in her pocket. No sense in hurrying. Then she asked timidly, "Could you possibly stretch it to four thousand, five hundred? I really need the money."

Knowing she had bagged her quarry, the older woman shook her head. "Take it or leave it, my dear. It's a fair price I'm offering because I sympathize with your predicament."

Who is conning whom? Chelsea thought, but she said, "Well, okay. But I've gotta have cash. My friend told me not to take any kind of checks."

"Naturally. My bank is just three blocks away. Would you like to meet me there or shall we walk?"

"Let's walk."

At the bank, Chelsea waited a good distance from the teller's window so that her image would not be picked up if there were cameras recording people making transactions. Keeping her face averted, she looked out the window at the pedestrians passing by. It had all been so much easier than she expected. No wonder crime was on the rise.

Holding the envelope with the cash, Mrs. Thornton asked for the ring. Chelsea reached into her pocket, pulled out the box without the label on the bottom and handed it to her. After checking to make sure that she had the ring in her possession, she handed the envelope to Chelsea.

"There are forty one-hundred-dollar bills in there, just as you requested. Do you want to count them?"

"I trust you, Mrs. Thornton, but my friend told me to

always count money. I can't afford to miss even one of those bills," she replied, quickly counting them without removing them from the envelope. When she finished, she tucked them into her pocket.

"Well, good-bye, Mrs. Thornton. You'll be the first person to wear the ring. Even if it's ten years old, it's brand new."

"It's really the most beautiful ring I've ever seen," the woman remarked enthusiastically, slipping it onto her finger. "Do you have anything else you might like to sell? Your father had beautiful taste," she remarked, and Chelsea saw the spark of greed in her eyes. The well-to-do Mrs. Thornton didn't feel the least bit guilty about having cheated a desperately needy young woman.

"If I had, I would never have sold that ring, Mrs. Thornton, never. You have no idea how much I wanted to keep it," she said, with just the right amount of regret in her voice. Who said there was only one actress in the family? she thought smugly.

The two women parted, and Chelsea took a circuitous route, passing the jewelry store twice to make sure Mrs. Thornton hadn't gone back there again. Reassured that the woman had taken her loot home, Chelsea hurried to her car. Once back on Highway 101, she ripped off the uncomfortable wig and looked for another service station where she could wash her face and change her clothes before going to work.

Later that night in the laboratory, long after Jake had left, Chelsea took the real emerald out of the setting and polished the enamel off the gold, which she then melted down, erasing all traces of the duplicate ring. The emerald had done its work so well, she was almost tempted to use it again, because she had a great idea for a new setting for it. Caution prevailed, however, and she decided against it. She had once read that most crooks got caught because they were too unimaginative to deviate from their chosen modus operandi, and she had no intention of falling into that trap.

Now it was time to sell the diamond pendant. If that

worked out as well as the emerald had, she would re-mount the stones in their original setting and still have the ring as well as several thousand dollars. Then she would sit down with her grandmother, go over the bills, and decide just what bills were the most important to pay. After that she could begin to think about how she would entertain her British friends.

Any guilt she might have felt was swept away by the knowledge that she had taken a definitive step toward putting her grandmother's house in order.

37

Because Chelsea was so busy pursuing her own agenda for financial salvation and avoiding both her mother and grandmother as much as possible, she was unaware that the situation in her home was changing. She was exhausted from fighting the traffic up the Santa Ana Freeway from Newport Beach, where she had succeeded in selling a replica of the diamond pendant for five thousand dollars, when she walked into the house one evening and thought her mind was playing tricks on her. Her senses were assaulted by the familiar and savory smell of food cooking, as well as something else. What was it? Bleach, furniture polish, something . . .

She stopped at the hall table and checked for the mail, but there was nothing for her. When she looked up at the mirror, she noticed that the haze was gone, the hall table dusted and shining. She looked at the staircase, and it too was clean. What the devil was going on around here?

She hurried to the kitchen to find dear, sweet Catalina was back!

"Catalina, my God, it's great to see you," she said, and gave the woman a warm hug.

"S'good·to be back, Chelsea. How you been?"

"What are you doing here?" Chelsea asked, and learned that Catalina had been spirited away from her former employer with the promise of a higher salary. Chelsea was delighted to have her, but she wondered at the woman's lack of common sense. Granted, she looked upon the Thomas women as family, but didn't she realize that they still couldn't pay her?

Chelsea learned from Catalina that a new Latino maid had been hired too, and a gardening service was busy replanting the flower beds, trying to make the garden look respectable once more. Where in the devil had Gran gotten the money?

Excusing herself, Chelsea ran upstairs and knocked on Laverne's door. She rushed into the room, ready to ask serious questions about the sudden wave of spending.

"Gran, last week you were moaning and groaning about being in debt, and now you're hiring a houseful of servants. Where is the money coming from?" she demanded.

Laverne looked up from her vanity table, where she was polishing her nails.

"Don't you talk to me like that! Who do you think you are? And keep your voice down, your mother is already asleep, and she has to get up early in the morning."

"The bills, Gran—doctor bills, hospital bills, the rent—how are we going to pay them?" Chelsea asked, lowering her voice and trying to sound less irritable.

Laverne leveled her gaze at her pugnacious grandchild and said archly, "That, my dear young woman, is none of your damned business. They're paid. And for your information, your mother has just been cast in the most important role in a movie this year. She's going to play Annabel in Mike Stern's film, *The Beyonder*. Hilda just finished the negotiation today. So . . . what do you think of that?"

"I think . . . it's great," Chelsea replied, nonplussed by the announcement. "How's Mom doing?"

"Naturally, she's thrilled. She's meeting with Mike in the morning for a read-through of the script. We've already had dinner, so you'll have to eat alone." Dismissing her granddaughter, she returned to the serious task at hand. One didn't go to meet producers or directors with chipped nail polish.

Chelsea did not go into the kitchen to eat dinner, because her stomach was in a knot. For the first time since she had embarked on her adventure to raise money, she felt the true impact of what she had done. She had committed two serious crimes, and for what? For nothing at all. Gran and Mom apparently didn't need her help, and now she was no longer a criminal with a higher cause, she was simply a criminal . . . period. She was afraid. Good God, what had she been thinking?

38

The next day Chelsea arrived home from school to be greeted at the door by a tall, dark young man wearing a white shirt, black tie, and charcoal-gray suit. Bowing his head slightly, he greeted her in a soft, modulated tone distinguished by the barest hint of a British accent, "Good day, Miss Chelsea. I'm Clark, Avery Clark, the new butler."

"Good for you," she said through clenched teeth, brushing past him. "Where's my grandmother?"

"In her room, I believe. Would you like me to tell her you're home?"

"I can do it myself, thank you," she said irritably, and hurried up the stairs. Without knocking, she opened the door and found Laverne lying on a massage table, while a brawny young man in white cotton slacks and a T-shirt with sleeves rolled up to reveal his rippling muscles manipulated her spine.

"Hello, darling," Laverne said. "Meet Raoul. He just

gave Bunny the most wonderful massage to relax her, and I decided to indulge myself and have one too."

"Gran, I need to talk to you now," Chelsea said, seething with anger.

"If it's anything that will disturb me, let's postpone it until later. Ooooh, Raoul, right there, work on that spot a little harder."

Frustrated, Chelsea backed from the room before she made the mistake of saying something that would be repeated in all the bedrooms where Raoul plied his trade. Damn! Butlers, massages, hairdressers, designer clothes. Her grandmother was running up exorbitant bills, and Mom hadn't even signed a contract yet! Didn't either of them have any sense at all?

She stomped into her room, slammed the door behind her, and was startled at the appearance of the room. The bed was made, the rug freshly vacuumed, the dimity curtains washed and ironed, and the papers and books on her desk were organized in neat little piles. She loved it, but the cost of it all overwhelmed her.

Disgusted with the mess they seemed to be forever getting themselves into, she threw herself into the chair by the desk and put her head in her hands. Suddenly she noticed a letter addressed to her propped up on her desk. The handwriting wasn't familiar, but her heart skipped when she saw that it was from London. She turned it over and saw the Ashford crest on the back. It wasn't Margaret's handwriting, so it must be from Wills!

Using the letter opener and slitting the envelope open neatly, she unfolded the brief note.

Dear Chelsea,

Yes, it's truly me. Sorry I haven't written for lo these many years, but I warned you I wasn't much of a correspondent when I was barely thirteen, didn't I? Can't say I've improved much with the years.

My sister told me she'd written to let you know that we'll be in your part of the world for four days

in May, and I wanted to be sure you'll be available
to spend a bit of time with us. Although it's been
a dreadfully long while since we last saw you, we
all think of you often. Do write and tell us if it will
be possible to see you. If the time is not convenient,
perhaps we can juggle our schedule about to fit in
with yours.

I'll look forward to hearing from you soon.

Your caring friend,
Wills

She read it again and again, and with each reading, the
anger she had felt moments before with her grandmother
slowly drained away, until the presence of servants and
the absence of money became benignly insignificant. She
lost herself completely in memories of the halcyon days
spent at Ashford Hall, riding with Wills, talking with
Margaret, having dinner with the family . . . the blessed
family. How she missed them still. In her thoughts,
Heaven was not somewhere in the clouds where angels
played harps and the streets were paved with gold, but
in the bosom of the Ashford family, surrounded by the
mists of evening, playing chess with Wills, her fingers
occasionally brushing his as she strove to give him a good
match even if she had no hope whatsoever of beating him.

"What did you want to talk to me about?" her grandmother asked sharply, suddenly appearing at the door of
her room and jolting her back to their most inauspicious
present circumstances. Chelsea was momentarily disoriented, but quickly regained her pique.

"Gran, why are you spending money we don't have
yet?" she asked with less irritation than she would have
shown before reading Wills's letter.

"Chelsea, I'm running this house, not you!" Laverne
said haughtily.

"Well, I think it's ridiculous for us to start having maids
and butlers and masseurs when—"

Laverne was startled by the girl's nerve. "Listen, young
lady, just because you have a little job that pays peanuts

doesn't mean you have any right to question my decisions. For your information, your mother has an image to uphold, and in this business, image is everything, absolutely everything. I know that's beyond your small, pedestrian mind to comprehend. The bills will get paid . . . in good time."

They glared at each other for a long, tense moment, and then Chelsea gave up. There was absolutely nothing she could do to change her grandmother's attitude about finance.

"When will Mom get her first check?" she asked quietly.

"Soon. And it will more than cover our expenses," Laverne replied, also lowering her voice. "Besides, Hilda is already lining up another picture for Bunny, which will start immediately after she finishes principal photography on this one, so you can stop worrying. Everything's going to be fine."

"I hope you're right, Gran. God, I hope you're right. By the way, Margaret and Wills Ashford are going to be in Los Angeles for four days in May. Is it all right if I invite them to stay here?"

Laverne's countenance brightened immediately. "The earl's children? How very nice! We'll have to arrange a party so everyone can meet them . . ."

"Gran!" Chelsea called out in alarm. "No! Absolutely no parties, and don't go trying to get their names mentioned in any of the columns. They're private people, very private, and they're coming to visit me. They're my friends. They have no interest in movie stars, understand?"

"The whole world is interested in movie stars, you silly girl. Most girls your age would be thrilled to have the great Bunny Thomas as their mother, but you—most of the time you act as if she's an embarrassment to you."

"Please, Gran, let's not get into another one of those 'you ungrateful child' conversations. We just wind up being mad at each other. Now, Wills and Margaret are not—I repeat, not—coming here to see the great Bunny Thomas. They're friends of mine, not fans of my mother."

"You not only look like your wretched father, you act like him too." Laverne sighed wearily. "What a shame you didn't get at least a little something from our side of the family. Life would have been so much pleasanter around here if you had." She turned and left the room in irritation, slamming the door behind her.

Accustomed to being the odd one out in her family, Chelsea had long ago ceased to be hurt by her grandmother's slighting remarks. She looked at the time and realized it was too late to sit down and answer both Ashford letters; that would have to wait until later. Now, she'd better grab a bite to eat and get over to the lab. She hoped the demonstration against the Vietnam war wouldn't clog up the traffic on Westwood Boulevard again. No matter what her grandmother expected in the way of jobs for her mother, Chelsea for one was never going to be sucked into that particular fantasy again. One of these days she'd be independent of everyone in this household, and from now on she'd do it with honest, hard work.

39

Principal photography on *The Beyonder* was scheduled to begin in less than a week, and Hilda still had not received executed copies of Bunny's contract. Every morning, she would arrive at the office to find that her secretary had already fielded six or more anxious calls from Laverne. Sometimes she wondered if handling Bunny was worth the stress of dealing with her mother, who seemed to get more difficult with each passing day.

Hilda poured herself a cup of coffee and looked out the window at the traffic along Wilshire Boulevard. Sweetened with two saccharin tablets, the brew was hot and strong, and she would need every drop of it to get her through the morning. When the cup was half empty, she buzzed for Ruth, her capable and patient secretary, who responded immediately.

"Ruth, before I call Mrs. Thomas, would you get Hart Baldwin on the telephone for me, please?" she asked. She might as well try one more time to get the lawyers over at Warners off the dime. Annoyed as she was with Laverne, the woman had good reason to be miffed at the delay. The final details on the contract had been ironed out more than two weeks ago, and still they hadn't delivered as promised.

"Come on now, Hart," she said upon being connected, "what's holding up those contracts now?"

"What can I tell you, Hilda? We're moving as fast as we can," he said, and the whine in his voice told her that he was as tired of her bitching as she was of Laverne's.

"Let me put it this way, my dear sir—from this moment on, Bunny Thomas will no longer be available for costume fittings, makeup tests, etcetera, etcetera, until she gets the first check, understand?" Hilda pronounced testily.

"You agents are beyond belief. You want everything but the kitchen sink put into the contracts to protect your clients, but you still want the money yesterday," he said, escalating the discussion.

"Don't you start giving me a hard time. I was the one who convinced Bunny to turn down a contract for two million to do this film for next to nothing, remember? The least you can do is see that what little she's being paid is given to her in a timely fashion."

"Save that crap for somebody who just got off the train from Peoria. You and I both know she was damned lucky to get the part. Every actress over the age of twenty-five wanted it."

"I don't know any actress in this town who admits to being over twenty-five, and neither do you," she snapped, adding, "and I won't be the one boarding a train back to Peoria when you-know-who starts calling to find out where the hell Bunny is today and I refer him to you.

Bye-bye," she said, her final words dripping in sugar laced with poison.

She slammed down the telephone and then punched the intercom to see who was waiting on the line to talk to her.

"Laverne Thomas is on line two, and Sergio is on line three," her secretary replied.

"Okay, I'll take Laverne first, but tell Sergio to hold on. I need to talk to him before he leaves the house."

"Will do."

She punched line two so hard she smashed her fingernail, causing it to crack at the quick. "Shit!" she exclaimed, which became her not wholly inappropriate salutation to Laverne.

"Well the same to you, lady," Laverne said in surprise.

"I'm sorry, Laverne, but I just broke a nail," she said apologetically.

"Sounds like your day is off to a great start."

"Look, I just talked to Hart Baldwin. Has Bunny left the house for the studio yet?"

"She's not supposed to be there until ten, so I haven't started the morning drill. It's such a struggle to get her out of bed."

"What kind of sleeping pills are you giving her?" Hilda asked distastefully.

"Just Seconals, and please, spare me the lecture," Laverne retorted. "You and Mike and everybody else want her thin, and the only way she's going to get that way is with diet pills, which as you know quite well keep her up all night."

"God, I wish you could just control her intake of food and keep her off those things," Hilda said. She hated drugs and had to be extremely ill before she would take any kind of medicine.

"So do I, but she just can't do it. She's down more than twenty pounds now, and her tummy is flat enough so her hipbones can be seen. Mike said he wanted ten more pounds off before final fittings."

"Well, I can understand his worry. After all, Annabel

is supposed to have an incurable disease. Anyway, let her sleep as long as she wants. And have your butler answer the telephone, okay? You're not at home to anybody but me."

Laverne was immediately apprehensive. "What's going on?"

"I talked to Hart Baldwin, the head honcho in legal over at Warners, and told him Bunny wouldn't be available for anything until we got a check. I have a feeling it will be on my desk within an hour after Mike finds out he can't reach her. I talked to him yesterday, and he's concerned about not having enough rehearsal time. You know what a perfectionist he is."

"Well, at last you're finally starting to get tough with those bastards," Laverne said with satisfaction.

The response irritated Hilda. "My dear," she said, biting her words sharply, "if I had started playing hardball too early in the game, they would have backed off and anointed somebody else with the prize role of the year. Once the news was leaked to the press that she had the part, the last thing she needed was the ignominy of being replaced, understand? For God's sake, Laverne, lay off and let me do my job, will you?"

"Well just do it then!" Laverne snapped, and slammed down the telephone.

The rift between the two women was getting wider with each confrontation, and it was apparent to them both that they were on slippery ground. Hilda herself was not at all sanguine about her relationship with the Thomas women. Only her belief in Bunny's talent kept her from telling Laverne off. Taking a deep breath, she punched line three and tried to erase the anger from her voice.

"Sergio? Good morning, darling. How come you're up so early?" she asked her husband of less than two years.

"Consuela rang the doorbell and got me out of bed, because you forgot to leave the key under the doormat," he said petulantly.

"Oh God, I'm sorry, darling. Why don't you go back to bed?" she asked, her voice full of contrition.

"You know how hard it is for me to do that. Besides, I have to get dressed and go pick up the laundry. I haven't got a clean shirt for the tryout this afternoon." The tone of his voice left no doubt whom he thought was to blame for the effort he had to make.

"I tried to pick it up on my way home last night, but I was too late," she explained sweetly, her tone of voice so different from the one she had used with both Hart Baldwin and Laverne. "I'm sorry, darling. I've got a call in for Mark Olson, who's doing the choreography, to remind him to be on the lookout for you. They need a strong, handsome dancer for the big solo in the second act."

There was silence on the other end. "Sergio, darling, are you there?" she asked several times, but the line was dead. He had hung up on her, as he always did when he was annoyed. She dialed her home number again, but she knew it would be useless. He never answered the telephone when he was pouting about something.

She sighed and dropped her face into her hands. God, what was happening to her? Why in the world had a forty-year-old woman married a young Italian stud like Sergio? Everybody had told her he was nothing but a pretty face and body with no talent, looking for an easy way to make it in Hollywood. Even worse, they had said he was lazy and just wanted a successful wife to support him. And everybody had been right. Oh God, how right they had been!

How could she have thought for a single moment that he really cared about her, or even wanted her sexually? Even now, when she often found herself the target of his contempt and distaste, why wasn't she able to get rid of him? Why? she asked, looking up at her reflection in the mirror over the couch. Why? Because then she would have to admit to the world that this pretty, brainless chunk of pectorals had made a fool of her. Hilda the smart, the clever, the cagey agent, who was succeeding in the man's world of Hollywood, would then be cut down to size, and she couldn't bear the humiliation. But it wasn't just concern for her reputation that held the marriage together, it was also sex. She still had an overpowering lust for his young body.

That afternoon, just as she had expected, a messenger delivered the final contracts for Bunny's signature. At five o'clock she had them back on Hart Baldwin's desk, signed and witnessed and with a note attached asking Hart to messenger a check immediately. As soon as she had it in her hands, although it was too late to bank, she sent her own company check to Laverne for the full amount less her ten percent.

Feeling pleased and relieved, she decided to reward herself and go home early. She'd stop at Chalet Gourmet and pick up something delicious for dinner, including a tin of Beluga caviar, which Sergio loved, as well as a bottle of Chambertin, his favorite wine. With a little firelight and her lace peignoir, perhaps she could buy herself a little loving.

She was waiting for the elevator in the hallway when Ruth rushed out with a message.

"Miss Marx, wait," she called, hurrying toward her anxiously.

Hilda backed away from the opening elevator door and turned toward her secretary. "What is it, Ruth?"

Ruth shook her head and moved closer so she would not be overheard. "Miss Marx, a Mr. Olson just called from the Music Center. He said to tell you that your husband is a—a—" she hesitated, her face going pink.

"A what, Ruth?" Hilda asked impatiently, hoping that at last somebody had perhaps seen the promise and talent she saw in Sergio.

Looking down, speaking in a hushed tone, Ruth finally got the correct word out. "An asshole, Miss Marx. That's exactly what he said."

"Good heavens, are you sure?" Hilda asked, startled.

"Yes, quite sure. He left his number and said he wants to talk to you right away. He's awfully angry."

"Get him on the telephone for me, Ruth. Immediately," Hilda said, leading the way back into her office.

"Mr. Olson?" the secretary asked.

"Yes, and then call my home and find out if Sergio is back yet."

Mark Olson, who had been a personal friend for years, and who was one of the greatest choreographers on the West Coast, was as furious as she had ever known him to be.

"Mark, for God's sake, what happened?"

"How could you have married a punk like that, Hilda? He's nuts!" he bellowed at her.

"Calm down and tell me what he did!"

Mark took a deep breath in a desperate attempt to bring himself under control. "Well, I went through a few steps for him, and he was fine—not the best we've seen, but because of my relationship with you, I decided to work with him a little before I took him to the director. There was one movement he refused to do the way I wanted, and so I explained it again and even showed him. He had the gall to tell me it was better his way."

"Come on, Mark. That's not so terrible, is it?" she said, relieved.

"Hey, that's only the beginning. You know me. I figured, what the hell, maybe he's right, so I let him do it his way for Chelli, who you know is probably one of the best directors of musical comedy in the world. Chelli watched, then thanked him for coming in and said he wasn't right for the part. Then your shit of a husband walked over to Chelli, who is half his size and twice his age, and before anybody could stop him, he threw a punch that broke Chelli's nose and knocked the caps off his front teeth."

"Oh my God," Hilda said with a sharp intake of breath. "I'm so sorry."

"Yeah, well, the other dancers jumped him and held him down while the police were called. He's in jail, and Chelli wants them to throw the book at him. Is he on something, for God's sake?"

Hilda felt sick with responsibility. Mark was a dear and kind friend, and Chelli was one of the world's great talents. "I don't think so, Mark, I really don't. He's just got a short temper and a mean mouth when he feels he isn't being taken seriously. Oh God, I can't tell you how bad I feel about this. I've never known him to be violent, never. Please, tell Chelli that I'll take personal responsibility for everything. Just send all the bills to me, and I'll see that they're paid."

"Don't be a fool, Hilda. Wash your hands of the bastard. Let him rot in jail."

"I can't do that, Mark. He's my husband."

"Jesus, Hilda, don't tell me you're going to throw your life and career away just for a hard cock!" he said furiously.

"What's the matter, Mark—are you mad because he only likes girls?" she asked cruelly, hating herself as she said it.

Stung, Mark retaliated, "You bitch! You deserve each other."

40

Chelsea had gotten her first job at the age of sixteen in the stock room of I. Magnin's in Beverly Hills, and with her first paycheck she had opened an account in a bank in Santa Monica where no one knew that Chelsea Hunter was Bunny Thomas's daughter. Each month she had added a little bit to it, determined one day to be secure and independent. Her balance had grown slowly through the years, then taken an enormous and sudden jump with her foray into the confidence game. Now she had a nice little cache of money to support her design ambitions. The man who had bought the pseudo-diamond pendant for his wife had been even easier prey than the woman who bought the ring, which made her feel guiltier.

Having aborted her life of crime, she reset both the emerald and the diamond into the original ring and destroyed the real pendant, which she hated to do. It was probably the most creative thing she had ever made. The man who bought it might have gotten a fake diamond, but he had bought a genuine piece of art, she rationalized. She returned the ring to the vault, and while she was there, decided that perhaps she could make better and safer use of the remarkable cache of jewels.

It was a miracle that she had gotten away with the switches anyway. Anyone with any knowledge at all could have recognized immediately that the eighty-cents-a-carat cubic zirconium she'd set in the pendant was not a diamond, because it was so much more transparent and glittering than the real stone. A diamond was whiter and more reflective of the light.

With Jake repaid for the materials, several thousand dollars in the bank, and her mother about to begin working again, Chelsea could concentrate on her own longer-term goals. She was just a few weeks away from getting her degree from the university, and it was time to find herself a job designing jewelry, a job where there was a future.

To create the necessary portfolio of designs, Chelsea went over the inventory and chose the pearls—the rich, large pink pearls. Pearls were so staid and predictable; they just draped around the neck in strands. Why not do something different and highly original?

She took the pearls from the vault and studied them for hours. After doing many sketches, she finally came up with an idea that intrigued her because it was a bold departure in the use of the oysters' contribution to ornamentation. Inspired by the channel-set baguettes in her mother's original wedding band, she made a slim gold bangle bracelet into which she set the pearls side by side instead of stringing them. When she was done, she was pleased with its simplicity of design but suspected it could be glitzier. Since she had a large quantity of the beads, she made a second bracelet, differing from the first only by the gold spacers set between the pearls. The bracelets were such a beautiful variation on a theme that she made a third, and on its spacers she set small diamonds from the clasp. When she was finished, she had not quite enough pearls for a fourth, and so on that one she filled out the bracelet with much bigger gold spacers, on which she set a tiny floral design of baguettes from her mother's wedding ring and sapphires from a platinum bracelet.

Working nights, it took her more than two weeks, but she was so encouraged by the results that she made sketches of other, more costly ways to embellish the design with bigger stones and additional rows of pearls. The design was exceptional, a new and exciting way to show pearls, and an inner voice told her that this line of bracelets might just possibly be her ticket to a career. She decided to chance it, and made an appointment with the manager of Tanager's for the Thursday before Wills and Margaret were due to arrive in Los Angeles.

With the bracelets wrapped in velvet and her sketchbook under her arm, she arrived at the pink marble entrance to the old, established firm. As she walked past the glass cases displaying the finest gems in the city, she congratulated herself for wearing a simple blouse and skirt instead of her usual denims. At first she thought perhaps she should look the part of the dedicated artist, wearing jeans, long hair, and love beads, but Tanager's was a temple of the conservative, catering only to people with money enough to spend on expensive baubles, and so she had settled on a nondescript appearance.

All the salespeople watched her as she softly traversed the thick green carpeting. There were no customers in the store, and everything was so quiet, she was certain she could hear the whoosh of the rug's pile as it recovered from the pressure of her footsteps. She climbed the grand circular staircase with its polished brass banister and gave her name to the secretary guarding the entrance to the office, which looked down on the store below.

"Mr. Corell is with a client at the moment. Please have a seat," the secretary said, and returned to her typewriter.

Chelsea noticed that the woman, who looked to be in her forties, was dressed in a simple black dress with a white collar, and she wore no jewelry at all.

"Will he be very long?" Chelsea asked. After all, she did have an appointment.

The woman did not smile. "I really can't say."

"Then I think I'll just stroll around the store and look while I'm waiting," Chelsea replied. "Please let me know when he's available." There was no way she was going to waste her time sitting when she could be examining all sorts of beautiful things.

The wait turned out to be quite long, but Chelsea barely noticed. The salespeople were happy to take even the most expensive pieces from the case and let her handle them and look at them closely. She was somewhat disappointed, however, in the singular lack of imagination in design. Most diamonds were set in platinum and were conservative in every aspect except size. She saw nothing that was new or exciting. Wasn't there a market for a more modern approach?

When she was at last called into Corell's office, she found herself smiling at the sight of him. He looked as if he had been designed and built to specification. Tall and slender, he had thick, softly waved white hair, clipped very short at the sides, and his skin was smooth and apparently untouched by the sun. Can't get a tan from the glow of diamonds, Chelsea thought. His eyes were a conservative gray, as were his suit and tie. He looked to be in his fifties, and he seemed quite fit. Racquetball, squash? she wondered. His smile was gracious but reserved, and his voice, when he spoke, was as deep and smooth as plush velvet. Though his manner was courtly, there was an amused sparkle in his eyes. She liked him immediately.

"I'm sorry to have kept you waiting, Miss Hunter, but I was in the midst of a trying discussion with an old customer who has fallen on hard times. I wish I could have helped him, but . . ." He spread his hands helplessly and allowed his voice to trail away.

Hoping he would tell her the whole story, Chelsea listened attentively, but he shrugged the problem away. "Now, let's see that bracelet you were telling me about on the telephone."

Chelsea unwrapped the black velvet cloth and laid the bracelets before him. Her heart leaped when she saw his look of surprise and pleasure.

"My dear, where did you ever get such perfectly beautiful pearls? Why, they're magnificent."

Disappointed that it was the pearls that attracted him and not the design, Chelsea murmured that they were from an old necklace she had bought at a flea market in Paris.

"Well, you have enough of these marvelous pearls for a necklace, but you are seriously misusing your materials, my dear young woman. Pearls of this quality are quite rare, and their value increases geometrically with the number you have. A single pearl is not worth all that much, but an entire string of matching ones of that size and quality could be quite valuable. I would certainly be interested in making you an offer for the lot of them," he said, examining the bracelet with a loupe.

Chelsea's hands were shaking. God, what a mess she had gotten herself into. There was no way she dared sell a strand of pearls supposedly destroyed in a fire.

"I wouldn't be interested in selling the pearls at all, Mr. Corell. I just used them in the design temporarily, to show a new and different way that pearls could be used. What do you think of the design itself?"

Corell looked disappointed. "Well, it's quite nice, as a matter of fact," he replied, laying the bracelet down on the velvet pad on his desk. "How much would you want for all of them?"

Thinking fast, Chelsea replied, "These are only prototypes, Mr. Corell. I just wanted to demonstrate how versatile the design is. I'm afraid I couldn't think of selling them as they are, because as you noticed immediately, it would be a waste to put pearls of this quality in a setting as closed as this one is. My plan was to use pearls with a blemish that could be hidden by the setting."

Corell looked up at her thoughtfully. "Interesting idea, but Tanager's would never sell inferior merchandise."

"You wouldn't be selling pearls, you would be selling a beautiful bracelet, and the cost could be kept to a manageable level. As you can see, I have kept the weight of the gold down, the diamonds are quite small and could be even smaller, and blemished pearls are quite cheap," she replied quickly, realizing that in her eagerness to deflect his attention from the pearls, she had moved into a hard-sell stance.

Warming to her pitch, she continued, "Think about all the young men who would love to give their wives a Christmas or birthday gift from Tanager's. Or I could even see this bracelet being promoted as an anniversary gift because it's a never-ending circle. It could be called the 'Eternal Love' bracelet," and thinking fast, she added, "You could sell a plain one and then add a diamond each year for the customer."

"Interesting idea," he said, continuing to look at her closely. "I see you brought a sketchbook."

"I certainly did," she replied, and as she opened the book, a sketch of the pendant she had just destroyed slipped from the back pages where she had tucked it and fell to the floor. Although Chelsea scrambled to catch it, it fluttered away and Corell picked it up.

Chelsea was speechless as he looked it over in great detail. "This is quite beautiful, Miss Hunter, but it probably wouldn't make up well, I'm afraid. The stone would be too heavy for the setting."

"But I did make it up, and it was even more lovely than the sketch," she said defensively, her pride in creation overcoming all caution.

"Well, I would be most interested in seeing it. I hope you brought it with you?"

"I sold it," she said, wishing he would change the subject.

"Pity. Would you consider doing another one for us?"

Shaking her head vigorously, Chelsea replied, "I'm sorry, but I promised the buyer I wouldn't repeat it. Ordinarily I retain the rights to all my designs, but in this case, the man was willing to pay so that his . . . ladyfriend would have one of a kind."

Corell shook his head despairingly. "I can certainly understand his feelings, but take my advice and never do that again, my dear. Sell the product, but never the idea. You are an extremely talented artist, but you'll be a poor one if you restrict yourself to producing only originals."

Chelsea sighed with relief, pleased with herself, if embarrassed, for having concocted all the baloney she had laid on this nice man.

Corell continued to leaf through the book, apparently fascinated by what he saw. At last he looked up at her again and asked, "And now, since the bracelets aren't for sale and you won't make a copy of this pendant, what do you want of me?"

What did she really want? she wondered, but the answer sprang off her tongue of its own accord. "I'd like to work for you as a designer."

Corell shook his head. "Our workrooms are all in New York. That's where the diamond and gem dealers are. On the basis of what I've seen, I could probably get you hired there, but—"

Chelsea shook her head. "I can't go to New York. I have family obligations here, but why couldn't I make jewelry in my own workroom and you could buy it from me?"

"Tanager's has never done that sort of thing to any great extent. Ordinarily everything we sell comes from our own in-house designs."

Chelsea bit her lip, then, thinking she had nothing to lose, said softly, "And that's why it's boring. Mr. Corell, look around at your display cases. The gems are magnificent, but the designs have changed little in the last thirty or forty years. The little stones are in little settings, the big stones in big settings . . . it's all so predictable."

Corell smiled and said in mock indignation, "You are

a very brash young woman. How dare you call us stuffy and boring. We're one of the oldest, most respected purveyors of fine jewelry in the country."

"I didn't say stuffy, you did," she said with a grin.

"But that's what people want, my dear. When they buy diamonds, they buy tradition. The very settings that you call predictable are just as you say, but that's how people know they're wearing the real thing and not costume jewelry. Besides, our clients are older, more settled."

"Mr. Corell, that's the way it used to be, but especially here in Los Angeles there's a whole contingent of young people making lots of money—rock stars, movie stars, agents, producers, directors. They can afford to spend, but you can't offer them things Grandma wears."

As she spoke, Chelsea realized that not only was she making a great sales pitch, but crystallizing her own ideas about jewelry design. She didn't want to design for the older generation, she wanted to design for now. "Besides, California is fast becoming the bastion of design—in clothing, architecture, and maybe, if we do it right, jewelry."

"You're a persuasive young woman, Miss Hunter. I'm going back to New York next month. Is there any chance that you could make up another piece or two for me to take along with these bracelets?"

Chelsea was elated. "Sure. Are there any sketches in there that you particularly like?"

"Yes, as a matter of fact. That ruby and emerald pin, and the ring with enamel and emerald."

"I'll see what I can do," she said, getting up.

"Give it your best effort, will you? I'll need all the ammunition I can get to keep from being strung up for heresy by those old, stuffy codgers back East. And reset the bracelets with lesser pearls, will you? No point having the old boys salivate over something they can't have."

"When would you like to have them?" she asked.

"As soon as possible, but no later than the fifteenth of next month. I leave on the sixteenth."

"It's a deal," she said with a grin.

Chelsea drove home with her mind filled with plans for the work she had ahead of her, and for the first time she almost regretted that she would lose four days while she entertained her old friends from England. Thank God Mama and Gran were busy and out of her hair. She was also grateful that she had plenty of money in the bank to buy the materials she would need to make the necessary pieces of jewelry, but she decided it might be sacrilegious to thank the Lord for her ill-gotten blessings.

41

Neither Sergio nor Hilda trusted themselves to say anything on the trip from the police station, and so they rode in tight-lipped silence with Hilda at the wheel. Once inside her home, however, she turned on him angrily.

"Just what in the hell were you thinking about when you threw that punch at Chelli?" And without waiting for him to answer, she continued, "He's sixty years old, for Christ's sake, and he's a serious diabetic, not to mention that he's one of the most famous, most powerful directors of musical comedy in the world. My God, Sergio, any dancer would sell his soul for a chance to work for that man!"

Almost chastened by the events of the past few hours, but not quite, Sergio turned his back on her and sauntered into the living room to get a cigarette from the silver box on the coffee table. Hilda watched him in a state of fury as he casually lit it with the heavy silver lighter and took a deep drag.

Irritated, she snapped, "Well? Are you going to answer me or not?"

He swaggered back to her, and when he was within inches of her face, he forcefully exhaled the smoke directly in her eyes. Then, caught up in his own sense of physical power over her, he shoved the palm of his hand against her face and slammed her head hard against the wall. "Go fuck yourself, bitch!" he snarled. "Nobody else wants to!"

Without thinking, Hilda slapped him across the face so hard that she caught him off guard. As he staggered back, he lost his balance and stumbled over the ceramic umbrella stand, which crashed to the floor and shattered. Horrified and frightened by the escalating violence, she quickly reached down and grabbed a cane that had fallen from the stand, to protect herself. Sergio was much bigger than she was and quite strong, and the very animalism that she found so sexually stimulating in him, now posed a serious threat to her.

"Get out of my house before I call the police!" she threatened, backing away from him.

"You're not calling anybody, you ugly hag!" he replied, strode to the telephone and ripped its cord from the wall. The menace in his voice and manner was deadly, and for the first time in her life Hilda was mortally afraid. Dear Lord, she was going to die if she didn't think of something to stop him from attacking her.

"Don't you dare touch me!" she commanded, her voice high-pitched and obviously filled with terror. Sergio had the upper hand now, and he knew it. As she backed away, he moved toward her, smiling, excited by the desperation in her eyes.

"You stinking cunt," he said, "I'll drive that pretty nose the doctor made for you into the back of your head, and then I'm going to fuck you to death!"

Hilda was terrified. Sergio was out of control.

"Stay away from me!" she said in a strangled voice, desperately holding him at bay with the cane while she tried to think of some way to get away from him. She'd seen his violent moods before, but they had never been directed so fiercely toward her. Good Lord, he must be popping something!

"You're gonna really enjoy it this time, bitch. You like it rough, don't you? You always wanted it hard and fast . . . well, that's how you're gonna get it. And when

I'm done, you'll be finished, but good. Hey, this is gonna be fun." One corner of his mouth dropped in a malicious smile. "Why, I'm even lookin' forward to it for a change. I always hated it, you know. I had to psych myself up and think of other broads when I was humpin' you."

Hearing his final insult, Hilda's fear suddenly metamorphosed to a fury more powerful than his.

"You bastard!" she screamed, and lunged at him, the end of the cane aimed directly at his swelling crotch. Startled, he made his second mistake by lowering his hands to protect that most precious part of his anatomy, but she skillfully outmaneuvered him by raising her aim and hitting him full force between the eyes. Stunned, he fell to the floor. With his vile words still ringing in her ears, she quickly grabbed the other end of the cane, switching it from a lance to a golf club. Then, with a swing Jack Nicklaus would have envied, she whapped him on the side of the head with the antique gold handle, rendering him instantly unconscious.

She wanted to hit him again and again until he was smashed to a bloody pulp, but Hilda suddenly became a rational human being again, with the ability to stop herself, which she did immediately. Good Lord, had she killed him? She started to move toward him, but her instinct for self-preservation made her wary. No, the first thing she must do was call for help, but his body blocked her way to the kitchen, where the other telephone was. She hesitated; she would have to step over him to get there. Suppose he was just pretending to be unconscious in order to grab her when she was near enough?

Now that her anger was dissipated, she became cautious. Sidling away, she moved slowly toward the front door with her eyes fastened on him, watching for any sign of movement, even a flicker of the eyelids; but he was still as death. Her heart was beating so rapidly that it thundered in her ears, and she was as breathless as if she had jogged a mile. At last she reached the door, fumbled with the dead bolt and pulled it open just as she heard a noise behind her. Terrified, she turned back, expecting him to pounce upon her. But he was still dazed and trying to get to his feet.

Without an instant's hesitation, she ran from the house. It was growing dark outside and there was no one on the block. The car was in the driveway, but she had no keys, and so she began to run as fast as her high-heeled shoes would carry her, not looking back, afraid she would find him chasing her. With her heart thudding inside her chest, she ran to the corner, where she saw the dry cleaner's truck approaching and threw herself into the street in its path.

"Stop!" she screamed at the driver, and he slammed on the brakes. Before he could get out to see what was wrong, she jumped into the vehicle beside him.

"Take me to a telephone, please. I've got to call the police."

Ten minutes later, seated in the back of a Beverly Hills squad car with two young officers up front, Hilda returned to her home. The front door was still open, and the police went in first. No one was there.

"Looks like you didn't do him too much harm, ma'am. He seems to have gotten up and walked away."

"Please search the house," she said nervously.

"You want to wait here or go with us, ma'am?"

"I'm not waiting here by myself," she replied. Hilda knew her fear would persist until she was certain Sergio was long gone.

They made a thorough search of the house and grounds, and there was no sign of Sergio, but the Porsche was gone.

"Looks like he took off, ma'am. I suppose he's got a key to the house?"

Hilda nodded silently, her mind now awhirl with dreaded possibilities.

"You said you just got him out of jail, right?"

"Unfortunately, I paid his bail. He hurt someone quite badly earlier today."

"Then if I were you, I'd call my attorney. The court'll revoke his bail and he can be picked up. No problem."

"Officer, would you mind waiting here until I get some things together? I don't intend to stay here alone until he's safely back in a cell and I have the locks changed."

"I wouldn't wait too long if I were you, ma'am. With nobody in the house, he might come back and ransack the place. Locksmiths work twenty-four hours a day, you know."

"Thank you, officer. That's probably an excellent idea," she said, hurrying up the stairs. "I'll be just a minute."

Upstairs in her bedroom she grabbed the boxy Vuitton train case that she always kept stocked with cosmetics and medicines, ready to take on business trips on short notice. She rolled up a nightgown, clean underwear, and panty hose and stuffed them on top of the bottles, then went into her closet, pulled aside the orderly row of silk blouses and gasped. Her wall safe was open and everything was gone! Desperately and futilely she swept her hand back and forth inside the vault, but there was nothing there. He had taken it. God help her, it was gone!

An hour later a subdued and frightened Hilda checked into the Beverly Wilshire Hotel and cautioned the desk clerk not to give out her name or room number to anyone. Once safely in her room, she called room service and ordered a double scotch on the rocks before placing a call to Sandy Shapiro.

She was halfway through the drink when the lawyer called her back.

"What are you doing there, for God's sake, Hilda?" he asked in his rough, cigar-stained voice.

"Sandy, I can't tell you what a mess I've gotten myself into over Sergio," she began. She related the entire day's misery, and when she finished, she cautioned him, "Please don't say I told you so, because at this point I just don't think I can handle it."

"Hell, I did tell you so, didn't I? I wouldn't even go to the goddamned wedding because I knew you were getting yourself in a mess with that brainless hunk of trash."

"I wish I'd listened, Sandy. I really do. It was the biggest mistake of my life."

"At least you've finally come to your senses. Now, I'll get his bail revoked and have him picked up. What's the license number on the Porsche?"

Hilda gave him the number, and then he asked, "Is the car in your name or his?"

"It's in both of our names," she said quietly.

"Good grief, girl, didn't I teach you anything? What about the house?"

"No, it's still in my name alone," she said. "After all, I inherited it from my parents."

"Thank God for small favors. We should be able to get you out of this marriage without too much damage to your net worth. We might even be able to bargain with him a bit, like in maybe not pressing charges."

"We've got to find him, Sandy, as soon as possible! The bastard wanted to kill me. He's crazy, you know."

"Look, I'll do the best I can. I'll call Mort Spencer and ask his advice. He's one of the best criminal attorneys in town, but don't expect too much. All the jerk's really done, you know, is hit you and threaten you. It's not exactly murder-one."

"But he would have killed me, Sandy," she protested. "As God is my witness, I know that if I hadn't gotten him with a lucky swing of that cane, I'd probably be lying in the front hallway in a puddle of blood."

"Okay, I believe you, but the plain truth is that the police and the courts usually don't interfere in cases of domestic violence . . . unless, of course, somebody gets killed. Now have a drink and relax. Have you called a locksmith yet?"

"No, my mind's been on other things."

"Look, I'm gonna call the police and ask them to keep an eye on the place tonight because that's where they might find him. Anything else I should know?"

Hilda took a deep sigh. "There's one other thing, Sandy . . ."

"What . . . tell me. I don't like surprises."

"You better come over here, Sandy. I'm in big trouble, and I can't talk about it on the phone."

Hilda was not one to cry wolf, so when Sandy heard that, he knew something was seriously wrong. "I'm on my way, sweetheart."

Less than half an hour later he was sitting on the couch in her suite with a highball in his hands.

"So tell me."

"He took my . . . my book," she said heavily, her words dripping with anxiety.

Sandy sat quietly staring at her, waiting for her to enlighten him.

"Ever since I started in the business, I've kept a journal."

"Jesus Christ, you didn't!"

"Dad told me to. He said that in this town you had to play a defensive game . . . protect your ass . . . all the time. I never intended to do anything with it. I just kept a record of names, dates, deals . . . things I learned . . . just to protect myself. I never used anything against anybody."

"Don't tell me, let me guess. The book is full of embarrassing facts about people in the industry, right? And if it falls into the wrong hands, it could blow the careers of a lot of your clients?"

She nodded, unable to look him in the eyes. "Not just embarrassing."

"God, don't you know that an agent is supposed to be like a priest—listen to everybody and talk to nobody? Christ, that book is worth a bloody fortune! Bad enough that you should write it, let alone leave it where a schmuck like Sergio could get his hands on it."

"I kept it locked in my safe!"

"Oh God, Hilda, you're really in a mess this time. We've got to get that book back or you're gonna have to leave town—hell, you'll have to leave the planet. You haven't got anything in there about Sy Christman and his mob connections, have you?"

Hilda nodded her head in misery. "In detail . . . all the

threats whenever I had a client working on one of his studio's films . . . the under-the-table payoffs . . . deals the agency cut to get bigger fees for some clients at the expense of others. It's a tough business, Sandy. Everybody gets their hands dirty once in a while."

"Don't tell me anything about this business, Hilda, tell me why you'd show that stuff to that asshole. Was he that good a lay?" Sandy had never spoken so roughly to her before.

"I didn't!" she cried defensively. "I never showed it to him or told him anything. I didn't even know he knew about it."

"Did he take anything else?"

"Mom's diamond earrings . . . a pearl necklace, some gold bracelets, uh—"

"The jerk went for the jewelry!" Sandy said excitedly. "He probably doesn't even know the book is as valuable as it is. I'm going to the police. We've got to find him as fast as possible . . . before he reads the damned thing and finds out he struck gold."

The elderly attorney got to his feet and was on his way to the door, when he turned to say one last thing.

"If we don't find him in time, I just hope to hell he gives you the first crack at buying that damned book back from him." He sighed in despair. "Too bad you didn't kill the bastard when you had the chance," he exclaimed, his words not said in jest. "I could have gotten you off on self-defense."

42

The flight on which Wills and Margaret were scheduled to arrive was late, and because she hadn't bothered to check before heading for the airport, Chelsea found herself sitting in the TWA waiting room. Ever since her

meeting at Tanager's, Chelsea had been torn between her
need to get started on the new pieces for Corell to take
to New York and her eagerness to see her old friends.
Even now, with the plane delayed only thirty minutes,
she was exasperated at the delay. As she waited, she con-
jured up images of how much Wills might have changed.
And what would he think of her? Would he be disappointed? She went into the bathroom to have one last
look at herself and run the brush through her long hair
one more time.

Well, at least things were ready for them at home. Her
grandmother's unfortunate penchant for spending money
had, for a change, proved to be of some value. Because
there were now capable and enthusiastic servants in the
house, Chelsea had been relieved of making any prepa-
rations for her guests, for Laverne had arranged for the
two spare bedrooms to be turned into comfortable, attractive guest rooms. This morning there were even bouquets of fresh-cut flowers in each room, along with bowls
of fruit and chocolates. Her grandmother had also announced at breakfast that she had engaged a limousine
and a driver to be available to Chelsea while her friends
were there.

It wasn't free, of course. Nothing ever was. In return
for her kindness, generosity, and goodwill, Laverne demanded that Chelsea bring the young aristocrats to visit
the set where *The Beyonder* was filming so that Bunny
could have her picture taken with them for release to the
society columnists, who loved British titles. If she hadn't
been so preoccupied with her own ambitions, Chelsea
might have registered a token protest, but under the circumstances, she was grateful to be relieved of some of
the burdens of entertaining, rationalizing that Wills and
Margaret would probably be thrilled to visit the set and
meet Bunny anyway.

Chelsea tried to concentrate solely on ways in which
to entertain her guests properly, but it had been almost
ten years since she had last seen either of them, and in
her mind they were still the innocent youngsters she re-

membered. Although she had changed and become an adult, it was difficult to picture Wills as a man, much less Margaret as a fully-grown woman.

At long last the plane arrived. Chelsea moved slowly toward the gate so that she would be at the back of the crowd waiting to greet passengers. She wanted to have a few moments to study the arrivals, for she wasn't at all sure she would recognize her friends.

The first two off the plane were men in dark business suits, next a flight attendant with an older woman in a wheelchair, and then Chelsea saw Margaret. It was not the same body or the same walk or demeanor, but it was the face of her old friend nevertheless. The awkward young girl was now a slender young woman who carried herself gracefully. She had filled out, become gently rounded, and she moved with a majestic bearing. Dressed in a short, fashionable dark blue Courreges suit, wearing ivory stockings and dark blue flats, Margaret looked every bit the English lady. Her hair was short and chic, and she carried a small leather case in her gloved hands. Chelsea was so startled by the change in her old school chum that she rushed to greet her without even looking beyond.

"Margaret!" she called in delight.

"Chelsea?" Margaret asked, smiling tentatively at the tall, smashingly beautiful young girl with the long blond hair, who was wearing flower-embroidered blue jeans.

"Margaret, I can't believe it! You are the picture of your mother, do you know that?"

Reassured that this was indeed her old friend, Margaret returned the hug. "Chelsea, it's so good to see you!"

Suddenly a deep voice announced, "I say, don't I rate one of those too?"

Chelsea looked up and up and up until at last her eyes connected with the blue eyes of the young man towering over both of them. Margaret had changed, yes, but it was Wills who had been transformed. One look at him and all the old feelings she'd had for him once came instantly alive again. He was not at all thin anymore. Underneath his perfectly tailored gray English-cut suit, she could see that he was quite muscular, his shoulders broad, his waist narrow. He had grown considerably taller than his father; his bright-cheeked, outdoor complexion set off his light brown hair, and his brown eyebrows and thick lashes formed a perfect frame for the piercing blue of his eyes.

"Is that really you, Wills?" she asked, and just as her eyes reached his perfectly beautiful mouth, she found it moving swiftly toward her own.

"In the flesh," he said, and kissed her. It was not a long, passionate kiss, just a brief, soft sweet touch of his lips on hers, but it affected her profoundly. For the first time in her life she had an inkling about the fuss people made over sex. For a long moment the two young people just looked at each other, and perhaps would have never taken their eyes away if Margaret hadn't asserted herself.

"You two! Already! Come on, we've plenty of time for that. Let's get the bags and be on our way. I don't want to miss a moment of our precious few days in California!"

Suddenly remembering her duties as a hostess, Chelsea laughed and said, "I just can't get over how much you two have . . . grown up. I guess I thought that while time was passing here, it was standing still in England, or maybe I just wanted for everything to stay exactly the same as I remembered it."

"Well, you've certainly changed, Chelsea," Margaret said as the three fell into step on their way to the baggage claim.

"You think so, really?" Chelsea asked. "I feel like an awkward kid next to you two in your grown-up clothes. I spend most of my life in grubbies."

"Do you suppose we might have a chance to buy some jeans like yours while we're here? They're all the rage at home," Margaret said.

"Of course. Now, give me your baggage checks. I've got a car and a driver who will take care of things for us."

When they finally arrived home, Chelsea was thankful that Laverne had already gone, and so she showed them

to their rooms herself and told them that the servants
would unpack.

"I don't want to rush you, but when you're ready, come
downstairs to the patio and we'll have tea, okay?"

"Do you often have tea, or is it just for the Brits?"
Wills asked mischievously.

Chelsea laughed. "It's just for you. But the cook has
made some delicious granola cookies. It will give you a
chance to wind down, and we'll plan the next few days."

Margaret demurred, however. "If you wouldn't mind,
I'd like a bit of time to bathe and change into something
more comfortable."

"I, on the contrary, will be down right away," Wills
hastened to say with a smile and a wink.

It was not long before they were both seated at the
umbrella table beside the swimming pool. Behind her
dark glasses, Chelsea at last had a chance to observe her
old love closely. Although she had found him immensely
attractive when he was just a young boy, now she found
him to be the most beautiful man she had ever seen, and
as she sipped at her cup of Darjeeling tea, she was thrilled
to have him so close beside her.

His blue eyes squinting at the bright reflections of the
sun, Wills said, "I can see that I'm going to have to buy
a pair of sunglasses or I'll go blind. We're not used to
this much brightness in foggy old Londontown."

"We have to wear them year 'round here, I'm afraid."

There was a moment of silence, and then Wills reached
over, took her hand and held it in both of his. He held
her fingers up so that he could examine them, and Chelsea
was ashamed of her short blunt nails and the discoloration
of her skin from working with metals. She tried to pull
away, but he would not let her go.

"Please," she said, "my hands are so ugly. I make jewelry, you know, and it's pretty hard to keep them looking
nice."

"They're beautiful," he said softly, and lifting her hand
to his lips, he kissed the tips of each of her fingers. Chelsea
suddenly felt a part of her that was deep down inside her

and sleeping begin to stir and awaken. She shivered with the intensity of the feeling.

"Wills," she asked softly, "what are you doing?"

Without even seeming to hear her question, he began to talk in a voice so low she had to strain to hear him.

"Ever since the first day I met you at Ashford Hall, you've been the only girl I've ever really wanted, Chelsea. When I dream, it's always of you. You're the girl I've held in my arms, the girl to whom I made love. I've been out with a lot of women in the past few years. I've kissed them, made love to one or two, but you're the only one who inhabits my dreams."

"Wills . . . I don't know what to say," Chelsea replied haltingly, uneasy with the abruptness of his approach and unbalanced by her own emotional responses. She was a novice at romance, completely unsure of herself.

"You know why we made this trip at this particular time, Chelsea?"

She shook her head.

"Because I've been seeing a girl that my family is set on my marrying when I graduate from the university next year. She's a good sort, really, very pretty, an excellent rider, and loves horses almost as much as I do. I didn't think it was right to mislead her if in the end I couldn't get you out of my mind. Since you wouldn't come to see us, I . . . well, I decided I just had to see you before things progressed any further."

The thought that Wills had been obsessed by romantic thoughts of her came as an enormous surprise to Chelsea. Because of the almost daily anxieties of her own life, she had, in fact, relegated all thoughts of the Ashford family to a little corner in her mind that, however special, was painted in watercolors of the past. It had no realness or connection to the world in which she now lived. She had never imagined that Wills might someday be a significant part of her future. Margaret's teasing about picking out a wife for him had been only girl talk, long forgotten. The touch of his lips and his hands, and most especially the words he had just spoken, however, abruptly altered her perception of the situation, perhaps for all time.

"I don't understand, Wills," she said, looking into his eyes questioningly.

"Take off the bloody sunglasses, will you? I can't relate to my own reflection when I'm speaking from the heart," he said with a grin.

"Oh, sorry," she said, pulling them off and trying not to squint.

"That's better. Look, Chelsea, it's quite simple really. I had to see you and talk to you to find out if I was still as infatuated as I was in puberty."

"And . . . are you?" she asked, suddenly realizing how important it was that he say the right words.

"Couldn't you feel it when I kissed you at the airport? For God's sake, tell me that you felt something, that I wasn't flying solo."

Before she had a chance to give him an answer, Margaret came through the French windows, now clad in a summery white linen skirt and pink blouse. Her complexion was scrubbed and glowing, and she looked refreshed and younger than the proper young woman who had gotten off the plane.

"My goodness, but you Americans do have the best plumbing. Wills, wait until you try that shower. Water comes right at you from six different sprays. It's glorious." Pouring herself a cup of tea, she then asked, "Well, have you two planned our visit?" Taking notice that her brother was still holding tightly to Chelsea's hand, she said wryly, "It looks as if we're a threesome again, um?"

Slightly flustered, Chelsea said, "Well, I thought you might enjoy having dinner at one of our most popular restaurants, and so my grandmother has made a reservation for us at Scandia this evening. It's very much like Belle Terrasse at Tivoli in Copenhagen. Then, tomorrow, I thought we'd go to Disneyland—"

"I say, do you really like that place? Isn't it mostly for children?" Wills asked.

Chelsea blushed. "I guess so. I've never been there

myself. Mom and Gran were never much interested, and since I've been grown, I've been too busy with work and school to drive all the way down to Anaheim."

"Then we'll pretend we're still twelve and all see it for the first time together," Wills said, smiling and squeezing her hand.

"I promised Gran I'd bring you to the set of Mom's picture day after tomorrow, and then we'll have a look at the studio, take the Universal tour if you like, and drive across Hollywood Boulevard and stop at Grauman's Chinese Theater and look at all the old stars' footprints in the cement."

"Well, those two days are filled up, then. Are we ever going to make it to the beach?" Margaret asked.

"We'll go on your last day, if that's all right?"

"Fine, is Scandia the kind of place where we might meet some of your friends?"

Chelsea laughed. "Not really."

Margaret frowned. "Pity. I really had hopes we could do something . . . well, young, you know."

"Say, I've got a better idea," Chelsea said, suddenly realizing that in spite of the fact that her friends were British aristocrats, they were her own age. "I'll take you to Westwood Village. That's where everybody goes to the movies, and the stores stay open in the evening. We can have pizza and walk around. There are lots of stores with great jeans and stuff. You'll love it."

"Sounds perfect. I'll take a quick shower and change and we can be on our way," Wills said, giving Chelsea's hand a light kiss before letting it go and taking his leave.

When the two young women were alone, Margaret opened the conversation. "I have a feeling by the stunned expression on your face that in his usual forthright way Wills has told you why we came."

"Well, sort of, and I'm still in a state of shock."

Margaret nibbled at a granola cookie and looked off into the distance thoughtfully. "Chelsea, Wills and I are barely twenty-two years old, and I am distressed just terribly by the fact that my parents are pushing him into a commitment already. Thank God there's no perfect suitor on the horizon for me at the moment or Mum would be picking out my wedding gown."

"I don't understand."

"It's really quite simple. Wills likes Pamela a lot, but he's had a thing for you forever. We're very close, you know, and he's never ceased talking about you."

"I had no idea," Chelsea murmured in wonder.

"Really? How curious. Well, anyway, perhaps some day it will work out for the two of you. Then again, perhaps not. However, I feel it only sensible that he keep his options open for a while," Margaret explained. "This trip was my idea, I must confess. Not that I'm trying to make a match, you understand, but my brother really ought to understand his true feelings before he makes a decision that might be quite irrevocable. Wills is so good-natured that I feel I have to protect him from our parents."

"What . . . what do you expect of me?" Chelsea asked, still unsure of what Margaret was really saying.

"Just be yourself, that's all. Let him see the person you truly are, and if you like him as much as he likes you, then please don't be coy."

"But I do like him, Margaret. I always have."

"Then tell him, please. By all means, tell him. We're on the same side, you and I," she said with a smile. "But then we always have been, haven't we?"

43

Laverne sat in the makeup room and watched as Fernando Ramon applied Bunny's makeup, but the chair was hard and uncomfortable and she wasn't feeling well. She would have liked to excuse herself and go home to lie down, but Chelsea's friends were arriving, and she'd promised her she wouldn't interfere in any way. She pulled herself to her feet. Bunny would be occupied for another hour and a half, at the very least, because the wig she was wearing for the part had to be carefully set into place and secured tightly to keep it from being blown off by the wind machine.

"Honey, I'm going over to the commissary for a cup of coffee, then I'll be in your dressing room if you need me."

"No problem, Mom, I'm in good company with Fernando here. I'll probably have to go directly on the set," Bunny replied, looking into the mirror at her mother and noticing the circles under her mother's eyes. "Look, why don't you just take a day off for a change and go home and relax? Are you feeling all right?"

"Of course, sweetheart. I'm just tired, but a short nap on your couch and I'll be fit as a fiddle. Fernando, go light on that brow pencil, will you? I don't want her to look like John L. Lewis."

"Who's John L. Lewis?" Fernando asked quizzically.

"A labor leader . . . with bushy eyebrows," Laverne snapped, and left the room.

Fernando and Bunny exchanged looks in the mirror, and he asked, "Doesn't it bother you to have your mother hanging around all the time?"

Bunny smiled her most sparkling smile. "Sometimes, but she means well."

Dabbing a triangular piece of rubber foam into the dark, contouring pancake makeup, Fernando shook his head. "My mother means well, but she lets me have a life of my own. Tell me, aren't you interested in men at all?"

Bunny looked up at him in surprise as he began to apply the makeup to the side of her nose.

"Of course I like men. You think I'm a dyke or something?"

Leaning closer, so that their faces were only inches apart, he said softly, "I know you're not a dyke, my love. You're every inch a man's woman . . . a blind man could see that." He paused then, and looking deeply into her eyes, said, "But that mother of yours is like a barrier between you and the men in the world, do you know that?"

"I never thought of it that way. Are you sure?" Bunny asked, mesmerized by the man's blatant sexuality. Of average height and build, and young—no more than twenty-five—Fernando was unremarkable except for the depth and size of his eyes, which she found fascinating. She loved dark eyes, and Fernando's were big and almost black and luminous.

"I know so," he replied, his voice a bare tone above a whisper. "If she were still here, I couldn't do this." His right hand suddenly slipped down into the wrap she was wearing and gently cupped her breast with it, his thumb gently rubbing the tip.

A sigh of surprise escaped from Bunny's lips, and he knew that once again he had not made a mistake. While his thumb gently continued to massage the now upright and hardened nipple, he leaned close enough so that the moisture from his breath would caress her lips with warmth as he whispered huskily, "I could lock the door and put a glow on your face unlike anything Max Factor sells."

"Do it," she replied softly, feeling the familiar pressure between her thighs as her desire bloomed.

Without wasting a moment or a gesture, Fernando kissed her breast, pulled her out of the chair and, taking her across the room with him, locked the door. He had no intention of releasing his hold on her flesh until he had finished what he'd set out to do.

With their privacy assured, he pulled at the sash holding the wrapper around her, and it fell to the floor, leaving her naked.

"You've been driving me crazy coming in here without anything on under that thin wrapper," he said, his voice low and sizzling with passion as he unzipped his pants, unfettering his most cherished possession and putting it in her hand.

Her tiny fingers explored the length and girth of the

engorged shaft, and she giggled with admiration, "Oh God, you're so big. You'll rip me apart."

"And you'll love every minute of it," he declared tensely, pushing her against the wall and lifting her so that he could ram himself inside her.

"Oh!" she gasped in surprise as she suddenly found herself taken. Fernando was demanding and relentless, and his mouth closed firmly on hers, forcing her lips apart so that his tongue could enter her also. His movements, top and bottom, were fast and hard and dominating, and she found herself sinking into a mindless passion. Her body invaded from both above and below, she surrendered herself abjectly, allowing him to do whatever pleased him. Although she wanted it never to end, the temperature of their passion rose so swiftly that within a few brief moments it exploded and then was over for them both.

Without a second's hesitation, Fernando withdrew, wiped himself with a towel and handed a fresh one to her. He zipped his pants, motioned her toward the bathroom and unbolted the door, briskly and efficiently. Once the sexual coupling had ended, Fernando was ready to go back to work. He was, after all, a professional. And just as he had promised, Bunny's color was bright and pink, her eyes shining, when she returned to the makeup chair.

"What did I tell you?" he asked as they both looked into the mirror, pleased with what they saw.

"You're amazing, Fernando," she said happily.

"I know. Keep that mother of yours at home, darling, and we'll do it every morning before you go to work. Wait till you see what it does for your performance."

"I might need more than one injection a day," she replied coquettishly. "Do you make house calls?"

Fernando smiled knowingly. "I could be persuaded."

When he was just a little boy in school, the teachers had told him that if he developed his natural talents, he'd be a success, and Freddie Thatcher had not become Fernando Ramon just so he could paint women's faces. He had better things to do. God wouldn't have given him such a phenomenal cock if He hadn't intended him to put it to good use, and now it was going to make him a lot of money.

44

Wills and Margaret loved Westwood Village, and the three friends spent their first day together walking the streets for hours, stopping to have beer and pizza, eating ice cream cones and buying blue jeans and fancy cowboy shirts. They talked and laughed, and throughout the entire time, Wills managed to keep himself in constant physical contact with Chelsea, either by holding her hand or putting his arm across her shoulders as he saw other young couples doing.

When they at last arrived home, it was well past midnight and everyone was asleep. Margaret was exhausted and excused herself immediately.

"Good night all. I'm awfully tired. Do you realize it's past three in the morning in New York?" she said. "I can't even think what it is in London."

"I'm still wide awake. How about you, Chelsea?" Wills asked.

Chelsea agreed. "So am I. Suppose we go in the kitchen for a snack?"

Margaret begged off. "Not for me, I'm afraid. I'll see you in the morning. What time is breakfast?" she asked, moving toward the stairs.

"Whenever you like, but we need to leave early, it's a long drive to Anaheim."

As soon as they were alone in the kitchen, Wills took Chelsea by the shoulders and swung her around to face him. Without a word he pulled her to him and kissed her softly and gently. It was the sweetest, most tender moment of her life, and she surrendered to it completely. When it was finished, Wills held her close, with her head tucked into his shoulder, and she felt warm and cuddled and protected. Chelsea had known so little affection in her life that the feeling of another warm body touching hers was unusually exotic. When she was a little girl, her mother had held her and cuddled her, but her grandmother, a cold woman, had little concern for Chelsea's emotional needs. As she grew older, no longer a cuddly child, her mother drew away too, so wrapped up was she in her own problems and insecurities.

"Lord, this feels so good," Chelsea whispered.

"I know. I could spend the rest of my life just standing here with you in my arms. You're so lovely, Chelsea, even more beautiful than I remembered," Wills said, lifting her chin with the tip of his finger and looking into her eyes. "Did you ever think about me at all?"

"You've always been there, Wills. The moment I saw you today, I realized just how much you've always meant to me."

"I want you to come back to England with me. I can't bear the thought of our being separated again," he said, his mouth moving close to hers, their lips touching as he spoke.

Their kisses became longer and deeper and more passionate as they pressed their bodies closer and closer together, until all attempts at restraint were abandoned and Chelsea proposed that they go to her room together.

Holding tightly to his hand, she led him up the back stairs and down the hallway, past her mother's room. When they were safely in her room with the door locked, Wills gathered her in his arms and whispered softly, "Are you sure you want to do this, Chelsea?"

"Yes, Wills, yes. More than anything I've ever wanted in my life," she replied, her long slim fingers unbuttoning his shirt.

When all their clothes were lying on the floor at their feet, they stood for a moment, not touching but just drinking in the beauty of each other's bodies. Chelsea was fascinated by the sight of his maleness. She had never seen a man undressed, and certainly had never seen an erection before.

"You're beautiful, Chelsea," Wills said, "even more beautiful than I had dreamed you."

Chelsea pulled off the coverlets on her bed, and they stretched out on the white sheet together. Slowly and gently, Wills ran his fingertips from the hollow of her neck around each rosy, upturned nipple, and finally down and into the golden triangle, and she said softly, "Wills, I've never done this before. You'll have to help me."

"Oh God, Chelsea. You're all my fantasies come true," he whispered.

Gently and slowly, they made love, and although it was painful for Chelsea at first, suddenly her maidenhead gave way and they were united in a passion that carried both of them to the pinnacle and beyond.

Holding each other closely, Wills whispered, "I love you, Chelsea. I've always loved you. Promise that we'll never be separated."

"I love you too, Wills."

"Will you marry me when I finish school next year?"

"Oh yes, Wills. I want us to be together forever. There could never be anyone for me but you now, never," Chelsea nearly wept with joy.

"Will you mind leaving your family and everything you have here to live with me in England? I have to stay there, you know. I'm the only son in the family."

"Oh God, Wills, there's no place I'd rather live. I've always loved your family, and I would be so happy to share your life."

It was six in the morning when Wills finally left Chelsea's bed to return to his room. "I know this is the new age of sex, but I don't want any trouble with your family, darling. Perhaps we should keep our liaison quiet until I formally ask for your hand in marriage."

"I don't want anybody—not even Margaret—to know, Wills . . . Promise?"

"It's our little secret," he whispered. Chelsea snapped on the light and got out of bed with him.

For a long, sweet moment they stood together at the door to her bedroom, tightly wrapped in each other's arms, hesitant to let go of the joy they had shared. Chelsea, who had never known the love or affectionate touch of a man, was mesmerized by the rapture and contentment she felt in Wills's embrace. Made wise by the revelation, she realized that all her life her feelings had been asleep, that she had only now been awakened to the bliss that one human being could find with another.

When they finally kissed for the last time and Wills reluctantly pulled away to go to his room, she felt the exquisite agony of separation. As she watched him move away down the hall, Chelsea knew that nothing would ever be quite the same again.

45

After her grim conversation with Sandy Shapiro, sleep was impossible for Hilda. All the demons that she'd encountered in her life came back to torment her as she tossed and turned in her hotel room bed. It was the worst night of her life. How could she have been such a fool?

The sun had barely broken through the horizon before she was out of bed. During her altercation with Sergio, the most important issue had been saving her life. But now her life wasn't worth a damn. If that journal were to be made public, a lot of people would regret Sergio's failure to kill her.

Dressing quickly, she checked out of the hotel and took a cab home. If her husband were foolish enough to come back, she wanted to be there to meet him. As soon as she entered her house, however, she raced upstairs, got the small handgun she kept in her lingerie drawer and put it in her purse. If she did encounter Sergio, she would have to threaten him if he wouldn't listen to reason.

What irony, she thought. She had bought the gun to protect herself when she lived alone, but when she married Sergio, she assumed that with a strong, virile husband in the house, there would be no use for it. Now she needed it to protect herself from him. He was a threat, not only to her, but to countless people she had named in her journal.

She picked up the telephone and called Sandy to let him know where she was.

"Sandy, I decided to come home. If Sergio shows up here anytime today, I want to be here to meet him."

"Stay there, I'll be right over. I've been giving this thing a lot of thought, and I want to talk to you. I've already checked with the police, and there's been no sign of the Porsche. I would guess he's holed up somewhere nearby, waiting for things to cool down."

"Reading the book, probably."

"Not necessarily. Make coffee."

Hilda's housekeeper arrived just before Sandy, and she took over in the kitchen. Sandy and Hilda sat down in the sunroom with their coffee.

"Last night you were scared to death of him. What's changed you?" Sandy asked. Although he'd had only a couple hours of sleep, Sandy looked fresh and rested. Hilda decided he must be one of those people who thrive on excitement.

"Lying in bed all night, remembering the things I wrote in that damned book. You know, some of the stuff goes back to when my father was the head of Gemini Studios. After he died, I went through a lot of his papers, thinking they might be of some use to film historians, but there was no way I could release them. Too many people who were involved in some of those deals are still alive."

"You put that stuff in your book too?" Sandy asked in surprise.

"Yeah, it was so damned fascinating. Once I started writing, I began to include stories he'd told me when I first got into the business. He thought I should know everything he knew. He detested Gordon Baker, you know. He actually paid to get evidence on his corrupt sexual life, and then didn't use it because he didn't want to destroy the lives and careers of the child stars."

"Like Bunny Thomas?"

"Yeah, she was the main one, because she had the biggest career. Dad could have blown the bastard right out of the water, but he didn't do it. That's one of the reasons I took Bunny on as a client. I felt sorry for her."

Sandy sipped his coffee and looked at her through narrowed eyes. "You lied to me, kiddo. You told me you took her because she had a 'wealth of unused talent.' Those were your exact words."

"I didn't lie. It's true, but she's such a bundle of neuroses that the talent sometimes gets buried."

"Her mother knew what was going on between her and Baker, didn't she?"

"Dad knew Baker's housekeeper, and he had sworn depositions from her that most of the mothers actually brought the kids to the house themselves. There were a lot of them, but she especially remembered Bunny because she cried all night."

"Oh Jesus. I don't want to talk about that anymore. Tell me what's in the journal about Sy Christman. You know he's under indictment for racketeering right now. If he ever got wind that there was anything out there that might add to his troubles, Sergio's life—and yours—wouldn't be worth a plug nickel."

Hilda sighed and shook her head. "There's a lot. He's always been fascinated with stars and Hollywood, you know, and he's had his fingers in the music business—"

"That's old stuff," Sandy said, waving his hand as if to brush the subject away. "I said anything new."

"He's the unseen partner in a film production company that's provided funding for some very big films."

"What partnership are we talking about?" he asked, his coffee cup poised in midair.

"Mezzaluna."

"No way!" he said, and the words exploded from his mouth like bullets from a high-powered rifle.

"My source is Lou Holton himself. The senior partner."

"Why would he tell you that?"

"My father was a close friend of his father's. I was about to pull Ghilly Jordan out of *Sandman* because she was having a lot of trouble with the director. She's not well, you know, and three weeks into filming she collapsed on the set. She's a serious asthmatic and needed to be hospitalized."

"But she finished the picture."

"Yeah, one lunch at Perino's with Holton and I caved in. I got them to provide a physician on the set for her and oxygen tanks, and she did manage to finish. It wasn't a very good movie, but that wasn't her fault."

Shaking his head, Sandy muttered, "Hard to believe."

"Well, Lou was just being a friend, warning me who I was going up against, and I'm not stupid."

"Did you tell Ghilly Jordan?"

"I'm not crazy either. No, I just talked her back, agent-like. Want some breakfast?"

"Sure. It's the custom to eat at wakes, isn't it?"

"Not funny, Sandy."

Getting out of his chair, Sandy followed her into the dining room. "I didn't intend it to be."

46

I can't believe the four days are over already, Chelsea. I've never known time to pass so quickly," Margaret said as the three friends stood at the TWA gate. The final call for the twins' flight to New York had just been announced over the loudspeaker, and they couldn't extend their reluctant good-byes a moment longer.

Wills was holding tightly to Chelsea's hand, the pain he felt at leaving excruciatingly evident.

"You have to spend the Christmas holidays with us in England. You promised. We'll tell my parents and plan the engagement announcement then." His tone was urgent.

Chelsea tried to smile, but the corners of her mouth quivered nervously. The past four days had been the happiest of her life, and even though she and Wills planned to get married in London next July right after his graduation, she was overwhelmed by sadness. She didn't want him to leave without her. "I'll be there. I promise," she said, and then added, "if I possibly can."

Suddenly, in a move most uncharacteristic for him, Wills dropped his formal public posture and pulled her into his arms. "It's going to be hell without you, Chelsea. I'll be counting every day, every minute, every hour until you're in my arms again," he whispered into her ear.

The flight supervisor approached. "We're closing the gate now," he said kindly. "If you don't get on now, you'll have to wait for the next flight."

Reluctantly, Wills let her go. Margaret pulled at his arm. "Come on, Wills. You can telephone her from New York. We've got a two-hour layover there. Good-bye, Chelsea. Thank you for just everything. I love Los Angeles, every freeway and palm tree. Too bad you and I couldn't just switch places. I'll send a note to your lovely mother and grandmother for being so very kind. Good-bye."

Not another word passed between Wills and Chelsea. They just looked at each other with feelings that transcended words, and suddenly she was alone again, but the aloneness was more desolate than ever, because now she knew what it was like to love and be loved in return.

Chelsea stood at the window watching the big jet pull from the gate and taxi toward the runway, and when it had passed from view, she still did not move until she saw it take off into the sky. Slowly, her feet dragging as if they were filled with lead, she walked down the long, tiled corridor, burdened with a sense of finality she could not shake.

The limousine driver was waiting for her at the entrance, and she climbed into the backseat and closed her eyes, realizing that she was completely exhausted. Four days of sightseeing and activity and four nights of blissful lovemaking suddenly had taken their toll on her young body, and would probably explain the dreadful feeling of melancholy that was crushing her.

"Would you like me to take you home, ma'am?" the driver asked, but Chelsea had no time for rest. Now that the Ashford days were over, she had to go to work with a vengeance.

"No. You can drop me off on Westwood Boulevard in the Village and then you'll be finished." She reached into her purse and realized that all she had left was a twenty-dollar bill for a tip. It wasn't enough.

When she got out of the car, she handed the money to him. "You've been great, and I'm sorry this is all I have. I'll tell my grandmother to add ten percent to the bill, okay?" she asked.

"Hey, no problem. It was a pleasure, ma'am. And I sure enjoyed Disneyland the other day. Thanks for paying my way in and not making me wait in the parking lot."

Jake was working when Chelsea arrived at the lab.

"Hey! So, how did your visit with the swells go?" he asked with a grin, happy to see her again.

"Wonderful, terrific, exhausting." She had intended to tell him about her plans to marry and live in England, but it was still too soon and too intensely personal to discuss with anyone.

"Well, I'm glad to have you back. The work is piling up around here, and I need to take a few hours off to go to the dentist. I've been taking aspirin, but it doesn't help this toothache."

Suddenly Chelsea realized that she hadn't yet told him about her visit to Tanager's.

"Jake, I hate to tell you this, but I'm not going to be able to work for about three or four weeks . . ." she began.

When she had finished telling him, she took the small

box from the safe where she kept her own projects and showed him the pearl bracelets.

Jake was impressed. "They're terrific, Chelsea. If Tanager's turns you down, don't give up. There's Tiffany, Cartier . . . somebody, somewhere, is going to recognize your talent and buy your stuff."

Chelsea heard his words, and something he said sent off an alarm bell in her mind. "No, Jake. That's not what I want, and I didn't realize it until just this moment. Tell me, would you go to an art gallery and buy a painting and not know who did it?"

"I don't get the drift. What are you talking about?"

"Well, I believe there's more to a piece of jewelry than the cost of the gems and the gold or whatever that make it up. It's more than just the sum of its parts. A beautiful piece of jewelry is a work of art. Why shouldn't the buyer want to know who created it? Is it enough to label the piece with the retailer's name?"

"Yeah, right, I agree with you wholeheartedly, but kiddo, you're barking up a very tall tree. I can't imagine any of the big guys promoting the work and reputation of a single designer. That would be giving too much power away. Besides, you're just a kid, and your experience in my puny little lab has about as much value as a rat's fart, excuse the expression."

"Then what have I got to lose, Jake? If the stuff is good enough, I can always sell it outright, can't I? It's not like a piece of canvas that isn't worth anything unless the paint on it is properly arranged," she said, suddenly pleased with the crystallization of her own goals.

"Go get 'em, then. But one of these days, when you're standing at Tiffany's drinking champagne and being honored, give my little place here a plug, okay? Tell everybody I was the one who gave the Picasso of the jewelry world her start."

Chelsea slid down from the stool and gave Jake a hug and a kiss on the cheek. "You're my best friend, Jake. I love you."

"Hey, hey . . . no sex in the lab please. After all, I'm a

married man," he said, pleased that she appreciated his friendship.

Chelsea worked until late in the evening. Jake went out and bought her a hamburger and a Coke before he left for the dentist. She finished two sketches for more variations of the pearl bracelet and compiled a shopping list of supplies she would need for the next day's work.

Since her car was at home, she called a cab, and didn't realize until she got home that she didn't have a cent in her purse to pay the fare. Rather than wake her grandmother, however, she borrowed the money from Catalina.

Too tired to shower or even wash her face, she brushed her teeth, slipped into a nightgown and fell into bed. It was only after the light was out that she thought about Wills for the first time in more than eight hours. How very, very strange. For four days she had been consumed with him, and yet the moment she had gone back to work, he had almost vanished from her thoughts. Fatigue began to glide slowly across her arms and her legs, making them feel heavy and lifeless. She would have surrendered to sleep, but was troubled by her feeling of sadness. Why did love make her feel blue and her work make her happy?

At last she succumbed to the irresistible embrace of Morpheus, the god of dreams, who banished all thoughts of gold and diamonds and ushered her once more into the arms of her beloved.

47

Laverne was on the set watching Mike Stern rehearse Bunny with Gene Sinclair, who had been cast as her father in *The Beyonder*. The scene was a pivotal one in the film, and Bunny had to hit it with full force. Although he was a tireless taskmaster, Mike was so impressed with the intensity of her rehearsal that he called for a take immediately.

"That's it, Bunny, you were right on the nose. Now let's see if you can do it again for the camera. Everybody ready?"

"Quiet on the set!" the assistant director called, and a young man with a clapboard stepped in front of the camera.

"Camera ready?" the assistant asked.

"Camera ready," came the response.

"Sound ready?" he asked again, and the sound man responded that he too was ready.

"Action camera," Mike said quietly, and the cameraman called back, "Camera rolling."

"Sound rolling!" the soundman called.

"Mark it!" Mike ordered, and the young man with the clapboard said crisply, "Scene forty-two, take one," snapped the clapper and moved out of range quickly.

"Just like you did it before, Bunny. Action," Mike ordered, and Bunny moved across the lavish living room set until she was standing navel to navel with Gene. Defiantly jutting her chin up toward the much taller actor's face, she said one word, "Never!" and getting no response from him, threatened, "I will not spend one more night in this house."

"Where the hell do you think you're gonna go? He's got a wife and family of his own. What would he want with a sick tramp like you?" Gene Sinclair responded, delivering his lines with just the right amount of disdain.

Drawing herself up with a dignity and self-assurance that her character, Annabel, had never known before, Bunny said, "He doesn't matter anymore. And you don't matter either, understand? You've never been a father to me. Never. All you ever wanted to be was my judge!" she declared, turned away from him and walked to the door. "Good-bye, you bastard, and please, spare me any of your worn-out threats to disinherit me. I'm sick of hearing them. Donate your money to charity. Maybe you can buy your way into Heaven. God knows, that's the only way you'll ever get there."

She walked out the door purposefully, her head high, her stride measured. Mike let the camera run for a few moments and then said, "Cut."

Bunny returned to the set just in time to hear the director say, "Print it. We can't get any better than that. Set up for Bunny's close-up."

"Aren't we going to do one more?" Bunny asked in astonishment.

"We can't improve on perfection, Bunny. Just see that you do it exactly that way for your close-up, okay?" he said, moving away to talk to his cinematographer.

Laverne had little time to reflect on her daughter's performance, because a male voice in her ear said, "How's that for a delivery?"

Laverne turned toward Fernando, who had also been watching the scene. "She was wonderful, wasn't she?" she asked him triumphantly.

"I was talking about my performance, not hers, Mrs. Thomas. I believe you have something for me?"

"I'll pay you tomorrow," Laverne whispered curtly, annoyed that he would approach her so brazenly.

"I don't give credit. I get paid after each time, cash. It's the only way I work, and we had a deal, remember?"

"I don't have that much with me today," she said.

"Then I might have to tell your sweet little girl that I've got no more time for her, that she's a rotten lay," he threatened with a sneer.

Knowing she was bested, Laverne hurriedly took all the bills from her wallet, crumpled them into her hand and offered them to him furtively. "Look, here's fifty. I'll give you the rest after the lunch break."

"Okay, but don't make me wait again," he snapped just as Bunny approached.

"Was I okay, Mom?" she asked, her eyes shining with pleasure.

"You were terrific, baby," Fernando offered. "And you looked gorgeous. What did I tell you?"

Taking her arm and leading her back to the makeup room, he said, "Come on. Let me touch up that makeup. Gotta be perfect for the close-up."

As they walked away, Fernando threw his last words to Laverne carelessly over his shoulder. "See you later, Mama."

"You little prick," she muttered, furious that she now had to go to the car and drive to the bank to get a check cashed and miss Bunny's next scene. God, men were bastards, every goddamned one of them.

48

The police spotted the Porsche on Sunset Boulevard at noon. Sandy's contacts at the department called him immediately, and he, in turn, called Hilda.

"They snagged him on Sunset Boulevard. Want to go with me?" he asked.

"You bet," Hilda replied, relieved. It was too soon for Sergio to have made any important contacts yet. She just prayed to God he still had her journal with him.

When they arrived at the police station, Sandy went into a huddle with one of the detectives whom he knew. Once their conversation was over, he reported back to the anxiously waiting Hilda.

"They searched the car and found nothing. He's stashed whatever he took from your house."

"Damn, can we talk to him?"

"Yeah, he's setting him up in a room where we can be alone. They want us to press charges for assault."

Twenty minutes later Hilda and Sergio sat across from each other. Sandy was engaged in a telephone conversation, and since his fate was the main topic, Sergio was listening closely, trying to figure out whether or not he was going to be off the hook legally.

"So you explained it to Chelli, and he's interested?" Shapiro asked, and listened for an answer. Then he said, "Fine. Call me back after you've talked it over and come to a decision. We want to end this mess with as little hurt feelings as possible. Hilda's very upset, as you can well imagine, and she wants to make everything right. I know it's not her fault, but she feels responsible anyway. You know what kind of a gal she is. Good. Talk to you tomorrow, then."

He replaced the receiver and looked at Sergio witheringly. "Young man, you've caused one helluva lot of trouble for some very nice people, you know that?"

Sergio tried to look defiant but managed only to look extremely uncomfortable as he replied, "Yeah, so I had a bad day, so what?"

"Don't give me that crap!" Sandy snapped furiously, his jowls quivering with indignation. "One of the world's great talents will have to spend hours of his valuable creative time in a dental chair because you can't control your temper, and it's damned lucky you didn't break anything more than his teeth."

Sergio tried to bluff it out. "They treated me like some shitfaced little—"

But he was interrupted by Hilda. "Listen, Sergio, you couldn't have even gotten your nose into that rehearsal hall if I hadn't begged them to give you a chance. You had no right to hit anybody!" Hilda said, pressing him hard about the attack on Chelli, as Sandy had coaxed her to do. No mention had yet been made about the journal.

"You're a fine one to talk! Look at the bumps on my head, will you? You coulda killed me with that cane."

Sandy shook his head wearily and said, "I wish to hell she had. No jury in the world would have convicted her. Now, let's cut out the bickering and get things straightened out. Here's the deal—we've offered to pay Chelli for all his medical expenses, which are going to be considerable, but not enough by half in way of compensation. Then, if he's not going to have the satisfaction of sending you to jail, he's gotta have something to make up for the pain and humiliation of being knocked on his ass. All the money in the world wouldn't satisfy him, so we hadta figure out something that would appeal to his good nature. Hilda and I talked it over, and she's offered to pick up the tab for a Rolls-Royce or a Ferrari or any kinda automobile he picks out. Chelli loves cars, and his attorney's gonna recommend he go along with it and drop the charges against you."

"Jesus, a Rolls or a Ferrari for just one little punch in the mouth!" Sergio remarked, impressed with the offer.

"You're not getting off scot-free, buddy," Sandy replied. "There are certain things that Hilda expects from you or there's no deal, understand?"

Avoiding his wife's eyes, Sergio looked up at Sandy and said, "Wait, don't tell me. Let me guess. I gotta fuck the broad every night, right?"

Before Sandy could respond, Hilda took the offensive. "You better watch out, you limp Casanova, or one morning you might just wake up with all your fucking privileges cut off at the stem!"

His hands moving instinctively to his crotch, Sergio recoiled. "Jesus, stay away from me, you bitch!"

Unable to control his amusement, Sandy laughed out loud. "That's telling him, sweetheart."

"What do you people want from me?" Sergio asked, a distinctive whine creeping into his voice.

"I want nothing from you ever again," Hilda snapped. "As far as I'm concerned, you can stuff that shriveled-up little prick anywhere you like as long as it's nowhere near me."

Although he was enjoying the nasty exchange which he had advised Hilda to instigate, Sandy waved his hand in an attempt to ameliorate the situation. "Now, now, let's be ladies and gentlemen in here. Everybody needs to calm down. Hilda, it's not entirely true that you don't want anything from him, is it?"

Hilda shook her head. "I want my jewelry back. I want everything back that he took out of my safe."

"Who said I took your jewelry?"

"Your fingerprints were all over the safe," Sandy lied. "We've got you cold on that. Have you any idea what it would be like for a handsome young man like you to go to the penitentiary? Just think of all the big studs in there who would love to ram it up that pretty little ass of yours."

"Did the cops find anything in my car? Did they?" he asked pugnaciously.

Sandy decided to try a different approach. "Sergio, it's in your best interests to give Hilda back everything you took from her. Then she won't press charges on the jewelry or the car, and she'll pay off Chelli. You'll be off the hook."

"The Porsche is half mine already," he argued.

"It's possible that we could make it part of the divorce settlement," Sandy said, putting his hand on Hilda's shoulder to keep her from saying anything.

"Who said anything about a divorce? I don't want a divorce!" Sergio cried.

"Well I do, you pissant!" Hilda declared. "You don't actually think I could go on living with you after last night, do you?"

Sergio looked beseechingly at Sandy, who just raised his eyebrows and shrugged.

"What am I gonna do? I can't get a job as a dancer. Nobody'll hire me after that story in the papers. Where'll I go? You gonna give me enough in the divorce settlement so I can go on livin' in Beverly Hills?" he asked, making one last attempt at keeping the good life from slipping through his fingers.

"I suggest you tell us where you put the jewelry, and then we'll talk about the future," Sandy said sternly.

There was a long pause, while Sandy and Hilda held their breath waiting for Sergio's response, which was not long in coming.

"No, first you draw up a paper that details everything the way it's gonna be, then I give you back your jewelry. You won't give me anything otherwise."

"Well, we'll have to talk it over . . ." Sandy replied.

Sergio got to his feet to go back to his cell. "Yeah, you

talk it over . . . and sharpen your pencil, because I know it's not the jewelry my wife wants back. She wants that brown leather notebook, don't you, bitch?"

The air in the room suddenly went very still, and the sounds outside the small office created a counterpoint to the paralyzing tenseness of the silence in the room.

"See you soon," he said, swaggering through the doorway.

Hilda and Sandy looked at each other without speaking.

49

Sandy and Hilda sat in stony, thoughtful silence for a long time after Sergio had left the room. Finally Hilda suggested that they go someplace where they could talk privately.

Later, sitting in Sandy's office, he offered the first hopeful suggestion.

"Look, the situation's not all that bad. Any problem that can be solved with money isn't fatal. We just gotta come up with a package that he'll buy."

Hilda shook her head. "You've got him wrong, Sandy, believe me, I know. He's one of those thick-headed people who will see every overture we make as a sign of weakness, and he'll greedily ask for more, no matter how much I offer him. Everything is never enough for this man."

"So what do we do?"

"He doesn't respond well to kindness. He has to be frightened and pushed around."

"So we scare the shit out of him. How're we going to do that without risking that damned journal of yours getting into the wrong hands. Suppose, just suppose, he got the bright idea to sell it to somebody like the *National Enquirer* . . . that's about his level, right?"

Hilda was too busy thinking to hear Sandy's remarks. A germ of an idea had begun to form, and she needed to concentrate. She got out of her chair, picked up her mug of coffee and went to the window. Sandy watched in silence. He knew Hilda to be a tough-minded negotiator, and he suspected she was already working out a solution to the problem.

At last she spoke. "Okay, here's how we do it," she said conspiratorially. "This is going to take some planning, but I think we can get the journal back for a reasonable price if we do it right."

Two hours later she and Sandy arrived back at the jail and Sergio was brought into the office where they waited. Throughout the next half hour of talk, Hilda sat near the window and did not participate.

"I've drawn up an agreement, which I'd like you to consider," Sandy began. "But first, I want you to know that it's a take-it-or-leave-it deal."

"What's that supposed to mean?" Sergio asked in his usual surly manner.

"I mean you say yes or no now, while we're here, or the deal's off. Hilda wants her jewelry and her journal back today, or we don't negotiate, we prosecute."

"Look, buddy, talk nice. I'm the one holdin' the cards, not you. So what's your offer?"

Sandy put the hastily drawn document in front of Sergio to read, but he was only halfway through it when he looked up and scowled at his adversaries.

"You think I'm nuts or somethin'?" he asked, pushing the paper away from him. "That book is worth a whole lot more than a Porsche and a lousy ten grand."

"That journal is her property, and if you don't accept our offer, she intends to press charges for—"

"Press charges, my ass. Her name'll be mud if that book gets circulated around this town. You think I'm a fool or somethin'?"

The argument escalated. Sandy kept offering more, but

just as Hilda had predicted, her husband kept upping his demands, until finally Hilda leaped from her chair, strode to the table where the proposal lay, grabbed it and tore it into pieces dramatically.

"You asshole, you're not going to get a dime. I'm going to walk out of this place forever. And you know where I'm going, you jerk? I'm going straight to the telephone, and I'm going to call Sy Christman himself and tell him about the journal and exactly what's in it. I'm going to tell him everything, that you stole it out of my safe and that you're blackmailing me with it by threatening to sell it to somebody who'll expose it to the light of day. Now what do you think he'll do when he finds out? Do you really think he'll sit on the sidelines and let you put on your little sideshow without any interference?"

"You're bluffin'," Sergio said warily, but with less bravado.

"I never bet on cards I don't hold, and you know it as well as anybody. Well, so long. Have a nice life, what little is left of it." She picked up the pieces of the contract, threw them in the air, and walked out of the room with Sandy right behind her.

Protesting, Sergio tried to follow them, but a policeman blocked his way.

"Hilda, for God's sake, come back. Let's talk this over," he yelled to his wife, but neither she nor Sandy bothered to look back.

50

When Chelsea finally managed to pull her leaden body out of bed and into the shower at eight o'clock the next morning, the soothing warm water did nothing to purge her desire for sleep, but in fact relaxed her so much that she actually felt herself beginning to doze off. Impulsively, she turned off all the hot water and was shocked into complete wakefulness by the cascade of icy water. Once all traces of sleep were banished, she allowed herself the privilege of retreat, stepping out of the shower and wrapping her now alert and recharged body in a warm, thick terry towel.

She pulled a fresh pair of jeans from the closet and noticed the sharp crease. Dammit, why did the new maid insist on ironing everything in sight? She brushed her teeth, ran a comb through her long hair, and checked the time. She had an appointment at nine at the Jewelry Mart, and she would have to battle the traffic on the Santa Monica Freeway. If she was late, the guy would be annoyed for having come in early to accommodate her, and he'd probably jack up his prices. Damn!

She grabbed her sketches, her car keys, and her wallet, raced down the stairs and saw the offending servant.

"Fabiola, have Gran and Mom gone already?" she asked the woman, who was polishing the mirror in the entry hall.

"Hour ago. You see the flowers?"

"What flowers?" Chelsea asked, not wanting to stop to talk to the garrulous maid, but curious.

"Florist boy bring them for you last night."

"Flowers came for me?" Chelsea asked. She had never received flowers in her entire life.

"*Sí.* They already in silver vase. I put on piano."

Despite her rush, Chelsea sprinted across the hall into the living room. There on the ebony Steinway grand was the largest bouquet of long-stemmed red roses she had ever seen. She went closer to bury her nose in the fragrant velvet of the flower petals and thought of Wills. Suddenly, her eye caught a tiny bit of engraving on the ornate silver vase. Squinting to read it, she saw that the dates of her friends' visit had been engraved in script along with the words, "Days to Cherish, with Love, Margaret and Wills." For the first time since Wills had gone, her defenses were down and an agonizing sense of loss engulfed her. She wanted to carry the flowers to her room and indulge herself in an orgy of memories they had created together, but there just wasn't time. She turned to go, but the roses had cast a spell on her and she could not leave without one to carry with her. Quickly, she pulled a flower from the vase and hurried to her car. Snapping the stem short, she stuck the flower into the top buttonhole of her white cotton shirt, close enough to her face so she could lower her chin and touch its softness and feel the spirit of her beloved close to her.

By the time she got back to the laboratory it was almost one. She had missed both her classes, but there was just no time for school now anyway. Jake was still at lunch, and so she spread all the little packages of pale blue tissue paper on the table to check out her purchases. Unwrapping the largest packet, she laid a dozen strings of pearls on the table and examined them with the magnifying glasses. She had chosen pearls of good color and luster but slightly blemished. The first thing she had to do was replace her mother's valuable pearls in the bracelets with these.

It was tedious and uninspiring work, since she hated to do the same task twice, but she finished it in that afternoon, driven by her desire to work on other things. Although she had intended to make another diamond pendant, she'd had an inspiration while examining the stones at the Jewelry Mart that morning. Seeing so many varied shades of pink and red tourmalines, she had impulsively bought a large quantity that graduated from dark to light, as well as a variety of various hues of green. In her imagination she had seen a wide gold bracelet, highly polished, and inset with a large rose of the tourmalines, and she was anxious to make a sketch to see if it could be done successfully.

Jake tried to engage her in conversation as they worked side by side, but she was too full of her plans to be very talkative. Because he understood her need to work every moment of the day, he volunteered to go out and bring back a sandwich for her before he left for the night. In parting, he cautioned her not to work too late, but it was obvious that she wasn't listening.

Taking the now withering rose, she laid it in front of her and began to sketch. When she was satisfied, she laid the tourmalines on the pattern to see how it would look, but found it far too gaudy, too much like costume jewelry if the petals were filled in completely. As she stared at the design, Chelsea was suddenly seized by pleasant memories of the join-the-dots puzzles she loved as a child, remembering the joy of making a picture by simply connecting one dot to another.

She took a piece of onionskin paper and laid it over the rose. Carefully she made a pattern of points on which she laid the jewels. Just as in the puzzles, however, it didn't make sense unless she connected the dots, and she decided to do that with lines of tiny diamonds between the colored stones. Endowed with the extraordinary ability to envision such things clearly, she knew she had created an original and stunning design.

The next problem involved the shape and size of the gold bracelet, which would need to be close to two inches wide with a nice convex curve to give it grace. Briefly, she considered buying a bracelet to decorate, which would save her a day's work, but decided it would be improper to submit anything to Tanager's that wasn't completely original. So she worked until her shoulders and neck screamed from the unremitting strain as she bent over the table. It was almost three in the morning before she got back home. Up in her room, she found a gold florist's box on her pillow.

She sank down on the comforter, hands shaking with fatigue, pulled off the red ribbon and opened the box. Inside there was another beautiful rose. With a smile, she put the rose in a glass of water on the table beside her bed, to preserve it until the next day, when she would wear it. Wills's flower had brought her inspiration, and she needed every bit of help she could get. Wearing it also gave her a warm feeling of being loved.

51

Laverne stared at Bunny, while her mind anxiously searched for words that might persuade her foolish daughter to stop and think before taking a step that would bring nothing but trouble into the house. Unfortunately, however, the pain in her head was so severe that it blocked everything except its own excruciating presence. She wanted to take a pill and lie down in the cool, dark quiet of her bedroom, but she felt forced to take a stand and oppose her daughter's ridiculous suggestion.

"Mom, what's so terrible about Fernando moving in with me? I thought you liked him," Bunny said peevishly as she stepped out of the tub and took the towel from her mother's hand. "He'll be here any minute, and I intend to tell him tonight that it's fine with you."

"But it's not fine with me, Bunny. It will never be fine with me. If you want to screw around a little, that's your business, but you'll look like a fool if you start being seen around town too much with a makeup man! And he's more than ten years younger than you are!"

"What's age got to do with it? Old men fall in love with young girls and nobody thinks anything of it."

"Bunny darling, you're one of the world's great stars. When this movie you're doing with Mike comes out, you'll be back on top where you're supposed to be. It's ridiculous for you to even think of satcheling yourself with this little pipsqueak. He's a nothing. Believe me."

The hammers inside Laverne's head suddenly began pounding at her skull with blows so ferocious that it seemed they might actually pierce the bone.

"If I'm such a big star, why the hell should I care what people think?" Bunny retorted, and handed the thick terry-cloth towel to her mother to dry her back.

Laverne took the towel to do what was expected of her, but the movement jarred her head, and suddenly the tenuous hold she had on her anger snapped. Throwing the towel at her daughter, she said, "Dry your own back for a change. I'm getting sick of waiting on you. I've got a terrible headache, and I'm going to bed." She turned and rushed from the room.

Bunny was startled by her mother's uncharacteristic display of temper, and she quickly slipped on her bathrobe and followed her. Something must be terribly wrong for her mother to be so cross and impatient.

In defiance of her doctor's orders to take no more than one of the green pills for her migraines, Laverne was in her own bathroom taking two when her apprehensive daughter appeared.

"Mom, you've been getting these headaches too often lately. Don't you think you should see a doctor about them?" Bunny asked nervously, her voice reflecting her concern.

"I saw him last week while you were working, and everything's fine. I've just been under too much stress, and he said I needed more rest. Better get your clothes on. Fernando will be here to do your makeup any minute now, and I ordered the limo for seven o'clock. Go on now, I'm fine," she said, for the first time in her life wishing her daughter would just go away and leave her alone.

"Well, okay, but . . . I told Fernando he could spend the night here tonight," Bunny said, once again childishly attentive only to her own wants and needs. "Do you mind?"

Suddenly, after a lifetime of jockeying for control of her daughter's every movement, Laverne let go and allowed all of the resistance to flow from her. In the grand scheme of things, what the hell difference did any of it make anyway?

"Make up your own mind, for a change, Bunny. Now just let me alone."

Now that she'd gotten what she wanted, Bunny hurried back to her room to get ready, all concerns about her mother's unusual behavior and obvious distress dissolved into her own anticipation of the night ahead. Ever since

Fernando had first seduced her, she had fantasized about spending an entire night with him with no worries about being interrupted and no need to hurry.

Wearily, Laverne undressed and climbed into bed, where she lay listening to the sounds of the evening. When Fernando arrived, she could hear them giggling and talking. Finally, the bell rang again, and she knew the limousine had come to pick them up. They were going to the annual fund-raising ball for the Cancer Society, of which Bunny was this year's honorary chairman.

Laverne moved, slowly so as not to jostle her aching head, to the cooler part of the sheets. Mercifully, the pills were beginning to numb the pain. Lifting her now heavy arm, she stroked her breast. The swelling was still there, and now when she pressed, it felt a bit harder, like a mass of ball bearings buried deep in the flesh. She really should go have it looked at, she thought, and foggily wondered why she had lied to her daughter about already having had a physical examination.

Heavily drugged, Laverne slept through the night, undisturbed by the noisy sexual antics in the room next to hers. Fernando more than earned his pay that evening, exhausting Bunny to the point where she could not get out of bed the next day, which fortunately was Sunday. Fernando was not just an inventive and skilled lover, he was a world-class sexual athlete.

Lying in the beautiful four-poster bed, on the Pratesi linens, Fernando toted up the evening's take, while Bunny slept beside him. Would that old biddy in the other room believe him when he claimed they'd done it five times and she owed him a hundred for each? Nah, she'd probably never been with a man who could get it up more than once a night, and she'd never buy it, even though the actual count had been six, a record even for him. It'd been easy with this chick, because she seemed to get off on pain almost as much as he enjoyed inflicting it. Before they got together again, he'd have to get a little hardware. She'd probably love some kinky stuff.

* * *

Because her bedroom was on the other side of the house, Chelsea hadn't heard anything, and so she was startled when the strange man appeared at the breakfast table.

"Who are you?" she asked, wondering if her grandmother had hired another servant.

"A friend of Bunny's. Who are you?" he asked, pouring himself a cup of coffee from the silver pot on the sideboard and hungrily eyeing the assortment of crisp cold melon slices and freshly baked rolls.

"I'm her daughter, Chelsea. Does my grandmother know you're here?" she asked forthrightly. Something told her that Laverne would not approve of this insolent young man. There was an aura of malevolence about him, and she disliked him immediately.

"I don't know. When I came to pick up your mom last night to go to the cancer ball, Laverne had already gone to bed. We got in pretty late." He looked up at Chelsea, who was perhaps six inches taller than he was, and in spite of his exhausting night, he found himself assessing his chances of getting her in the sack, but decided they weren't very good. She was a piece of ice.

"Is my mother still asleep?" Chelsea asked.

"Yeah, she's pretty tired. As soon as I have something to eat, I'll be on my way." He turned his attention once more to the delectable bounty before him. In spite of what he'd said, he planned to spend a very long time eating. He didn't want to leave until the old woman came downstairs, so he could collect his night's pay along with a little bonus. If the old lady was as opposed to his moving in as Bunny said she was, she'd probably pay plenty to keep him out of the house on a permanent basis, which was fine with him. He was interested in Bunny Thomas for one reason, and that was financial. He had no intention of letting any broad put a leash on him.

52

The next few days passed quickly for Chelsea as she struggled to get the bracelet finished. Her join-the-gems design turned out so well that she drew a large medallion using the same concept, with both a bail for hanging it on a chain around the neck and a pin on the back. She did detailed sketches for a new diamond pendant and the emerald ring she had sold. Although she wanted to make a ring out of the pink diamond on the clasp of her mother's pearls, she simply ran out of time.

The day before Mr. Corell was scheduled to go to New York, Chelsea appeared at Tanager's with the results of her round-the-clock efforts. There were dark circles under her red-rimmed eyes, and her untended hair hung lank around her shoulders as she sat across the desk from him, watching nervously while he looked over her work.

For a long time he inspected the magnificent bracelet, which was the high point of her presentation, and when he at last looked up at the young woman sitting before him, he smiled kindly, searching for the proper words. Chelsea could tell by his reluctance to speak that the news was not going to be good.

"Your work is beautiful. It's original and imaginative. Inspired, really, but . . ."

A mantle of doom suddenly enveloped Chelsea and choked off her breath. Good God, he was going to turn her down.

"But you don't like them?" she asked.

"No, that's not what I'm saying. I love them, but I'm afraid they're too, how should I say it . . . too witty and amusing for a traditional firm like Tanager's. We take our jewels quite seriously, you know."

"You're not going to take them to New York, then?" she asked, trying to breathe, trying to draw life-saving breath into her lungs to keep from drowning in the agony of disappointment.

Corell looked surprised. "You misunderstand me, my dear young woman. We had an agreement, and I always honor my agreements, but I just want you to know that the chances are quite slim that Tanager's will take them."

Chelsea grasped desperately at the slender thread of renewed hope. "Then you've got to convince them that everyone, even Tanager's, must change with the times or go the way of the dinosaurs. Take me with you, Mr. Corell. Let me show the designs myself. Let me talk to them."

The older man was mesmerized by her passion; it gave life to her eyes and her voice as she spoke. Her fervor delighted him, but he was a cautious man.

"Well . . ." he began, unable to say no to the eager child before him.

Taking advantage of his hesitancy, Chelsea pressed her argument. "Look, let me go with you. I'll pay all my own expenses, and it won't cost you a thing. Just let me have ten minutes of their time. That's all. Just ten minutes!"

"I suppose that might be possible. But it will have to be done the day after tomorrow. Although it's highly irregular, I could probably let you speak just before I give my annual report." He stopped to think the matter over, and when Chelsea started to speak, he raised a hand to quiet her. "My dear, you understand that if I permit you to accompany me, I will have committed myself irrevocably to your cause. I'd look foolish if I did otherwise," he said, and Chelsea knew that, miraculously, she had succeeded in changing him from disinterested observer to outright advocate.

Before he could change his mind, Chelsea closed the debate by getting to her feet. "Good. Tell me what flight you'll be on, and I'll join you," she said, and began to gather up her treasures.

"No," he said, stopping her. "Please let me keep your things here. I want to show them to our employees and get their reactions. After all, they're the ones who have to sell the jewelry, and if their reactions are positive, it will be helpful. I'll carry them in my special case. Ask my secretary to give you the information on my flight."

"See you at the airport," Chelsea said, and hurried from the room. To her dismay, she learned that Corell was scheduled on a flight at eight-thirty the next morning, first-class, of course, and it was already after two. If she didn't get across town before the bank closed, she wouldn't have any money to buy her ticket.

The traffic was terrible. She was stuck in a line of cars on a freeway on-ramp for more than fifteen minutes because of a stalled truck, and when she finally got on the freeway itself, the cars were inching along. As the minutes ticked away, she left the freeway in frustration and found herself lost in an unfamiliar neighborhood. For more than ten minutes she drove up one street and down another trying to get her bearings. By the time she got back to Beverly Hills, the bank was closed. She banged on the door to get the attention of the employees still working inside, but no one would even look in her direction.

Desperately, she drove to the laboratory to ask Jake for help, but he had less than a hundred dollars on him. She needed a lot more than that if she were going to buy a first-class ticket so she could sit next to Corell and keep his enthusiasm from wavering.

"What about your grandmother?" he asked.

"Oh Lord, I'll have to explain the whole thing to her, and she'll probably say no anyway. I can't remember once in my life asking her for anything and getting it, Jake. And that's the truth," she moaned, sitting down at the worktable and putting her head in her hands.

"I sure wish I could help you, but I cut up all our credit cards a year ago, after we got ourselves in debt buying stuff for the house. I think you should put the screws on your family. If your grandmother says no, go to your mother. Don't let them off the hook so easily. That's the least they could do for you."

"You're right, but I'd almost rather stop a stranger on the street than go to Gran for anything," Chelsea said morosely, not mentioning that she could not ask to borrow from her grandmother because she didn't want to reveal that she had money of her own in the bank and could pay her back.

It was an afternoon of missed connections and frustrations, one on top of another. At the studio she learned that they were filming on location, but no one could tell her exactly where, even though she identified herself and begged for help. Having decided that her grandmother was her only hope for getting money quickly, Chelsea was not about to give up, so she called Hilda Marx.

For the first time that day, the tide of fortune finally turned her way. Hilda was in her office and took her call immediately.

"Hi, Chelsea, what's up?"

"Hilda, I need to talk to my grandmother. Where are they shooting today?"

"God, honey, they're somewhere in the Angeles Forest, but I have no idea exactly where. Is there anything I can do for you?"

Hilda had always been friendly and understanding. So, under duress, the ordinarily independent and self-reliant Chelsea did something she had never done before. She asked for help.

"Hilda, I know this sounds just terrible, but I need two thousand dollars right away. If you could lend it to me, I promise I'll give it back next week. I have the money, but the bank's closed, and I've got to fly to New York early tomorrow morning."

"Two thousand dollars!" Hilda exclaimed in surprise.

Chelsea knew she had to explain quickly or risk being turned down. "Look, the manager of Tanager's here in L.A. has agreed to let me present some of my jewelry designs to their people in New York, but I've got to go tomorrow or the deal is off. It's a chance of a lifetime for me, Hilda."

"Your designs?" she asked in bewilderment.

"Yeah. That's what I do."

"Your grandmother never mentioned it to me."

"She doesn't know. You know she and Mom don't

really have much interest in anything besides the movies, so I just don't talk much about myself around the house, Hilda. You know what they're like."

"Indeed," Hilda replied. She seemed impressed that Chelsea had the talent to even be considered by Tanager's. The fact that the people closest to her knew nothing about such an important part of the girl's life made Hilda eager to help.

"Chelsea, I don't have the money—but wait, don't panic. I can work it out for you. Give me the flight number, and I'll have your ticket charged to our office account and sent here. Then let me see how much cash I can scrape up. Give me until about six, okay?"

Chelsea was stunned. No one had ever gone out of her way to do something so generous for her.

"Gosh, thanks, Hilda. That's great. I promise I'll pay you back every cent. I've got to sit near the man from Tanager's who's sponsoring me, because I need to talk to him. So I have to be in first-class," she said apologetically.

"It's the only way to fly. See you here at six."

At five minutes to six, Chelsea arrived at Hilda's office. Most of the staff had gone, but Hilda was waiting for her.

"Come on and sit down," Hilda said, looking dismayed by the young woman's unkempt and wilted appearance. "I've got the ticket here, and I borrowed fifteen hundred dollars from the petty cash fund, which, added to the two hundred I had and fifty I got from my secretary, should more than take care of you. How long are you going to be in New York?"

"I'm not sure," Chelsea replied, and told Hilda the whole story.

"That's amazing. Look, if you find that you have to stay longer and need more money, just call me and I'll wire it to you," Hilda said.

"I don't know how I can ever thank you enough, Hilda. I'd have been lost without you," Chelsea said, overwhelmed with gratitude.

"Hey, that's my line of work, honey. I like to help talented young people get started in the world. And you're lucky you caught me. I just finished negotiating a very big contract," a slight, ironic smile quivered at the corner of her mouth, "and I've been out of the office all day. Say, would you mind if I offered a suggestion?"

"Not at all."

"Don't go into Tanager's in jeans, okay? They're a conservative group of old fuddy-duddies who think denim should stay on the farm. And, use your mother's name."

"What?" Chelsea asked, startled.

"When you're on the bottom rung you have to use everything and everybody if you don't want to stay down there, understand? Get rid of those silly ideas that you have to go it completely alone. That's just pious bullshit. Everybody in this world who ever made good got help from somebody, somewhere. Tell them that Bunny Thomas is your mother, and that if they take your designs, she'll wear the jewelry in public and get her picture taken. Got it?"

"But—"

"No buts about it, young lady. Talent isn't enough. You've also got to be smart." Hilda watched Chelsea as she struggled with the concept.

"Have you got the right clothes to wear, sweetie?" Hilda asked.

Chelsea shrugged. "I've got a few things that should be okay. I've never been much interested in clothes. I hardly ever wear anything but jeans."

"What size are you?" Hilda asked.

"A ten, but I'm tall. Most things are short-waisted on me, and I buy all of my shirts in the men's department because the sleeves are long enough for me."

"Come on. Let's go over to my place and do a little shopping in my closet. I've bought a ton of designer things in sizes from eight to twelve, depending on my weight, which goes up and down like a seesaw."

"I couldn't . . ." Chelsea protested, but Hilda would

not listen. Motherly in her approach to all of her clients, she had just taken on a new challenge.

"Let me call my housekeeper and tell her there'll be two for dinner. When you taste her cooking, you'll wonder why I'm not a size forty."

53

The cast and crew of *The Beyonder* were back in the studio after some location shooting, and Mike Stern was in good spirits. In less than two weeks they would finish principal photography, and the dailies reassured him that he had cast the film wisely. Each day, Bunny Thomas seemed to grow more and more like Annabel, and on several occasions he had noticed that she remained in character even when the camera wasn't running. Watching her curiously, he saw that whenever anyone spoke to her, her right hand invariably clutched at a piece of hair and began to twist it nervously, an affectation he had suggested early in the filming to demonstrate Annabel's insecurity when talking to strangers. To test his thesis, several times he had called Bunny by her character's name, and she responded just as Annabel would.

Eerie as it was, the continuity served the film well, although he hoped that Bunny's transformation would reverse itself once the picture was completed. Annabel, after all, turned killer at the end of the film, pushed too far emotionally by the demands of the men in her life. But that wasn't his problem. He had an overbudget, overschedule big movie to complete. Bunny's emotional problems were not his concern.

Mike walked through the set, thinking through the shots of the day one more time. Today's scenes would constitute the big climax of the picture, and he wanted to be thoroughly prepared. Reassured that the physical setting looked the way it should, he decided to stop in the dressing room and talk to Bunny alone and make sure she was in the right frame of mind.

Stepping over the cables and skirting camera paraphernalia, he stopped occasionally to bid each crew member a good morning. Mike believed in making everyone who worked on his films feel they were an integral part of the process. As a result, he got good work and maintained a high level of morale. The gossip and backbiting that marred many crews were absent from his pictures.

When he approached Bunny's dressing room, he noticed that her mother was outside the door pacing back and forth angrily, and he wondered why she was so uptight, since everything seemed to be going smoothly.

"Hi, Laverne. How's our star this morning?" he said breezily. Hoping not to get involved in a conversation, he ignored her surprised warning, "Wait, don't—" Although Mike had had no significant interference from Laverne, there was something about the scrawny woman he just couldn't stand, and he sailed past her. Without bothering to knock, he turned the knob and walked into the room unannounced, but the scene he encountered made him wish he'd been a little more circumspect. There was his star, his beautiful, touching, sensitive Annabel, draped over a chair, hanging virtually upside down with her bare rear end exposed. Standing over her, with his pants down around his ankles, was Fernando, pumping at her like a dog with a bitch in heat. The urbane and normally unruffled director backed away speechless, quickly pulling the door shut once more.

"I told you not to go in there, didn't I?" Laverne snapped angrily.

"What the hell's going on between those two?" he asked.

"Couldn't you tell?" she asked sarcastically, pulling a cigarette from her purse and lighting it with shaking hands.

"How long?"

Laverne shrugged and exhaled the smoke. "Practically

ever since shooting started. They do it in there every morning, most afternoons, and they'd like to do it every damned night too."

Mike was shocked. "At night? Has he moved in with her?"

"Over my dead body. Last night I gave in and let him stay, but I'm not going to put up with that crap."

"He's half her age," Mike protested, still not ready to accept the situation.

"He'd have to be to perform as often as he does. God, I'll be glad when this picture's over."

"What does the picture have to do with it?" he asked.

"Ask your leading lady. She's standing behind you."

Mike turned around and saw Bunny standing there, her silk kimono wrapped tightly around her, her hair and makeup in perfect shape.

"Mother!" Bunny said sharply. "You were supposed to keep people out. You know I need my privacy in the morning."

Mike did not hesitate to assume the blame. "Look, she tried, but I didn't listen. Bunny, what's Fernando's humping you got to do with my picture?" he asked indignantly, outraged that something so patently base could have anything to do with the art he was creating.

Bunny glanced irritably at her mother and replied, "Well . . . every morning, Fernando gives me a little something to heighten the color in my cheeks and make me glow." She looked down demurely and continued, "I call it my daily injection of love. It's working pretty well, don't you think?"

With his mouth agape, Mike absorbed the astonishing information. "So help me, now I've heard everything," he mumbled, and walked away, calling back over his shoulder, "Be on the set in two minutes without fail!"

Bunny hurried back into her dressing room and donned her costume with her mother's help. Not a word was spoken until Bunny left the room. Then Fernando looked up from the sink where he was washing his brushes and said to Laverne, "I'm gettin' tired of this crap. You owe me more than two thousand bucks, and I wanta get paid."

"I don't owe you a cent more than I've already paid you."

"Before I ever touched your nympho daughter, you promised to pay me a hundred bucks each time I screwed her. We had a deal, and now you're tryin' to welsh on me."

Laverne pulled a hundred-dollar bill out of her purse and laid it on the makeup table. "There's your pay for this morning. When we made that agreement, it never occurred to me that you were going to do it morning, noon, and night, for God's sake. I've told you that I'll pay for one time and one time only each day, and that's it. If you don't like it, keep your cock in your pants."

"Yeah, well, maybe I will. Let's see how your daughter feels when she finds out she can't get it anymore."

"She's had enough in the past month to last her for the rest of her life. Get lost, Fernando," she snapped peevishly, and walked out of the room. Laverne began to feel the little fingers of pain pinching inside her head and realized that she was about to have another migraine. Rummaging in her purse for the bottle of pills, she was relieved when her fingers found the smooth plastic cylinder, which she opened quickly. Only one pill slid into the palm of her hand, and she realized that she was in trouble. She had become accustomed to taking two, and one simply would not do it for her.

She went to the telephone and dialed the number of the pharmacy on the label, but was told that the prescription was not refillable. She tried to call her old friend, Dr. Jack Shepherd, and was told that he had retired to Mexico. Drat. Resigned to the inevitable, she called Victor Cableshaw, who was the current doctor of choice among the stars. He had a cancellation for the following morning but no sooner, so she made an appointment. Good God, it was going to be a long and miserable day and night.

It turned out to be much worse than she had anticipated. She arrived home late in the afternoon to find a note from Chelsea saying she had gone to New York on business and would call later. What in the hell kind of business would her granddaughter have in New York? And where in hell had she gotten the money to go? Reeling from the escalating pain in her head, she went to bed and fell into a fitful slumber, only to be awakened by Bunny's return in the early evening.

"Mom!" she wailed, standing at the foot of the bed and causing Laverne to sit upright immediately, jarring the pain back to life.

"For God's sake, what, Bunny?" she asked foggily.

"You're ruining my life!"

"What do you mean?" Laverne mumbled, disoriented and confused. Was it night or morning?

"Fernando said you told him he could never set foot in this house again. Why would you say a thing like that? You know how much he means to me!" Tears were running down her eyes, the mascara creating black rivulets on her cheeks.

Remembering the ugly episode of the morning, Laverne said impatiently, "Bunny, he's nothing more than a screwing machine. He doesn't mean anything to you, understand? Jerks like him are a dime a dozen in Hollywood. Let him go." Wearily she lay back down on her pillow, longing to return to sleep, tired of everything and everybody.

Bunny, however, had no intention of crying alone. When she suffered, the world must suffer too. When she wept, she expected an audience of millions, and if that were not possible, one would do, but there had to be at least one.

Sobbing loudly, Bunny moaned and groaned, tore at her hair, pulled the buttons from her blouse, stormed from the room, only to return minutes later, the intensity cranked up a little higher. Through it all Laverne clung to her pillow, clamping her eyes shut, begging a God whose acquaintance she had not yet made to turn off the noise and give her peace. But it was not to be. In her own way, Bunny had determination that could wear through the toughest shell of emotional armor, and when at last the intensity of her lamentation reduced her to a sodden heap of temperamental rubble lying on the floor, Laverne conceded defeat.

With great difficulty she pulled the neurotic mess that was her daughter to her feet and helped her into the bathroom. In spite of her own misery, she comforted her child, bathed her, and put her to bed. Hours later, when Bunny was at last deep in exhausted sleep, her mother limped back to her own bed, where she lay awake all night, tense from the pain that had become her constant companion.

By the time she arrived at the doctor's office the following day, Laverne was ready to step in front of a speeding truck. Resentful that Chelsea had left her to cope alone, and crippled with blinding head pain, Laverne had solicited the assistance of Fabiola to force Bunny out of bed and get her to the set. Although it was her custom to linger until things were well under way, Laverne simply turned Bunny over to the wardrobe mistress and Fernando and left. She had intended to have a talk with him and offer a compromise, but there was no immediate opportunity, and she couldn't take the time to wait.

Fortunately, the doctor was on time. Despite his popularity with the rich and the famous, Dr. Cableshaw did not let it interfere with his practice of good medicine. His finely chiseled features and thick gray hair were perfectly suited to deal with his Beverly Hills clients, but he was not a toady, nor was he a source of supply for medications not needed to cure an illness. He had successfully treated Bunny the year before when she had developed severe bronchitis.

"Here's a paper gown," the nurse said briskly. "Take off everything but your shoes, and the opening goes down the front."

Laverne was annoyed. "Look, I just need something for my headache. There's no reason for me to undress," she protested.

"Doctor's orders, Mrs. Thomas. He needs to do a

workup to see if there's a reason you're having so much trouble lately. Headaches can come from almost anything, you know. Just press this little green button when you're ready," the nurse said briskly, and left the room, closing the door with a determined snap.

If the pain hadn't been quite so terrible, Laverne might have walked out and looked for a physician who would have capitulated and just written a prescription for pain pills, but she was weak and desperate, and so she obediently took off her clothes. Just before slipping her arms into the paper gown, she glanced down and saw the swelling on her breast. There would be no more excuses now. No more chances for running away from the truth. No more silly denials. Truth had at last caught up with her.

An hour later she was dressed again and sitting opposite Dr. Cableshaw, who was busy writing a prescription. When he looked up, he stared at her thoughtfully for a few moments before asking, "Why, Mrs. Thomas? Why did you wait so long?"

More relaxed now that it was finally over and done with, she could not meet his eyes. "I honestly don't know. I suppose I just didn't want to admit it to myself."

"But you knew what it was, didn't you?"

"I suppose so."

"It's quite large on the left, and there are several palpable tumors on the right side too. There are a lot of things that I would do ordinarily, but at this point we've got to get you into the hospital today for a biopsy and lymphectomy to find out exactly what it is and if it has metastasized."

"I couldn't possibly go into the hospital today, Dr. Cableshaw. I've waited this long, surely another week or two wouldn't make any difference. You see, Bunny is just finishing a big film with Mike Stern, and it would upset her if I weren't around to take care of things."

"Mrs. Thomas," the doctor said sternly, "have you listened to a word I've said? It's precisely because you've waited so long that you can't waste any more time. We're not talking about a pimple, we're probably dealing with a major life-threatening illness. There's a very good chance that the lumps in your breast are the source of your headaches."

"Am I going to die?" she asked weakly.

Victor Cableshaw's impatience with her melted instantly. "We're all going to die, Mrs. Thomas. We just want to postpone it as long as possible, okay?"

Taking a deep breath, Laverne compromised. "I've got to have two days. Then my granddaughter will be back from New York, and Bunny will have someone to rely on, all right?"

The doctor was a pragmatist. Obviously if he was too inflexible, she might leave and get no treatment at all. "If you insist. Day after tomorrow, I want you at the hospital first thing in the morning. Shall I arrange for a surgeon for you or do you have someone in mind?"

"No, no. Please, you take care of everything for me, and thank you, Doctor. Thank you for being so understanding." Strangely, she felt that he had just given her a reprieve.

"Have this prescription filled downstairs. That injection I gave you should cool down that headache, but I don't want you to drive. Can you have someone pick you up?"

"I have a driver."

"Good. As soon as that head starts up again, take two pills, then one every three hours. But do not exceed more than six in one day, understand?"

Laverne nodded. She was anxious to leave. She had a million things to do before she checked into the hospital.

54

Chelsea sat quietly beside Mr. Corell and looked out the window of the plane at the white clouds below. She'd had two glasses of the champagne the hostesses had poured so generously, and had eaten every bite of the breakfast, and now she felt sleepy and relaxed for the first time in weeks. Fortunately, her traveling companion was engrossed in the *Wall Street Journal,* and so she closed her eyes. What an exciting adventure.

She felt flattered that Hilda had been so helpful and had taken so much time with her. Despite all the years that she'd been her mother's agent, Hilda had rarely talked to Chelsea without Laverne or Bunny being present, and Chelsea was surprised to find out what a warm, wonderful woman she was. They'd had great fun rummaging through Hilda's closets. The neat little Dior suit in navy-blue she was now wearing was Hilda's, as was the softly tailored pale blue Anne Klein suit she planned to wear to the meeting tomorrow, and the simple little black Adele Simpson cocktail dress Hilda had insisted she take in case she was invited to dinner. All were packed neatly in her mother's Vuitton suitcase, along with one pair of clean denims and cotton shirt and her own pleated skirt and only silk blouse.

She glanced down at the briefcase under the seat in front of Mr. Corell. All her hopes and dreams were packed in that case. Well, maybe not all. There was still Wills, and the life they would share. How wonderful it would be to live in London, to have children who would learn to ride at Ashford Hall on weekends and in the summer. They'd have a town house big enough so that she could have her atelier, where she could create beautiful things that perhaps Garrard's, the world's oldest and perhaps finest jewelers, might consider showing. For the first time in her life she saw the infinite possibilities stretching out before her, and she was inspired and happy and filled with hope.

In New York they checked into the Pierre Hotel, and Mr. Corell bid her good night.

"I would love to take you to dinner, my dear, but I already have plans, I'm afraid. There are a number of good places within walking distance, but if you're too tired to go out, room service here is excellent."

Chelsea was relieved. "I'll be just fine, Mr. Corell, and I'm much too tired to explore New York tonight, so I'm going to bed early."

"Good idea. I have a car picking us up at nine-thirty in the morning. Tanager's is actually less than a dozen blocks away, and although I prefer to walk, it's not a good idea to carry this bag of goodies. All right?"

"I'll be ready," Chelsea said, and followed the bellman to her room.

Once unpacked and undressed, Chelsea snapped on the television set to watch the news. Briefly she considered telephoning her grandmother to tell her where she was, but something told her not to call. Laverne would undoubtedly be annoyed that she had gone without telling her, and Chelsea didn't need any negative thinking in her life that night. What she needed was a light dinner and a long sleep, but first she wanted to look over some of her notes. Standing in front of the mirror, she began to say the words she had written and memorized.

"Until the nineteenth century, men were more important than women as buyers and wearers of jewels, but at the very time when gold prospectors were the busiest and discoveries were being made of huge new diamond resources, men ceased to wear jewels. At that time women came to be regarded more as the property of men than individuals in their own right. Therefore, a man's success could be proclaimed to the world by the amount of expensive baubles worn by his wife."

She stopped speaking and groaned. Oh God, this all seemed so school-teacherish. If she said things like that, they'd laugh at her, but she continued, hoping her little talk would get better as she got into it.

"Fashions and customs revolve in a never-ending cycle. Just as women are beginning to demand equal rights in the seventies, we now see men beginning to wear jewelry again, perhaps not yet here in New York, but in California men are wearing gold chains on their necks, diamond-encrusted watches, and identification bracelets."

Well, that was a little better, she thought, but still dull

and obvious. Frustrated, she tore up the paper, got a piece of hotel stationery and started to write again. Everything seemed too stilted and awkward. To hell with it all, she decided. She'd wing it.

In spite of her exhaustion, she was too excited and nervous to sleep soundly, and when the hotel operator called at eight the next morning, Chelsea was glad to get out of bed and get the day started. Corell came downstairs to find the pretty young woman already waiting for him, dressed smartly in a light blue suit that enhanced her eyes, her blond hair shining. Heeding Hilda's advice, she had tied her hair back with a ribbon, which made her look older.

"Well, young lady, you look very nice. Shall we go?"

Chelsea sat in the reception area outside the boardroom on the top floor of Tanager's with her portfolio of jewels and designs in her lap as she waited to be called into the meeting. She resolved to forget all the stuff she had planned to say and try to relax and be natural, but she was beginning to wonder if this great opportunity had not happened too soon. Another year or two of seasoning after graduation might have been better in the long run. She told herself that her whole career did not hinge on the coming meeting, but it didn't do anything to alleviate her anxieties.

At eleven-thirty a tall slender woman in a black suit opened the door and beckoned her into the boardroom. Gripping her wares in hands that suddenly began to quiver uncontrollably, she got to her feet uncertainly. Taking a deep breath, she went into the room.

To her surprise, the gentle Mr. Corell was sitting at the head of the conference table, apparently conducting the meeting. Was it possible that he had more influence than he'd led her to believe? The idea encouraged her.

"Sit down, Miss Hunter. We've saved a chair for you," he said, indicating an empty chair immediately to his left.

When she was settled, he wasted no time. "Now, I'd like for you to show my colleagues your designs and tell us how you think they might be of benefit to Tanager's."

Chelsea looked around the table of men. There was only one other woman in the room, and she was taking notes. Suddenly, she realized why Mr. Corell had been so doubtful. How was she, barely into her twenties, going to convince this group of mature men that she knew anything about selling jewelry?

"Gentlemen, I can't thank you enough for giving me a few minutes of your valuable time. Before I show you the things I've done, I hope you won't mind if I say a few words." Seeing that they were listening intently, she began. "Tanager's is an establishment that deals in the finest jewels, beautifully set, and that's great, but it also limits your customers to a very select few. It is my hope that you might consider developing a boutique line, a line of good jewelry that could be bought by younger people, those who are on the way up. Right now you've got a great opportunity to attract a whole new generation of buyers because costume jewelry is out of style. Everywhere you look, you see young girls and women wearing gold chains, very light and thin, but of real gold. And they are not necessarily waiting to get them as gifts. These women are buying real jewelry for themselves. It is for these potential customers that I've created my designs."

Quietly, she opened her portfolio and took out the gold bracelet and matching medallion and the series of pearl bracelets and handed them to the gentleman next to her for his inspection. She then took her drawings and handed them to Corell to pass around the room.

"The rose bracelet and medallion are from my 'Anytime a Rose' collection. The stones are tourmalines, and although I could have used rubies and emeralds, the quality of the design would not have been enhanced but the price would have made it prohibitive for my targeted buyers."

The man sitting across from her interrupted. "Miss Hunter, Tanager's deals only with precious stones. You're trying to sell us semiprecious stuff, which just isn't good enough."

Chelsea was delighted to be drawn into a debate. "There's more to jewelry than just precious stones. The artistry of the setting is just as important. Isn't it a shame that we've destroyed so many beautiful works of art from the Renaissance just to recover the precious stones to make more fashionable jewelry? Even now everybody has the diamond in Grandma's engagement ring reset, right? Suppose the canvases of Rembrandt had been recycled for younger painters to use?"

"What does that have to do with Tanager's, my dear?" Mr. Corell prompted, enjoying her perspicacity.

"Just this—that Tanager's ought to offer jewelry that is beautiful because of the design, and not necessarily because it's set with big rocks. The Art Nouveau movement recognized craftsmanship and brought the jewelry designer out of the ranks of anonymity, and I think that's the wave of the future. People are going to start buying jewelry the way they buy other art, by the name of the creator. Just in the last decade, important artists like Calder and Dali have turned their talents to making jewelry. The intrinsic value of their work lies in their design, not just in the amount of the gold or the diamonds."

"You put yourself in their class?" the portly gentleman at the end of the table asked, but Chelsea refused to be insulted.

"I consider myself both an artist and a craftsman, and while I may not yet be in 'their class,' remember that I have only just begun my career. I would hope the things I'm showing you will be the least of what I do, not the best."

The man holding the bracelet looked up from his examination and said, "Well, it's something I think we should consider. Frankly, I believe my daughter-in-law would love this bracelet. She hasn't had the diamond necklace I gave her as a wedding gift out of the vault since her wedding day. She says it doesn't go with any of her clothes."

Corell decided that was the thought on which to close the discussion.

"Thank you very much for your presentation, Miss Hunter. It has given us something to think about. If you'll be so kind as to leave your collection with us, I will see that it is well cared for. By the way, gentlemen, I learned on the plane that Miss Hunter is the daughter of Bunny Thomas, who has promised to begin wearing her designs in public. Isn't that interesting?"

Chelsea smiled and nodded her head demurely, acknowledging her tie to the famous star, amused that he had come up with the idea himself about her mother promoting her designs. Was it possible that, like Hilda, he understood the influence of star power?

She was out of the boardroom and on her way to the elevator when the woman who had been taking notes caught up with her.

"Miss Hunter, Mr. Corell asked me to tell you that he would like you to join him for dinner this evening, if you don't have other plans."

Chelsea was delighted. "Well, I'd love to."

"Fine, I'll tell him."

"What time?"

"Seven-thirty, I believe. The board members and their wives always get together when Mr. Corell is in town for a little dinner party. Tonight, Mr. Standish, the manager of the New York store, has invited everyone to his home."

Chelsea was startled. "You mean I'll be going there . . . with them?" she asked.

"Why, of course. Mr. Corell has to be there. The dinner is, after all, for him."

"Tell me," Chelsea said, lowering her voice, "just what is Mr. Corell's position in Tanager's?"

"He's the chairman of the board. Didn't you know?"

"No kidding? I thought he was just the manager of the Los Angeles store!"

"Well, yes, he's that too. You see, he was married to the granddaughter of the founder and chief stockholder in the company, and for years he was president and operating officer. Then when Mabel died ten years ago, he turned over the management of the company to Mr. Sells, stepped up to chairman of the board, and went out to

Los Angeles to be near his only daughter, who lives out there."

"Good grief, I guess I should have known that!"

"Not necessarily. It's a very closely held company, and he keeps an extremely low profile. He took over management of the store out there because . . . well, I better let him tell that story. Nice meeting you, Miss Hunter. Tell your mother I'm one of her biggest fans."

Chelsea spent the afternoon walking along Fifth Avenue, looking in the shops, checking out Harry Winston's, Tiffany's, and Cartier's. She walked all the way down to Forty-seventh Street and browsed through some of the little shops and stands in the diamond district. Amid the bewildering displays of gold and platinum and jewels, it was hard to believe in the rarity of the product when there was such an abundance of it in that one long block.

Posing as a potential buyer of a diamond engagement ring allowed her to listen to the pitches of the salesmen, which she found hilarious. With absolutely straight faces they showed her gems that were big but of inferior color and cut and filled with flaws, "crushed ice" as they were known in the trade. In one store she was intrigued by the uniformly gray color in every one of their stones of more than three carats. They were of decent cut and comparatively free of flaws, but she was almost certain that if they were dipped in ethyl alcohol, they would suddenly revert to their natural yellow color, not deep enough to be valued as "canary" diamonds, but too off-color to be worth a fraction of the asking price. She had read about painted stones, and she was certain that was what she was trying on. When it came to diamonds, the best advice was caveat emptor, let the buyer beware.

She had intended to call Laverne when she returned to her hotel room, but it was almost six when she got back, and she needed time to dress. Now that she knew the power of her mentor, she was more assured than ever. This was going to be an interesting evening.

55

Okay, you're outta here," the guard said as he opened the door of Sergio's cell.

"Whattya mean?" Sergio asked, getting to his feet and quickly exiting the place where he had been jailed for almost twenty-four hours.

"Your lawyer bailed you out. He's waitin' for you out front."

"I don't have a lawyer," Sergio said suspiciously.

"Well, you got one now," the guard said, opening the door and indicating a tall, thin young man nattily dressed in a dark blue pinstriped Armani suit.

Sergio walked over to him with his hand outstretched, but the young man pointedly ignored it. Rebuffed, Sergio said, "Who hired you?"

The man hesitated briefly, looked around him, then said softly, "The court appointed me since you had no representation."

"So, who put up the bail?"

The young man smiled. "Uh, a friend of yours. He's outside waiting to speak to you," he said, opening the door and waiting for Sergio to go first. A long black Lincoln limousine was parked at the curb.

Sergio asked, "Is that him in there?"

The young man nodded.

The chauffeur opened the door and smiled. Sergio should have been suspicious, but he was unduly impressed with the trappings of power and money, and so he got into the car. Immediately he was pulled into the backseat between two burly men, one of whom said, "Let's go."

The door was banged closed and locked. As the car sped off, Sergio realized he was in trouble.

"Who're you?"

"We work for a man who wants to talk to you. You've got something he needs."

"Who do you work for? Sandy Shapiro?"

The man with the ugly scar across his cheek narrowed his eyes and said, "Who's he?"

"Well, if you don't work for Sandy Shapiro, then you must work for my wife."

"I don't work for no woman, I can tell you that, punk," the other man said. Sergio looked up at the man's weather-beaten face, partially hidden by dark glasses, and the lips stretched out in a cobra smile.

"Then who the hell do you work for?"

"He'll tell you himself. So relax, punk. It's a long drive."

For the remainder of the ride neither man deigned to respond to any more questions. The limousine drove up the San Diego Freeway and exited in the north valley. Sergio tried to keep track of where they were taking him, but the area was unfamiliar and he was completely lost when they entered an area of wilderness. Driving up a long dirt road, they came to a chain-link gate. The driver got out, put a key in the padlock and opened the gate. Back in the car, he drove past the gate, then got out once more to lock it behind him. By then Sergio had grown extremely nervous.

"Listen, you guys, you could go to jail for this. This is kidnapping."

"You wanta go back to jail, punk? Just say so, and we'll take you back, okay? Nobody's makin' you do nothin', understand?"

After a drive up a narrow and rocky road, the car stopped at a small, commercial building and they hustled Sergio out.

"The man you want to talk to is inside," the ruffian with the sunglasses said. "We'll wait for ya out here." He leaned against the car and lit a cigarette.

His apprehension building, Sergio opened the door and went into a room that looked like a small field office. Behind the desk, talking on the telephone, was a dark man with slicked-back black hair and a mustache. He too wore dark glasses. Motioning to Sergio to sit down in the chair in front of the desk, he continued his conversation.

"Sorry, friend," the man said, "but we made a deal. I

don't give a shit if the contract's signed or not, you gave me your word, and I'll hold you to it."

He listened for another few moments and then said angrily, "Listen, you asshole, nobody fucks around with Sy Christman, understand? As far as I'm concerned, we got a deal, and that's it. The contracts will be on your desk at three this afternoon, and I want them back on mine at five o'clock . . . signed!" With that he slammed down the receiver. Without even looking at Sergio, he jumped out of his chair and ran to the door.

"Blades, get your ass in here!" he called.

The man with the sunglasses hurried toward him. Standing at the door, the two men had a conversation too low to be heard. Sergio was awed to be in the presence of the powerful and legendary Sy Christman. He owned one of the biggest recording companies in the industry, and it was rumored he was backed by the mob.

Their conversation ended, Blades left again, and the mustached man with slicked-back hair returned to his desk.

"Now, we have some business to discuss. I understand you've got a diary kept by my old friend, Hilda Marx. I want that diary, and I want it today." There was about as much warmth and friendliness in his tone of voice as one might expect from a talking rattlesnake.

"Uh, what makes you think I've got it?" Sergio asked, startled.

"You threatened to make it public, and she was just doing an old friend a favor. You know that's what this business is about—making friends . . . and enemies. And you gotta always make sure that your friends are more powerful than your enemies." There was more than a hint of menace in his tone.

Sergio was confused. "Why would she tell you?"

"Because she's smart. Maybe she shouldn't have put some of those things down in her book, but she had the brains to figure a way out. So she called me, and now we're in this together. And you, friend, are the enemy. So . . . how much?"

"A hundred grand?" Sergio asked boldly. "That's peanuts to you."

The man laughed out loud, then, leaning closer to Sergio, he said, "A hundred grand is not peanuts to me . . . but your life is worth nothing to me. Ten grand, take it or leave it."

Sergio never knew when to quit. "Why should I take ten grand from you when my wife offered me more?"

"Your mistake. You should have taken it before she told me. It was worth more then. We gotta deal?"

"That's highway robbery."

The man laughed. "You oughta know, buster."

"Okay," Sergio said reluctantly, "but I—"

The man got to his feet. "Good. Blades will take you to wherever you've got it stashed. When you give it to him, he'll give you the cash."

Sergio tried to delay. "Uh, well, why don't I bring it to you tomorrow?"

"And give you a chance to shop around? You must think I'm stupid. It's today or never, but then . . . if you decided to do something that dumb, I'd be very upset, and I'd really be your enemy, wouldn't I?" His words were laced heavily with threat.

Intimidated, Sergio capitulated.

"I'll get it in cash? What about Hilda? Is she still going to—"

"Buster, what goes on between you and your wife is none of my business. Although I did promise to retrieve her jewelry . . . as a gesture of goodwill, you know, for coming clean and calling me. So give the jewelry to Blades too, will you?"

Stung, Sergio protested, "That wasn't part of the deal!"

The man smiled. "It was if I say it was . . . and I say it was. Good-bye." He edged Sergio out the door.

Immediately, the two husky men hustled Sergio into the car. Just as they were about to drive away, the man called from the doorway, "Make him sign a receipt for the dough!"

*   *   *

At five o'clock Hilda picked up the telephone in her office to take Sandy Shapiro's call.

"Just like you thought, we got it cheaper," he announced with a laugh.

"You sure it's the right one?" she asked, but there was no mistaking the joy and relief in her voice.

"Yeah, yeah, I paged through it and it's definitely the right one. You mind if I read the damned thing before I burn it!"

"Be my guest, but I want to be the one who lights the match."

"Let's do it over dinner tonight at your place. I would really enjoy one of Emma's baked Alaskas. Say about eight o'clock? Mind if I bring Junior?"

"Terrific. I want to hear everything."

Sandy didn't arrive at Hilda's home until almost eight-thirty, and she opened the door to welcome him and his son, Sanford Shapiro, Jr.

"Sorry we're late, but I was reading this great potboiler and I couldn't put it down. Here it is, sweetheart. Don't say I never gave you anything."

Taking the diary, Hilda put her arms around Sandy, hugged him, and gave him a big kiss on the cheek.

"Hey, how about me?" asked the tall, dark man, who looked to be in his early forties. Hilda laughed and kissed him on the cheek too.

Sandy handed her the package he was carrying. "The jewelry's in there too."

"You got my jewelry back?" she asked, clearly delighted.

"Yeah, that was my idea," Sanford Jr. replied. "When it was obvious that I had him on the ropes, I figured, what the hell? He stole it, didn't he?"

"He's a law and order man, didn't I tell you? He keeps threatening to vote Republican," Sandy chortled proudly.

With glasses of Dom Pérignon, they toasted success, and Hilda asked for details.

"Well, the actors you got to play the hoods were terrific. They worked for scale, but I gave them each twice that, because they were so convincing," Sandy said. "I told 'em that if they ever needed an agent, to call you. I briefed them on exactly what to do and say so they would in no way be in violation of the law, in case that jerk ever wises up and realizes he's been had."

"Yep, we were very careful. I never once told him that I was Sy Christman. I just let him put two and two together," Sanford said. "Incidentally, that makeup artist was terrific. He used a wig and mustache and darkened my skin. I didn't even recognize myself."

"Good thing Sy Christman never lets himself be photographed. He's small and wiry and has bushy white hair," Hilda remarked. "And Sanford, I can't thank you enough for volunteering to do this. I would hate to have hired some actor I didn't know to get involved in this mess."

"He loved it," Sandy said.

Sanford laughed. "He's right. I wanted to be an actor, but Dad wouldn't let me. He made me go to law school."

"And aren't you glad he did?"

"Well, I was until today," and then with a mischievous twinkle in his eye, he added, "but I really got into that part this afternoon, and now I'm wondering if maybe I might not have been destined to be another Brando."

"That diary's evil. Let's burn the damned thing and be done with it, before it causes any more trouble," Sandy suggested.

"There's the fireplace. Let's tear out the pages and go to it," Hilda said.

As they watched the pages curling and crackling in the flames, Sandy softly quoted the words of Omar Khayyam, " 'The moving finger writes, and having writ moves on. Nor all your piety nor wit, Shall lure it back to cancel half a line.' "

Picking up the verse, Hilda finished it solemnly and softly, " 'Nor all your tears wash out a word of it.' "

There was a long silence, which Hilda broke with a deep sigh. "It's hard for me to believe it's finished. Sergio read that damned thing, and he's dangerously stupid. I'll bet I haven't heard the last of him."

"Call off the deal with Chelli. Let that dumb jerk go to jail for what he did to him," Sandy said vehemently, but Hilda shook her head.

"That's not fair to Chelli. I'm buying him the Rolls-Royce anyway, but with no strings attached. If he wants to go after Sergio for assault, that's his affair."

"God, I wish you'd never married that jerk," Sandy said.

Hilda led the way to the dining room in her starkly modern and beautiful home.

"It was worth it for a while, Sandy. Too bad I have a tendency to choose men who don't know the difference between roses and poison ivy."

56

Much to Chelsea's surprise, the dinner party with the board members of Tanager's turned out to be an amazing success for her. Several of the older men had wives who were close to her own age, and the women were friendly and appreciative of her "Anytime a Rose" bracelet. Mr. Corell, thoughtfully, had brought it back to the hotel for her to wear that evening. Having been raised in a household where her grandmother had often given elaborate dinner parties, her attendance at which had been de rigueur, she was socially at ease among the affluent New Yorkers. They were all intrigued by her relationship to a superstar.

Mr. Corell, who had suggested in the limousine that she drop the Mister and begin calling him Jonathan, was an attentive and gracious escort. For the first time since her visits to Ashford Hall as a young girl, Chelsea found herself the center of attention, and she liked it immensely.

Although she preferred to believe everyone was deferential because of her talent and persuasiveness, she was realistic enough to suspect they were probably just following Jonathan Corell's lead. He made it quite evident that he wanted her to enjoy herself, and he stayed at her side constantly, encouraging her to talk, delighting in her thoughtful discussion of jewelry.

It was not until they were returning to the hotel, however, that he gave her the news she had been so eagerly anticipating.

"My dear Chelsea, I suppose you've guessed by now that you've endeared yourself to everyone at Tanager's."

Two glasses of champagne and a sense of triumphant euphoria brought a response that was more flip than she intended. "Do you mean they liked my smile or they admired my work?"

Far from being offended, Corell laughed out loud. "My God, you're a cheeky young lady. I meant that everyone liked not only what you've created with your own two pretty little hands, but they were impressed with your suggestions."

Chelsea felt her cheeks burn and her blood began to throb at her temples. "Oh, Mister . . . Jonathan, that's wonderful!"

"Indeed, and we want you to work exclusively for us, my dear, in the Los Angeles office."

"Designing?" she asked timidly.

"Naturally. However, I must warn you that there are strings attached to the proposition. Nothing ever comes free in this world, you know, but I believe that there's nothing you couldn't live with comfortably. We do, after all, want you to be happy."

"What kind of strings?" she asked dubiously.

"First of all, we've decided to reopen our jewelry workroom on the coast. We closed it three years ago, but that, I've decided, was a mistake. We tried sending things back and forth across country, but customers of Tanager's were not being served as well or as promptly as they desired, and so we have taken to contracting with local jewelers for repairs, sizing and such. Unfortunately, the results have been mixed at best."

"And that's where you'll want me to work?" she asked.

"Not exactly. We have an entire floor that's empty in the building, and I am considering carving out a space to serve as your design studio. The laboratory will be staffed with the best goldsmith from our Paris store as well as a skilled gem setter from New York. These men will take your designs and execute them for you. Someone as creative as you should not waste her time doing the actual work."

"It sounds terrific," she said, impressed by the completeness of the plan.

"Yes, but here's the rub, my dear. Everything you design will be the sole property of Tanager's."

"That's only fair," she commented, wondering where the catch was in the arrangement.

"I'm glad you feel that way. When the pieces are finished, they will be marketed under your name, which we intend to promote heavily. You will be a star, my child, but . . ." and he paused dramatically, "in return, you must sign an exclusive ten-year contract with us. Everything you design during that time becomes our property in perpetuity."

So that was it. Ten years! How could she commit herself for that long a period? In less than two years she would be married to Wills and living in London. She slumped back into the seat to deal with the possibilities.

Corell patted her hand and tried to reassure her.

"It is a long time, my dear. A very long time, but it would not be feasible for us to embark on such an adventure unless we could be assured of enough time to make it work. How old are you now?"

"Almost twenty-three," she murmured, looking out the window, deep in thought.

He chuckled softly. "You'll still be very young when the contract is ended, but I predict you will be one of the world's great names by then. It's a golden opportunity, my dear, but you should take your time about making a decision. I want you to go home and think about it carefully. There's no rush."

Chelsea turned to look at this stranger who had become her friend and advocate, and smiled. "You're one of the nicest men I've ever met in my entire life. Why are you doing this for me?"

"Because I like you? Yes, absolutely. You've made me feel young and hopeful and excited about doing something new and different. But that's not the reason, my lovely child. I'm doing it primarily because I believe Tanager's can make a lot of money from you and your ideas, and that, as they say, is the bottom line. The board feels the same way."

Corell walked her to her room, took her key and opened the door for her.

"Thank you for a lovely evening, Mister . . . Jonathan. It was the best—almost the best—night of my life. No matter what happens in the future, I'll never forget it." She reached up and kissed him on the cheek.

"The pleasure was all mine, my dear. Our plane leaves at ten-thirty, so the car will pick us up here at eight-thirty. Good night. Sleep well."

As he turned and headed back to the elevator, she admired the straight way he walked. He was so assured and yet so gentle. Next to Wills, she liked him more than any other man she had ever met, and she hated the fact that she was going to have to say no to his generous offer. She was just going to have to find some other way to get her career started.

57

Mike Stern found the relationship Bunny had formed with her young makeup man to be very strange, but he was not about to complain. Every actor he had ever met had his own idiosyncratic way of getting up for a role, and if it worked, he couldn't care less how it happened. Bunny was giving a brilliant performance, and that was all that mattered.

When she walked on the set the next morning, he caught her eye and they both smiled at the memory. He was glad she suffered little or no embarrassment at being caught with Fernando, and he wondered if he would have as much poise as she had if the reverse had happened.

Filming went smoothly. Bunny hit all her marks and her cues exactly right. In fact, she was so thoroughly into her character's skin that Mike gave her a greater latitude in her interpretation than was his usual custom. Several times he found himself watching the scene as a fascinated spectator rather than as the director. Given her freedom, Bunny took off like a rocket, sweeping her co-star along for the ride.

Things were going so well that Mike would have continued without breaking, but union rules prevailed, and they called lunch at two-thirty. He took Bunny aside to talk to her privately.

"Sweetheart, you were sensational this morning. I don't want you to change anything about Annabel in the next scene. It's going to be tough, because every single little movement has to be done exactly right so nobody gets hurt, understand?"

Bunny nodded, but it was apparent that she wasn't paying attention. Her mind seemed to be on something else, because she kept looking around as he spoke, avoiding most eye contact.

"Listen to me closely, Bunny. What I said is extremely important. In fact, I think we should rehearse it once or twice before we shoot it, don't you?" he asked forcefully, demanding a response.

"No, Mike," she responded, "I'll walk through the motions once, then you better shoot it. I want to give it everything I've got, and I'm not sure I can work up to the intensity of the kill more than once. I don't want to hold back anything for a second or third take."

They stood and looked at each other while Mike considered her approach. At last he nodded. "Okay, babe. We'll do it your way. Now go on back to your dressing room and take it easy for a while. If we get this scene in the can today, we're home free." He patted her on the arm and turned his attention to the assistant director, who was waiting to talk to him.

When Bunny returned to her dressing room, she was annoyed to find it empty. This was her big day. Where in the hell was her mother? Unaccustomed to being alone, she sank down on the couch, lit a cigarette, and dialed her home number, only to learn from the butler that he had not seen Laverne since early in the morning.

"My daughter's not there by any chance, is she?" Bunny asked. Although Clark knew that Chelsea had gone to New York, he revealed nothing, wisely deciding that if Laverne hadn't told Bunny, it was certainly not his place to do so.

"She's not home either, ma'am."

Slamming down the telephone, Bunny turned on the television. She was emotionally keyed-up and restless. After five minutes she got to her feet and began to pace. She called makeup, asked for Fernando, and was irritated to learn he'd taken the afternoon off.

"Debbie, his assistant, is here. Would you like us to send her over?" the man asked.

"No," Bunny snapped, slamming down the telephone. "Not unless she's got a hard-on," she added bitterly.

The star was back on the set ten minutes before the end of lunch break. Like a racehorse at the starting gate, she was anxious to get going.

Fernando's assistant arrived carrying a comb and a bottle of water mixed with glycerin to spray on the actors' faces to simulate perspiration just before the filming began. The gaffers drifted back to check the lights, and Mike, holding a cup of coffee in his hand, was in deep discussion with his cinematographer. The property master arrived carrying a butcher knife.

"Is that the real one?" Bunny asked, but her co-star,

Mel Holland, who was right behind her, said, "God, I hope not."

"Yes, Miss Thomas, this is the real thing."

"Whoa!" Holland protested. "Mike said we were going to use the rubber one and he'd do an insert with the real one. It's too risky to have her holding a steel blade while we're rasslin'."

Bunny, who took the comment as an insult, snapped back at him, "For God's sake, I'm not going to stab you. If you're unfortunate enough to get hurt, it will be because you made the mistake yourself. It won't be my fault."

"Uh, easy for you to say. You're the one holdin' the knife. Mike!" he called, turning away from her and striding to the director to register his protest.

Bunny raised her eyebrows and looked around for support, but everyone avoided eye contact with her. As the filming had progressed, she and her co-star had carried their escalating on-screen hostilities into their relationship off-screen, and Bunny's recent reference to Holland as a "muscle-bound queen" had not gone down well with the crew. Mel Holland was a handsome and popular star, a good actor, and well-liked by people in the industry. Although it was generally known that he was homosexual, few people ever mentioned it.

After a few minutes of discussion, Mike led Holland back to where Bunny was waiting. "Come on, Mel. Bunny needs to hear this."

"Bunny, dear, Mel is worried that you might hurt him, but I've assured him there is no danger. So, let's walk through the scene once, show him exactly how you're going to handle the weapon and let him see that everything's okay."

Bunny let her eyes travel slowly from the middle of Mel's chest, her eye level, up to his face, and she replied mockingly, "Why would a great big 'man' like you worry about little old me? You're twice my size."

"Yeah, I'm a lot bigger'n a rattlesnake too, but I

wouldn't rassle one a them either," he said, his normally kind eyes filled with distaste.

Mike made no attempt to ameliorate their animosity, because he hoped it would transfer to the screen.

"Okay, take your marks. Keep that eyelight on her all of the time," he ordered the gaffer.

Once Bunny and Mel were ready, Mike gave them a quick refresher.

"Mel, right after you shout your line at her, she turns away from you, but you grab her shoulder roughly and pull her around to face you. Pull your arm real far back when you swing at her, okay? The audience needs to see how badly you want to hurt her."

"I'll make it look good," Mel replied seriously.

"After he hits you, Bunny, pop your head back hard and fast, recover, and then stagger to the kitchen counter where the knife is lying, then turn around slowly and face him. As he moves menacingly toward you, you grasp the knife with your left hand behind your back. Look up at him, and with your right hand pull open your blouse and expose your breast. Don't lose eye contact with him for a moment. Open your mouth sensually, lick your lips, and let your knees start to buckle so you'll begin to sink toward the floor. Mel, don't react too fast. Violence and sex are already mixed up in your mind, but you've still got to give it time for your anger to develop into lust. Let it ripen slowly, let the camera see it happen. Okay?"

"Got it, Mike."

"That goes for you too, Bunny. With you it's love gone to hate, but don't cross over the line from passive submission to violent action too quickly. Submit to his embrace, let the audience think that sex will conquer all, then let him have it. Stop the knife, however, as soon as it touches him, understand? At that point, we'll cut to an insert, okay?"

They walked through the scene perfectly, and when it was over, Mike said it was fine and told his actors to get a final once-over by the makeup people. Casually, however, he strolled over to the camera where his A.D. was standing and said sotto voce, "I want you to call a delay. Say there's something wrong with the camera, then get Mel into wardrobe without letting Bunny know what's going on. Have them put one of those bulletproof vests on him. Bunny's acting strangely aggressive. I just don't want her getting carried away with this scene and inadvertently hurting somebody."

"Jesus, Mike, it'll show under that cotton shirt of his, won't it?"

"Put it on 'im and let me take a look."

An hour and a half later they were ready for the scene. Wardrobe had taped a stuntman's protective vest to Mel's back so there would be no bulk visible from the front. Mike compensated by changing the camera angle slightly, and they were ready to go.

"Thanks, pal," Mel said as he passed the director on his way to his mark.

By this time Laverne was back on the set to soothe and comfort her daughter's irritation with everyone in the entire world. When the cameras rolled, however, true to her promise, Bunny gave it everything she had. She was by turns browbeaten, sensual, angry, murderous. When she at last delivered the deadly blow to her violent lover, she was Annabel, pushed beyond the level of endurance. Fortunately, her submersion in the character stopped at the exact moment the point of the knife touched Mel's shirt and went no deeper.

There was a hush on the set after Mike said "Cut!" and then the entire crew, which had been holding its collective breath, exhaled and applauded appreciatively.

"Print it," Mike said, and pronounced the take perfect. He walked over to his actors and said, "That was just superb. It couldn't have been better. Every jaded person here was caught up in the scene emotionally. It was dynamite. I wish I didn't have to ask you to do it again for close-ups, but I think we should keep on till we finish today. I don't want to let your feelings go cold overnight, all right?"

Emotionally exhausted, both stars just nodded, and Laverne led Bunny back to her dressing room.

"Boy, she's really somethin'," Mel said admiringly. "We were both wrong about her, weren't we?"

"Maybe," Mike said enigmatically. "But keep the thing on till we're finished for the day."

"What for? It's scratchin' the hell out of my back."

"Please, Mel. Just do as I say," Mike insisted.

58

The limousine dropped Chelsea off at home at about five o'clock, and she was delighted to find that three more roses had arrived in her absence. The maid had put them in a vase on her bedside table along with a letter from her darling Wills. She sank down on the bed to read it, and she found her cheeks growing hot as she read his rather explicit words of love. Wills was apparently suffering from the separation even more than she was, and she was both surprised and thrilled that he was able to be so unrestrained. She was not sure that she could have written such an erotic love letter, although she certainly had the feelings to match his words.

The letter contained other important information too. Wills had told his parents of his engagement to Chelsea, and much to his and Margaret's relief, they had accepted his decision, but only on the provision that he finish school first. He, of course, had assured them that he intended to do just that, and he closed with words of his undying love and longing for her. Chelsea went to her desk to answer the letter, feeling guilty for having been too busy with her work to write sooner. She needed to respond to him and tell him that she loved him more than anything in the world and that the hours she had spent with him had been the most beautiful of her entire life.

She was still struggling for words to match Wills's ardor, and trying to find a tactful way to explain the offer from Tanager's as well, when there was a soft knock at her door. Clark, the butler, announced with unmistakable distaste, "Miss Chelsea, your mother's young friend is downstairs. I told him that both your mother and grandmother had not yet returned, but he insists on waiting. What would you like me to do?"

"Is it Fernando?" Chelsea asked, making a face.

"I'm afraid so," he said with a pained expression.

"Tell him to wait in the living room, Clark. They should be home in an hour or so, and for God's sake don't tell him I'm here, or he'll insist on talking to me."

"Well . . ." He hesitated.

"What's wrong?" she asked impatiently, anxious to go back to her letter.

"Your grandmother gave me strict instructions never to leave him in the house unattended. She's afraid he might steal something."

"Damn. Well, then tell—no, I'll go downstairs and tell him myself. Thanks, Clark. I'll get rid of him."

Without bothering to put her shoes back on, Chelsea hurried down the stairs.

Fernando was standing in the entry hall examining the antique grandfather clock.

"Hi, beautiful," he said with a smile. "This is some clock. I bet it's worth a fortune."

"I wouldn't know. It was here when we moved in. How come you're not on the set?" she asked suspiciously.

"I took the afternoon off. I had some business to take care of. They must be workin' overtime, huh? Just my luck to miss out on it. I coulda used the extra dough."

Ignoring his attempts to draw her into a conversation, she approached the situation forthrightly. "I haven't got the slightest idea what time Mom will be home. I just got back in town myself, and I haven't seen anybody here in three days. I really don't think you ought to wait. Mom will be extremely tired when she gets home after working so long. Perhaps you just ought to plan on seeing her tomorrow on the set," she said, retreating a step as he moved uncomfortably close to her.

He smiled in his usual oily manner, and she noted with revulsion that there was a piece of yellow food stuck between his two front teeth. "S'okay. I'll wait. I've got business with the old lady too, and time passes fast when there's a pretty young girl like you to talk to. How about we go in the other room and have Clark bring us a little of your mom's champagne? I'll bet you love champagne," he replied, lowering his eyes and giving her his significantly sexual look.

God, he was disgusting, Chelsea thought. How in the world could her mother get involved with such a jerk?

"I don't have time," she snapped frostily. "I've got classes tomorrow and a lot of work to catch up on, so you better go now." Her tone was cross and forceful, for this was a man on whom subtleties would be wasted.

He reached for her hand, but she pulled away at the first moment of contact.

"Come on, don't be such a party pooper. Let your hair down and have a little fun for a change. You're too uptight."

"Look, I'm not interested in spending any time with you, understand? Now leave, or I'll call Clark and have him throw you out!"

Her angry ultimatum was still hanging in the air when Bunny and Laverne suddenly walked into the hallway, having entered the house through the garage.

"Well, you're finally back, young lady," Laverne said, deliberately ignoring Fernando's presence. "Come up to my room. We need to have a little talk." Brushing past the visitor as if he didn't exist, she started up the stairs with Chelsea beside her, but Fernando protested loudly.

"Wait a minute! You and I have business to discuss—private business, Mrs. Thomas," he said.

Laverne turned and snarled at him, "I have nothing more to say to you ever! Bunny, get him out of this house. Immediately!" Now that Bunny's performance was essentially finished on the picture, there was no need for his services any longer, and Laverne didn't intend to give him any more money. Taking Chelsea's arm, she proceeded up the stairs. She had much more important things on her mind than that lecherous little vermin downstairs.

Bunny was amazingly calm, however, and if Laverne and Chelsea hadn't been so absorbed by their own concerns, they might have noted her unusual behavior. Bunny had *never* been an island of reason in a tumultuous sea of emotions. Smiling glassily at the man who had bedded her so often and so well, she took his arm and steered him forcefully into the library. "Come on, Fernando. My mother's just tired. Let's have a nice quiet drink all by ourselves. By the way, where were you today? I was counting on you to be there for my big scene," she said smoothly, closing the door firmly behind them.

Chelsea might have wondered what Fernando had to discuss with her grandmother, had she not been so preoccupied with her own problems. How in the world was she going to explain her trip to New York without also revealing the offer from Tanager's? There was certainly no point in telling her grandmother about that, since she was going to turn it down anyway because of Wills's proposal. But she was not yet ready to reveal that particular plan to her family. She needn't have worried, however, for Laverne had little interest in her granddaughter's affairs at the moment. Her own problems were far too pressing.

Chelsea sat down on the satin chaise longue in her grandmother's room and listened attentively, managing as usual to thrust her own concerns to the back of her mind.

"Chelsea, there's something we need to discuss. I went to the doctor this morning, and . . . well, I'm going into the hospital in a couple of days."

"What's wrong, Gran?" she asked with alarm.

Laverne sank down on the bed and put her face in her

hands. "They think it's cancer. I have these lumps in both my breasts, and it's not certain, but he thinks it's pretty advanced."

"Oh my God, Gran, I'm so sorry!" Chelsea moved toward her grandmother and, putting her arms around her thin body, held her, while Laverne allowed herself to weep at last. Crying did not come easily to her, and unlike Bunny's emotional storms, Laverne's was intense but brief. When she had herself in control again, she wiped her eyes and they began to talk quietly.

"I have a feeling that the next few months may be very difficult for all of us. I just don't know how Bunny's going to make it without me," Laverne said morosely.

"She's going to be fine, Gran. Mom's stronger than you think she is. When are you going to tell her?"

Laverne took her granddaughter's hand and said, "I don't want her to know what it's all about, and I need your help in keeping her reassured that nothing's seriously wrong."

"But Gran, you're going in the hospital. What are you going to tell her?"

"I'm going to tell her that it's minor surgery and I'll be out in a day or two. Promise you'll help me convince her of that," she urged.

Chelsea objected strenuously. "No, Gran. It's not right. If it turns out to be really bad, then it'll make things even harder for her to accept. I think you should tell her the truth now so she'll have a chance to get used to it while there's still hope. We're a family, and we'll fight this thing through together."

"No, no. You and I are strong, and we can handle it. Bunny isn't . . ." Her words trailed away as her thoughts turned to the real question. Was it possible that she was going to die and the world would go on without her?

The two women sat quietly for a long time, silently assessing their futures, both contemplating life without Laverne. Then Chelsea realized what her grandmother wanted from her. Laverne fully expected her to step in and take her place as Bunny's guardian and keeper. The idea was overwhelming. How in the world could she do it without sacrificing everything that was important to her?

Although she was wrapped in her own worries, Laverne suddenly picked up a danger signal; either it was the sound of her daughter in distress or merely the force of her own intuition, but she leaped to her feet and started for the door.

"I better go downstairs and see what's going on. I should never have left Bunny alone with that creep."

Having heard nothing, but sensing her grandmother's worry, Chelsea got up to follow her.

"No, it's not necessary to go with me, Chelsea," she said. "I can handle that jerk. Go on back to your room. After I've gotten Bunny to bed, we'll talk some more."

"You want me to call Clark?" Chelsea asked.

"Not yet. I don't like to get him involved in family matters unless it's absolutely necessary. Butlers like him are hard to find, and I can't afford to lose him now."

Bunny followed her grandmother to the head of the stairs and watched as she hurried down to the library. Something told her to follow, but the prospect of talking to the odious Fernando stopped her, and she turned back to finish her letter to Wills and get ready for bed. Deciding that perhaps a warm shower might steady her nerves, she undressed, turned on the water, and stepped in.

As she stood under the cascade of warmth, she tried to relax, but the shattering news she'd received from Laverne prevented that luxury. Her life was beginning to break up into little pieces. She had a lover and prospective husband to consider, a career that looked to be detoured because of him, and now, a grandmother who expected her to assume a responsibility for which she had no inclination. Come on now, she tried to reason. Mom was an adult. Surely she didn't need her daughter to arrange her life for her as Gran had.

Suddenly she was overwhelmed with guilt. How could she be so consumed with herself when her grandmother might be facing death?

Disgusted, she turned off the water and stepped out of the shower to dry herself. It was comforting to rub her skin briskly with the thick terry-cloth towel, and when she was dry, she combed out her wet hair and put on her pajamas and robe. As she was brushing her teeth, she heard a knock at the bathroom door. She opened it to find her grandmother standing there ashen-faced.

"Chelsea, you must call the police. There's been a terrible accident . . ." she said, in a voice so muted it was almost inaudible.

"Accident? What kind of accident? Is Mom okay?" Chelsea asked anxiously.

"I—I— Come downstairs with me," the older woman said, and turned abruptly. Chelsea followed her down the stairs. The library door was closed, and Laverne hesitated before opening it.

"Brace yourself, Chelsea," she murmured, and turned the knob.

Suddenly Chelsea didn't want to go into the room, sensing that whatever was in there was going to change her life forever, but she followed her grandmother anyway and stepped in to find her worst nightmare come true.

Bunny was sitting on the leather chair in front of the fireplace, gazing beatifically at the figure of Fernando, who was lying at her feet with the silver letter opener sunk to the hilt in his heart. His eyes were wide with astonishment that death had claimed him so swiftly and unexpectedly.

"My God!" Chelsea gasped. "Is he dead?"

Bunny looked up and smiled. "Was that a print, Mike? Did I do it right?" she asked sweetly.

For a long, long moment the three women were frozen in a tableau vivant so grisly it might have been staged by Hitchcock, and then Laverne spoke, ignoring her daughter's words. "I'm not sure, Chelsea. Maybe you ought to check."

Carefully, Chelsea knelt beside the body, trying to avoid looking at his open, staring eyes. She had never seen a dead person, much less touched one, but she forced herself to take his wrist and feel for his pulse. Backing away, she said, "He's dead, Gran. What the hell happened?"

Laverne chose her words carefully, and as calm and reasoned as they were, they did not ring true. "As you know, I sensed that Bunny was in trouble," her grandmother began, "and I came downstairs and found him with his hands around her throat. I tried to pull him away, but he was like a madman and wouldn't let go. He kicked at me and knocked me to the ground. I was scrambling as fast as I could to get to my feet when I saw the letter opener on the desk and I grabbed it to defend myself . . . But he's much stronger than I am, you know, and I can't tell you exactly what happened then, only that suddenly he was on the floor . . . like that."

"You . . . killed him, Gran?"

"I . . . yes, I must have," she said softly, her eyes fixed on her daughter's face.

It didn't make any sense. "Why was he trying to kill her, Gran?" Chelsea asked.

"I don't know. Maybe she was trying to get rid of him. He was becoming a terrible nuisance."

Chelsea turned to her mother. "Mom, are you okay?"

Her mother smiled and said, "Fine, honey. Tell Mel he can get up now. The camera's not rolling anymore."

"Mel?" Chelsea asked in bewilderment.

"He's her co-star. I think she's in shock. She doesn't seem to understand what happened," Laverne said. "Call the police, Chelsea. We mustn't wait too long or they might become suspicious."

"Suspicious of what, Gran?" Chelsea asked, moving gingerly past Fernando's body to get to the telephone.

"Oh . . . I don't know. Anything. You know how police are," she said vaguely, sitting down on the couch and putting her arm across Bunny's shoulders.

Chelsea picked up the telephone and then put it back down. She wanted to believe her grandmother's story but it was just too pat, too contrived. She sighed and turned to her grandmother for one last measure of reassurance. "Gran, are you certain this is the story you want to tell?" she asked softly. "You can't change your mind once you've made a statement to the police, you know."

"That's my story, and I'm stuck with it, I'm afraid," Laverne replied.

Chelsea stared at the vacant-eyed expression on her mother's face. Nothing made complete sense to her, but she picked up the telephone and asked the operator to connect her with the police. If she had trouble believing her grandmother's account of what happened, wouldn't they have trouble with it too?

59

The place was soon swarming with uniformed policemen, plainclothes detectives, men taking pictures and dusting for fingerprints. Chelsea sat in a corner, her arm around her mother, who was curled up against her shoulder, sleeping soundly.

Across the room Laverne was giving her statement to the detective, and Chelsea was scheduled to be questioned next. She was worried that her own story would sound as fabricated and phony as her grandmother's.

Suddenly the door opened and Hilda Marx sailed into the room with an older man right behind her. When she saw that Laverne was occupied, she went directly to Chelsea.

"Thank God you called me right away. I went by and picked up Sandy. Is Laverne talking to police without a lawyer present?"

Chelsea nodded mutely, wondering why she hadn't thought of that.

"Let me go talk to her," Sandy said, and hurried over to help Laverne protect her rights.

"How can she sleep through this? Did she take something?" Hilda asked, looking down at the curled-up actress.

"No, but she's really out of it, Hilda. She has no idea what's going on," Chelsea whispered so that no one could overhear her.

"No kidding? What happened exactly? Were you in here when it happened? What did you see?"

Chelsea's mute and abrupt shake of her head sent off bells of suspicion in Hilda's mind. Narrowing her eyes doubtfully, Hilda pressed the younger woman for more information. "Why in God's name did Laverne kill him? There were people in the house who could have helped her. Didn't she call anybody?"

Chelsea looked down at her hands, which seemed to have developed a reaction of their own as they nervously folded and unfolded themselves in her lap, reflecting the miserable and confused state she was in. She would have given anything to talk it over with rational, sensible Hilda, but she could not. If she had doubts, she would have to find some way to squelch them.

Watching the young woman, Hilda sensed she wasn't telling everything she knew or suspected. Bunny had flipped out; Laverne was insisting she killed a young man because he had been trying to hurt her daughter; and Chelsea would say neither yea nor nay.

Hilda leaned down to speak softly. "Listen to me, Chelsea, if you can't tell the truth, don't say anything at all until you've had a chance to talk to a lawyer, understand? Whatever you do, for God's sake, don't lie. Don't lie to the police, don't lie in court. That's one of the worst things you can do."

"I'm not going to lie, Hilda. I wasn't in the room when it happened. I only know what Gran told me," she replied in a monotone.

"Okay, okay, but take my advice and don't say a word until you've talked to an attorney. Whatever you tell him will be protected by the lawyer-client privilege, understand?"

Impulsively deciding to confide her predicament to her new friend, Chelsea said, "Hilda, look, I know I can trust you more than I can some stranger, even if he is an attorney, and I need some—"

Hilda shook her head vigorously. "Chelsea, you're not listening. I don't want you to tell me anything, understand? I'm not an attorney, and I can be subpoenaed to testify to anything you reveal. I may be your friend, but I will not perjure myself for anyone. And neither should you. Sandy's not a criminal attorney, but he'll get somebody for you to talk to, okay?"

Chelsea nodded, and when the detective came over to talk to her, she said she did not want to talk to anybody until she had an attorney present.

"Look, kid, your grandmother has already confessed. You're not a suspect. I just need you to corroborate her story, that's all," he insisted, but Sandy was at his elbow and he stopped the interrogation immediately.

All attention was suddenly diverted to Bunny, who had finally awakened. Sitting upright and looking around her in bewilderment, Bunny asked, "Who are all these people?"

Laverne went to her. "Nothing to worry about, babydoll. They're just policemen doing their job."

"Why are they here?" she asked in confusion. "Were we robbed?"

Laverne put her arm around her daughter protectively and said, "The poor thing must have gone into shock. It was a ghastly thing for her to see. I think we ought to get a doctor for her. She's in no state to answer questions right now."

As always, Laverne prevailed. A physician was summoned to care for Bunny, and eventually the group dispersed. Laverne was taken down to the police station to be charged. Sandy followed immediately after calling one of the most prestigious firms specializing in criminal law in California and convincing them to represent Laverne. Upon Hilda's advice, he decided that Chelsea should have her own attorney, which he promised to provide as soon as he could reach someone.

Just about every paper in the Western world carried a banner headline story the next morning describing the bizarre and brutal killing. Photographs of Laverne leaving the house with the police ran side by side with pictures of the shrouded corpse being placed into the police ambulance. There were also file shots of Bunny and Chelsea.

In Carmel, Anne Hunter handed the *Chronicle* to Frank, and he swore as he read the messy story. "I knew that one of these days those two silly women were going to make a mess of my daughter's life!"

"I think you ought to go to her, darling," she said softly. "She's probably feeling very alone right now. She needs your support."

"It wouldn't be fair to drag you and the kids into something as rotten as this," Frank said, but it was apparent he wanted her blessing.

"We'll be fine. Really, we will," she said, putting her arms around him and holding him close.

At two o'clock that afternoon Frank got out of the cab in front of the house where his daughter lived. There was a crowd of people hanging around, newspapermen and curious bystanders. Clark answered the door.

"I'm here to see Chelsea Hunter," Frank said.

"Whom shall I say is calling?" Clark asked warily, fully prepared for another lie from a pushy reporter trying to get into the house.

"Frank Hunter. I'm her father."

Clark was momentarily stunned. If that was a lie, it was a bloody good one. "Sir?"

"Just tell Chelsea that I'm here."

The claim was an audacious one, but the butler believed him. There was something so quiet and unassuming about the well-tailored, handsome man that the butler brought him into the foyer and asked him to wait while he went upstairs. "Miss Chelsea's had a very bad day, sir, as you can well imagine. The telephone has been ringing off the wall, and she doesn't dare step outside the door because there are newspapermen everywhere. The gardener even found a photographer up in the tree outside her bedroom window," Clark explained before taking his leave.

Upstairs, Chelsea was lying on her bed looking at the ceiling, relieved by the attorney's advice. He said she was obligated only to tell what she knew and nothing else. Patiently, he had explained that it was not deceitful or unlawful to keep her suspicions to herself.

Clark knocked, and she jumped nervously, thinking that perhaps it was her grandmother.

"Who is it?" she asked.

"You have a visitor, ma'am. He says his name is Frank Hunter, and he's your father."

The announcement shocked her. Why was he coming here now after a lifetime of silence? She closed her eyes and remembered all the missed birthdays, all the years of never having a father to hold her close and protect her from the vicious world. Whatever he brought her now would not be enough to make up for her whole lonely childhood.

"Tell him I'm not home to him, Clark," she said firmly. "Tell him he's too late."

"Are you sure, Miss Chelsea?" Clark asked, hoping she'd reconsider. "He seems to be a very nice gentleman."

"Very sure, thank you. I've never been surer of anything in my life," she replied flatly.

Closing the door behind him softly, Clark went downstairs and turned Frank away.

"I'm so sorry, sir, but I'm afraid Miss Chelsea does not want to see you," he said as gently as he could.

Disappointed, Frank asked, "Do you mind telling me exactly what she said?"

Clark hated being involved in other people's conflicts, but today he felt a strong inclination to be honest. "She said to tell you it was too late, sir. Those were her exact words, I'm afraid."

For a long, long moment the two men just looked at each other, and then Frank spoke. "Thank you. I guess there's not much point in my staying here any longer. Tell her . . . tell her . . . I'm sorry, will you?" Reaching into his pocket, he took out a business card and scribbled a telephone number on it and handed it to the butler.

"If you wouldn't mind giving this to her. I've put my private home number on it. Tell her to call me . . . if she ever changes her mind or needs my help."

"I'll do that, sir," Clark said, and watched as the man got into his car and drove away.

Chelsea took the card silently and stared at it for a long time when it was handed to her.

"What was he like, Clark?" she asked.

"A very nice man, Miss Chelsea. Tall, quiet-spoken, gentlemanly. He seemed quite disappointed."

Chelsea snickered bitterly, "I know just how he feels. What does he look like?"

Clark thought a moment. "Well, actually, I'd say he looks quite a bit like you. In fact, the resemblance is extraordinary."

60

Laverne was fingerprinted and booked, and although her attorney requested that she be released on her own recognizance, bail was set at fifty thousand dollars. Because Laverne did not have the money readily available, Hilda volunteered to advance it, and the older woman was able to return home.

The following afternoon, escorted by Hilda and Chelsea, Laverne was admitted to Cedars-Sinai Medical Center. Although she used a false name, an employee in the admitting room recognized her from the pictures that had been splattered all over the evening news, and he tipped off the media. Hilda and Chelsea tried to keep Laverne from finding out about the reporters hanging around downstairs, but she learned about it anyway and was amazingly sanguine.

"Don't worry. I'll be old news in a day or two. They're the least of my concerns. Are you sure that nurse you hired to take care of Bunny is qualified?"

"She's an experienced psychiatric nurse, Gran," Chelsea reassured her. "Now stop worrying. I'll be there too. The doctor said he'd have to keep Mom on tranquilizers unless we agree to hospitalize her, which he thinks we ought to do."

"No! She's going to be fine, I tell you. She's just in shock, that's all. Anybody would be after that awful experience," Laverne said firmly, glaring at her granddaughter.

"Gran, come on now. You've gone through even a worse experience than she has and you're all right," Chelsea persisted.

"Don't compare Bunny to an old warhorse like me. She's always been emotionally delicate."

Not wanting to be caught up in a family argument, Hilda tried to leave them alone. "Look, you two have a lot to talk about. I'll just go downstairs for a cup of coffee."

"Don't leave, Hilda. You and I have important things to discuss," Laverne said briskly, dismissing her granddaughter's concerns. "Chelsea, just be a good girl and sit still and listen. Now, Hilda, have you called Mike and asked him if he'll need Bunny for any additional scenes?"

Chelsea backed away. Good God, nothing had changed. Her grandmother had stabbed her mother's boyfriend to death and was now facing surgery for what might possibly be inoperable cancer, her mother had gone completely bonkers, and yet the only matter of any importance at all was the career of Bunny Thomas! Incredible. Chelsea did as she was told and sat down to listen. Was she crazy or were they?

Hilda's response was quiet and reasonable. If she found the discussion macabre, she did not let on. "I had a long talk with Mike this morning, and he's extremely sympathetic. He's shut down production for a day or two while he goes over the footage with his editors, but he said he was pretty sure he could go with what he had."

Laverne became agitated. "That's not what I want! This is Bunny's last chance, Hilda, can't you see? The film can't be just good enough. It has to be great!"

"We've got to trust Mike, Laverne. If he says he has all he needs, he does. The real problem is if he doesn't. From what I've seen, Bunny's in no condition—"

"You're wrong! She'll be fine as soon as I get out of this hospital."

Chelsea could not keep her mouth shut. "Gran! You're going to be here for a while. The doctor said—"

Laverne whirled on her granddaughter angrily. "To hell with the doctor! I've given him permission to do biopsies, nothing more, understand? Even if the tumors are not benign, I've given him explicit orders to do nothing, nothing whatsoever, without my express permission. There's no way I'm going to let him work over my body with his little scalpel while I'm lying there helplessly anesthetized." There was lightning in the spirit in her eyes and the thunder of a determined will in her voice.

"Well, it's your body, Gran, but—"

"You're goddamned right it's my body! And I want you and the doctors to remember it. Don't you dare give permission for them to do anything I don't want, you hear me?"

Chelsea nodded. She had never disobeyed her grandmother; this was certainly not the time to start.

When the surgery resident arrived to do a preliminary examination, Hilda and Chelsea went downstairs for coffee. Sitting at a long table in the back of the room, they waited for the hot brew to cool and talked.

"Your grandmother's something else."

"She's a tough customer," Chelsea said with a sigh. "When it comes to Mom, she's a lioness with her cub."

"Chelsea, Laverne's really sick, isn't she?"

"The doctor thinks it's too late. I had a long talk with him on the telephone this morning. I made the mistake of asking for the truth, and he gave it to me in spades. She's had this lump in her breast for months, but she just ignored it. Why would she do something so stupid?"

"Typical. She's always shaped the world to suit her own view of it, or at least she tried. She probably felt that if she ignored the lump, it would go away. Unfortunately, things don't always happen the way we want them to." Hilda sipped her coffee and changed the subject.

"Chelsea, I'm going to level with you. I don't expect you to comment or agree or anything. I just need to air my own feelings about this mess to somebody I can trust," she began.

"Go ahead."

"Just between you and me, I don't think for a minute that your grandmother killed that guy," she commented, watching Chelsea closely for her reaction.

If there was one thing Chelsea had learned from years of living in the same house with Laverne and Bunny, it was to keep her own feelings private, and so the expression and tone of her voice were noncommittal as she replied, "Surely you're not suggesting that my grandmother's taking the blame for something my mother did?"

"Look, this isn't idle speculation, Chelsea. I've thought about it constantly, and I'm worried. Suppose, just suppose, that your mother went over the edge in the library before the killing, not after," she said very softly.

"What's the point of this kind of conjecture, Hilda?"

"It's okay if Laverne wants to take the fall and protect her daughter, but—and this is a very big but—isn't it possible that she's doing her daughter an injustice by denying her the treatment she needs? And isn't it also possible that if Bunny is seriously disturbed, she may be a threat to those around her? Like you, for instance."

"For God's sake, Hilda! You don't believe that, do you? My mother a threat to me? It's preposterous."

Gently, Hilda leaned forward and spoke softly and maternally. "Chelsea, dear, listen to me for a few minutes and then decide whether or not my reasoning makes sense."

The young woman looked up and nodded.

"The way I see it," Hilda began, "is that your mother's been gradually getting farther and farther from reality, and she no longer knows what's real and what's just film-making. Because you've been busy with your own life and Laverne's been obsessed with this movie, not to mention her own illness, nobody really noticed. Your mother's a bit of a cypher anyway, you know, the fire and the gumption was all supplied by Laverne."

"Don't underestimate my mother. There's more to her than people usually see on the surface," Chelsea said.

"Well, maybe, but anyway, Bunny did her big emotional scene—brilliantly, according to Mike, who also, by the way, told me the intensity was so palpable he thought for a single excruciating moment that he had actually watched her commit murder on the set."

"She's a good actress," Chelsea said, but her voice was tight with emotion.

"Along with the movie, Bunny's had this sex thing going with the makeup guy. I've asked around and heard that he screwed everything in sight, but Bunny has never been content with just a nice roll in the hay, has she? She wants romance and love and devotion along with it. Just like in all her movies. Then suddenly something goes wrong, just like it does in the script of *The Beyonder,* and when Fernando doesn't show up for work, she starts thinking weird things, like he's cheating on her maybe. The guy is waiting at the house, and you and your grandmother make the fatal mistake of leaving the two of them alone."

"Oh God, I keep playing that moment over and over

in my head, thinking that if we had only done things just a little differently, that man would still be alive," Chelsea said, obviously tortured by her own small part in the events.

"It wasn't your fault, Chelsea, and I suspect it wasn't Laverne's either . . . not directly anyway, but let me finish—something happens, they argue, he says he's not interested anymore, whatever, and Bunny grabs the letter opener and stabs him, only this time there are no cameras recording the action. Laverne sizes up the situation in a glance, quickly rigs the evidence and takes the blame herself. Why the hell not? She's an old woman, and she knows she's dying anyway, right? Bunny is a star, and unless her mother protects her, everything Laverne has worked for will be destroyed."

"Suppose you're right. What do you want me to do about it?"

"I believe in facing the truth, Chelsea. I know that's strange talk from an agent, but I do believe the truth sets you free, and I'm worried about you. If you allow yourself to be drawn into this weird fantasy of your grandmother's about Bunny's stardom being the only thing in life, you'll become a slave to it too. Look at your mother. What in the hell has stardom ever done for her?"

Chelsea looked across the room and answered thoughtfully. "You're talking to the wrong person, Hilda. I have no power in this family," she said with regret. "I've never had any, and I won't as long as my grandmother is alive. Even if I believed that my mother was dangerously psychotic, I couldn't do anything about it. Sick as she is, my grandmother is still very much in charge. Do you think for a single minute you could convince her to put any kind of blame on her daughter . . . for anything . . . especially murder?"

Her tone of voice was so filled with hopelessness that Hilda almost wished she hadn't broached the subject. Nevertheless, she had one more point to make.

"Chelsea, I just want you to be alert, that's all. I think Bunny is seriously disturbed, and if it's also true that

Laverne might not have much longer to live, the entire responsibility for her care will fall on you. Don't let it ruin your life."

Chelsea listened to Hilda's words of caution, and although she agreed with her in principle, she felt helpless to do anything about it. An evil destiny had taken control of the lives of the women in her family, and Chelsea felt trapped.

61

Hilda and Chelsea stared at the doctor sitting across from them in his green cotton hospital clothes as he confirmed their worst fears.

"I'm sorry to have to tell you this, but it's just too late to offer any hope of a cure. The cancer probably started in her left breast, that's where the largest tumors are, and it has apparently metastasized to the lung. We did X rays just before we took her into surgery, and there's a large mass in her left lung, which explains the persistent cough she's had for the past few weeks. The amount of cells in the lymph nodes confirms the spread, and although I'm not sure, I would guess that it's also attacked her spinal column and bones."

"Are you going to do a mastectomy?" Hilda asked.

The doctor shook his head. "There's no point in putting her through any further surgery. I'm calling in Polly Grover, who's one of the best oncologists in town. She'll look at all the lab reports and decide if it's feasible or desirable to administer chemotherapy, although she may want to use radiation on the lung tumor to try to shrink it. God knows, we don't want her to die of suffocation. That's a terrible way to go."

"Is there any hope at all?" Hilda asked.

The doctor shook his head solemnly. "I'm afraid not.

If she'd come to see me three or four months ago, maybe, but now the best we can expect is perhaps to buy a little time," he said sadly.

Hilda spoke up. "Doctor, you know the situation she's in legally, don't you?"

He nodded. "That's the least of her worries now. I will most certainly certify that she is far too ill to be either incarcerated or to stand trial. She's already under a death sentence."

"Are you going to keep her in the hospital?" Chelsea asked.

"For a few days, at least until Dr. Grover has a chance to make a full examination and assessment of her condition. After that, I think she should be wherever she'll be the most comfortable. It'll be up to her."

"When can I see her?" Chelsea asked anxiously.

"In a little while, but I'd appreciate it if you'd let me talk to her alone before you go in to see her. She tried to make me promise not to tell you if the news was bad, but I refused. I don't think it's fair to keep these things from the family. Besides, there's absolutely no way she'll be able to conceal her illness much longer. Her good days are pretty much all behind her."

Chelsea suddenly found herself overcome by the doctor's prediction that her grandmother would die—and soon. How would she and Bunny cope? Laverne had always taken charge of everything, and now all the responsibility would fall on her shoulders. Hers and hers alone. Could she handle it? And how could she possibly ever leave her mother and go all the way to England to marry and live? Would her mother consent to leave Hollywood and go with her? What would Wills think of the whole terrible scandal?

It was a crushing burden for a young woman not yet twenty-three, and if her thoughts were momentarily diverted to her own situation rather than to the tragedy that was her grandmother's, it was not because she was callous or uncaring, but because she was faced with the loss of most of her freedom and all of her hopes.

She and Hilda sat in silence for most of an hour until a nurse came to fetch Chelsea and take her into the room to see her grandmother. Tentatively she approached the bed where Laverne lay with her face turned to the window, her closed, unseeing eyes lifted to the sunlight.

"Gran, it's me. Are you okay?"

Without turning her head, Laverne whispered, "Did you understand what Dr. Cableshaw told you?"

"I think so, Gran, but he's only one person. We can get a second opin—"

Laverne's head spun quickly around until her now opened eyes locked into those of her granddaughter, and she snapped, "No! No more doctors, do you hear me?"

Chelsea protested, taken aback by her grandmother's intensity. "But, Gran, Dr. Cableshaw said—"

"Forget what he said. It's my life, and I'll damned well do with it whatever I choose. He can't help me anyway. The only thing he and all the bloodsucking vampires can do is use up my money, and you're going to need every penny we've got to take care of Bunny. I will not spend one damn cent more on doctors or hospitals or tests. I wish to God I'd never let him put me in here anyway. A fat lot of good it did me," she complained, anger pouring over her words, her fingers nervously plucking at the sheet covering her body, fear and anxiety overcoming the effects of the anesthesia.

"But, Gran—"

But Laverne had no time for contrary opinions. "Chelsea, just shut up and listen to me! I want you to go downstairs and find out what my bill is, then come back here and get the checkbook out of my purse in the drawer over there. I intend to pay the bill and sign myself out of this place today. There's no point in spending the money to sleep here when I've got a perfectly comfortable bed and servants to take care of me at home," she ordered in a manner that demanded compliance.

A lifetime of obedience could not be subverted in an instant, and Chelsea did as she was told. An hour and a half later, after having run the gauntlet of the head nurse, the hospital administrator, and Dr. Cableshaw, who finally acquiesced, Laverne prevailed. She was brought in a wheelchair to the front doors, where Chelsea waited for her in the car to take her home.

Clark helped Laverne upstairs so she could check on her still-drugged daughter to make sure she was sleeping quietly before she allowed herself to be ushered to the bed. Catalina had no sooner brought her a cup of tea than Laverne summoned Chelsea and demanded that she call Hilda.

"She was at the hospital with me all morning, Gran. I think we ought to let her—"

"I'm not dead yet, my dear young lady, so you will kindly do as I ask. Call her and tell her I want to see her—now! And bring me a bottle of brandy to put a little bite in this insipid tea."

"Do you think you should?" Chelsea asked uncertainly. "You just came out of the anesthetic a little while ago."

"Young lady, let's get one thing straight this minute. You are not my keeper, my nurse, or my conscience. God knows how long I'll be able to control my life, but while I do, butt out and do as you're told!" The timbre of her voice was thready and weak, but the ironclad determination in her words propelled her granddaughter to carry out her orders.

Hilda responded immediately and was at the house by the time Laverne had finished her second cup of tea, laced lightly with the best cognac in the house. Feeling more relaxed, Laverne motioned Hilda to a chair beside the bed, but when Chelsea started to leave, she was ordered to sit down and listen.

"Stay here, young lady, and learn something. You have to know everything that's going on in this house, so you'll be able to carry on without me." Turning to the agent, she wasted no words. "Have you talked to Mike?"

Hilda nodded. "Yes, and it's bad news. He says he's got to have Bunny for one more day of pickup shots or they'll have to cut a couple of scenes, including the one where the little girl tells her what she saw in the bedroom."

"Oh my God," Laverne exclaimed with agitation. "They can't cut that! The story won't make sense at all without it. What went wrong?"

"Somebody goofed, and everybody's pointing fingers at everybody else. They didn't get enough coverage so they can cut away from the kid to Bunny's horrified reactions, and the kid's performance looks lame without it. Do you think there's any possible way she could understand direction enough to do it right?"

"She's got to," Laverne said with finality.

"It's going to be tough, you know that. It's a long scene, and her attention span is probably very short." Hilda was doubtful.

Laverne listened and drummed her long red fingernails nervously on the edge of the cup. It was an irritating sound, and Chelsea wanted to snatch the china away from her, but she did not move. Suddenly the noise stopped.

"I know how we can do it," Laverne announced. "Tell Mike to set it up for next Friday, but make sure that nobody knows we're coming to the set. I don't want any reporters crawling up my back, understand? Tell him to shoot the scene M.O.S. . . . that way he can talk her through the emotions . . . you know, smile, be surprised, get angry. If he keeps the directions simple and treats her like a child actor, I feel sure she'll do whatever he tells her to do."

"Are you sure it will work?" Hilda asked doubtfully.

"We'll make it work. We've got to make it work," she said fervently.

They talked for another half hour about the studio's plans for the picture and the release date, and when the subject had been thoroughly exhausted, Hilda got up to leave.

"Call me and let me know the exact timetable, Hilda. I need at least twenty-four hours to get the tranquilizers leached out of Bunny's system so she'll be awake enough to perform, okay?"

"I hope you can deliver, Laverne. It'll cost them a bundle if the day is wasted, and Mike's already over-budget."

"You do your job, I'll do mine," Laverne said softly, and closed her eyes.

Chelsea followed Hilda out of the room quietly. When they were down in the entry hall, the agent studied the strained, tired girl and said, "You look awful. Are you going to be able to handle it, honey?"

"I haven't got much choice, have I?"

"My dear," Hilda said softly, "when Laverne dies, you'll be the one to make the choices, and you're going to have to assert yourself. For God's sake, don't let Laverne control you from the grave. What she did with her life was one thing, what you choose is another. I hope you're not thinking of stepping into your grandmother's shoes and devoting your life to nurturing Bunny."

"She's my mother," Chelsea said quietly. "I have to take care of her."

"What about Wills? What about your plans to live in England? You can't take her with you if she's still acting crazy, you know."

Chelsea's response was almost inaudible. "I know."

"Oh God!" Hilda said, turning away and marching out the door in anger and frustration. "What a fucking waste!" she muttered under her breath.

62

Chelsea wanted to make sure that everything was under control with her mother and her grandmother before she left the house to meet Jonathan Corell for dinner. He had called just an hour before, and since the household was relatively peaceful and no new crises loomed in the immediate future, she decided to go. The car he had sent for her was waiting out front, and although there were still a few free-lance photographers hanging around hoping to get a picture of someone going in or out of the house, most of the media mob had dispersed.

Gently, she knocked twice on her grandmother's door, and when there was no response, she entered quietly and found the older woman asleep, exhausted by the horrors of the past few days. Distressed that Laverne had left the hospital so quickly, Dr. Cableshaw had stopped in to see her, and after a long talk, he had bowed to Laverne's wishes and assured her that he would help her every step of the way. Before he left, he insisted on giving her a shot to relax her, and he left a prescription for pain and sleep medication. At Laverne's request, he checked on Bunny and recommended a reduction in the number of tranquilizers she was being given, because she was sleeping too much.

Finally, Chelsea thought, the day's terrible tensions had begun to ease. Relieved, she hurried down the stairs and out to the car. Her circumstances had changed so drastically in the past few long hours that she desperately needed to cement her relationship with her mentor at Tanager's. Now she needed his well-paying job.

At the California Club, the most exclusive men's business club in the city, she was escorted to the bar upstairs, where Jonathan sat in a corner waiting for her. Her heart skipped with pleasure at the sight of the tall distinguished man getting to his feet to meet her, and she hurried across the dark-wood-paneled room, unaware of the people who looked up to watch the beautiful young woman rushing past them.

When she put out her hand, Jonathan took it in both of his and squeezed it warmly, and Chelsea realized how happy she was to see him again. He was so calm, so reassuring.

After they were seated, Jonathan ordered a glass of wine for them both, and then he asked how she was bearing up under the strains of the past few days. Without feeling she had to hold anything back, she described in detail what had happened, and he listened attentively and sympathetically. When she finished, Jonathan found just the right words to comfort her.

"Sometimes we have to stop fighting and accept things as they are, my dear. Your grandmother has chosen the course she wishes to take, and it really is her life to do with as she wishes, now isn't it?"

"It's different in our family, Jonathan. My mother has never lived her own life, really. She's lived it the way Gran wanted her to. Now, I just can't imagine what's going to happen to her. She's utterly helpless without Gran."

"They must be very close," he commented.

"My mother and Gran? Oh Lord yes. They're two bodies and one soul."

"Did you ever feel excluded from that relationship?" he asked softly.

Chelsea smiled and shook her head. "Not really. I grew up believing that the only thing that mattered in our house was Mom and her career. No, I never envied my mother anything. She's a sweet, lovable woman, but very fragile. When I was a little girl I used to have nightmares about her getting sick and dying. She spent a lot of time in bed when she wasn't working." Chelsea's voice quavered slightly, but she continued, pausing only occasionally to sip her drink. "When things went well for Mom and she was happy, we were all happy. When they went badly, a cloud of gloom settled on the house and everyone in it. Now . . . I just don't know what's going to happen to us."

Jonathan clearly was impressed with the strength and character of the young woman before him. Though she'd never been coddled or spoiled or had the love and support of doting parents, she had turned out so well. She was intelligent, thoughtful, caring, and unselfish. She was also extremely talented, and she deserved to have someone help her with her own dreams.

"There's an old saying, Chelsea, that God places the heaviest burdens on those people who have the strength to carry them. I feel sure that whatever happens, you'll handle it. Take things as they come, and don't try to plan your entire life in the next five minutes."

"Jonathan, you make me feel so . . . peaceful."

"I think that a nice dinner will make you feel even better. I'll wager that you haven't sat down to a full meal since we left New York, right?"

"New York, God, it seems like an eon since we were there. It's almost as if it was in another life."

"Let's think of it as the beginning of your new life, Chelsea. A rich, rewarding, fulfilled life. You have a great future ahead of you. Don't be afraid of it."

When the evening ended, Chelsea went home to bed, and for the first time since the night of the murder, she was able to sleep. Telling Jonathan that she would sign the contract if he still wanted her was, in her mind, the very best decision she had ever made. It was in reality the only decision she could make, under the circumstances. Taking care of her mother would mean that she'd have to support her financially as well as emotionally. The best way to do that was to pursue her own career as far as it could take her. And, bless him, Jonathan was going to help her, all the way.

63

"Gran, I can't believe you're doing this! You must be crazy," Chelsea said, with more anger than she had ever displayed to her grandmother.

"I know what I'm doing, Chelsea, so shut up and help me get out of here," Laverne responded, tying a scarf around Bunny's hair to cover the thick, auburn mane that would identify her to anyone who might be watching them leave the house.

"I'm tired, Mom. I want to go back to bed," Bunny said lethargically, her eyes still glazed with sleep.

"Look at her!" Chelsea insisted. "She can hardly hold up her head. How in the devil are you going to get her in shape for the camera?"

"Just go down to the kitchen and get me a thermos of coffee to take in the car, Chelsea, and quit worrying. This won't be the first time I've had to glue your mother together to go to work, and you damn well know it. Believe me, when I get finished with her, she'll do fine," Laverne snapped, her own adrenaline surging to get her through the coming ordeal.

Stomping into the kitchen, Chelsea asked Catalina for the coffee, and while she waited for a fresh pot to be brewed, she sipped at her own cup, which had gone cold. By the second sip, however, she felt a sudden queasiness, and she put the cup down. God, what was wrong with her? She'd always had a cast-iron stomach, but ever since Fernando's killing, she got nauseous at even the thought of food.

As soon as Chelsea left the bedroom, Laverne scurried into the bathroom and inserted a key into her locked medicine chest. Taking two disposable syringes from the shelf, along with a vial of medicine, she quickly gave both Bunny and herself an injection of amphetamine. She was careful to use just enough to arouse Bunny from her torpor and to give herself a burst of energy. It was going to be a long, tough day. When that was done, she put the vial and a handful of syringes into her purse. Long experience had taught her that even when her daughter was in the best of health, she needed a boost to keep her alert on extended days of filming.

Fifteen minutes later, mother and daughter descended the stairs to the front door, where Chelsea was waiting with the thermos, a startled look on her face.

"Mom!" she said, as she appraised the woman walking toward her.

"Chelsea, darling, you look awful. Do go get your hair done, will you? It's so stringy," her mother said in her lilting voice.

"Bunny's right," Laverne chimed in. "Start taking better care of yourself, will you? There are still photographers hanging around outside, and most of the time you look like something the cat dragged in."

Chelsea paid no attention to their remonstrations. Being nagged about her appearance was nothing new. What really surprised her was the sudden transformation of her mother from a sleepy, mumbling vegetable to an alert human being. It was the first time since the murder, now more than a week ago, that her mother had said an intelligible word. What the hell had happened in the past few minutes?

"Mom, do you feel like working today?" she asked doubtfully.

"Darling, the show must go on, you know that. Besides, I feel wonderful. Is that coffee? You sweet thing," she said in the stagy voice she used in public as she took the thermos from her daughter's hand. "I don't suppose you thought to get me a bagel or a Danish too, did you? I haven't had breakfast yet . . . have I?" she asked, turning to Laverne.

"No, darling, you just got out of bed a few minutes ago. Go on and get in the car. I'll get you something to nibble on." Laverne handed her daughter over to the driver who was waiting just outside the door and headed for the kitchen with Chelsea right behind.

"Gran, what the hell did you give her?" she demanded.

"Oxygen, darling, just oxygen. It's a little trick I learned years ago. She's always been hard to awaken, but a few whiffs usually does the trick."

"Where did you get oxygen?"

"I always keep a tank, just in case. You're such a nosy thing, I'm surprised you never noticed," Laverne replied airily. Seeing the cook, she asked, "Catalina, I hope you've got some fresh rolls or something for Bunny to eat on the way to the set. Do you?"

Catalina too was startled by the sudden change in her employer, and she threw a questioning glance toward Chelsea as she responded, "I baked some caramel nut buns. That okay?"

"Lovely, just lovely," Laverne replied archly. "And while you're at it, perhaps some juice. Did you squeeze any this morning?"

Nodding, Catalina wrapped some foil around the plate of rolls and then got the bottle of freshly squeezed orange juice from the refrigerator. As she passed Chelsea, she raised her eyebrows conspiratorially.

Laden with goodies, Laverne hurried out to the limousine, which quickly disappeared from view, leaving both Catalina and Chelsea gaping in astonishment.

"Your mama gonna work and eat today, no foolin'?"

Chelsea shook her head. "Sure looks like it."

"Madre de Dios, es un milagro."

"I'll say. I saw it with my own eyes and I still don't believe it," the young woman replied in wonder.

"Even the eyes play tricks, *chiquita*. Even the eyes," she mumbled on her way back to the kitchen.

Chelsea hurried upstairs to shower and dress. She had places to go and things to do today, things that had been delayed too long. But first she had a telephone call to make. Sitting down at the desk, she dialed a number that she had committed to memory. It was only seven in the morning, but she knew it was not too early.

Hilda picked up the telephone on the first ring. Not many people had her special private number, and she was quick to answer that particular telephone, assured that it wouldn't be some client with a gripe about the director or producer.

"I hope it's not too early," Chelsea said when Hilda answered.

"Honey, I've already run two miles. I'm just getting ready to take a shower. How are things going this morning?"

"Weird, Hilda, very weird."

"Lord, don't tell me that your grandmother couldn't get Bunny out of bed," she asked apprehensively. She had personally guaranteed Mike Stern that Laverne would deliver Bunny in good shape, both mentally and physically ready to work. If Laverne didn't do it, it would be Hilda's ass on the line.

"Oh, not at all. In fact, they just left for the set."

"Already? That's great!" Hilda exclaimed, relieved and astounded at the same time.

"I'm not at all sure about that."

"What do you mean? Wasn't Bunny with it?"

"Not when she first got out of bed, she wasn't, but when she left, she was as chipper as ever. She was even nagging me about my appearance."

"No kidding? Sounds like a miracle."

"It was. She could hardly hold her head up while Gran dressed her. I went downstairs to get coffee, and fifteen minutes later she was marching down the steps as la-di-da as you please."

"Oh shit!" Hilda replied. "Your grandmother must have given her something." She'd been around this town too long not to recognize the result of drugs.

"That's what I thought, but when I asked her about it, Gran insisted that all she'd given her were a few whiffs of oxygen. She said it was what she always uses."

"And you never knew about it before? Never saw an oxygen tank in the house?" she asked suspiciously. If Bunny was on drugs, Hilda wanted to know about it.

"Come to think of it, no. I've never seen a tank around here."

"Well, maybe she's got it hidden. Thanks for calling, honey. Cross your fingers that things go well today. I'll keep tabs on the filming, so you can check with my office anytime for an update. Have a nice day, sweetie."

Hilda put down the receiver, pleased that her relationship with Chelsea was so close. It was patently obvious that Chelsea needed a friend, and she fully intended to be one. Maybe she ought to warn her that Bunny, who was already psychically on the edge, was in even greater danger if Laverne was giving her amphetamines. She'd seen enough in her career to know that tampering with the brain's chemistry was just like playing with dynamite.

It had happened in her own house, in fact, she thought, recalling Sergio's rages.

The telephone rang again; it was Sandy.

"Morning, Hilda. There's good news for a change," he said without preamble.

"Tell me quick, I need a fix," she replied.

"The charge against Laverne has been reduced to involuntary manslaughter, and the D.A. has postponed taking it to the grand jury. I had dinner with him last night, and he's got bigger fish to fry than Laverne, especially since they found out that Fernando Ramon, as he called himself, had an outstanding indictment against him."

"No kidding, what for?"

"Raping a fourteen-year-old girl. He was called Freddie Thatcher then, and he jumped bail in Nebraska four years ago, changed his name, and went to one of those theatrical makeup schools in L.A. Laverne's timing was perfect too. They've got their hands full down there with that hospital ghoul case. Even if it takes a year for her to die, Laverne'll probably never see the inside of a courtroom again. Unless, of course, there's some miracle and she gets cured." There was a long silence, and Sandy asked, "Hilda, are you still there?"

Arousing herself from her thoughts, she replied, "Yeah, sure, that's great news. It'll save the taxpayers some dough."

"You don't think she did it, do you?" he asked.

"No, but what do I know?"

"Forget it, kiddo, it's all over."

64

Mike Stern was patiently waiting on the set, which was lighted and technically ready, when Bunny finally emerged from makeup to make her way delicately across the cable-strewn floor. With Laverne at her elbow, Bunny smiled at the crew, blew kisses to the gaffers above, chatted sweetly with everyone nearby, and acted for all the world as if nothing had happened in the days since she had shot the climax of *The Beyonder*. Satisfied that she'd made an entrance, Bunny stopped at the director's chair. Mike got to his feet and greeted her with a warmth that was more feigned than real.

"Bunny darling," he said. Taking both of her hands in his, he brought them close to his face and touched each lightly with his lips. "It's so good to see you looking as fresh and beautiful as you always do. I want you to promise me that if you start feeling tired, you'll let me know immediately, okay?"

"Don't worry, I'll let you know," Laverne interjected.

Mike smiled stiffly and felt his teeth began to clench as he replied, "I have no doubt that you will, Laverne. Now, since the crew has been waiting for more than twenty minutes, I think we better get started. Bunny, this is the scene where you close the door behind Marvella. She's just told you about having an affair with Jack, but you acted as if you had known all along and didn't mind. You assured her, very sweetly, that you didn't hold her to blame. She's been your best friend for years and you still think of her that way. Remember?"

"Yes, I think so," she said, and turned to her mother. "Do you remember that scene, Mom?" she asked uncertainly.

"Yes, of course I do, and you were wonderful, wasn't she, Mike?"

Nodding, Mike agreed. "It's a great scene, Bunny. Would you like me to have the editor run it through to refresh your memory?"

Bunny started to nod, but Laverne answered for her. "That won't be necessary, Mike. Just tell her exactly what you want from her. There are no lines, right?"

"Right," he said, feeling more nervous than ever about finishing the picture properly, but aware that he'd have to get as much footage as he could today. It would not be the first Academy Award performance created in the editing room.

"Come on over here, Bunny, and stand at the door with your back resting against it, your hand behind you still clutching the knob tightly. You're stunned . . . okay?"

"Stunned?" Bunny asked vaguely.

"Surprised and angry . . . shocked, understand?"

"Oh yes, I can do that. Should I open my mouth or just purse my lips?"

Mike looked at Laverne quizzically, but she seemed to be made of stone. "Mike will shoot it both ways, honey. Won't you, Mike?"

Startled, Mike nodded and said uncertainly, "Both ways, right. Let's try for the pursed lips first. You're surprised now, Bunny, but while the camera is rolling, you begin to be angry, you begin to plan revenge. Can you do that?"

"Yes, she can, can't you, darling?" Laverne responded before her daughter had a chance to answer.

Bunny smiled and took her mark. "Ready when you are, C.B.," she said with a laugh.

Mike took a deep breath. "I hope she meant that as a joke," he muttered.

Laverne made no comment.

"Let's do one rehearsal . . ." Mike said to his assistant, but Laverne dissented.

"Take my advice, Mike, shoot everything she does today. I don't think she'll be able to remember from one scene to the next what's gone on before."

Ordinarily Mike hated to have someone second-guess him on the set of his own film, but he had enough savvy to realize Laverne was probably giving him excellent advice.

"Whatever you say, Mama. I'm sure you know your daughter better than anyone."

"You're the first director to understand that," Laverne replied, but there was no rancor in her tone of voice.

Mike gave Bunny explicit directions, and when she was

ready, the cameras rolled. She did exactly as she was told, and within minutes the scene was in the can, usable, if not inspired. With that insurance, Mike felt free to experiment, and Bunny cooperated. When he had five good takes, Mike moved on to the next scene, and by the time the day ended, he had everything he needed to finish his movie.

Feeling generous and expansive, and mightily relieved, he thanked his star and her mother, and retreated quickly to the privacy of his office, where Len White, his executive producer, had gone to wait for him.

"Len, where the hell's the champagne? We ought to celebrate," he said, striding into the office and closing the door behind him.

Not interrupting his steady gaze out the window, Len White replied quietly, "I don't feel much like celebrating, Mike. Sorry."

"Why the hell not? You sick or something?"

"I guess you could say that," he replied quietly. "I'm sick at heart." Then, after a moment's pause, he turned and looked at Mike and asked, "You ever worked with a child star, Mike?"

"God, no. I've never found a story that was worth that kind of abuse, and you know what, I never intend to," he replied.

"Bunny was the best, Mike. The absolute best. I was a lowly assistant editor on *Good-bye, Mommy,* and she couldn't have been more than ten years old when she starred in that picture. But I gotta tell you, buddy, she never once spoiled a take. She was always letter perfect in her lines and movements."

"So what's bothering you?"

"I was the producer on *Ask Me No Questions.* She was about twenty-five or -six when she made that film, and she was marvelous . . . passionate, sexy, and knowing. She wasn't a kid actor then, she had become an actress, a real actress."

Mike had poured himself a scotch on the rocks as Len

talked, and he settled down on the couch to listen. "Go on, Len. I can tell you're not finished."

"My God, Mike, your press agent calls you the most sensitive, intuitive director in the world. Couldn't you see what was going on out there all day?" he asked in exasperation.

Swirling his glass so that the ice cubes tinkled, Mike finally replied, "She was following directions like an obedient child."

Rolling his eyes toward the ceiling, Len said, "Thank God you got it right. I thought I was going to have to bar you from the editing room. She's back in her childhood, isn't she?"

"Yeah, you're right. I couldn't quite put my finger on the problem, but I think that's it."

"Sad, isn't it?"

"Maybe, but let's not look a gift horse in the mouth. Bunny the child is better than no Bunny at all. I'm just glad she didn't have any lines to say. Child stars always sound so damned perky," Mike replied. "Come on, I'll take you to dinner . . . on second thought, you take me. You're the guy with the dough."

"Send her flowers, Mike, first thing in the morning. Two dozen pink roses. Tell her she was wonderful," Len said firmly.

"I usually send them when the picture opens," he protested.

"She needs them now," Len replied as he led the way out the door.

65

When she arrived at Tanager's, Chelsea was escorted into Jonathan Corell's office without delay. He got up from his chair to greet her at the door.

"My dear, I hope things are starting to settle down a bit," he said, sincere concern evident in his voice. "I know how terrible this all has been for you. Come in and sit down. Can I get you some coffee?"

He put his arm around her shoulders and escorted her to the deep leather chair beside his desk.

"If you have tea, I'd love a cup. Coffee seems to upset me nowadays," she replied, sinking down into the softness of the well-worn chair. How peaceful it was there in the hushed confines of his orderly office. Had there ever been an emotional crisis in this room?

"I'll have some brought in immediately. Lemon or milk?" he asked.

"That's a question not many people ask here in the States. Milk, please. I learned to drink it that way in England."

He sat down in the chair beside her, eschewing his own chair behind the desk in order to be closer and less formal.

"I gather from what I read that the district attorney is postponing action against your grandmother until she's well. That's good news, at any rate. It is, isn't it?"

"I suppose so," she said distractedly, "but it's hard to focus on that when my grandmother refuses to do anything, anything at all to fight this disease. She's just going to give up and die."

"I'm sure that's very hard for you. How is your mother doing now? You were very concerned about her the other evening."

"She seems better, but she still doesn't talk much. Most of the time she sleeps, although she managed to arouse herself enough to go back to work today."

"That's a good sign," he said, and patted her hand. "When life is difficult, one is forced to find comfort in very small things."

"Mr. Corell . . . Jonathan," she began hesitantly, "I've been doing a lot of thinking since our dinner the other evening, and I want to be sure that you really still want me to work for you. If you feel that I might be an embarrassment to you or the firm, and you'd like to withdraw the offer, I'll understand."

"Withdraw?" he asked, puzzled. "Why in the world would we want to withdraw the offer?"

"The notoriety . . . I know what a conservative and—" she began, but he interrupted her.

"Nonsense, my dear. If we avoided artists who have family problems, we'd never have anything worthwhile to sell. Of course we still want you, on exactly the same terms as before. The contract is on my desk waiting for you to sign."

Chelsea's spirits lifted considerably. Her career was now the only glimmer of hope she had for some life of her own. "I'll do it now, then," she said eagerly, afraid the golden opportunity would slip through her fingers.

"Wait a minute now, my dear. Don't you want your own attorney to look it over for you?"

"It won't be necessary. I trust your judgment, Jonathan. And I trust you. I hope we have a long and profitable association. I just pray I can live up to your expectations," she said with sincere humility.

Jonathan Corell appraised the young woman beside him. The haunted look in her eyes contrasted sharply with the youthful dewiness of her skin and the luster of her silver-blond hair. She had the beauty and vitality of youth but the soul of a much older woman.

"You'll have no trouble living up to my expectations, Chelsea. I just hope you'll be able to live up to your own."

The tea tray was brought, and after Chelsea finished signing, they chatted comfortably for a long, long time. When they finished, he took her through the old workroom, which had been closed, and discussed the equipment they would need to refurbish it.

"Dennis Petalski, who has been with Tanager's in New York for more than ten years, has volunteered to make the big move out here to L.A. He's a wonderful technician, Chelsea. His standards are the highest," Corell explained. "He'll be here, ready to work, next Monday. What about you?"

"If it's all right with you, I'd like to work just part-time until the middle of next month. I've fulfilled most of the requirements for my classes, but I have a few exams to take before graduation."

"Come in whenever you can, but we'll consider you a full-time staff member as of Monday and you will be paid accordingly."

"Paid?" Chelsea asked in surprise, suddenly realizing she had no idea how much money she was going to receive. She felt incredibly stupid for neglecting a matter of such importance.

Jonathan shook his head in mock distress. "Young lady, I told you to have your attorney look over the contract, didn't I? Now take a copy to him. If he wants any changes, let me know. It's not too late. Most contracts aren't worth the paper they're printed on anyway. What's important is the good will between the parties involved."

"I'm so lucky to have met you, Jonathan."

"I'm the lucky one, Chelsea," he replied, taking her hand and squeezing it gently.

On the way home, Chelsea stopped at Sandy Shapiro's office and left the contract for him to look over for her. When she was back in her car, she had time to think through the sudden change in direction her life had taken. For the first time ever, she had not just one, but two concerned and influential men in her life—a wonderful employer, and a lover. Dear God, why couldn't she keep them both?

Just the thought of Wills sent her back into a depression. Now that she had taken the irrevocable step toward a career here in Los Angeles, she should set him free. It would be cruel to allow him to continue believing that she could join him in England anytime in the near future. She knew she should have told him when he telephoned right after the killing that there was no way she would ever be free to leave, but the sound of his voice had been so sweet, and she loved him so much that all she could do was return his words of love with her own, all the while feeling that terrible ache of separation in her heart. Why was life so wretched?

She had known from the moment her grandmother had told her about her illness that the future she'd planned with him was not meant to be. No matter how much it hurt, she had to sit down and write a letter telling Wills how her situation had changed. She loved him far too much to involve him in her family's messy problems, she told herself, but the idea of never seeing him again, never being held in his arms, was almost unbearable. Just when she felt herself losing courage and longing for his touch once more, she drew herself up short by remembering Fernando's body on the library floor. Not only did she have an obligation to care for her mother, but the sordid scandal in which they were now embroiled would be an embarrassment to the Ashford family. Surely they would not want their only son and heir to marry a young woman whose family was so dreadfully tainted.

It took her hours to compose the letter, hours punctuated with pain, and when it was done, she stretched out on her bed to read it again. It was a good letter, she decided, and should settle the matter once and for all. The last paragraph was an effective coup de grace to their love affair.

> . . . and so, Wills, I'll always remember your smile, your warm touch, and the beautiful moments we had together. I wish we could stretch those moments into a lifetime of loving, but we can't. You have your responsibilities there in England, and I have mine here with my family. Please remember me and the sweetness of discovery that we shared. You will always live in my heart.

Under her signature she had drawn a tiny rose.

Chelsea folded the letter carefully and sealed it in an envelope. Today she had opened the door to her new life, and closed the door to her love. She couldn't remember ever feeling quite so miserable.

66

The day after Bunny finished her work on the film, Mike Stern called Laverne, as he had promised to do, and told her he'd seen all the dailies. They were fine; Bunny would no longer be needed.

"Does the studio still plan to release it in December?" Laverne asked.

"I suppose so, but you never know how these things go," he hedged. "We'll have a rough assemblage by next week, and if it looks all right, I'll let the studio see it before I start fine-tuning. I can't promise anything."

"Will you keep me posted?" she asked. There was a humility in her voice that Mike had never heard before, and it touched him. Laverne Thomas, the creator and architect of her daughter's career, might not live to see Bunny's best picture.

"Of course I will, Laverne," he said softly, "and I'll do everything I can to get it released on schedule. I promise you."

"Thanks, Mike. You're a great director, and I ought to know. Bunny's worked with the best."

"Thanks for yesterday, Laverne. With everything that's happened to you lately, I appreciate the concern you showed for the picture. I'd have been in trouble if you hadn't helped me with Bunny."

"Mike," she said, "make this her best performance yet, will you? It might be her last one, you know."

"Don't say that, Laverne. She's just in a state of shock, that's all. She's still a young woman. She has years of good work ahead of her," he protested, but he knew they were hollow words. Laverne was probably quite close to the truth.

"I won't be around much longer, and she can't make it without me. Funny, isn't it?"

"What's funny, Laverne?" he asked, not wanting to get

involved in her personal life but too sensitive to shut off the discussion.

"I was always afraid she'd find somebody else to take my place, and so I never let anybody get too close to her. Never. It was a terrible mistake," she mused aloud, and then suddenly realizing that she was putting too much of her personal misery into words, she changed her tone. "That's enough of that. God, how I hate women who get maudlin. I'd like to see the assemblage, Mike . . . when it's ready, of course," she asked, back to her usual high-pressure tactics.

Taken aback, Mike started to refuse. "I never let—" he began, and stopped himself. "Sure. Why not?"

"Thanks. I'll look forward to hearing from you when it's ready."

As she got up from her chair, Laverne felt a sudden stabbing pain in her back. Great, she thought, the last thing I need is to pop a vertebra. She moved slowly and carefully, and the pain diminished, only to recur when she started up the steps. It was so severe that she could hardly stand, and she stood frozen in place, clutching the banister and gasping. At last she called out for help.

"Clark!" she screamed, and the pain in her voice was so commanding that within seconds the butler and Catalina were both at her side.

With their help she was finally able to make it to her bed. "Call Dr. Cableshaw," she whispered, her eyes glazed with agony. "I have to talk to him. Catalina, get me a glass of water and give me two of those red capsules."

Fortunately, the doctor was in his office, and he left his patient to take the call. After Laverne described the pain, he offered to stop by to see her that evening.

"Can't you just send me some medicine?" she asked.

"I want to check you over, and I'll give you a shot that will keep you comfortable through the night."

By the time he arrived, Chelsea was at home. She had taken two difficult final exams and was exhausted and ill, but she forced herself to sit down at the dinner table with

Bunny. She had decided that some semblance of normalcy had to be restored to the household, and she had personally gotten her mother out of bed, dressed her, combed her hair, and brought her down to the dining room. Nauseated and tired as she was, Chelsea nevertheless tried to make conversation, but Bunny seemed not to hear anything she said, so busy was she consuming every bite of food placed in front of her.

After Dr. Cableshaw had examined Laverne, he asked her granddaughter to join them upstairs.

"Are you feeling any better, Gran?" Chelsea asked.

"A little. Chelsea, Dr. Cableshaw wants to teach you how to give me injections. I could give them myself, but he apparently doesn't trust me with the medication."

The doctor took issue. "It's not a matter of trust, Laverne. Your judgment will be severely impaired after one shot, and you could overdose easily by taking too much. Do you mind doing this, young lady?"

"Whatever you say. It's not too hard to do, is it?" Chelsea asked.

"Bring me an orange, and we'll use that for practice," he said quietly.

Skilled at doing work with her hands, Chelsea learned easily, and when at last the doctor was ready to go, Chelsea walked him to the front door. "What's the pain in her back, Dr. Cableshaw?"

"It's the cancer. It's in her spine, I'm afraid. Without any kind of treatment, this is going to spread like wildfire."

"Then why is she refusing everything?"

"I think she realizes that the most we can buy is a little time, and the cost is very high, not only in dollars, but in effort and illness."

"It's not like her to try to save money. She's a terrible spendthrift," Chelsea countered.

"The prospect of death changes everything, Chelsea. Everything. Man is the only animal who knows he will die, but yet refuses to believe it. Your grandmother has accepted the fact that she will not live long, but her main concern is still her daughter. She doesn't want to spend any money on herself, money that her daughter will need when she's gone."

"But I can take care of Mom," Chelsea protested, "and I will."

"Tell your grandmother that. I think it'll make her feel better. Now, you can give her an injection every four hours, but only if she needs it. Stretch the time between injections as far as she can go. Good night, young lady."

Chelsea went upstairs and sat at her grandmother's bedside quietly, waiting for her to open her eyes. When she did, her first words were, "Where's Bunny?"

"She's fine. She came downstairs and ate a good dinner. Now she's sitting in front of the television set watching *The Big Valley*."

"She always loved Barbara Stanwyck," Laverne said with a sigh, and closed her eyes again.

"Gran, don't you think you ought to reconsider taking some of the treatments for this thing? What could it hurt? You have nothing to worry about as far as money goes. I'm going to a great job at Tanager's right after graduation, and I'll be able to take care of Mom."

Laverne opened her eyes. "What in the hell are you doing taking a job selling jewelry?" she asked.

Chelsea chuckled. "You don't understand. I'm not going to sell it. I've been hired to design it, Gran. They're going to put out a line of jewelry for younger women under my own name. Isn't that wonderful?"

"Does it pay much?"

"It will . . . eventually. It's all tied in with sales, I believe."

"I hope you know what you're doing."

"Gran, I have something to tell you. Maybe it will change your mind about taking treatment."

"Nothing will change my mind. I'm not going to give every last cent we have to doctors and hospitals when I'm going to die anyway," she said, her voice beginning to fade as the medicine took effect.

Chelsea took her hand and tried to arouse her. There

was no time to wait. If something was going to be done, they could waste no more time. "Don't fall asleep yet, please. I have something important to tell you."

Laverne opened her eyes and looked at her grand-daughter. "What?" she asked listlessly.

"If I could lay my hands on a lot of instant cash, would you go to the hospital and begin treatment? Maybe buy yourself some time?"

In spite of the medication, the prospect of money caught the older woman's attention. "Money? What kind of money? Where would you get it?"

"Remember Mom's jewelry, that stuff that burned up in the fire that you collected insurance on?"

"What about it?"

"Well, it didn't burn. I have it, every single piece."

"How?" Laverne asked with astonishment. "How did you save it?"

"I took Mom's jewel case into my bedroom to play with that afternoon. I used to do it all the time in secret. Then, when the fire started, I stuffed the box inside my pillowcase. Remember, there was a picture of me in the newspaper clutching my pillow?"

"Why . . . why didn't you tell me?" Laverne asked, but her voice was getting thick and her words were slurred.

"I overheard you saying you were glad everything had burned up because of the insurance, and I was afraid you'd be mad at me."

In spite of her fascination with Chelsea's revelation, the effects of the medication became too strong for her to resist any longer, and she began to fade away. "Tell me the story in the morning, Chelsea. Please. Don't let me forget," she whispered, and closed her eyes.

Chelsea tucked the blanket around her, turned out the light, and went back to her own room. Taking the key for the safety deposit box from her top drawer, she stuck it on her key ring. Tomorrow she would begin to sell off the pieces, one by one.

Wearily, she went downstairs and curled up in a chair in the room where Bunny was staring at the television set and smiling. What was going on inside her mind? her daughter wondered. And why had she retreated from the world?

67

Dr. Cableshaw was surprised to get a call from Chelsea the next morning.

"Doctor, I've managed to convince my grandmother to begin taking treatment," she said, explaining her reason for calling so early. "She knows how bad the odds are, and so do I, but I still think she shouldn't just give up and die. So, we're ready to start when you are."

"She agreed?" he asked, still not quite believing that the determined Laverne Thomas ever changed her mind about anything.

"Yes, she's finally become convinced that she needs to stay alive as long as she possibly can."

"You know it's going to make her sicker, don't you? Her hair will fall out, and she'll be quite miserable," he warned, "and the best we can offer is perhaps a few extra months, if we're lucky. It would be unrealistic, given the advancement of the disease, to expect any kind of a miracle cure."

"She knows that and so do I. She's decided that she wants those months if she can get them. I've also managed to convince her that it's important for us, my mother and me, to be assured that everything humanly possible has been done and that her life wasn't just written off. Can you understand how we feel?"

"Of course. Let me call Dr. Grover immediately and explain the situation to her. I'm pretty sure she'll want to start chemotherapy or radiation treatments as soon as possible. I'd like for her to see your grandmother this afternoon."

"Is this a woman doctor you're talking about?" Chelsea asked doubtfully. "I'm not sure Gran will like that. She disapproves of women physicians."

"That's unfortunate, because this particular doctor is the best qualified. Dr. Grover specializes in breast cancer and has done a lot of important research. If she understands that, I certainly think your grandmother will accept her. If not, I'll try to find somebody else, but I strongly recommend that she not reject Dr. Grover just because she's a woman."

"I'll talk to her."

"I'll call you as soon as I know something. You're at home?"

"Yes, I'll wait for your call."

Chelsea took her mother in to see Laverne, who was sitting up in bed with a breakfast tray in front of her. Although she had drunk the orange juice and coffee, nothing else had been touched.

A smile appeared on Laverne's face when she saw Bunny. "Darling, did you have a good night's rest?" she asked her daughter.

"Yes, Mama. Can I sit on the bed beside you?" Bunny asked softly.

"By all means. Come sit right here," Laverne said brightly, patting the coverlet near her, but when Bunny sat down, the movement of the mattress caused her mother to wince with pain. Chelsea noticed and moved forward.

"Mom," she gently suggested, "why don't I pull the chair up close to the bed and you can sit on that. It hurts Gran for you to sit on her bed."

Laverne waved her away. "It's okay, Chelsea. Let her stay. What did the doctor say?"

"He's going to call an oncologist. You may have to go into the hospital this afternoon," she began, and noticed that Laverne was shaking her head, afraid that any mention of hospitals might upset Bunny. Bunny, however, was too busy picking at the bacon and eggs on her mother's plate to take notice of anything being said.

"Didn't you give her any breakfast?" Laverne asked.

"Gran, she had an omelette, three slices of bacon, two rolls with butter and jam, orange juice, and coffee. I think she would have kept on eating if I hadn't stopped her."

"Then for God's sake get rid of this tray before she eats anything else. Has she had any exercise at all?" Laverne asked impatiently.

"I can't get her to do anything but sleep and eat. After breakfast I tried to take her out into the backyard for a little walk around the pool, but she balked when I opened the door and absolutely refused to go outside with me."

"You've got to be firm with her, Chelsea, you know that. She's lazy, and she's always hungry. As tiny as she is, she'll be a blimp within a week or two if you don't control her," Laverne snapped in irritation.

Chelsea wanted to tell her grandmother that it didn't make much difference, that without Laverne to scold and push, Bunny was probably never going to work again, but she kept her silence. If Gran was going to die, let her take her illusions with her. Chelsea extricated the tray from her mother's grasp and carried it out of the room.

Once Chelsea had closed the door behind her, Bunny leaped to her feet and declared angrily, "For God's sake, stop talking about me in the third person as if I were deaf, dumb, and blind!"

"Shush!" Laverne cautioned forcefully. "Somebody might hear you talking and figure out what's going on."

"I don't know how long I can keep up the pretense, Mama. It's driving me really crazy," she said, her voice filled with frustration. "Have you any idea how hard it was to act like a child on the set yesterday and still give a performance?"

"You've got to keep it up, honey. You just can't trust yourself to be questioned by the police. There are just too many holes in our story."

"I hate it all, Mama. Here you are sick and dying, and I'm slugging about the house pretending I don't know what day it is."

"Lower your voice!" Laverne commanded. Bunny

was getting out of control, and she had to reign her in quickly.

Bunny sank down in the chair disconsolately. "We should have told the truth. It would have been better in the long run."

"No, it would not! They'd have sent you to jail, you silly woman. Can't you understand that? It would have all been over for you. Everything we've worked so hard for would have gone up in a torrent of publicity so scandalous nothing could have been resurrected. Your daughter's life would have been ruined too. You don't want Chelsea to live under the cloud of having a murderer for a mother, do you?"

"Mother, grandmother, what's the difference?"

"There's a big difference. I killed him to keep him from killing you! That's justifiable. Your killing that little creep because he insulted you is not. God, can't you see the distinction?"

"He was lying, wasn't he? You weren't paying him to screw me, were you?" she asked, her huge eyes rimmed with bright tears.

"Of course not! I would never do such a thing. He was a creep and a liar and I'm glad he's dead, understand? It's almost a pleasure to take the credit for ridding the world of such a parasite."

Bunny's tears had started, and Laverne knew it would be a long, wet thunderstorm. "Come lie down here beside your mother, darling. Everything's going to be all right."

"It was so awful, Mama," she sobbed. "I didn't mean to kill him. I thought we'd have a drink and make up and everything would be fine, but he was so cruel. He said I was an old woman and a lousy lay and he wouldn't have touched me if it hadn't been for the money you were paying him. But I never meant to kill him. It just happened."

"He was just another vile man, darling. The world is filled with them," Laverne crooned softly, wondering what would happen to her little girl when she was gone.

* * *

Chelsea was halfway down the stairs when the telephone rang. Dr. Cableshaw must have some news for her. She dropped the tray on the hall credenza and picked up the telephone.

"This is the overseas operator. I have a call for Chelsea Hunter. Is she there?"

"Yes, I'm Chelsea Hunter," she replied, and before she realized what was happening, Wills's voice came over the wire as clearly as if he were in the next room.

"Chelsea, I got your letter this morning. What the devil is going on?" he inquired anxiously.

"Didn't you read it?" she asked, still trying to recover from the surprise of hearing his voice.

"Of course I read it, but what difference does it make what's going on with your family? They're not us, Chelsea. What we feel for each other is more important than anything or anyone," he said passionately.

"I can't come to England to live, Wills. I just can't," she began, her throat dry and tight with emotion.

"Why not?" he demanded.

"I told you. My grandmother is going to die soon, my mother's helpless and needs care. I can't just run away from my family, Wills, could you?"

"Of course not," he said, his voice softening, "but you can bring your mother with you, darling. We'll take care of her together."

"Oh Wills, I can't . . . I can't impose that kind of burden on you," she protested, but her determination was wavering.

"Darling, look, don't rush into making a final decision right now. We've lots of time. Promise me you'll think it over through the next few months, will you?"

"Wills . . . I just signed a ten-year contract with Tanager's. I had to. Nothing else I could do would pay the kind of money this job does, and I'll need every cent."

"Damn the bloody contract. We can't let a piece of paper stand between us. Now promise me you'll think about this, or I'll stay on the overseas line until I've spent every shilling of the Ashford estate."

"I'll think about it," she said.

"That's all I ask for now. I love you, Chelsea. I'll always love you."

Dr. Cableshaw's call came in almost as soon as she finished talking to Wills, and he told her that Dr. Grover was willing to oversee Laverne's treatment. To Chelsea's surprise, her grandmother not only accepted the prospect of being cared for by a woman, but she also agreed to go into the hospital at UCLA immediately. Although there was a bed available on the VIP floor, Laverne refused because of the expense, opting instead for a standard private room. Clark and Chelsea helped her downstairs and into the backseat of the Lincoln with a pillow and blanket, and they took her to the hospital. She had just settled into her room when a pretty young woman with short, straight black hair suddenly appeared at the door.

"Hello, Mrs. Thomas," she said, approaching the bed. "I'm Polly Grover, your oncologist." Turning to Chelsea, she smiled and asked, "Are you the granddaughter?"

Chelsea nodded and smiled. The woman was so strikingly pretty and young, it was hard to imagine that she was a trained specialist.

"Good. Now, your grandmother is going to be very busy for the next few hours. I'd suggest that if you have errands or shopping to do, you go do them now. I'll give you a call around dinnertime, all right? Then if you want to stop in for a brief visit this evening, you may," she said crisply, dismissing Chelsea.

Back in her car, Chelsea checked the time. Though it was past two, if she hurried, she could get to the bank before it closed and get started on her liquidation plan.

By three o'clock she was back on the San Diego Freeway with the valuables in her purse. After sorting through the jewelry, she had decided to bring it all home so she could decide what to sell first. It would probably be wise to start out with the least distinguished piece, a diamond brooch. Although it had been more than ten years since the fire, she knew she had to be very careful to feed the pieces back into the market slowly.

Jeth Goldstein took the brooch without the slightest hesitation. Chelsea had removed all the distinguishing marks from the signed Tiffany piece, thereby lowering the value considerably. Under the circumstances, it was the only safe thing to do. Private sellers could never get anywhere near the price that jewelers could charge their customers anyway, she figured. Although Goldstein would have given her a check for five thousand dollars, she insisted on cash, which meant she had to settle for four, and with the money tucked into the band of her panty hose, she left the Jewelry Mart to head home. So far, so good. By the time she had sold everything and put it with the money she already had in the bank, she should be able to pay for Laverne's treatments and keep the household going. At least for now. When her grandmother died, Chelsea intended to make a radical change in their lifestyle. But not now. The least she could do for Gran was to keep her in her home, surrounded by servants, living the luxurious life that was so important to her.

As she drove home, Chelsea's mind was filled with plans for the next sale. She would dismantle the pink pearls and sell them without the clasp. She'd unmount the pink diamond and reset it in a platinum ring with baguettes on the side; then, with a bit of reworking, she'd replace the pink diamond with an emerald taken from another piece. When that was done, she'd either make a small pin or a large dinner ring, depending on which would work best. Since her time and energy were limited, she knew she had to sell off the jewelry with only enough preparation to avoid the risk of exposure.

At home everything was quiet. Clark reported that her mother had been in her room all afternoon, and she said she'd check on her. Bunny was sleeping, and although Chelsea knew she should probably get her up and take her for a walk, she just didn't have the energy. As soon as exams were over and she had stockpiled enough money to pay for Laverne's treatments, perhaps she'd have Dr. Cableshaw do a complete physical examination of Bunny. Maybe she was anemic or something.

Going into her own room, she found a message on her desk from Hilda asking her to call. She stretched out comfortably on her bed and picked up the telephone.

Fortunately, Hilda was available, and they chatted easily. It was so nice to have a friend in whom she could confide. When Hilda learned that Laverne had suddenly changed her mind about treatment, she was sure she knew the reason.

"She wants to see the movie, Chelsea," Hilda said with finality.

"The movie? What movie?" Chelsea asked.

"Honey, get with it. Your mother's big movie—*The Beyonder*. Laverne wants to live long enough to see her daughter's greatest performance. That movie."

"Right, why didn't I think of that? How could I be so dumb? Do you think she'll make it?"

"I wouldn't put it past her."

"Have you seen any of the dailies? Is Mom as good as Gran thinks she is in it?" Chelsea asked.

"She's fantastic, she really is. I talked to Mike this morning, and he's thrilled. He's even going to let your grandmother see the rough assemblage. He says there's not much doubt that Bunny will be nominated for an award, unless, of course, there's too much conjecture about her part in the killing."

"I hope to God that doesn't spoil it for her."

"How's Bunny getting along with her psychiatrist?"

"Gran doesn't believe in shrinks, Hilda, you know that. Mom hasn't seen him in weeks."

"Look, young lady, you're going to be the head of that household from now on. You make the decisions. There are a couple of doctors here in town who could probably help her a lot. Let me research it for you, okay?" Hilda insisted, putting on as much pressure as possible. She knew she should bring up the subject of drugs, but she wasn't quite ready to make such serious accusations.

"Um, well, sure, Hilda," Chelsea replied reluctantly, with dollar signs dancing in front of her eyes. Psychiatrists cost a lot of money.

"Promise you'll give it serious consideration?"

"Yeah, I will, sure," she promised, wondering how in the world she was going to pay for everything.

As she put down the telephone, Chelsea closed her eyes for only a brief respite, but there was no time for relaxation. She had to spend the next few hours studying for her last college final, which she was going to take in the morning. After she visited her grandmother at the hospital later, she would go to the lab and work on the jewelry. And once classes were over tomorrow, she would make a trip to the Jewelry Mart to sell another piece.

Would there ever be time for her to rest again?

68

Laverne stayed in the hospital for her first week of chemotherapy, and although she was quite ill, she was anxious to go home because she could not bear to be separated from her daughter. Chelsea had brought Bunny to the hospital, and the first visit went well, but on the second evening, her mother had simply refused to set foot inside the place. Chelsea tried to coax her, but Bunny had collapsed into hysterical weeping.

The doctor finally agreed to let Laverne go home. He advised Chelsea to hire a private nurse, but Laverne decided it would be too expensive, and so the burden of caring for her grandmother fell on Chelsea's shoulders. Fortunately, she was not alone, for Clark and Catalina were extremely helpful. Since chemotherapy is a delicate process whereby the patient is poisoned to the point where the cancer cells are destroyed without quite destroying the host, it was necessary that Laverne's physical condition be monitored closely. Clark was assigned to drive her to the doctor's office daily. In addition to cooking and cleaning, Catalina was also responsible for taking care of Bunny, who was relatively placid unless she was deprived of food. As the days passed, however, Bunny began to sleep less, and she often sneaked into the kitchen to stuff herself with whatever was available.

Hilda did her best to persuade them to put Bunny under the care of a psychiatrist, but as Chelsea had predicted, Laverne would not hear of it.

"She's just in shock, Chelsea," Laverne insisted. "She needs time to recover, that's all. Besides, if word gets out that she's seeing a shrink, people may start to get ideas. You know the district attorney would like nothing more than to blow this whole thing open." Then, almost as an afterthought, she muttered in exasperation, "Besides, I don't want anybody poking around in my daughter's mind and finding out . . . things."

Chelsea thought the comment rather odd, but when she tried to press the point further, Laverne changed the subject. The matter was obviously closed, and frustrating as it was, Chelsea could not bring herself to openly defy the skeletal figure that had once been her strong and active grandmother. As she sat beside her bed, Chelsea wondered how long her grandmother would have to suffer so terribly. Catalina cooked things she liked, and Laverne forced herself to eat, knowing how important it was to have nourishment. It was not in her nature to be bested by anything, including cancer.

"Gran, I have to start work next week. The money is going out so fast, and I really need this job. Are you going to be all right alone here all day?"

"I'll be fine. Have you sold all the jewelry yet?"

"Most of it. I still have Mom's engagement ring, which I hate to sell, but I will of course, and although I've shown the pink pearls around to a couple of dealers, nobody's come close to what they're worth, and I hate to give them away."

"How much have you gotten for everything so far?"

"Almost forty thousand," Chelsea said softly.

"My God, they must have been worth four times that much," Laverne responded accusingly.

"I know that, Gran, but they're hot, remember? You'd already collected the insurance on them. Besides, I was limited by the need to sell them for cash only, and I had to be very careful about the people I dealt with. You know I could go to jail for this," Chelsea said defensively.

"You're worrying too much," Laverne replied, her voice now reduced to a coarse whisper. "That happened more than ten years ago, who'd remember?"

"Somebody might," Chelsea said softly, wondering how she'd managed to get herself into such a miserable mess. Not only was she guilty of fencing jewels that belonged to the insurance company, but she'd sold a fake emerald ring and diamond pendant. Good Lord, how had they managed to turn a family of three simple women into a den of thieves and murderers?

She was suddenly jolted out of her morbid reverie by a coarse, cackling laugh. "Don't worry so much, Chelsea," her grandmother said bitterly, "you can always plead ignorance and put the blame on your dying, evil, murderous grandmother. After all, if I could kill a man, why would I hesitate to cheat the insurance company? Besides, you were only a child when the house burned down."

"Gran, what are we doing?" Chelsea asked, longing for deliverance from guilt and the resurrection of order and peace in their lives.

"We're doing the best we can, that's all," the older woman said, closing her eyes and turning away. "For a woman to survive in this rotten world, she has to use everything she's got . . . every damned thing, or the bastards will crush her under their heels."

After a moment, Laverne turned back, and her piercing eyes shone with fury as they bored into those of her granddaughter. Her next words spilled out of her mouth like vomit. "This cancer is going to kill me, Chelsea. Who's to say that I haven't got a right to use it any way I please?"

Chelsea didn't answer her, and so there was a long, long silence in the room. Changing the subject at last, she asked, "So, when do you begin radiation?"

"About three weeks, if I'm still alive."

"You will be," Chelsea said with a greater confidence than she felt as she reached to answer the ringing telephone. It was Hilda.

"Does Laverne feel like talking?" she asked.

"I think so," Chelsea said, handing the receiver to her grandmother, grateful for the sound of another human voice.

"Laverne, are you up to a little outing tomorrow?" Hilda asked.

"What for?"

"They've got the film together, and Mike called and said you and I were invited to see it. Bunny too, if you want to take her along."

"No, not Bunny," Laverne responded quickly.

"Why not?" Hilda asked.

"I don't want her to see that stabbing scene. She's starting to get better, and it may be a setback for her, but I will definitely be there. What time and where?"

"Two-thirty tomorrow. I'll pick you up."

"I'll be ready, but would you mind if Clark drove us? I'm awfully weak, and he's very helpful."

"No problem. Why don't I just meet you at Technicolor? Okay?"

"Fine," Laverne said.

When Hilda had hung up, she gave the telephone back to Chelsea, who asked, "You're going to see the film? When?"

"Two-thirty tomorrow."

"But you have a doctor's appointment at three!" Chelsea protested.

"Cancel it."

"I'll call Dr. Grover's office and try to schedule you in the morning," Chelsea said, not giving in completely.

"Did I say change it? Did I?" Laverne asked querulously. "I said cancel it. It will take every ounce of strength I have to make one trip tomorrow, much less two. Now, it's almost time for my pain shot. Just give it to me and go away so I can sleep in peace."

"I think you're making a mistake not taking Mom to see the movie. It might just give her a push in the right direction," Chelsea commented as she prepared the injection.

"Mind your own business!" Laverne said with a fierceness that was almost frightening. "Bunny must never be allowed to see this film . . . never!"

"But why, Gran?" Chelsea asked, bewildered.

"You don't want to know. Just make sure she never sees it or we'll have more trouble on our hands than we can ever handle."

Later that evening Chelsea received a call from the university reminding her to pick up her cap and gown for the graduation ceremony.

"I won't be attending," she said, "so just cross me off the list, okay?"

"Do you want the diploma mailed to your home address?" the woman asked.

"That will be fine," she replied, and with a sigh she pulled out the stack of bills to be paid. Tomorrow she would put just enough cash into her checking account to cover the checks she had to write. If the money kept flowing out as fast as it had been lately, it wouldn't be long before they'd be in serious trouble.

When she had finished, she sealed all the envelopes and stamped them. Then she took out her sketchbook and tried to concentrate on her jewelry designs, but her mind seemed to have gone blank. After an hour staring at the paper, she set it aside and went to get herself a glass of warm milk. She wondered if she was developing an ulcer. She found Bunny sitting in front of the television set, with a huge bowl of popcorn in her lap, watching *The Doris Day Show*.

"Mom," Chelsea snapped, reaching over and snatching the bowl away. "Who gave you this?"

Bunny said nothing, angrily pursing her lips together and frowning furiously, just as she had so many times in her childhood films. Chelsea looked at her hopelessly. As Laverne had predicted, Bunny was blowing up like a balloon. Her cheeks were so puffy that her eyes seemed to disappear, and her swollen belly sat on her lap like a beach ball.

Chelsea sighed again. There was so much in this house that seemed to be out of control, and her mother's waistline was the least of it. "Come on, Mom. It's time to get ready for bed. I'll help you tonight. I think Catalina's getting worn-out." The last thing Chelsea needed was to lose the best housekeeper in Beverly Hills.

She turned off the television set and walked her still pouting mother up the stairs. At the landing, she caught a glimpse of herself in the mirror. What a strange sight they were: the tall, skinny daughter, and the round little puffball of a mother. Bodies were so strange, Chelsea mused. Here were three women, all bearing many of the same genes, living in the same house, breathing the same air, eating the same food, but weight seemed to be flowing off two of them and settling comfortably on the third. Poor Mom.

69

Six weeks had passed since Laverne began her treatments under Dr. Grover, and although she was still weak and in a great deal of pain, to everyone's amazement, she had not given in to the disease. Every morning she would drag her emaciated body out of bed, dress, and pull the handmade wig over her barren scalp, apply powder and rouge and false eyelashes to the death's head that was her face, and make her way downstairs on Clark's arm.

At her mother's insistence, Bunny was also routed out of bed and dressed and brought down to the breakfast table. When they finished eating—a few bites for Laverne, a carefully monitored portion for her daughter—the two women would walk arm in arm to the solarium. Clark would play old records on the stereo for them, and they would sit on the couch together and talk until lunchtime. A visiting nurse came every afternoon to check Laverne and give her the shots necessary to get her through the day.

Although the chemotherapy and radiation treatments had ended, Dr. Grover had proposed another series of experimental medications, and Laverne had agreed to try it. She wanted desperately to stay alive until *The Beyonder* was completed. Having seen the rough assemblage, she hungered for the day when the film would be released and her daughter's talent acclaimed once more. Every afternoon, Hilda would call to report on the progress of postproduction and the advertising campaign being planned.

Chelsea was at home only in the evenings. She had started her new job at Tanager's, and there was so much work to do that she often didn't get home until both her mother and grandmother were in bed asleep, courtesy of modern chemistry. She felt a bit guilty for being away from home so much, but the atmosphere in the house was depressing, whereas her job was challenging and exhilarating.

The laboratory was in full operation, and her first design, the rose bracelet and medallion, were put on display. Within a week all four pieces in both the New York and the Los Angeles stores were sold. To celebrate, Jonathan invited Chelsea to have dinner with him at the Windsor, and although she felt guilty about going, feeling she was needed at home, she rationalized that it was business and accepted the invitation.

Over a glass of Roederer Cristal, Jonathan informed her that the board had approved her request for additional artisans, and he had advised Dennis Petalski to hire two goldsmiths from Italy in order to expedite production.

"There's a condition, however, my dear," he warned.

"And that is?" she asked, the dimple in her cheek deepening.

"You're spending too much time in the manufacture of the pieces. We want you at the drawing board designing." He smiled and put his hand on hers.

Chelsea looked up from the long slim fingers adorned with a handsome signet ring to the face that had become such a fixture in her life. She loved working with him. He was bright and reasonable and understanding. If there was a problem, he always found the solution.

"Jonathan, whenever I'm with you I feel as if I'm swimming in a sea of tranquility. You make me believe that all things are possible."

He laughed softly and withdrew his hand. "They are when you're young, my dear, but for those of us in the third act of life, there are fewer options."

"Don't say that. You've the youngest, most vigorous mind I've ever known."

"Ah, the mind, yes!" he replied ruefully.

"I can't tell you how much working at Tanager's means to me, Jonathan . . . I'm not sure I'd have made it through these past terrible weeks if it hadn't been for my job."

"How's your mother doing?"

Chelsea shook her head. "It's hard to say. She's all

locked up in a cocoon of silence. Catalina, our house-keeper, says that she hears her talking to Gran, but she never says anything to me. I wanted to take her out for a drive last weekend, but Gran said no, and I suppose she's right."

"But why? She hasn't been out of the house for weeks, has she?" he asked.

"Gran is afraid somebody'll spot her and take her picture . . . and Mom, well, she's gained a lot of weight."

"Does that worry your grandmother?"

"Oh God, it used to, but it doesn't seem to bother her as much anymore, although the food is kept locked up and Mom's served small portions. But I don't want to talk about that. I'm the one who's gaining weight. Ever since I started work, my appetite has gotten enormous."

"I hope it's because you're happy in your work."

"That must be it," she said, smiling.

The house was quiet when Chelsea got home. She picked up her mail from the credenza and tiptoed up the stairs. There was a letter with the Ashford family crest on the envelope, and she tore it open, disappointed that it was not in Wills's handwriting.

Dear Chelsea,

Wills has been terribly busy and so he asked me to write to tell you that Father died unexpectedly two weeks ago from a heart attack. We are grateful that he did not suffer, but it has been most difficult to adjust to his loss. He was an extraordinary man, kind and loving and generous. Life will never be quite the same for any of us, ever again.

Father's title passes to Wills, and he has assumed the mantle with his usual grace and courage. He asked me to convey his love to you, and to tell you that he will write when things settle down once more, although I suspect it will be some time before that happens.

I hope you and your family are bearing up under

the withering effects of the murder in your home.
The tabloids have been filled with the unfortunate
story as well as ugly speculations about your
mother, who used to be a quite popular star here.
It must be very difficult for you to have any kind
of a normal life. I'm not sure I could handle it if
that sort of scandal ever touched anyone in my own
family.

                              Affectionately,
                              Margaret

Chelsea dropped the letter onto her desk and sank
down on the edge of her bed, stunned. If she had ever
harbored the hope that her present difficulties might work
themselves out enough for her to marry Wills and become
the mistress of Ashford Hall, they had been crushed by
that delicately scripted piece of paper. Margaret was telling Chelsea that she was tainted by the "scandal," "ugly
speculations," and "murder," words that had leaped off
the page and scalded her with their intensity.

In her own civilized, British way, her friend, her ally
Margaret had told her to stay away from her brother. He
was an earl now, and there was no place in his life for
her and her Hollywood family. To hell with them all!

Filled with anger and hurt, and raging at the unfairness
of a life that conspired to thwart the love two people had
for each other, Chelsea threw herself on the bed. If ever
she needed the release of a long soggy bout of weeping
and sobbing, it was now. She tried to let herself go, tried
to squeeze one little drop of moisture from under her
eyelids, but it was useless. Her eyes were as dry as the
desert at high noon in the middle of August. What was
wrong with her? Why couldn't she cry?

It was after midnight when she finally pulled herself
off the bed and got to her feet. Her head hurt and her
body seemed to be heavy with an unexploded bomb
wedged deep inside her. The rage had become a numbing

ache that throbbed through the bone, flesh, and organs of her body, and her soul bled despair.

Wills was certainly a part of her past now. She would never regret a moment of the delight they shared, but their love was dead. All their hopes and dreams of a life together would never be fulfilled. They had been the fairy-tale fantasies of a child anyway. Every little girl dreams of marrying a handsome prince and living in a castle and riding beautiful white horses. Wills had been her dream prince, but she was an adult now, and grown-ups know those kinds of dreams don't come true. It was time to pack them away with her toys and her dolls, and never, ever, look at them again.

70

Hilda called Chelsea at work one morning to tell her that she was going to New York to meet with some important clients. Her firm was putting together a package to make a very large budget film, and it was her job to sell the deal to the two stars who hated each other passionately. She did not expect to be back in Los Angeles for a while.

"How's it going with you these days?" she asked.

"Everything's just great here at work, Hilda, but it's really tough at home," Chelsea responded.

"I know. I stopped in to see Laverne yesterday, and she's gotten so thin she's almost invisible. How can she hang on? She's lost so much weight, it's like talking to a disembodied voice, although her morale is amazingly high for someone so terribly ill."

"You really have to admire her. She's so tough and so brave, isn't she?" Chelsea said. "She had a miserable time last night. She's in excruciating pain, and the medication just isn't doing it for her anymore."

"Didn't the chemotherapy and radiation help at all?"

"Not much, maybe a little. Dr. Grover says the radiation shrank the lung tumor somewhat, but the chemotherapy had no effect on the cells in her spine. God, here it is, almost 1971, and they still haven't figured out how to cure this disease." The exasperation and fatigue were evident in her voice.

"Hell, they can't even free those 150 airline passengers that are being held hostage in the desert by a small group of terrorists. But enough of that, at least I've got some good news for you. The release date on *The Beyonder* has been moved up. The score is finished and recorded, and Mike says it's great."

"So it's not going to be a Christmas release, after all. Well, that's good, isn't it?"

"I think so, it's really not a holiday-type picture, and so they're going for the last week in October."

"This is only September, Hilda. I'm not sure Gran's going to make it that long."

"Don't underestimate the power of your grandmother's will, Chelsea. Look, I haven't seen you in weeks. Why don't you quit a little early today and have dinner with me? It's been ages since we've had some nice, private girl talk."

"Oh, I couldn't, I'm afraid. As soon as I get finished here, I need to get home," Chelsea protested.

"Now stop that! You need a night off occasionally. You're working too hard."

"You know I'll feel miserably guilty all through dinner and won't enjoy myself," Chelsea protested, although the idea of a quiet evening and one of Emma's dinners was very tempting. Besides, the prospect of delaying her return home, where misery seemed to bloom in every niche and corner, was exceedingly seductive.

"Emma's fixing a rack of lamb. I promise we'll just have a quick dinner and then you can go. What do you say?"

"You said the magic words, Hilda. I don't know what's gotten into me lately, but I'm hungry all the time. Must be my mom's genes. The only thing that fits me comfortably is an elastic-waisted cotton skirt. I've been wearing it every other day."

"You're under a lot of stress, kiddo. Speaking of waistlines, how's Bunny's doing?"

"She started to smoke again, and she's already up to three or four packs a day, but she's not eating constantly, and she's lost weight. Laverne, by the way, has quit smoking altogether. She needs oxygen constantly now, and the nurse warned her that she might burn herself up."

"What time can you get out of there?" Hilda asked.

"I'll leave at five sharp."

Hilda's call had lifted Chelsea's spirits considerably, and in spite of her lack of sleep, the afternoon was a productive one. She phoned the house at four-thirty and talked to Martha, the day nurse she'd hired when she went to work full-time. The nurse reported that everything was fine but said Laverne had been asking for the pain shot every two hours, although she'd managed to delay it to three.

"Every four hours is not often enough, Miss Chelsea," Martha said. "I think you ought to talk to the doctor."

"She told me to use my own discretion, Martha. Go ahead, give it every two hours and try to keep her comfortable. I'll call him and talk to her tomorrow."

"When you do, ask her if it would be okay to give Laverne some heroin. It's really the best drug for people like her. Too bad those druggies have caused it to be made illegal."

"But that's addictive!" Chelsea reacted, shocked that this pleasant, jolly, middle-aged woman was suggesting something so radical.

"Do you think that would be a problem for Miss Laverne?" the woman asked.

Chelsea felt stupid. "You're right, Martha. One needn't worry about long-term problems for a life that's become short-term. I'll ask her. By the way, would it be possible for you to stay overtime tonight? I've been invited to a special friend's house for dinner, but I'll be home early. I'll pay you extra, of course."

"I'd be happy to do it, Miss Chelsea, and I do need the extra money."

Chelsea then put in a call to Dr. Grover, who, after a long conversation about drugs for cancer patients, revealed that if it were legal, heroin would probably be the drug of choice for patients like her grandmother.

"I can get it from a drug dealer, but I can't get it from a drugstore? Is that what you're telling me, Dr. Grover?" she asked in frustration.

"I was speaking academically, Chelsea. It's not in your grandmother's interest or yours for you to break the law."

Chelsea walked across her office and stared at herself in the mirror. This unlined, pretty face with the wide cheekbones and dark eyebrows was the mask of a crook. "Sorry, Gran," she whispered to her reflection, "I'm going to have to pass on this one. I wouldn't even know where to start."

Driving through the rush-hour traffic, Chelsea's thoughts drifted to Wills, but she dismissed them immediately. She'd had three letters from him, but she had answered none of them. One of these days he would call again, and she was ready with a response that would end it once and for all. There was no room in her life for him, and there was certainly no place in his for a woman with a notorious family as well as shabby secrets of her own.

Hilda was shocked when she saw Chelsea. "Chelsea, is that really you?"

"Oh God, Hilda, don't tell me I'm that fat!"

"Well, no," she answered hesitantly, "it's just that you were so damned skinny the last time. Hey, if you had a boyfriend, I'd swear you were pregnant. Come on in, dinner's ready. Want a glass of wine first?"

"Great," Chelsea said as she entered the room, but Hilda's remark had stunned her. My God, she thought distractedly, how could I have been so stupid?

Hilda chattered as she poured the wine, but Chelsea didn't hear a word she was saying; her mind was too preoccupied with the terrible suspicion that Hilda had seen something that she had been too stupid or too ig-

norant to figure out for herself. God, when had she last
had a period? It had been weeks . . . no, maybe months.
They were always irregular and scanty, but she hadn't
seen Wills for over three months, so it just couldn't possibly be true. Could it?

"Hello, hello, is anybody home?" Hilda asked, and
suddenly she had Chelsea's attention.

Shaking her head, Chelsea replied, "Oh God, sorry,
but . . ." She hesitated for a moment, then seeing the
concerned expression on Hilda's face, added, "Heaven
help me, Hilda, but I think you're right."

"Well, I usually am . . . about what?"

"I think I'm pregnant. It all fits . . . I can't remember
when I last had a period . . . I was sick for a few weeks,
but I thought it was just a nervous stomach because so
many things were happening at the time. And now I'm
hungry all the time and I'm gaining weight."

"You must be kidding, right? Oh God, you're not!
Should I be looking into the East for a star or did you
do something that would make it likely? And when, for
Heaven's sake, did you find the time?" Hilda asked. The
wisecracking tone of her voice indicated that she was not
for a minute taking Chelsea seriously, until the younger
woman suddenly put her face into her hands.

"Oh Lord, who was it?" Hilda asked.

"Wills."

Setting her wineglass down, Hilda got up from her
chair and moved over to the sofa where the distraught
young woman was sitting and put her arms around her.
"Everything's going to be fine. You love him, don't you?
You told me how wonderful he was. So, if it turns out
that you really are pregnant, then I'm sure he'll want to
marry you as soon as possible."

Suddenly, Chelsea found tears streaming down her
cheeks. She wept and wept as Hilda held her, unable to
talk, her sobs were so deep and strong. When at last the
weeping began to subside, Hilda got a cold, wet wash-
cloth and wiped her face.

"There, there, sweetie. A good cry bathes the soul, my

mother used to say. Now, suppose we go have a little bite of dinner and talk."

Chelsea obediently followed Hilda to the dining room, and although she tried to eat the delicious rack of lamb with mashed potatoes and string beans, the food just wouldn't seem to go past the lump in her throat.

"I'm sorry," she apologized. "I guess I've lost my appetite."

"I'll have Emma bring some vanilla ice cream. It's the world's great comfort food. Now, how long has it been since you've seen a doctor—for yourself, I mean?" Hilda asked.

"When I got hit on the head, you know, the night Mom tried to kill herself."

"So you don't go for regular female-type checkups?"

Chelsea shook her head.

"I'll have my secretary make an appointment with the woman I go to. She's an ob-gyn specialist and just the person you need to see." When Chelsea began to protest, Hilda raised her hand for silence. "No buts, no excuses! You have to go, preferably tomorrow. You've got to find out one way or the other as soon as possible, because if you are pregnant, surely you'll want to tell your young man right away. You don't want too much time to elapse between the wedding date and the birth of the child, do you?"

"I can't marry Wills," Chelsea said flatly. "His father died, and he's now an earl. There's no place for me in a family like his. Besides, I have responsibilities here. I couldn't drop everything and rush to the other side of the world, now could I?"

"What are you going to do?" Hilda asked.

"I can't have the baby. I simply can't," she said in a tone of such great finality that the words continued to hang in the air, reverberating through the room long after they had been spoken.

Hilda's sympathetic and understanding voice finally broke through the walls of her misery. "Chelsea, my dear, for the right price, there are people who will do this for you. When did you last see your young man?"

"The fifteenth of May," she said softly.

"It's pretty late, Chelsea. The kind of person who'd do it now . . . Well, you'd be risking your life."

Chelsea turned from the window, her face a mask of pain. She looked at the woman who had become her best friend and asked, "What am I going to do, Hilda?"

"It's your decision, Chelsea, but whatever it is, I'll stand by you."

Chelsea sighed. "I've got to go home. It's getting late, and the nurse will be waiting for me so she can leave."

"Try to get some rest tonight."

"It was a lovely dinner. Thanks for . . . everything."

71

The doctor confirmed Chelsea's pregnancy, estimated the date of delivery on George Washington's birthday, gave her bottles of calcium and vitamins, and sent her on her way with another appointment scheduled three weeks later. As she was driving across town on the Santa Monica Freeway, the terrible import of her own personal tragedy descended on her in full force. Instead of exiting the freeway at the appropriate off-ramp, she continued driving east. Once past the downtown area, the traffic became lighter and she was able to increase her speed.

With her foot pressed hard on the accelerator, she found release in maneuvering the speeding car as she headed toward the San Bernardino mountains. The farther she traveled from the city, the better she felt. When she got past Riverside, heading toward the desert, she depressed the accelerator harder, and as the car rocketed ahead on the now open road, she felt free at last. Free from concern for her own life. Free of the burdens of her family. She wanted never to stop, to go faster and faster until she came to . . . where? If there was a Heaven, she wouldn't be welcome. She was a thief and a wanton, and when she died, nobody would care. Life on earth was over for her now. She had nowhere to go. Just a quick twist of the wheel and she could smash into a pole, and all the misery would be ended. She'd do it. She'd pick the right spot so that nobody would be hurt but herself, and she'd be going so fast that when she hit, there would be no chance that she'd survive. One quick swing of the wheel and it would be over.

Life, however, is one of those things that happens while people are busy making other plans, and just about the time that Chelsea was seriously considering that most fateful decision, the car ran out of gas and coasted to a stop.

Frustrated, she slammed her forehead on the steering wheel and groaned, "God, I can't do anything right!"

The car's interior temperature rose dangerously, and if help hadn't arrived promptly, the heat of the desert on a summer afternoon might have done what she had failed to do herself. A highway patrol officer appeared, however, in less than twenty minutes, and by the time the service station truck arrived to start her car again and lead her to the station where the tank was once more filled, the terrible, desperate urge to destroy herself had passed. In life, timing is all, she thought.

Quietly, she headed west, battled the traffic through the interchange, and although everyone would be gone, decided to return to her office, where she would have peace and quiet. She was not yet ready to confront the problematic Bunny and the dying Laverne in her psychologically delicate state.

It was almost seven o'clock when she sat down at her desk, feeling utterly, hopelessly defeated. Ignorance and stupidity had finally gotten the best of her, and she could not blame luck, destiny, her family, or even the father of her child.

How could the wonderful, beautiful relationship she'd

had with Wills have brought her so much unhappiness
and pain? Regret filled her, and once again tears began
to spill slowly from her eyes. It wasn't long before she
was sobbing, again. She had never been so miserable.

Nothing would ever be the same. Unlike other young
women in such circumstances, she could not go somewhere and quietly have the baby and give it away. She
needed to work to support her mother and her grandmother, but the extreme visibility of her family would
put her job in jeopardy. She had lived in the cruel glare
of publicity all of her life, and she knew what the press
would do to her when it was learned she was pregnant
and unmarried. The search would be on for the father,
and even Jonathan Corell would not be able to withstand
that kind of muck. He would have to let her go to protect
the name of his venerable firm.

In just twenty-three short years, she had managed to
make a mess of her entire life. She had failed at everything.
She couldn't even manage to kill herself properly.

The telephone rang, but she didn't answer it. Sobbing,
she faced a future that stretched out before her like a
long, bleak, and dusty road that had to be traveled on
foot, all alone and carrying a heavy pack, and she had
neither strength nor courage nor direction.

She was still weeping when there was a knock on the
door a little after eight. When she didn't answer, the
sound became more insistent, and then she heard Jonathan Corell's voice. "Chelsea, is that you in there? Are
you all right?"

"Go away," she croaked through her sobs. "Leave me
alone."

There was a moment's hesitation while he reacted to
her strangely belligerent response and distressed tone of
voice, and then he pounded on the door forcefully. She
was obviously in trouble and needed help. "Open it up
this minute, or I shall call security and have them come
up to unlock the door!" he ordered in a voice that commanded obedience.

Chelsea was nothing if not obedient, and she went to

the door and unlocked it. Without looking at him, she returned to the desk, where she covered her face with her hands once more.

Striding in, Jonathan stopped when he saw the depth of her anguish, and he rushed to her.

"My God, Chelsea, what's wrong? Did your grandmother die?"

She shook her head and began to sob again.

"Tell me, my dear, tell me," he said softly. "Maybe I can help."

"Nobody can help me, nobody," she said, turning away from him.

He sat down beside her, and putting his hand on her arm, said, "Come here, Chelsea. The least I can do is give you a shoulder to cry on." Gently he pulled her around toward him and took her in his arms. With her head tucked under his chin, she continued to cry, but it was warm and comforting to be held. Affection was something that she needed, and even though nothing had been solved, she began to feel a little bit better.

When the storm had finally run its course, Jonathan gently wiped her face with his handkerchief and said, "Now I want you to tell me everything. Maybe I can do nothing, but at least let me be your friend and listen, all right? You'll feel better, and since I'm older and wiser, maybe I might have some answers for you."

Haltingly, she began the story. She told him about Wills and Ashford Hall. She told him about their love affair and their plans to marry. She told him about the letter from Margaret who no longer wanted Wills to marry her. She told him about needing to care for her mother and her grandmother. And then she told him about the baby. And when she was finished, she added, "I know you won't be able to let me stay here, and I'll understand. I intended to dismiss the servants and move out of the house when Gran died, but I suppose I'll just have to do it sooner."

He pulled away and looked at her. "See, what did I

tell you? You're already starting to think in terms of solving the problem."

"I'm sorry I made such a mess of your shirt collar. It's all wet."

"Leave it. A lovely woman's tears are like holy water. Now, have you had anything to eat today?"

"No, but I have to get home. Martha will be wondering where I am."

"Call her and tell her you'll be late. We're going out to eat and talk about how to solve your problems," he said softly but firmly.

"I . . . I have to pay her to stay longer," she protested.

"Then do it, my dear young lady, and stop worrying about money. You have more important things to think about. Now call her and go wash your face with cold water. I'll call Chasen's and have them save a quiet table for us."

Less than an hour later they were comfortably ensconced at a table far from the other diners, and Jonathan watched as Chelsea sipped at a cup of vegetable soup.

They stayed there for a long time. Jonathan tried to convince her to call Wills and even offered to pay her plane fare to England to talk to him, but Chelsea would not hear of it.

"No, Jonathan, no! Please take my word that there are very good, unemotional and sound reasons that I can never go to him and can never be his wife," she stated flatly. "Don't ask me what they are." She couldn't bear to think about the jewels and the insurance company, nor her own escapade in crime.

"You are absolutely sure?" he asked.

"Yes."

"Wills was the only man in your life. You have no other young men in whom you're interested?"

She smiled. "Afraid not. I haven't been what you'd call sexually active. By the time most of my contemporaries were tall enough to ask me out, I was too busy to accept. I worked my way through college, you know."

There was a long, long silence. Finally Jonathan had

the words he needed. "If that is truly the case, then Chelsea, why don't you marry me?"

"What?" she asked, unsure that she had heard his proposal correctly.

"Why not? Your child will have a father and you'll have a husband . . . quite a lot older, I admit, but I'd take good care of you both. There would always be a place in our home for your mother, if she needs it. I'm sure my daughter will give me good references as a parent, and I will love and cherish your child as if it were mine . . . which it will be."

He took a sip of his coffee and continued quietly. "I could offer you a marriage in name only, but the truth is, I've become very attracted to you, and I would like to be your husband in all ways."

"Jonathan . . . I don't know what to say," she said.

"I would prefer that you think it over for a bit. Please don't say yes or no right now. I'm not yet sixty years old, I'm in excellent shape physically, and, I might add, financially. You will never have to worry about working again."

"Oh, but I want to work . . . I love my work," she protested, and he smiled.

"Well, that's something else we can do together then, isn't it?"

"But . . . won't the men on your board think you hired me because . . ." she asked dubiously.

"Possibly, but then it's not true, really, and time will prove it was your talent that got the job and not my lust for your pretty face and figure, right?"

Chelsea looked deep into his eyes for a long time. "Jonathan, you're the most interesting, remarkable man I've ever met, and I cherish—"

"Please don't refuse without thinking about it," he said, putting his fingers to his lips to shush her.

Chelsea smiled. "I won't, Jonathan. I will think about it."

She looked around and saw that the restaurant was

empty and the waiters were standing around watching impatiently.

"I'd better go home now. Would you mind taking me? I don't think it would be safe for me to drive by myself. I'm much too distracted."

Reaching over and kissing her lightly on the lips, Jonathan replied, "So am I. Thank God, I have a driver."

He held her close on the drive home, and when they arrived at her house, he walked her up to the doorway.

"Chelsea, my darling, I have one more thing I must say to you. I was happily married to the same woman for almost thirty years. When she died, I was certain that my life was over. Now for the first time since I told her good-bye, I'm looking forward to the future."

As Chelsea let herself into the house, she thought despairingly that she wished she could feel the same.

72

The glare of the morning light exposed all the obstacles to marrying Jonathan Corell that had faded into the shadows of candlelight the night before. Chelsea lay in her bed looking at the ceiling as the dawn seeped slowly through the curtains on her window. How could she have believed, if only momentarily, that everything was ginger-peachy when in reality nothing had really changed? Bunny wasn't capable of working, Laverne still had to be taken care of, and she surely could not bring Jonathan into the craziness of her own home.

Before Chelsea managed to get out of bed, Hilda was on the phone demanding to know where she had disappeared the day before. "My God, girl, I called you every hour, both at the office and home, where the hell did you go? I was worried about you."

Chelsea explained that she had just taken a drive, that

she was fine, and that she'd talk to her later. She had no reason to tell Hilda anything about Jonathan because when she had finished talking to him today, there would be nothing to tell.

After showering and dressing, she went in to see Laverne, who was awake and demanding a shot.

"Where the devil were you last night?" she croaked in a voice that got thinner and raspier by the day. "That damned nurse made me wait three hours yesterday. Hurry up."

Although Chelsea had spent a greater part of the night at her grandmother's bedside, she was patient with Laverne.

"I'll talk to Martha, Gran. She's only doing what she thinks is best for you."

"Tell her I want to take a bath in the tub today, will you? I hate having her wash me with a soapy cloth. My skin is beginning to itch. Is Hilda coming this afternoon?"

"Yes, Gran. She promised to stop in after her lunch appointment."

"Damn bitch has made a lot of money off us. It's the least she can do."

"She's not a bitch, Gran, she's a very kind lady. By the way, she's got some good news for you," Chelsea said, busying herself with preparing the needle.

"What? What? Don't play games. Tell me now, I might not be alive this afternoon," she whispered crossly.

After giving her the injection, Chelsea leaned down, kissed the withered cheek and with great patience and affection said, "No fair. It's Hilda's news to tell, not mine. What would you like for breakfast?"

"Nothing. I can't stand that garbage Catalina feeds me. Garbage on a silver tray, that's all it is."

"Gran, don't hurt Catalina's feelings. She tries so hard to please you."

"She's lazy, and she cooks garbage," she said, but the bite and malice were gone from her voice as she drifted once more into a haze of pain and medication. Laverne's moments of awareness and lucidity, as ill-tempered as they were, were getting shorter and farther apart. Chelsea looked down at what little was left of her grandmother and felt a terrible guilt. How could she have possibly considered giving up her own life voluntarily, when her grandmother was struggling so valiantly to hold on to hers?

No matter what anybody said about Laverne, Chelsea knew her grandmother was a tough, relentless, and courageous woman who had taken on the world and fought for a place in it for her daughter. If poor Bunny had only inherited a fraction of her mother's grit, her life might have been entirely different. How could it happen that mother and daughter were so entirely different?

Determined not to let her troubles get the best of her, Chelsea got ready for work. Since her car was still at the office, she decided to walk to Wilshire Boulevard and take the bus downtown. She was just finishing her coffee when Clark came in to tell her that a car had arrived to take her to work.

Surprised, she hurried outside to see Jonathan's black Lincoln and his driver standing by the open car door. What would it be like to be married to someone who never missed a single detail? she wondered, as she climbed in to ride to work in style.

She hadn't been at her desk more than five minutes when Jonathan's secretary called and said he wanted to see her in his office. Since the laboratory was in a small building behind the store, Chelsea ran down the steps and across the alley, her mind moving as fast as her feet. What was she going to say to him?

Without stopping, she rushed past his secretary and into his office. "You wanted to see me?" she asked breathlessly.

"Close the door behind you. We have things to discuss, my dear," he said, getting up from his chair and walking toward her.

Oh God, she thought, closing her eyes momentarily, he's changed his mind. Now I won't have to tell him anything. Spared the ignominy of confession, she found that her relief was colored by the illusion of rejection. In the cold light of day, he had probably realized he had made an impetuous mistake and didn't want her after all.

As she grappled with her thoughts, he moved quickly toward her, and before she knew quite what was happening, he gathered her into his arms and kissed her. Only this time it was not a dry, friendly kiss, but a real, urgent, and passionate expression of sensuality. Stray impressions dappled her surprise, like little sparkles of light from a diamond: he was considerably taller than she was; beneath his English-tailored suit, there was more solid bulk than one would suspect; he was strong; and he was far more passionate than she had ever expected he would be. My God, he really wanted her!

Then suddenly, as quickly as it had begun, he released her and stepped back. "I'm sorry I didn't do that last night," he said with a smile. "I was so exhilarated that I didn't get a wink of sleep. How about you?"

"I . . . didn't sleep much either," she replied, completely flustered. Who was this man? she wondered, as she looked at him through different eyes. He was tall and strong and handsome. She had always thought of him as quiet and genteel, and the realization that he was also sexual suddenly embarrassed her, and she began to blush.

"Did I startle you? I'm sorry," he said gently. "Come sit down on the couch and we'll talk. Shall I order some coffee?"

"No, no," she replied, allowing him to take her arm and lead her gently to the brown leather couch near the window.

"Now," he began, "I've given this a great deal of thought, and the last thing I want to do is take advantage of you at a most vulnerable time in your life. Perhaps we can find some other solutions to your present and most pressing problem."

"What do you mean?" she asked, curious.

"Well, I decided that to be fair, you should have other options from which to choose. I gave you only one, you see."

"What other options do I have?"

"That's the problem. Therefore, suppose I give you the money to go away to have your baby in private, away from the public's relentless intrusion. While you're gone, I'll provide for nurses for your grandmother, as necessary, and I'll continue to pay you your salary while you're away."

Chelsea looked at him intently. "Why would you do that? Jonathan, this isn't your child. You're not responsible for it, or for me."

He looked down for a moment and then said, "I wish it were my child, Chelsea. It would make things all so very simple. Maybe it's just an old man's fancy, or a last-ditch attempt to regain my youth, but I want to be responsible for you and the child."

Having said the words, he suddenly rose from the couch and walked to the window. "God help me, I actually think I've fallen in love with you," he said softly, looking down at the street below with unseeing eyes. "I have been inappropriately besotted since the day you came into my office in your plain blouse and skirt, your shining blond hair covering your face because you were too shy to look up." He paused thoughtfully. "Lord knows I've tried to divest myself of this foolish schoolboy crush, because it's so damned unseemly for a man of my age to feel this way."

One person's love, if it is fervent and passionate enough and pure enough, can often infect the beloved with an appropriate response. For a young woman who had spent all her life giving love to others and expecting little in return, Chelsea found Jonathan's emotional revelations nearly irresistible, and she felt an outpouring of affection for the man. Yes, Wills loved her too, but circumstances would never permit her to be the wife he needed. She and her baby would be an embarrassment to him, whereas Jonathan wanted her just as she was.

"Last night you asked me why I couldn't go to the father of the child and tell him I was pregnant. As I mentioned, he's from a prominent and respected family in England, the only son, as a matter of fact. His father just died and he's now an earl, and he's interested in politics. Aside from my family's unfortunate notoriety, I've done a few things of which I'm not particularly proud."

"Is there anything I can do to help?" he asked kindly.

"I'm afraid not, Jonathan. I don't want someone else solving my problems for me."

"Does this mean you've decided not to accept my proposal of marriage?" he asked, his tone gentle and understanding.

She looked into his eyes and smiled. How could she feel alone and bereft when she had friends like Jonathan and Hilda?

"No, it just means that I haven't come to terms with anything yet. Can you wait a little while for my answer?"

"Take all the time you want. And whatever you decide, I'll still be here to help in any way I can."

73

At Jonathan's insistence, Chelsea did not work that day but went home to rest. She tried lying down, but she was too jumpy, and so she went downstairs to the library and opened the drawer where her grandmother kept the bills. It was time to see where they were financially. Her grandmother was quite obviously past the stage where she could manage the household accounts. Chelsea checked through the mail first to see if there were any checks that needed to be deposited, and she found three. There was a good-sized check from Hilda's office, probably the last payment for Bunny's work in *The Beyonder*, a residual payment for *Wintersong*, which was now in syndicated television, and a check from the Chelsea Hunter Trust. What the devil was that?

She saw that the check had been mailed from the law firm of Sheridan, MacDonald, and Delaney in San Francisco. Curious, she went upstairs to ask her grandmother about it, but Laverne was sound asleep. Feeling frustrated, Chelsea went back to the desk and dug out the cancelled checks and bank statements for the past year. She learned that every month there had been a check deposited in her grandmother's account from the same trust, for the same amount, except once when there had been an additional check for a much greater sum. Where was the money coming from, and why had she never heard about it? After all, her name was on the trust, and it added up to a significant amount of money. Impulsively, she picked up the telephone and called the law firm in San Francisco. When she stated that she wanted information on the Chelsea Hunter Trust, she was referred to Brian Delaney's office. She spoke to the secretary, told her she was Chelsea Hunter, and almost immediately she found herself talking to the attorney himself.

"Hello, Chelsea. It's nice to talk to you after all these years. What can I do to help you?"

All these years, she thought, all these years? What in the world did that mean?

"Yes, I wonder if you could explain the Chelsea Hunter Trust to me. My grandmother is quite ill, and I was going over the accounts, and I found the check for this month."

"Well, it's quite simple, really. Years ago, when your mother and father were divorced, your father set up a trust to take care of you, to pay for your schooling and clothes and anything else you needed. As you grew older, he increased the amount to keep up with expenses, and from time to time your grandmother has asked for additional funds for emergency situations. Didn't you know that?"

Chelsea was stunned by the news. "No!" she said reflexively. "I don't believe it! Gran would never have done something like that. This must be one of my father's tricks—" She had begun to protest, but the truth often has a way of rising above the most ingrained perceptions of life, and she stopped in mid-sentence to listen for the facts.

"I have handled your trust from the beginning, Chelsea. We have cancelled checks endorsed by Laverne Thomas through the years, bank statements," he insisted, not about to let this golden opportunity pass him by. "And since you didn't know anything about the trust, you probably don't know either that on many occasions your father has asked Mrs. Thomas to let you come visit with him and his family, do you? That he has often asked for permission to see you?"

"Wha-What did she say to him?" Chelsea asked, stunned by the news that her grandmother had been deceiving her and lying to her about her father all her life.

"Frank was told repeatedly that you didn't want to see him. Wasn't that true?" Brian Delaney persisted, determined at long last to lay the truth before her.

"Not . . . not exactly." Chelsea's words were so faint they were almost inaudible. Her mind was filled with images of school days when other fathers were there to visit but hers never was, of nights wishing she had a father to hold her and comfort her. Dear God, was it possible that he had missed her as much as she missed him? No, it was too cruel to believe. Surely her grandmother would never have done such a thing.

The long silence on her end of the telephone made Brian Delaney worry that she'd hung up on him. "Hello, Chelsea, are you still there?"

"Yes . . . I'm still . . . here."

His voice softened. "I know this has probably come as a terrible shock to you, but I'm extremely happy to be able to speak with you at last. And your father is going to be most anxious to talk to you. If you'll give me the telephone number where you're calling from, I'll see that he gets it right away . . ."

Chelsea thought of the day her father had come all the way to Los Angeles to see her after Fernando Ramon's death and she had refused to see him. Her heart sank. Would he be able to forgive her? Could they now forgive each other? After a long pause, she said, "I'm at home. If my father wants to call me, I'll be here."

Chelsea's hand was shaking so violently that she had difficulty replacing the receiver on its cradle. All of her long-held beliefs about her life and her father had suddenly exploded in her face, and she was almost blinded by the fallout. After all these years, she would suddenly have to look at herself differently. She had never been deserted; in fact, her father had cared about her enough to continue to provide for her even though he had never been permitted to see her, to talk to her . . . to hold her. He had been deprived of her love and her gratitude, but had remained steadfast—despite rejection. He loved her. He really and truly loved her.

The telephone rang, jarring her out of her reverie, and she quickly picked it up.

"Hello," she said tentatively.

"Chelsea . . . is that you at last? This is your father."

A lump welled up in her throat and made it almost impossible for her to speak. "Hello," she finally managed to say as tears streamed down her cheeks.

Gently, Frank said, "Chelsea, this is the happiest moment of my life. I'm going to get on the first plane available and come down to see you. Is that all right with you? Oh baby, I'm so sorry for all the years . . . so sorry," and it was obvious that he too was overwhelmed by the moment.

Through her tears and her emotion, she finally choked out the word that she had wanted all her life to say: "Dad?"

"Yes, honey?"

". . . I've missed you."

"Wait for me. I'll come as fast as I can."

"I'll be here."

74

Hilda was sitting at her desk when a call came in from a reporter on the *Hollywood Tattletale,* a newspaper sold in supermarkets, which was filled with half-truths and distortions about celebrities.

"Tell'm to go screw himself. I don't talk to anybody on that rag," she snapped, and went back to reading the script she had to finish before going to lunch with a client who had been offered the leading role.

A few moments later her secretary came back on the line. "I'm sorry, Miss Marx, but I think maybe you better talk to this guy. He says your husband gave him an exclusive on Bunny Thomas, and he wants verification from you."

"Oh shit!" Hilda snapped, and punched the button on the telephone.

"Hilda Marx here. What do you want?"

"Hi, Hilda, this is Harry Spetlman. Your husband called me yesterday and wants to meet with me regarding some information he has on Bunny Thomas, which he said he got from you."

"What do you want from me?" she asked impatiently.

"Well . . . some kind of verification, I guess. He's askin' for a big chunk of dough, and unless I know he's got somethin' worth buyin'—"

"Let me tell you something, Mr. Spetlman. I have no way of knowing if the man you talked to is my husband. However, if it's the man I kicked out of my house, he's been in jail for assault, and I can tell you right now that whatever he's trying to sell isn't worth a dime, understand?"

"He says he has inside information that Bunny Thomas got to be a star by screwin' a big movie mogul."

Hilda howled with laughter. "No kidding? He said that? He must be really heavy into the stuff now. His imagination has gone out of reach."

"Then you deny it?"

"Deny it? Who the hell am I to deny it? I was just a kid myself. Bunny was only ten years old when she became a star. She wasn't exactly some hot chorine who rehearsed on the casting couch."

"Yeah, but he says—"

"Hey, look, don't take my word for it, check out her first big films and see for yourself," Hilda said, trying to keep her voice offhand and uncaring. "She was box-office dynamite. She was the screen's greatest talent then, and as far as I'm concerned, she still is. Did you ask that jackass where the hell he got that fairy tale? Is he still hearing voices in the night?"

"He said he read it in your diary."

Jesus Christ, Hilda thought, that coward Sergio was too intimidated to peddle stories on Sy Christman, so he had decided to pick on somebody who couldn't defend herself.

"Have you seen this guy yet? Tall, dark, handsome, with muscles that won't quit? Restless, sort of like a caged panther?"

"No, I just talked to him on the telephone," the reporter said, somewhat unsure of himself.

"Okay, then hear me out, if you know what's good for you. If you decide to meet with this guy, don't go alone. He's nuts, and if you say something that sets him off, like maybe questioning his source or something, you could wind up without a face. He's strong, very strong, and he's heavy into drugs. He'll say anything to get money, anything."

"I'm not afraid of him," the reporter said, although his words carried more bravado than the tone of his voice.

"Good for you, because I'm scared to death of the bastard. He tried to kill me. But it's your funeral. I should warn you, however, that if you print any information you get from him, you'll probably be sued six ways to Sunday. Bunny Thomas has an attorney who'll slap you with a suit that'll tie you up in court for years."

She took a deep breath and then went on. "There

absolutely is no such thing as a diary. Never was and never will be. God, it gripes me to think that anybody would believe for an instant that I'd be stupid enough to write things about any of my clients in a damned diary. He's telling you a lie he concocted just to get some money out of you."

Hilda hoped to hell she was convincing the guy. She didn't want to overprotest, but then neither did she want him to put any credence in anything Sergio said. If Sergio was desperate enough to go to the *Tattletale,* which was the cheapest rag in town, then he'd probably already been rebuffed by every other paper.

"He's into the hard stuff," she continued, "and probably desperate for a fix." That was a good line. Nobody trusted or believed junkies. "But I can't tell you what to do. Meet with him if you don't believe me, but remember what I said. Don't go alone. You know Chelli Davis?"

"The stage director? Sure. God, is he still alive?"

"Just barely. He had the gall to turn my husband down for a small part in his new show, and for that he got his teeth bashed down his throat. You can check it out, but I oughta know—it cost me a new Rolls-Royce and all his medical and dental bills."

"No kiddin'?"

"No kidding. Sergio's a maniac. That's why I now have a license to carry a gun, which I do."

"He's that dangerous?"

"Yeah. So good luck."

"Thanks a lot."

Hilda slammed down the telephone, swore, and hoped she'd been successful. All Laverne and Bunny needed right now was to be smeared in the press by that old story.

God help her, was she going to spend the rest of her life paying for one rotten mistake? Was there some way short of murder to shut Sergio up for good?

75

After her telephone conversations with Brian Delaney and then with her father, Chelsea found herself at war with her own emotions. Although she was filled with rage at her grandmother for deceiving her so terribly, she was also elated by the realization that all her life she'd had a father who cared about her and loved her and apparently still did. Anger and happiness struggled for control of her emotions.

She realized it was time to check on her grandmother to see if she needed anything, but she couldn't bring herself to even look at the woman while her feelings were in such turmoil. So she sat quietly in the library, reassessing her life and trying to come to some sort of terms with it. As the result of just a few brief words on the telephone, her entire world, which was already seriously skewed, had gotten enormously complex.

How could her grandmother have been so cruel? And her mother . . . had dear, sweet, gentle Bunny been part of the scheme to keep her in the dark about her father? Why had they done it? Why?

Why? she asked herself, and then cynically answered her own question. It was the money, of course. That had to be it. With Gran, it was always the money. Keeping the money from the trust under her exclusive control gave her grandmother a guaranteed source of income, and that was the cushion that had carried them through some seriously lean times. But what about the many days of plenty when money had been spent lavishly? Surely there was no reason to have kept her in the dark then; but again, her own intimate understanding of her grandmother supplied the answer. The money Frank Hunter had provided for his child's welfare had gone instead into the trappings of stardom for Bunny Thomas.

Bitterly, Chelsea reasoned that by keeping her innocent of her father's support, her grandmother had found it possible to be as parsimonious with her as she was generous with Bunny. But why had she felt it necessary to treat her granddaughter like Cinderella? Chelsea looked back with regret upon a life in which she had been taught to expect little in the way of worldly things and even less in the way of emotional support. That was the worst of it. She had been denied the love of her father, and that she found unforgivable.

Filled with anger, Chelsea got up out of the chair determined to get some answers. Her mother wouldn't be any help, but she would go to her grandmother and demand an explanation from her. If there was a culprit, it was Gran, of that she was absolutely certain.

As Chelsea stood over her grandmother's bed looking at the ailing woman, compassion began to erode some of the anger. Her grandmother would surely be able to give her a reason for the things she had done. No one could be as cruel and lacking in consideration as she seemed to have been.

Laverne's eyelids fluttered and she looked up at her distraught grandchild.

"Chelsea, what's wrong? Is your mother all right?" she asked, lifting her head off the pillow in alarm. It was unlike the tranquil Chelsea to be so upset.

"Mom's fine. Gran, I just talked to my father on the telephone. Why didn't you tell me about my trust fund?"

"Your father is a no-good liar! You can't believe a word he says," Laverne retorted angrily.

"Gran, I saw the checks! I talked to the attorney," Chelsea said in a reasonable tone of voice. "It's time for the truth. God knows there's been little enough of it around this house."

Laverne sank to her pillow and turned her face away. "You've no right to talk to me like that, you ungrateful child," she retorted, overriding Chelsea's quiet inquisition with a rasping fury. "Here I am on my deathbed, and you're treating me like I was some kind of criminal. I raised you, didn't I? I gave you a home, a good home, even when I could barely afford an extra mouth to feed. You've never wanted for anything."

"Haven't I, Gran? Haven't I? What about love, Gran? What about love?" Chelsea asked, her own emotion rising to match her grandmother's tone. "Why did you lie to me and tell me all those terrible things about my father?"

"You dreadful ingrate! I gave my life to you and your mother. Don't you dare talk to me like that!" Laverne said, summoning all her strength to lift her head from the pillow and glare at her granddaughter.

"My whole life was a lie, Gran. Did I deserve to be treated like that? Did I?"

"If I'd had my way, you would never have been born," Laverne said, closing her eyes. "Now let me alone."

Frustrated and desperate for some kind of answer, Chelsea went to Bunny's room. God, what she wouldn't give to have a mother she could talk to, someone who would listen to her and answer questions. A mother who would explain why she had been deliberately denied a father.

Bunny was taking a shower, and Chelsea sat down on the pink satin boudoir chair to wait until she finished. Her mother wasn't much, but she needed to talk to somebody in their tiny family before she came face to face with her father.

It was a long wait. Bunny was accustomed to leisurely baths or extended scalding hot showers. When she at last emerged, pink and wet, with a towel wrapped around her body, she reacted sharply at the sight of her daughter. For a split instant Chelsea detected a spark of cognition in her eyes that she had not seen in a long, long time. It was the tiniest fleeting moment of an awareness of reality, but almost immediately Bunny's eyes dulled again, her jaw went slack, and the real-life Bunny disappeared once more, her spirit deadened to the world around her.

"Mom, I want to talk to you," Chelsea began, but Bunny acted as if she heard nothing. Slowly and plod-dingly, she continued to rub her body with the towel, scraping her tender flesh over and over with the rough texture of the terry cloth. When she finished, she carefully massaged a rose-scented lotion on her skin, donned the fresh dressing gown laid out by the maid, picked up a brush and began to burnish her auburn tresses, which fell long and loose about her shoulders.

Chelsea observed the ritual with interest. Little by little over the past weeks, her mother had begun to assume responsibility for her own care. She filed and polished her fingernails and her toenails, shampooed her own hair and rolled it up, and in the past week she had even started putting a little mascara on her lashes. Strangely, it seemed that as Laverne drifted closer to death, Bunny was coming back to life.

"Mom, do you understand anything I say to you—ever?"

Bunny turned slowly from her reflection in the mirror, smiled, and said softly, "Yes," but the intonation was bland and meaningless.

"Do you know that Gran is dying?" her daughter asked, hoping the shock of the words might force her out of her torpor. Bunny's only reaction was a slight wavering pause in brushing her hair, and silence as she continued to concentrate on her own image in the mirror.

"Do you remember my father, Mom? Do you? If he was as bad as Gran said he was, why did you marry him?"

There was no response from her mother at all.

"Mom, why did you let Gran keep it a secret that my father was sending me money? Didn't you know how important it was for me to know that my father loved me? Why wasn't I ever allowed to see him?" she asked in an emotional outburst that brought tears to her eyes.

"Didn't you and Gran ever stop to think that you were hurting me? For God's sake, tell me—why did you do it?" Chelsea raged, now so caught up in the tragedy of her childhood that she put her face in her hands and began to sob.

Bunny turned and looked at the tall, vibrant young woman who had inherited so many of her father's features, including his strength. The mask of pretension was suddenly washed from her eyes with her own tears.

"Darling, I'm so sorry, I'm so sorry," she said, getting up from her vanity bench and going to her daughter. Putting her arms around the shaking shoulders of her child, Bunny held her close, and softly began to cry. "We didn't know what we were doing, darling. We didn't mean to hurt you, honestly we didn't. We were just two stupid and ignorant women, and we were afraid."

"Afraid of what?" Chelsea said, marveling at her mother's sudden transformation as she looked into eyes that were tear-filled, but knowing and alert.

"It wasn't your grandmother's fault, darling. You mustn't blame her. She did it for me. I was afraid I'd lose you. Frank was so smart and so strong. He came from a family with money and power," she said haltingly, her words punctuated by sobs. "I was sure he'd try to take you away from me. Even though I was a star, I had no education, and there were . . . oh God . . . secrets . . . things in my background that he might use to prove I wasn't a fit mother for you. Most of the time you don't have to worry about fathers getting their kids, but he . . . was so devoted to you that it scared me."

Chelsea sat transfixed, listening to her mother's confession, lucid and cogent and reasonable. Bunny seemed not to notice her daughter's fascinated scrutiny, so caught up was she in explaining away the past.

"I loved Frank so much, but after you were born, he changed. All he seemed to care about was you. He hated my career and thought I ought to give it up and stay home to take care of you. He hated everything about Hollywood and the movies, and he was always talking about leaving and going back up to San Francisco. He was homesick I guess," she said softly, pausing to blow her nose and wipe her eyes before continuing. "I knew sooner or later he'd leave me."

She stopped and looked up into her daughter's eyes, her tone becoming less mournful and more confidential.

"You can't trust men, Chelsea, none of them. Sooner or later, after they get what they want, they get tired of you and there you are, all alone in the world, just like Mama was when my father left us." She smirked slightly as she said, "He came back, you know, my daddy did, after I became a big star."

"Really, when did that happen?" Chelsea asked. It was a story she had never heard.

Bitterly, Bunny explained. "Oh yes, he tried to hop on the gravy train, the bastard. He walked out on us and didn't give a damn, but when I was the number-one box-office star, my father showed up like the leech that he was. He brought me a doll, a cheap, ugly little doll . . . I had a roomful of expensive dolls. He said he loved me, but I knew better. All he loved was my success and my money. Mama let me see him. She let me be the one to tell him to go away and never, ever come back again."

"Didn't that make you sad, Mom?"

Bunny stopped and thought for a moment. "I don't remember. It was almost like a scene in a movie. I got angry and stamped my feet and pouted and pointed to the door. Just like Mama told me to do," she said, and her voice broke and she began to sob again.

The roles had reversed once more, and Chelsea found herself back in the accustomed role of comforting her weeping mother, but also marveling at her sudden emergence from her cocoon of silence.

"Tell me, Mom. Tell me all about how it was back then when my father left us," Chelsea said softly and encouragingly.

"She knew I was afraid. Mama always knew exactly how I felt. She promised me she'd get rid of Frank once and for all, and she did it. From the day he left the house, she never mentioned his name to me again. Never. It was almost like he'd disappeared from the face of the earth. She could do anything. Oh God, what's going to happen to me now? How am I going to get along without her," she wailed, but Bunny's tears did not frighten her daughter. She had seen her mother shed far too many of them to be seriously moved.

"You're aware then that she hasn't got long to live, aren't you?" Chelsea asked suspiciously. A pragmatic person, she didn't quite believe in miracles or sudden revelations. If her mother knew Laverne was dying, how much else did she know?

"Mom, do you remember Fernando?" she asked, stretching toward the vanity table and pulling a box of tissues within easy reach. She handed one to her mother and wiped her own eyes with another.

"Don't ask me about him, Chelsea. I promised Mama I'd never speak his name, never."

"Do you remember what happened to him? Do you remember that night in the library? And the letter opener?"

There was a long, long silence until at last Bunny responded in words that were so softly mumbled that Chelsea could barely understand them, and she asked her to repeat them.

"I don't remember anything about that night," Bunny said again.

"Are you sure you don't remember anything?" Chelsea asked, and Bunny nodded her head mutely. Chelsea sensed that if she pressed her mother too hard, the veil would be dropped again, and so she changed the subject quickly.

"Mom, it's so wonderful to be able to talk to you. Gran won't be with us very long, so we have to stick together, don't we?"

"I'm not sure I can make it without her," Bunny said dolefully.

"Yes, you can, Mom. You're much stronger than you think you are. You'll see," Chelsea encouraged her. "Just don't ever stop talking to me again, will you?"

Bunny smiled through her tears, shook her head, and snuggled happily into her daughter's loving and protective arms.

76

Hilda was usually in her office by nine every morning, but she'd had a number of calls at home from clients, and she'd finally had to get her answering service to pick up so she could get dressed and out of the house. It must be the full moon, she groused, pulling into her parking space and getting out of the car.

As she walked through the aurora-rosa marbled entry, she was annoyed to see the receptionist with her nose buried in a newspaper and not watching the lobby. Damn that girl. She'd been warned before not to read at her desk, and now she was doing it openly. Hilda was just about to reprimand her when her eye suddenly caught the headline on the copy of the *Hollywood Tattletale* in which the young woman was so engrossed.

"Excuse me, but could I have a look at that rag you're reading?" Hilda said, snatching the paper out of the startled receptionist's hand. "You've been told not to read on the job, haven't you?"

Sheepishly, the young woman apologized. "I'm sorry, Miss Marx," she replied, but a sly grin of amusement slid across her lips.

"Well, don't do it again."

Hilda folded the paper so the front page couldn't be seen and carried it into her office, her pulse beating a tattoo in her ears so loudly that she could hear nothing.

She sailed past her startled secretary with nothing more than a grim "Good morning," and locked herself in her office. Without sitting down at her desk, she threw her purse and briefcase down and opened the tabloid.

Good God, there in vivid, garish colors was a picture of her coming out of Chasen's with Sergio, which must have been shot at least a year ago. Her mouth was open and she looked like a fishwife, whereas Sergio looked sharp and young and handsome. The headline read:

"I MARRIED A MANIAC"
HOLLYWOOD AGENT NO MATCH FOR VIOLENT YOUNG STUD

Good Lord! That creep Harry Spetlman had snookered her! Quickly she scanned the short article, which continued inside with pictures of her with many of her famous clients. While the facts were basically true, it was written in purple prose that made her look to be a sex-starved broad who had sold her soul for the attentions of a younger man; which she supposed wasn't far from the truth. But it sure as hell made her look like a jackass. He had even used some exact quotes about Chelli and getting his teeth knocked down his throat and about her covering it up with a new Rolls-Royce. The bastard had no doubt had a tape machine going when he called her. Jesus!

She threw the paper down angrily and sank to the couch with her head in her hands. Once, just once in her life, she'd made a mistake—Sergio—and now it looked as if it were going to haunt her forever.

Her secretary buzzed her to say that Sandy Shapiro was on the line.

"Morning, Sandy, forget it, I don't have a case for slander. It's all true."

Sandy laughed. "Hey, I know you don't. I hate to say I told you so, but—"

"You don't hate it, you love it. God, am I never going to get rid of that bastard?"

"Before we go into that, tell me why for God's sake you talked to that sleazy reporter?"

"I was being real clever, trying to divert him from talking to Sergio and doing a story about Bunny and Gordon Baker. What I wouldn't give to go back a few years and erase that husband of mine from my life."

"All he wants is moola, honey. Why don't you pay him off?"

The idea appealed to her. "Think it'll work?"

"It's only money."

The rest of the day went from bad to worse. Contract negotiations bogged down, deals fell through, clients complained, and in fact nothing seemed to go right for the agent who prided herself on sleek, clever manipulation. Like vultures circling a dying man, the Hollywood sharks suspected that Hilda was on the ropes, and they were not only laughing at her behind her back, they were also moving in for the kill. By the time the day was over, she felt thoroughly mauled.

The building was deserted when she finally left her office and headed for the garage downstairs. She'd go home, pour herself a long drink and get into bed, she decided, and try to shut the world out. Tomorrow had to be better.

Only a few cars were still parked in the underground garage, and the attendant was gone. Her high heels echoed on the concrete, and she noticed to her dismay that the fluorescent lights over her parking space were out and the area was very dark.

Great, she thought, I'll probably get mugged tonight, which will make it a perfect day. She quickened her pace and looked around to make sure no one was following her. Nervously she inserted the key into the car door and realized that it was already open. That's strange, she thought. She couldn't remember when she'd last forgotten to lock her car.

She opened the door of her Mercedes sedan and slid behind the wheel. Feeling safe at last, she locked the doors and put the key into the ignition when suddenly she sensed a presence, a slight movement in the backseat. The nerves in her neck stood at attention. Someone was in the car with her!

She had to get to where there were people. Hesitating only a moment before she turned the key, she was about to shift into drive when a hand shot out from behind her and grabbed her wrist.

"Wait." The voice was familiar. "I want to talk to you alone."

Terrified, Hilda turned her head and found herself face

to face with Sergio. She was scared but thought: Better a known enemy than a strange assassin.

"Sergio!" she squealed. "You scared me half to death! What do you think you're doing, skulking around in the dark like this?" she asked, trying to keep the fear out of her voice.

"I been sittin' in this damned car since six o'clock. What took you so long?" he grumbled, climbing over the seat and sitting down beside her. "How about taking me to dinner?"

Hilda took a deep breath and tried to rein in her jangled nerves. "Where do you want to go?" she asked as she put the car into gear and drove toward the exit.

"Let's go to Scandia. We can sit in that back room with the big leather chairs and talk, and I can have one of their special salads with the shrimp and cheese toast and some of that frikadiller stuff and maybe a piece of rum cake."

"What the hell, why not?" she replied, relieved that Sergio seemed almost friendly. She hoped that she could convince Leonard to seat them deep into the tavern room where nobody would see them.

"So, what do you want to talk about, Sergio?" she asked. "The article in *Tattletale*?"

"Yeah, it sorta finished me around town, you know. I guess nobody will hire me after that."

"It sure as hell didn't do me any good either. It's perfectly all right for my clients to make asses of themselves, but they want an agent who has her shit together. I've had one helluva day, I can tell you."

"I can't understand why he was more interested in the story you told him than the one I was tryin' to sell," Sergio replied.

"You haven't got the diary anymore, Sergio. All you're selling is old rumors."

"How do you know I haven't got the diary?" he asked suspiciously.

Thinking quickly, Hilda replied, "Because if you had it, he wouldn't have had to call me for verification, and you wouldn't be panhandling for a free meal. Sy took it from you, didn't he?"

"Yeah. He's one scary dude."

Hilda suppressed a smile. There was no reason not to embroider the fairy tale a little more. "You're lucky to be alive, buddy. In fact, if you know what's good for you, you'll get out of this town. If he ever hears about you trying to peddle anything, anything at all out of that diary, he'll shut you up for good. Believe me, he will," she warned, pleased that her little trick had worked so amazingly well.

"Your neck's on the line too," he retorted.

Hilda pulled the car into the covered driveway off Sunset Boulevard and they got out. Leonard, who presided over the front desk with efficiency and cool politeness, always took care of his regular customers. Within two minutes after requesting a back table, they were led past the bar filled with noisy customers and into the quiet, darkened room. Seated in the alcove to the right, they settled into the huge, womblike red leather chairs and ordered drinks. Hilda had a vodka on the rocks—it was a day for a stiff drink—and Sergio asked for aquavit. The moment they entered the plush and popular restaurant, he had preened like a peacock. He loved the good life, and he was always treated like the important person he wanted to be when he escorted Hilda.

The drinks came in icy crystal glasses along with two baskets of breads, one assorted, the other with thin, hot and crispy slices of pumpernickel slathered with butter and melted Parmesan cheese.

Hilda took a sip of her vodka and got right down to business.

"What do you want from me, Sergio?"

"I want to come back."

Confused, she asked, "You want to come back where?"

"To you. I want to come back to you. I'm still your husband, remember?"

Hilda collapsed back into her seat and laughed. "No shit?"

"Yeah, I do. I miss you, babe," he said, looking into her eyes and making a vain attempt to look sexy.

"Give me a break, Sergio. You don't want to come back to me . . . you want to come back to this," she said, sweeping her arm around, indicating the surroundings.

"No, I don't. I want to be your husband," he insisted.

"You don't want to be *my* husband, Sergio. You want to be the Big Hollywood Agent's husband. The one who gets a prime table at every restaurant . . . who can afford to buy you expensive cars and clothes . . . who hobnobs with the rich and famous."

"What's the difference?" he asked.

She looked at him pensively. Good Lord, she thought, he really doesn't understand.

"It's out of the question, Sergio. Even if that article hadn't appeared in the *Tattletale* today, I wouldn't have taken you back, and now I can't. Agents have to look smart or nobody will trust them, and with you on my arm, I look stupid, understand? You see, smart men can marry young bimbos and get away with it in our society, but women can't."

"You're calling me a bimbo?"

"Sorry, I shouldn't have used that term, but the truth is, that's how you look to people."

"So what'm I gonna do?" he asked, signaling the waiter to pour another glass from the iced bottle sitting on the table.

"Have you got any money at all?" she asked, wondering if he'd tell her about the ten thousand he got from "Sy."

"I'm flat broke," he lied.

"Okay, tell you what I'll do. I'll see Sandy Shapiro tomorrow and we'll get a divorce agreement drawn up. How much do you want?" she asked, not wanting to initiate the sum herself. If his price wasn't outrageous, she'd pay.

"Two hundred grand. And the Porsche, of course. I could go to New York, get myself an apartment on the river, and try to get some work there."

"That's way too much," she hedged. No sense agreeing right away or he'd think he'd asked too little.

All through dinner, dessert, and coffee, they haggled. He was on his second glass of cognac when they finally reached a price.

"Okay, that's it. Six grand a month for the next year, then five grand a month for two years more, and then finish, understand? That'll give you three full years of support, and you should be earning some additional money yourself long before it runs out."

"Here's to you, baby," he said, lifting his cognac glass in the air.

Hilda wondered if everybody's bimbos were as expensive to get rid of as hers had been.

77

When Frank Hunter rang the doorbell at eight o'clock that evening, Chelsea herself opened the door. They stood there, father and daughter, looking at each other in amazement. Both immediately recognized their physical resemblance; features that to members of a family who see each other daily, are taken for granted, but which to Chelsea and Frank seemed miraculous. For a long, long moment they surveyed each other in wonder, and then Frank broke the silence.

"My God, Chelsea, what a lovely young woman you are!" he exclaimed softly, and stepped toward her with his arms outstretched.

Chelsea was so moved she was speechless, but she allowed herself to be taken into his arms. With her head on his shoulder, she closed her eyes and remembered all the nights of her childhood, lying alone in her cold bed, wishing for a father who would protect her and make her feel safe.

Gently, with his arm still around her, Frank led her inside the hallway and shut the door behind them. He tilted her face up to his and kissed her on the forehead.

"It's probably a vain thing to say, honey, because you look so much like me, but my God, you are the most beautiful sight these old eyes have ever seen. Is there somewhere we can go to talk? We have so much to say to each other."

Because her emotions seemed to have struck her dumb, Chelsea just nodded, and they walked toward the living room, passing up the quieter, more private library where Fernando had been stabbed.

Seated together on the couch, Chelsea finally found her voice. "It's so good to have you here. Would you like something to drink?"

"Maybe later," Frank said, taking her hand. "Where shall we begin?"

"Just tell me why you stayed away . . . that's what's most important to me," she said, looking down because tears had filled her eyes.

"It's not a very nice story, but I want you to know the truth, Chelsea. That's the very least you deserve," and then he told her everything just as it had happened, and when he finished, he explained further.

"And so, you see, for all these years your grandmother has held that one youthful transgression and that letter over my head, and I've had to keep away because I didn't want to bring embarrassment or scandal on my family or my friend. He's the son of a nationally prominent judge, and he's never told his family that he's a homosexual, although he's never married. And, like his father, he's been appointed to the bench, where he is serving with great distinction."

Chelsea, who listened eagerly to every word, understood and admired Frank for his integrity. He had done what he felt was right.

"You were wise to fear Gran. Nothing, not even murder, would stand in the way of her protecting Mom," she commented.

"Tell me about you. I have a whole lifetime to hear about," he said.

Chelsea smiled. "Well, my life story is really dull, I'm afraid. Should we have some tea, or would you like a drink?"

"Tea will be fine. I had a couple of drinks on the plane to bolster my courage. I was worried about making a good impression," he said with a grin.

Chelsea rang for Clark and ordered a tea tray and cookies and then returned to the couch.

They talked for hours, and Chelsea found herself telling him everything about growing up, about her ambition to be a jewelry designer, and about her offer from Tanager's, but it was very late in the evening before she had the courage to tell him about Wills. She hadn't intended to burden him with the news that she was pregnant, but there was something about her father that drew the truth from her.

"I feel so ashamed for having to tell you that," she said, forlorn.

Frank quickly moved nearer to her on the couch and pulled her close to him. "The first thing you'll learn about being a parent, honey, is that there's a lot of fear and pain in the job description. Now, have you told your young man yet?"

"I can't do that," she exclaimed with regret. "I'd never be welcomed into his family now. Margaret—Wills's sister, who used to be my best friend—has let me know in no uncertain terms that I've been tainted by this miserable murder . . ."

"Look, my dear sweet little girl, I didn't come here to start telling you how to live your life, but . . ." He paused and took a deep breath. "I think you need some fatherly advice."

"Before you say anything more, I should tell you that I'm not desperate. Jonathan Corell has asked me to marry him. He wants to give my child a home and a father. He says he's in love with me."

"Who's Jonathan Corell?" Frank asked, confused.

Chelsea told him all about Jonathan, and when she finished, Frank looked perplexed.

"Why would you consider marrying a man older than I am? You said you were in love with Wills."

Chelsea pulled away and got up to pace the floor as she talked. "It's not all that simple. Even if Wills did want to marry me, I can't just up and leave Los Angeles. Gran has very little time left, and I'll be needed here."

"What for?" he asked gently. Although he was sure he knew the reason, he wanted to hear it from his daughter.

"Mom needs me. She can't take care of herself," she said looking down at the floor.

Frank sighed and shook his head. "Chelsea, I've been part of this family, and so I understand the position you think you're in. Has Laverne extracted any promises from you?"

"Not exactly, but—"

"Your mother is an adult. It's high time she started taking care of herself," he said firmly.

"She can't," Chelsea said equally firmly. "Gran has always—"

Frank interrupted. "Yes, I know very well that she's always been a helpless child and Laverne has treated her like one. Don't you think it's time everybody in this family let Bunny grow up and become a normal human being? Doesn't she deserve the chance to try at least?"

Frank saw that his words weren't moving his daughter or changing her mind. That damned harpy Laverne had done her work well. Everything was for Bunny. Everyone was to subordinate their lives to Bunny and her career. Goddamn them all, he swore to himself, but he tried not to let his anger show too clearly.

"Look, let's talk about you and your baby, honey. That's the human being you have to take care of first. Please, I beg you, just grant me this one favor. Call Wills and tell him. Don't deny him the love and companionship of his first child the way I was denied you. Even if you choose not to marry him and live in England, let him know about his child. If he turns away, you'll always have

other options . . . and more importantly, you now have
me. I'll take care of things for you, you'll have whatever
you and the baby need, and I'll always be there for you
both. After all, this will be my first grandchild, you
know."

Chelsea hesitated, not because of what Frank was saying but because of the thought that his words had inspired. Did Wills have the right to his child? Perhaps.
But more important, did she have the right to deny her
unborn child his father as Laverne and Bunny had denied
her hers? Frank's reasoning was powerful enough to
change her mind. How could she have even considered
for a moment doing to her own child what had been
done to her?

She looked up and smiled, all doubt suddenly erased
from her eyes. "Thank you for making things clear. I'll
call Wills and tell him about the baby."

Frank couldn't believe that he had convinced her so
easily. "What did I say that changed your mind so suddenly?"

Chelsea smiled uncertainly. "I just don't want my baby
to grow up without Wills the way I grew up without
you."

Her words brought tears to Frank's eyes, which he
made no attempt to conceal. "Thank you, Chelsea. I'll
never forget what you just said."

He got to his feet. "Well, I'm going to a hotel. It's
getting late, and you have an important call to make.
Suppose I pick you up in the morning and take you
someplace where we can have a quiet breakfast together?
Then you can tell me some more about the father of my
grandchild."

"I'll be ready at eight. Is that all right?"

"Perfect," he said as they walked arm in arm through
the hallway to the front door.

When he had gone, Chelsea hurried up the stairs. Although she thought she probably should say good night
to her mother, she headed straight to her own room. She
had to call Wills before her courage deserted her.

78

As she dialed the telephone, Chelsea prayed that she would not have to talk to Margaret. Please let Wills be there, she begged silently while the telephone rang. The connection was clear, and when the servant who answered asked who was calling, she gave her name and waited. It took about two minutes, and then she heard the beloved voice that spoke to her nightly in her dreams.

"Chelsea, darling, what a grand surprise! I was just thinking about you . . . but then, I usually am. How are you?"

"Fine, Wills. It's so good to hear you," she said, her voice trembling.

Wills picked up on her nervousness immediately. "I say, you don't sound fine. Is something wrong?" he asked.

Chelsea didn't know where to begin. This was going to be every bit as difficult as she imagined it would be. "No—well, yes, I guess so. Wills, I'm . . ." She paused, as her courage failed her.

"Chelsea, sweet, are you still there?"

"Yes, I'm still here."

"I can barely hear you. Can you speak a bit louder?"

"Wills, I'm pregnant!" she blurted out loudly.

"What?" he asked, astounded.

"I'm carrying your baby."

"Oh, my Lord, well . . . that is a surprise, but a wonderful one nevertheless. We must have the wedding just as soon as possible then, mustn't we? Let's see, I suppose your grandmother is too ill to travel?"

"Yes," Chelsea said, amazed at his response.

"I see . . . then I suppose you can't come over here for the wedding, right? So, we haven't much choice—I shall have to hop on a plane and get myself over there as quickly as possible, and we'll have just a small wedding at your place. Would you mind awfully if I asked you to make the necessary arrangements?"

Chelsea was astonished by his easy acceptance of the situation.

"Wills, are you sure you want to do this?"

"Do what, darling? What are you talking about?"

"Are you sure you want to marry me?"

Suddenly, Wills understood her anxieties. "Chelsea, my sweet Chelsea, how can you ask such a question? I've wanted to marry you since I was fourteen years old!"

"But your family? What will they think of me?"

Wills chuckled. "Well, I would suppose that Mum's distress over not having a big wedding will be thoroughly overcome by her joy that you'll be producing an heir so promptly."

"Are you sure?" she asked in disbelief. How could something that had seemed such a tragedy to her bring such unremitting joy to Wills?

"Quite. Her greatest fear is that I might marry a barren woman. Heirs and property are most important over here, darling. Now hear me, stay by the telephone. As soon as I have my reservations, I'll call you back and give you the details of my arrival."

"I'll be waiting. And Wills, I love you," she whispered.

"I love you too."

Chelsea put down the receiver and stretched out on her bed. There hadn't been a second of hesitation on Wills's part. How could she have considered for even a moment keeping this momentous event from him? Thank God for her father. He had stepped back into her life just when she had needed him the most.

Wills called back within the hour to tell her that he would be arriving on Wednesday afternoon at three-thirty and had arranged to stay for a week.

"Can we get everything done in that time?" he asked anxiously. "I can't miss too many days of classes or my degree will be at risk."

"We'll manage, darling. I can't wait to see you," Chelsea said happily.

"I'm terribly relieved we won't have to wait until next year. Have you told your mother yet?"

"Not yet. I wanted to talk to you first."

"I say, your family won't make things difficult for us, will they?" he asked apprehensively.

"I won't let anybody make things difficult for us, Wills. Besides, now I have my father on my side. He's here in Los Angeles with me now."

"Wonderful. I'm eager to hear everything. See you in a few hours, my love."

When the call had ended, Chelsea looked at the clock and realized it was too late to break the news to anyone now. Mom had probably taken her sleeping pills, and Gran her pain shots. Tomorrow would be soon enough to tell them her plans. The thought of facing her mother's fear and her grandmother's anger filled her with despair.

Chelsea did not go to sleep until the early hours of the morning, and she had been asleep only a couple of hours when she was aroused by the jangle of the telephone.

"Good morning, sleepyhead. Did I awaken you?" Hilda asked.

"Oh God, what time is it, Hilda?" she asked, sitting up instantly.

"Almost eight o'clock. Are you feeling all right?"

"Look, Hilda, I've got to go now, but could I stop over at your office later this morning? I need to talk to you."

"Well, I was going to come over to the house around noon. I have some things to discuss with your grandmother."

"Great, but before you go up to her room, tell Clark you want to talk to me first, okay?"

"You got it. See you then."

"Oh, and Hilda? Would you be my maid of honor?"

"Jesus! Yeah, sure . . . who's the groom?" Hilda asked warily.

"Wills."

"That's terrific!" Hilda exclaimed, relieved and happy.

"I'll tell you all about it later. Don't mention a word of this to anybody," Chelsea warned before hanging up the telephone and rushing toward the bathroom. She had just ten minutes to shower and dress for her date with her father.

When she was ready, she raced down the stairs, not stopping to check on her grandmother. She went straight to the kitchen.

"Catalina, can you manage Mom and Gran till I get back in a couple of hours?"

Catalina nodded. "Your grandmother slept all night last night, for a change. Not once she ring the bell for me."

"Is she okay?" Chelsea asked, alarmed.

"*Sí*, I already give her pain shot. Now I fix her breakfast," Catalina said with a sigh, "but she probably no eat it again."

Chelsea heard the doorbell, and she hurried to meet her father. She could hardly wait to tell him the news.

79

During a lovely breakfast with her father in the garden of the Bel Air Hotel, where he had taken a suite, Chelsea and Frank came to several decisions. Because of her grandmother's failing health, they would have just a small wedding at home. Frank would give her away and prevail upon a judge who was a close friend of his to conduct the ceremony. Anne and their children would fly down from San Francisco for the event. He also insisted on paying for everything, and encouraged Chelsea to buy a special dress that afternoon.

Although Frank had wanted to be at her side when she broke the news to Bunny and Laverne that she was marrying Wills and would soon be leaving for England, Chelsea vetoed the idea. She didn't want to expose her father to the nasty scene she knew was coming. They parted with the agreement that he would come to the house that evening to meet with Laverne and Bunny. It promised to be a full, emotion-charged day.

Hilda was waiting when she got home, and the two retired to Chelsea's room to talk privately. Chelsea told Hilda everything that had happened, beginning with the information about the trust. When she finished, she was surprised to find Hilda less outraged than she had expected.

"Look, honey, don't be too hard on the old lady. I'm sure she loves you in her own way. She was a lone woman with a kid trying to buck the system out here, and I can tell you that's no piece of cake. Most of the women in this town find themselves doing things they'd never do somewhere else. Believe me, I know from experience."

"Maybe, but it's going to be very hard to forgive her for denying me my father."

"Maybe you wouldn't appreciate him as much if he'd been around all your life," Hilda said with a smile. "Most of us don't really appreciate our parents until they're gone. I know I didn't."

"Will you go in with me to tell them? Gran's going to accuse me of deserting them, and she's right. I just don't know how I'm going to ever leave my mother," Chelsea said anxiously.

"Your mother is going to be fine, I promise you she will. I'll be here to take care of her, and things are starting to go her way for a change. So let's go break the news, and then when you're finished, I have something to tell Bunny that will cheer the room up considerably."

They found Bunny in her mother's room, where she was holding a cup of tea for Laverne to sip. Both women looked up in surprise when the visitors arrived.

"Well, well," Laverne said, her eyes glittering with hostility, "here comes the poor little rich girl. Where've you been? Counting up all the money you think I owe you?"

Surprisingly, Bunny immediately jumped in to reprimand her. "Mama, don't talk to Chelsea like that. You owe her an apology."

Bunny's sudden return to clarity startled Hilda, but

before she could say anything, Bunny smiled and said, "I'm okay, Hilda. This time for good." Then she turned to her daughter and added, "I sneaked downstairs and peeked into the living room when you were talking to your father last night. I'd forgotten how handsome he was. Did you have a nice visit with him, honey?"

"Why didn't you come in, Mom? Dad's anxious to see you again."

Bunny smiled. "Is he really?" she asked, and then frowned. "Is he very angry with me?"

Chelsea went over, kissed her on the cheek and said, "He was never angry with you, Mom. And he's coming over this evening to talk to you and Gran."

Furious, Laverne raised her hand and pushed the cup and saucer out of Bunny's hand, sending it swirling to the floor. "No! He can't come into my house! I won't permit it! He's a pervert!"

Patiently, Bunny picked up a towel, wiped at the tea now staining the sheet and said, "He's not a pervert and you know it, Mama. Anyway, I want to see him and talk to him. I think you and I both need to tell him we're sorry."

"Never!" Laverne croaked, turning her head toward the wall and closing her eyes.

"Gran, don't go to sleep. I have something to tell you. Wills is coming here from England, and we're getting married later this week."

Laverne's eyes snapped open as she whirled her head about and glared at her granddaughter. "You can't marry him. You have to stay here and take care of your mother!"

Bunny said nothing, and Chelsea continued, but it was apparent from her tone of voice that she was shaken. "I'll always take care of my mother, and she's welcome to stay with us, but I'm going to live in England with Wills. I'm carrying his child."

"So that's it, you little slut," Laverne said nastily. "I knew one day you'd mess things up for us. You're just like your father."

Hilda watched the young woman absorb the abuse

gracefully, and although her heart ached and she wanted to step in and tell the old woman off, she kept her silence. It was Chelsea's show, and she was holding her own.

"Gran, I hope you're right that I'm like him, because contrary to everything you've told me, he's a wonderful person. Now let's not spend our last weeks together being angry. Wills and I are going to be married here in my home, and I want you and Mom there. No matter what's happened in the past, we're still a family. We always will be. And, Gran, even though I'm getting married quickly for the child's sake, I am not going to leave you and Mom while you're sick."

Bunny put her hand on her mother's shoulder to keep her from making any more troubling remarks, and she said quietly, "Your grandmother and I will be at your wedding. And you mustn't worry about me. I'm going to be all right, honey. Really I will." There was a strength and determination in her voice that no one had ever heard off the silver screen, and even Laverne was impressed.

"Mom, you'll love Ashford Hall—" Chelsea began, but Hilda interrupted.

"Sorry, Chelsea, but your mother's going to be too busy to take any trips to England for a while. The word's out about her performance in *The Beyonder,* and I've got a desk full of screenplays that she's been offered. There's one that she needs to make a decision on right away, and I think it's a beaut."

Hilda had waved her magic wand, and Laverne's mood did a complete turnabout. "Which one is it? Tell me," she asked, her eyes suddenly bright and interested. As Hilda began to give the details, Chelsea found herself mercifully no longer the center of attention. Relieved that the big scene was over, she went back to her room to get ready to meet with Jonathan Corell. That was another door in her life that was going to be painful to close.

At Tanager's, Chelsea climbed the grand staircase just as she had that day months ago when she first came to the store looking for a job, and her heart was heavy. The career she had begun here, with all its attendant dreams of glory, was coming to an end much too soon. Although she loved Wills and wanted to bear his children and create a wonderful family, it would be very hard to let go of her professional aspirations and her ambitions. Why was it that only women had to make such choices?

When she walked into his office, Jonathan greeted her warmly. They sat down on the couch together, and she told him that Wills was coming from England to marry her.

Gently, Jonathan took her hand and held it in his.

"Are you happy, Chelsea? That's all that really matters."

"Yes, of course I'm happy. I love Wills, and I'm grateful that he loves me, but I'm greedy, I guess. I want my career at Tanager's too."

"Just because you're marrying, my dear, doesn't mean that you have to give up your dreams. You can still go on creating beautiful jewelry."

"Just being Wills's wife and mother of his children and the mistress of Ashford Hall is going to take all my energy, I'm afraid," Chelsea said. "I'm not Superwoman."

"Don't plan your life too far ahead, Chelsea. I feel sure that you'll eventually have it all," he said with a twinkle, "but maybe not all at once. I don't believe that diapers and crying babies smother the spark of genius indefinitely, and I do believe you have that spark."

Chelsea looked up into the eyes of the man she respected and had come to love as a friend. "I'll miss working with you, Jonathan. I hope I haven't caused you too much trouble."

"You've caused me no trouble, and I shall miss you too, Chelsea. More than you'll ever really know. By the way, Tanager's has a branch in London, did you know that?"

"Well, yes, but—"

"When you have time, stop in and see the manager. His name is Harrison Wadsworth. I'll tell him to be looking for you."

"Will you call me whenever you get to London?" she

asked, her eyes moist, hating the thought that she might never see him again.

"Perhaps. But I'll not forget you, Chelsea Hunter. You taught me something very important."

"What's that, Jonathan?"

"That my life isn't over yet."

80

If Chelsea had doubts about the turn her life had taken, they vanished the moment that Wills got off the plane and ran to take her into his arms. Oh God, she thought as she clung to him, this is where home is.

She looked up into his eyes and saw all the love and reassurance she needed so desperately to see.

"Chelsea, darling, this is the second best moment of my life," he said softly, his lips closing quickly on hers for a long, loving, and tender kiss.

"The second?" she asked quizzically, pulling away slightly, but he held her firm.

"Surely you haven't forgotten already? I do believe you're carrying the little bugger we created on the first," he said with a grin, kissing her again, quicker this time but with obvious relish.

"Oh God, it feels so good to touch you, Wills, and no, it's not likely I will ever forget a single moment we spent together."

"We'll have a lifetime of them. Now, tell me every-thing . . . and is it possible that we could have some time together, alone, when we get back to your place?"

"We can try," she said with an impish grin.

Chelsea drove and they talked constantly. They had so much to say to each other.

"By the way, I've got good news. At least I hope you'll think so. Mum and Margaret are flying in tomorrow, and would you believe this, so is my dear, fussy sister Nancy. They're all pleased about the turn of events and couldn't bear the thought of missing my wedding."

"Wills, don't start out our life together by lying to make me feel better. I know Margaret has severe reservations about our marriage. What did they honestly say? Tell me the truth," she insisted, but her heart skipped a beat apprehensively. Did she really want to know?

Wills put his hand on her knee gently and said, "Well, the truth is, if you really insist, they greeted the announcement with stunned silence and typical old British stoicism. Margaret had the gall to ask if I was sure it was my child, but Mum came through with flying colors. 'Don't be such a little prig, Margaret,' she said, 'actually, I was pregnant with Nancy when your father and I married.'"

"Really? She said that?"

"Yes, she did. Then she turned to me and said I was my father's son. He liked American girls too, and if she did say it herself, she'd been a bloody good wife to him, as she expected you would be. Then she headed upstairs to help me pack and ordered Margaret to start getting herself ready to leave."

Chelsea felt as if a giant weight had been lifted from her shoulders. If Wills's mother had come around, she was sure Margaret would too.

When they reached the house, they were greeted by Clark, who carried Wills's luggage in.

"What room shall I put these in, Miss Chelsea?" he asked, lowering his eyes so the twinkle in them would not reveal his amusement.

"In my room, Clark. We're having two more house guests tomorrow, and we'll need the other rooms for them." She and Wills looked at each other and repressed a giggle.

Holding hands, they followed the butler upstairs, chatting casually.

"Wills, my father and his family are staying at the Bel Air Hotel. I promised them we'd be over for tea this afternoon, and I'm quite excited about meeting my half brother and sister for the first time."

"This is a very special occasion."

"Isn't it, though? If it's all right with you, I think it would be nice if you asked Jeremy to be best man. He's seventeen. Lisa is fifteen, and I'll ask her to be my bridesmaid. Do you think I should ask Margaret to be one too?"

"Well, she doesn't deserve it, but let's be generous. She'll love it."

Clark put the suitcase in the room and then discreetly left them alone, closing the door firmly as he left.

Grinning, Wills began unbuttoning Chelsea's shirt.

"Do you think we might have time for—" he began softly, his finger lightly tracing circles on her breasts.

"I think so," Chelsea responded, "but first let me lock the door."

81

With a lot of help from Hilda, Frank, and Anne, the wedding took place on Thursday afternoon in the living room of Laverne's leased house. At Chelsea's request, Frank had the florist decorate the room with red roses. Chelsea and her new family had taken to each other immediately, and Wills invited them all to visit Ashford Hall after the baby was born.

Chelsea wore an off-white gown of antique lace, and she carried a single red rose. Frank was the image of the proud father as he accompanied his daughter down the curving staircase.

Lady Ashford and her daughters had arrived as promised, and even Margaret participated in the wedding plans with enthusiasm. Bunny and Catalina managed to get Laverne into a blue satin dressing gown, and Clark carried her thin, wasted body down to the couch, where she reclined through the brief ceremony. To Chelsea's great relief, her grandmother was nice to everyone, except Frank, whom she ignored.

The occasion was a happy and sentimental one for all. When Wills placed an Ashford heirloom, a ruby and diamond ring, on Chelsea's finger, there wasn't a person in the room who was unmoved by the joy and love in the young couple's eyes. After the ceremony, Margaret was the first to congratulate the bride and groom.

"Chelsea, you must forgive me," she said, her eyes moist with emotion. "If you'll recall, this was all my idea originally . . . remember?"

Chelsea took Margaret in her arms to reassure her. "Of course I forgive you, Margaret. You've always been my dearest friend."

Jake, who had brought his wife, kissed Chelsea and shook Wills's hand, telling him gruffly, "You better take good care of her, young man. She's mighty precious." And to Chelsea he added, "And don't give up all your dreams, kid."

Chelsea gave him a warm hug and replied, "I won't, Jake. Wills is just the first of my dreams to come true."

Clark poured champagne, and everyone rejoiced. Bunny played the part of mother-of-the-bride so well that at the reception she was the cynosure of all eyes, much to Laverne's delight.

A sharp observer, Wills noted the situation and commented, "Your mum certainly commands the attention, doesn't she? Do you mind?"

Chelsea just laughed. "Of course not. There's only one movie star in our family. Thank God it's not me."

Slipping his arm around his wife's waist, Wills whispered, "I'll wager we could slip out of here and be on our way and not a soul would notice. Shall we?"

Chelsea shook her head. "Let's tell them all good-bye first. They've been so wonderful to us."

"Yes, but it's a short honeymoon, and I don't want to miss a moment of it," he replied.

*　　*　　*

Before Wills returned to England, he and Chelsea had three glorious days together in a bungalow at the Beverly Hills Hotel, where she told him in precise detail of her adventures with her mother's jewelry and her forays into a life of crime. Much to her relief, he found the story merely hilarious, and was even impressed with her courage in attempting something quite so risky.

Although it was painful for them to be separated, they both agreed that she should stay in Los Angeles with her mother until Laverne finally succumbed to the cancer.

"I've got to help my mother get through it, Wills. I hope you understand."

"Of course I do, just as you understand my need to finish school this year. We'll have our whole lives together, darling. We'll never be separated again."

The few weeks after Wills and his family's departure were difficult for everyone. Ill as she was, Laverne clung tenaciously to life, determined to live until her daughter's film was released. When at last *The Beyonder* opened, the film itself received mixed reviews, but it did well at the box office. More importantly, Bunny's performance was hailed as the best of her long career. Everyone declared that she had finally come into her own as an actress of maturity and range, and it was generally agreed that she was still the superstar she had been as a child.

Through her last days and nights, Laverne listened happily as the reviews praising her daughter were read to her over and over again by Chelsea, who stayed at her bedside, while Bunny fulfilled her commitments to publicize the film.

Right after Bunny appeared on the Johnny Carson show, however, Laverne slipped into a coma, and two days later she died with both her beloved daughter and her faithful granddaughter beside her.

Laverne was buried in Forest Lawn in Glendale. The sky was clear and blue, and the bright California sun illuminated the green of the grass, the white of the marble, and the sprightly reds, yellows, blues, and pinks of the numerous floral pieces surrounding the open grave. It was a funeral in Technicolor, complete with stars of all magnitudes. Unloved as the deceased was, her burial was a media event, and people came to be seen. It was a genteel way to bring oneself to the attention of casting agents and producers and perhaps be glimpsed on the evening news.

According to Laverne's wishes, the service was held only at the graveside, in the open air and under the sun. Mourners gathered around, tramping across adjacent graves, trying to put themselves in sight of the portable TV cameras. Although the studio wanted the lead actor of the film to read the eulogy prepared by the publicity department, Bunny and Chelsea opted instead to have Hilda do it. She read a moving and brief tribute to Laverne's courage.

Though Bunny was distraught by the loss of her mother, she rose to the occasion. Dressed in a sleek, black silk suit by Dior, with her radiant hair shining through a gossamer black veil, she looked stunning. She had eaten little in the last weeks of her mother's agony, and she had lost all of the pudge that often encased her body. With Hilda Marx on her left and her daughter on her right, Bunny was seen on all the TV news shows, both at six and eleven o'clock.

The producers of *The Beyonder* were ecstatic at the opportunity to grind out sad stories about the poor mother who had managed to live just long enough to see her daughter's triumphant comeback, and the theme was picked up by newswriters all over the globe. Suddenly Laverne's culpability in Fernando's death began to take on the glow of self-sacrifice—she was only a mother protecting her daughter from the brutal attack of a scorned and twisted lover. It made great copy. Cancer was, after all, the dreaded disease of the time, and if its victim had sinned, her soul had surely been burned clean in the purgatory of suffering. Laverne had timed even her death with impeccable precision and to maximum effect to promote her daughter's career.

Bunny's transition from a weak, blubbering child to a sensible adult seemed like a miracle to those who knew her best. It was almost as if at the moment of death, Laverne's spirit had left her body and settled comfortably into her daughter's, for Bunny began to be decisive and alert and more in control of her life. Both Hilda and Chelsea had been prepared for a storm of weeping, but it never happened.

A reception was held at their home after the burial. Once all the visitors had departed, the three women sat down on the couch and kicked off their shoes. Chelsea, now nearing her third trimester, was wearing maternity dresses.

"Well," Bunny said, "that's over. Chelsea, darling, there's really no need for you to hang around here any longer. I think you should pack up and be on your way to England. You've been separated from your darling Wills long enough."

"I can't leave you yet, Mom. If you're really going to give up this house and move to an apartment, there's a lot of work to do."

"There's no hurry. I haven't even begun to look for something else yet, and God knows how long it will take to find the right thing. Hilda, have you talked to that Martin Flekman about becoming my business manager?"

"No, but I will tomorrow, for sure," she commented, and a look of wonder passed between Hilda and Chelsea. Where had this assertive woman been hiding all of her life?

Hilda then added her voice to Bunny's. "Your mother's right, Chelsea. You really should be on your way. The further along you get in your pregnancy, the tougher that long trip is going to be. Besides, Bunny starts rehearsals for her new film in two weeks, and then she'll be on location in Wyoming for three months. So there's no need for you to hang around."

"Well, if you really think you'll be okay, Mom. I hate to leave you, you know."

"I know you do, darling, but your place is with Wills

now. Don't throw away a wonderful man as I did. Learn from your mother's mistake," she said, and her voice was filled with warmth and encouragement. Chelsea loved her mother more at that moment than she had ever loved her before.

As soon as she was alone in her room, Chelsea picked up the telephone and dialed Wills to tell him she was coming, and then she eagerly started to pack up her things.

In less than a week she was ready to leave, to begin her own life, at last.

"Mom, promise that as soon as you finish this film you'll come for a visit. I'm so anxious to show Ashford to you. You'll love it there," Chelsea said after kissing her mother good-bye.

"I'll try, darling, but you know with a career as demanding as mine, it's awfully hard to make promises. Just be happy, honey," she said, and her lips quivered slightly. Although there was a hint of moisture in her eyes, Bunny did not break down into tears, but bravely maintained her composure.

"Mama, I think we're both growing up," Chelsea said, putting her arms around her mother and hugging her one last time before boarding the plane.

82

Hilda arrived at Bunny's home early on the fourth day after they had put Chelsea on the plane for London, and Clark opened the door.

"Good morning, Clark. I know I'm a little early, but Bunny called last night and asked me if I'd mind picking her up this morning."

"She said you'd be coming, Miss Marx, and she specifically told me not to awaken her until you got here."

"No kidding? Well, I better get her up. Ask Catalina for some coffee. Today's her first day of rehearsal, and I don't want her to get there late," she said as she hurried up the staircase.

She knocked briefly, but without waiting for an answer, she opened the door to Bunny's bedroom.

"Up and at 'em, sweetheart. This is a big day for you," she called, striding across the darkened room and pulling the blinds open.

As the sun sent a shaft of light streaming across Bunny's cluttered vanity table, Hilda noticed a pink envelope taped to the mirror. Curious, she looked closer and saw that it was addressed to "Hilda Marx, for her eyes only," and cold fingers of fear suddenly clutched at her. Whirling about, she looked at the still figure sprawled on the bed, and she did not need to touch her or shake her to know that Bunny Thomas would never awaken again. Several empty bottles of pills on her bedside table gave mute testimony to the star's last rites.

Stunned, Hilda understood it all. Bunny had not grown up. There had been no miracle. She had been acting, damn her, acting. . . .

Her hands trembling, Hilda took the envelope from the mirror and opened it to read Bunny's last words:

Dear Hilda,

Forgive me for choosing you to be the audience for my last dramatic performance, but you always said it was an agent's job to do the bad stuff.

Tell Chelsea not to feel sad, because I'm doing the only thing I can. When Mama died, so did I. Without her, there is no such person as Bunny Thomas. There never was.

And please tell Chelsea I love her and that she must not feel guilty. Nor should you. Neither one of you could have stopped me from doing this. No one could.

Good-bye, and thanks for everything.

Bunny

P.S. Make sure I have a big funeral.

Coda

Twenty Years Later

Chelsea looked at her watch and saw that it was time to get her family downstairs into the limousine. The car had been waiting half an hour in front of their spacious London town house for them.

"Wills," she called impatiently from the foot of the stairs, "will you please see if the boys are ready yet. They're going to make me late."

"Don't be so nervous, darling. We've more than an hour before you need to be at the store, and it's only a ten-minute drive from here," he said, heading up to the back bedrooms that belonged to their sons, James, who was nineteen, and his younger brother, Thomas, who was seventeen.

"Jamie! Tom! Hurry now. Your mother is getting nervous," Wills said brusquely, knocking sharply on one door then the other.

Within moments their doors opened and the two handsome young men emerged, both dressed in gray slacks and navy blazers, smiles on their faces. They were almost as excited about the day as their parents, but tried not to show it.

"We're ready, we're ready," they said, and raced down the stairs to where their mother was waiting. Wills followed at a more dignified pace.

Although both sons were tall and well-built, Jamie had Bunny's auburn hair and Chelsea's facial features, whereas Tom looked just like his father. In inclination and tem-

perament, however, it was Tom who was artistic and
Jamie who excelled in athletics and was a top tennis
player. Both boys were good, industrious students, and
although they were excellent riders and loved horses, neither had achieved the honors their father had garnered
in that sport.

Wills, at forty-three, was slightly gray at the temples,
still slim and muscular, and even handsomer than he'd
been in his youth. He had been a member of Parliament
for ten years, but had retired recently because he found
the business of running their estate at Ashford more sat-
isfying than politics.

"Don't be nervous, Mother," Jamie said impishly,
"after all, it's only Her Majesty the Queen who'll be kept
waiting if we're late."

"Stop that. I don't need for you to make me any more
anxious than I already am. Come on now, let's go. I want
to be sure everything is just perfect before anybody arrives, including the Queen."

Quickly, they filed out of the house into the waiting
car and were on their way to the opening of the new and
enlarged Tanager's of London, to which the Queen was
paying a special visit later that day.

As Wills had said, it took less than ten minutes, and
they were in Knightsbridge at the site of the new store.
As Chelsea emerged from the limousine, she felt a surge
of pride. The windows were fully dressed, and in each,
as she had directed, along with the usual display of jewels,
there was a large crystal vase of red roses. The effect was
breathtaking. Diamonds and roses had a natural affinity,
she decided.

For more than six years Chelsea had been in charge of
the London branch of Tanager's, although she had been
designing for them since her arrival in England as a young
bride. On the basis of the exciting changes transpiring in
the new European community, she had in just the past
two years convinced Tanager's board of directors to ex-
pand in Europe. At her urging, they had opened stores

in Paris and Munich too. Successful as a designer, she also had a keen instinct for retailing.

Because she believed in the timelessness of good jewelry design, Chelsea had campaigned vigorously for its preservation by discouraging the mutilation of older pieces in order to reuse their stones in newer fashions. She had a staff of technicians who specialized in the restoration of antique pieces. Consequently, Tanager's of London had the largest and finest collection of estate jewelry in the world, which was displayed alongside the most avant-garde jewelry designs. Chelsea's changes had attracted a large clientele of buyers from both Europe and Asia. The pressures of running the operation now kept her from doing much designing, but the little she managed to create was highly prized and quickly sold.

Chelsea was at the high point of her career now, and as she walked through the room, with its sparkling new display cases, she felt the thrill of accomplishment. Today the new store would open for the first time, and Queen Elizabeth herself would be there for the unveiling of the Tanager Rose. The "Rose" was a 116-carat pink oval diamond which the corporation had acquired in its rough state due to Chelsea's nimble machinations and ability to outbid the competition. Although it had been a costly adventure, the publicity and notice had been worth twice the expense.

Cut from a stone weighing more than three hundred carats, the signature gem was not for sale. Rings and pins and necklaces, which had been created from peripheral cuttings, however, were on display in a beveled glass case sitting beside the "Rose." Every single piece in the case had already been sold in advance to chosen customers. Wills had insisted on buying one of the largest stones for Chelsea, and she now wore the chunky, ten-carat cushion-cut stone in a modern platinum ring of her own design.

To celebrate the occasion, a cluster of smaller stones had been used to create a pink rose pin, and that piece, also designed by Chelsea, would be presented to the

Queen as a token of appreciation for her visit. It promised to be an exciting day.

"I'm going upstairs to my office for a minute, Wills. Would you mind checking with Mrs. Burnham to make sure the caterer is ready?" she asked as she stepped into the modern, diamond-shaped glass elevator at the rear of the store.

"I'm sure everything is fine, my dear," Wills replied, but he moved toward the back room anyway. He was and had always been proud and supportive of Chelsea's career, much to the astonishment of his friends and family. Raised in a patriarchal society where wives were expected to adhere to traditional roles, Wills had nevertheless encouraged Chelsea to continue with the work she loved. After the birth of their second son, he'd built her a beautiful and spacious atelier at the edge of the forest in Ashford, and he had been impressed when the managerial job at Tanager's was offered. Their marriage was one of mutual consideration, and Chelsea had been equally supportive of everything Wills attempted. Even when the rigors of campaigning for election got in the way of her work, she made every effort to be at his side. Raised in a family of women, she had found fulfillment in her family of men.

Back downstairs, after checking on the details of the coming festivities, Chelsea looked regal and poised, despite her excitement. Dressed in a simple black wool dress by Oscar de la Renta, she wore only her mother's pink pearls, saved for special occasions, with matching pearl studs in her ears, and the new pink diamond ring. Her blond hair was pulled back smoothly into a small knot at the nape of her neck, and she was a vision of cool beauty and grace. Without being aware of it, she had inherited much of her mother's magnetic charm.

The guests began to arrive, and just ten minutes before Her Majesty's car was due, an attractive elderly couple were admitted to the showroom. As soon as she saw them, Chelsea rushed forward to greet them warmly.

"Jonathan! Kathleen!" she cried. "What a wonderful surprise. I had no idea you were coming."

Accompanied by his wife of eighteen years, Jonathan smiled proudly at the woman whom he considered his own special discovery.

"I wouldn't miss this, Chelsea," he said, hugging her. "Besides, on the Concorde, it's not such a bad trip."

Wills joined them, and the four conversed like the old friends they were. If there was one person responsible for Chelsea's success, it was the retired head of Tanager's, who had prodded and pushed and insisted that she continue her work, even engaging Wills in his campaign. After his marriage to Kathleen, Jonathan and his wife had often been guests at the country house, and he was Jamie's godfather.

Just as Queen Elizabeth's limousine was pulling up to the curb, Hilda Marx scooted through the door, followed by Anne and Frank Hunter. Seeing Chelsea occupied greeting other arrivals, they waved and smiled and melted into the crowd. There would be time for talk later.

Her Majesty stepped out of her car onto the purple carpet that was ringed by a row of security guards holding back the crowd of onlookers and photographers. Gracefully, the Queen paused briefly for photographers, waved to the crowd and then walked into Tanager's, followed by her entourage.

Chelsea welcomed the Queen warmly, and they shook hands. Slowly, Elizabeth II walked about the room greeting everyone there. She was dressed in blue, and Chelsea noted that she was wearing Queen Mary's Bar Brooch, a large pearl crossed by a curved diamond bar that ended on each side with a three-leaf clover of diamonds. On her ears she wore the Devon earrings, made of pearls and diamonds, which had been a royal wedding gift. Through the years and many occasions of being in the Queen's presence, Chelsea had become familiar with the extensive collection of Elizabeth's jewels.

With Chelsea at her side, Her Majesty circled the room, first stopping to admire the Tanager Rose, while Chelsea gave her an abbreviated explanation of the process used in cutting the huge diamond. Then the Queen looked over the case of additional pieces that had been cut from the stone, and she asked to look at the case where Chelsea's own designs were displayed. Finally, Chelsea presented her with the rose brooch, which she graciously accepted. Tanager's photographers, along with a selected group of the press, were then permitted to enter the room and take pictures.

It was a subdued and elegant event. At a signal from Chelsea, a harpist began to play background music, and waiters arrived bearing silver trays of Tanager's own crystal glasses filled with Roederer's Cristal champagne, followed by another dozen waiters carrying trays of canapés made with the finest Beluga caviar, smoked salmon, and other delicious tidbits. A half hour after her arrival, the Queen took her leave.

Immediately the hushed atmosphere evaporated and the conversation became noisier and more jovial. Tanager's board of directors, all of whom had attended the opening, congratulated Chelsea heartily.

When she felt that it was appropriate, Chelsea gathered her family and closest friends upstairs into her office, while the party continued downstairs. It was not long before Jamie and Tom were in a corner with Frank planning their next visit to their grandfather's home in Carmel. Both of them loved their mother's country, especially California. Frank was very close to his grandsons, and he did his best to lure them Stateside at every opportunity.

After talking to her father and Anne, inquiring politely about the latest husband of Margaret, who was on her third marriage, greeting Nancy and her husband, and listening sympathetically to her mother-in-law's problems with arthritis, Chelsea finally managed to get in a corner alone with Hilda.

"So, have you decided to retire yet?" she asked with a grin, already knowing what Hilda's answer would be.

"I was going to do it next month, but the agent I'd planned to turn my clients over to got busted for smoking crack, can you believe it? God, people are dumb. So, is everything going okay? Now is that a stupid question or what?"

"I'm quitting, Hilda," she announced softly, so that no one could overhear.

"You're what?" the agent asked in astonishment.

"Well, not really quitting I guess, at least not yet. Starting the first of the year I'm going on an indefinite leave of absence from Tanager's."

"How come? What with all the exciting things that are going on in your life, the opening of the new store, the Tanager Rose. Why, you're at the peak of your career. Why would you quit now?" she asked, and then struck with another thought, her eyes widened and she said, "Oh my God, you're not pregnant again, are you?"

Chelsea laughed out loud. "No, I'm too old to want that. I'm tired, Hilda, and if there was one thing I learned from my mother and my grandmother, it was not to hang on too long. You see, all my life I've taken life too damned seriously. Just like my grandmother did. I can't remember a time I wasn't working hard at something. Then, as you know, I became a wife and mother at almost the same time. Wills and I both looked at each other one day and asked if maybe there wasn't more to life than this. That's why he left Parliament. While we're still young enough, we want to have some time together . . . and alone. To be just a couple, to travel, have fun, do things on impulse."

"I give you three months, and then you'll both be anxious to get back in the saddle," Hilda said with a smirk.

"What do you know about saddles?" Wills said joining them. "Hilda, I've never been able to get you on a horse."

"And you never will, my friend," she replied with a laugh.

Later that night, when all their guests had retired to their various hotels, Chelsea sat at her vanity table brushing her hair. Wills came up, kissed her on the shoulder and then looked at her in the mirror.

"How is my lovely star feeling after her triumph?" he asked with a smile.

Chelsea looked up at him and said, "Funny you should mention that word just now—star. When everybody was praising me to the skies today, I kept thinking about my mother, and for the first time I understood how she must have felt being a movie star, getting such big doses of attention. No wonder she was so depressed when it stopped. Even after my short little moment in the spotlight today, I felt a slight letdown when it was over."

"The desire for adulation is habit-forming, I suspect," Wills said, sitting down beside her and taking her in his arms. "Are you sure you want to give up all the excitement and the glory?" he asked, nuzzling her ear with his lips.

Chelsea tucked her head on his shoulder. "I do, Wills. I really do. I never had a real childhood, you know. It's time I learned how to play."

"Then I say we start your lessons now," he whispered, getting to his feet and leading her to bed.

Tonight, Countess Dani diPortanova will be the envy of the international social set. In a gala, star-studded ceremony, the cutting edge of the fashion world and ultra-rich glitterati will honor her as the undisputed queen of fashion design.

To many who will attend tonight, the radiant, ravishing Dani is a woman who has it all. To others, however, she is a woman to be scorned and detested...and there is one who is even willing to kill her...

BORN RICH

Georgia Raye

"Has everything going for it—murder, passion, reckless ambitions, and an unforgettable love story."
—Burt Hirschfeld, author of *Fire Island*

UNFORGETTABLE FICTION FROM ST. MARTIN'S PAPERBACKS

MODERN WOMEN
Ruth Harris
Three extraordinary women and one explosive man, fueled by passion and ambition, prepare together to take New York by storm...
_____ 92272-8 $5.95 U.S./$6.95 Can.

OLIVIA AND JAI
Rebecca Ryman
An epic novel of forbidden love, dark betrayal and shattered loyalties set in the splendor of 19th-century India.
_____ 92568-9 $5.99 U.S./$6.99 Can.

SPECIAL INTERESTS
Linda Cashdan
An ambitious Washington reporter uncovers the scoop of her career—a scoop which might prove disastrous for her well-connected lover...
_____ 92512-3 $4.95 U.S./$5.95 Can.

ICONS
Caroline Winthrop
Married to a bloodless American diplomat, jet-setter Judith Marlowe risks her reputation—and her life—when she meets a dashing, mysterious Russian officer...
_____ 92430-5 $5.95 U.S./$6.95 Can.